NEW YEAR
WEDDING FOR
THE CROWN PRINCE

MEREDITH WEBBER

FIREFIGHTER'S
CHRISTMAS BABY

ANNIE CLAYDON

MILLS & BOON

First Published in Great Britain 2018
by Mills & Boon, an imprint of HarperCollins*Publishers*
1 London Bridge Street, London, SE1 9GF

New Year Wedding for the Crown Prince © 2018 by Meredith Webber

Firefighter's Christmas Baby © 2018 by Annie Claydon

ISBN: 978-0-263-93380-2

MIX
Paper from
responsible sources
FSC® C007454

This book is produced from independently certified FSC™ paper
to ensure responsible forest management.
For more information visit www.harpercollins.co.uk/green.

Printed and bound in Spain
by CPI, Barcelona

Meredith Webber lives on the sunny Gold Coast in Queensland, Australia, but takes regular trips west into the Outback, fossicking for gold or opal. These breaks in the beautiful and sometimes cruel red earth country provide her with an escape from the writing desk and a chance for her mind to roam free—not to mention getting some much-needed exercise. They also supply the kernels of so many stories that it's hard for her to stop writing!

Cursed with a poor sense of direction and a propensity to read, **Annie Claydon** spent much of her childhood lost in books. A degree in English Literature followed by a career in computing didn't lead directly to her perfect job—writing romance for Mills & Boon—but she has no regrets in taking the scenic route. She lives in London: a city where getting lost can be a joy.

NEW YEAR
WEDDING FOR
THE CROWN PRINCE

MEREDITH WEBBER

MILLS & BOON

CHAPTER ONE

CHARLES EDOUARD ALBERT CINZETTI, Crown Prince of Livaroche, gripped the armrest of his seat as the small plane in which he was travelling—foolishly, he now conceded—was tossed around in gale-force winds and lashing rain.

The journey had been interminable: long hours in the air, lengthy delays at foreign airports and now this. The pilot's laconic apology for the rough flight—'Sorry about the bumps, folks, bit of a low off the coast'—had hardly been reassuring, although Charles began to see lights through the rain, growing steadily brighter, and then they were down, with every passenger on board heaving a huge sigh of relief.

Not that Charles's journey had ended. He had to find his way to the seaside town of Port Anooka, another thirty miles from the airport.

'Just down the road,' the travel agent had told him. 'You could hire a car.'

Which had been a good idea back in Sydney, where the weather was clear and bright, but in this deluge?

No way!

'Just a bit of a low off the coast,' the cab driver told him, as he steered his vehicle through practically horizontal rain. 'Port'll be cut off, and that place you want, the old lady's house on the bluff—well, you won't even be able to get back to the village once the tide comes in and the road floods.'

Charles wondered if it was jet lag that made the conversation—carried out in clear, everyday English words—unintelligible.

A village that was cut off and flooded at high tide?

Coming from a tiny, landlocked principality, he knew little of tides but surely villages were built above high-tide marks?

And what was this low everyone was talking about?

He gathered it was a meteorological depression but he didn't know much about them either. At home, it might mean rain, or in winter snow, but obviously here it brought a deluge and wild wind.

'The old lady's barmy, ya know,' the driver continued, breaking into Charles's consideration of the limits of his very expensive education. 'Livin' out there on her own, the place fallin' to bits around her.'

Place falling to bits? Charles thought. He thought of the comfortable apartment he'd left behind at the palace. Of the snow, already deep on the mountain slopes, and Christmas lights slung along the streets; rugged-up carollers knocking on doors, and the city's Christmas tree ready to be raised into pride of place in the city square.

Had he made a mistake, coming here?

But how else could he get to know at least something of the mother who'd died giving birth to him—the woman his father had loved, married and buried, all within eighteen months of meeting her?

His father would talk of how she had made him laugh, how kind she had been to everyone she'd met, and how they'd fallen in love at first sight.

Not much help in putting together a picture of the whole woman, but Charles did know they'd met at Christmas, which was why he'd chosen to come now to see what she'd seen, do what she'd done, and hopefully get to know his grandmother—and to learn why she'd never contacted them. Something his father had never been able to explain—or perhaps had not wanted to explain.

As far as Charles was concerned, someone as loving and giving as his mother—gleaned from his father's description of her—must have grown up in a warm, loving family. He wasn't personally familiar with normal families, but anyone who'd worked in children's wards in a hospital had seen loving families up close, and knew they existed. Not in every case, of course, but in enough to have learnt how strong the bonds of family love could be.

His father had encouraged him to come, perhaps hoping once his son had it out of his system, he'd settle down, marry and have the children so important to the continuation of the royal line.

Charles sighed.

It wasn't that he didn't want to marry, but no woman he had ever met had made him feel the way his parents must have felt when they'd run away together.

'Port Anooka!' the driver announced, breaking into his thoughts as they entered another lit-up area. 'Not that there's much of it these days, and you're still ten minutes from the house.'

He half turned.

'Sure you want to go out there? Look how high the tide is already. You won't get back in an hour.'

Charles peered through the streaming windshield and was startled to see huge waves crashing onto the promenade along the foreshore, not a hundred yards from the cab.

Was he sure?

Shouldn't he book into a hotel, and perhaps go out tomorrow?

But the journey had already been too long.

'Of course,' he said, hoping the words sounded more positive than he felt. He'd come all this way, so there was no turning back.

Not now he was so close…

Besides, there, ahead of him, was the house, rising up two stories, high on a bluff above the ocean, looking for all the world like something out of a horror film, wreaths of sea mist wisping around it in a temporary lull in the rain.

He paid the driver, thanked him for his further warning of being stuck out here on the bluff, grabbed his hold-all, and headed for the two low steps leading up to the front door.

He'd barely raised his hand to knock when the door flew open and a bucket of water was tossed onto him.

Barmy old lady?

He knew that in England barmy meant a bit mad.

But was she really mad, and this her way of repelling intruders?

Perhaps not as good as the boiling oil of olden days, but still reasonably effective as it had sent him tripping backwards into a large puddle at the bottom of the steps.

He struggled to his feet, still clutching his bag, and faced his opponent.

But the thrower wasn't an old lady. She was a heavily pregnant woman, surely close to giving birth, who was turning away from him, shouting up the stairs to some unseen inhabitant.

'Of course you knew the roof was leaking, Dottie. Why else would you own twelve buckets?'

She was swinging the door shut when she must have

caught a glimpse of him, hesitantly approaching the bottom step, drenched in spite of the umbrella he still held with difficulty above his head.

'Who are you? Where did you come from? What are you doing here?' A slight pause in the questions, then, 'You're wet!'

He watched realisation dawn on her face and saw her try to hide a smile as she said, 'Oh, no, did I throw the water over you? You'd better come in.'

'What is it? Who's there?'

The querulous questions came from above—nothing wrong with the barmy old lady's hearing apparently.

'It's just some fellow I threw water at,' the woman yelled back, not bothering to hide her smile now.

She was gorgeous, Charles realised. Tall, statuesque, carrying her pregnancy with pride. And the condition suited her, for her auburn hair shone and her skin was a clear, creamy white tinged with the slightest pink of embarrassment across high cheekbones.

'Don't let him in,' came the instruction from on high, but it was too late. He was already standing, dripping, in the black and white tiled entry, watching the woman disappear into the darkness beyond.

She returned with a large towel, but as she handed it to him she laughed and shook her head.

'That won't do, will it? You're drenched. Come through, there's a bathroom off the kitchen—a little apartment from the days when the house had servants. Mind the bucket! Have you dry clothes in your bag or shall I find something for you?'

Of course he'd have dry clothes in his bag, Jo thought, but she was in such a muddle she barely knew what she was saying. It was shock, that was what it was! Opening the door to find a man standing there—a man at whom she'd just hurled a bucket of water. A man so stunningly attractive even her very pregnant body felt the heat of attraction.

And Dottie was probably right, she shouldn't have let him in. But he'd been drenched, and he didn't *look* like an axe murderer.

In fact, even wet, he was the visual representation of tall, dark and handsome.

Was she out of her mind?

Tall, dark and handsome indeed.

All this was flashing through her head as she led him through the kitchen to the minuscule bathroom beyond.

'Servants obviously didn't get many luxuries,' she said as she waved him through the door and watched him duck his head to get in.

Which was when she recovered enough common sense to realise she had no idea who the man was!

Or why he was here!

Well, she could hardly ask now, as he'd shut the door between them, and she was *not* going to open it when he was doubtless undressing.

Or think about him undressing…

She didn't do men—not any more, not seriously…

She shook away painful memories of that long-ago time when a man had betrayed her in the worst possible way.

Had being pregnant brought those memories back more often?

Think of this man. The stranger. The here and now.

She'd ask his name later.

The growling noise of the stair lift descending told her Dottie had tired of waiting for an answer and was coming to see what was going on for herself.

Jo hurried back through the kitchen, meeting Dottie in the hall.

'Who is it? What's going on?' the old lady demanded.

'It's a man,' Jo explained. 'He was on the doorstep and I didn't see him as I emptied the bucket. He was soaking wet so I've put him in the downstairs bathroom to dry off.'

'You invited him in?'

Incredulous didn't cut it. The words indicated total disbelief.

'Dottie, he was wet. I'd thrown a bucket of water over him, on top of whatever rain he'd caught getting to the house.'

'He had an umbrella!' Dottie retorted, pointing to where the large black umbrella stood in a pool of water in a corner of the hall.

Jo took a very deep breath and changed the subject.

'I need to check the buckets upstairs,' she said. 'According to the radio reports, the weather is going to get worse.'

Better not to mention that the road to the village was likely to be cut, and the man, whoever he was, might have to stay the night.

Would have to stay the night most probably!

'You can't leave me down here with your stranger,' Dottie told her.

He's hardly *my* stranger, Jo thought, but said, 'Well, come back upstairs with me. I've just emptied the one down here.'

She waved her hand towards the bucket responsible for all the trouble.

Dottie glared at her for a moment, five feet one of determined old lady, then gave a huff and stalked into the living room, which was bucket-free as there were bedrooms or bathrooms above most of the downstairs rooms.

'I won't be long,' Jo promised, taking the stairs two at a time, glad she'd continued her long walks up and down the hills around the village right through the pregnancy.

There were six buckets upstairs and she emptied them all into the bath before replacing them under the leaks. How Dottie slept through the constant drip, drip, drip she didn't know. For herself, too uncomfortable to sleep much anyway, the noise was an almost welcome distraction through the long nights.

She was back downstairs when their visitor returned to the hall.

'I left my wet clothes over the shower, if that's all right,' he said, his beautiful, well-bred, English accent sending shivers down Jo's spine.

'That's fine,' she said, 'although I could put them in a plastic bag for you if you like, because you really should be going. The road to the village will be cut off any minute. The weather bureau's warning that the place will flood at high tide.'

'So everyone keeps telling me,' the stranger said with a smile that made Jo's toes tingle.

But Dottie was made of sterner stuff. Ensconced in her high-backed armchair in the living room, she made her presence known with an abrupt, 'Fiddle-faddle! Stop flirting with the man, Joanna, and bring him in here. If he had any manners he'd have introduced himself before he came through the door.'

Jo shrugged and waved her hand towards the inner door.

'After you,' she said, smiling at the thought of the diminutive Dottie coming up against the stranger.

'Who are you?' Dottie demanded, and Jo watched as the man pulled a chair up close to Dottie and sat down in it, so he was on a level with her, before replying.

'I'm Charles,' he said. 'And I believe I'm your grandson.'

His voice was gentle, so hesitant Jo felt a rush of emotion that brought a wetness to her eyes. Pregnancy sentimentality!

She held her hand to her mouth to stop her gasp escaping, and waited for Dottie to erupt.

She didn't have to wait long.

'Are you just?' Dottie retorted. 'And I'm supposed to believe you, am I? You turn up here with your fancy voice and good shoes and expect what? That I'll leave you my house?'

Trust Dottie to have checked his shoes, Jo thought. Dottie was a firm believer that you could judge a person by his or her shoes...

'No,' Charles was saying politely. 'I wanted to know more about my mother and her family—my family—and you seemed like the best person to tell me.'

'You can't ask her?'

Not a demand this time, but a question asked through quivering lips, as if the answer was already known.

The stranger hesitated, frowning as if trying to make sense of the question, or perhaps trying to frame an answer.

Maybe the latter, for he leant a little closer.

'I'm so very sorry but I thought you'd been told. She died when I was born.'

The words were softly spoken, the stranger bowing his head as he said them, but Jo was more concerned with Dottie, who was as white as the lace collar on her dress.

But even as Jo reached her side, Dottie rallied.

'So, who's your father? No doubt that lying vagabond she ran away with. I suppose you've proof of this!'

If the man was disturbed by having his father labelled this way, he didn't show it.

'My father is Prince Edouard Alesandro Cinzetti. We are from a tiny principality in Europe, a place even many Europeans do not know. It is called—'

'Don't tell me!' Dottie held up her hand. 'I've heard it

all before. Some place with liver in the name, or maybe the vagabond's name had liver in it.'

'Liver?' Jo repeated faintly, totally gobsmacked by what was going on before her eyes.

The stranger glanced up and smiled.

'Livaroche,' he said, imbuing the word with all the magic of a fairy-tale.

But Jo's attention was back on Dottie, who seemed to have shrunk back into the chair.

'Go away, I don't want you here,' she said, so feebly that Jo bent to take her arm, feeling for a pulse that fluttered beneath her fingertips.

'Perhaps if you could wait in the kitchen. This has been a shock for Dottie. I'll settle her back in bed and make us all some supper.'

Dottie flung off Jo's hand and glared at the visitor.

'You can't stay here!' she said. 'If you *are* the vagabond's son, next thing I know you'll be making sheep's eyes at my Jo, and whispering sweet nothings to *her*.'

Dark eyes turned towards Jo, his gaze taking in her bloated figure, and the man had the hide to smile before he answered Dottie.

'Oh, I think someone's already whispered sweet nothings to Jo, don't you?'

The rogue!

But he'd turned her way again, serious now, frowning.

'That's if you are Jo! I'm sorry, we didn't meet—not properly. You know I'm Charles, and you are?'

His aunt? Charles wondered, though why that thought upset him he didn't want to consider.

No, Dottie had said 'my Jo', but it was impossible she could be Dottie's daughter. Dottie must be touching ninety, and if Jo was much over thirty he'd eat his hat.

Maybe a cousin…

But the statuesque beauty was talking.

'I'm Jo Wainwright, local GP in Port Anooka. I took over the practice a couple of years ago, but I have a locum there at present.'

'Then why are you here? Is D— my grandmother ill?'

Somehow saying Dottie seemed far too informal—inappropriate really.

Jo was shaking her head, the red in her hair glinting in the lamplight.

'Dottie is probably the fittest eighty-five-year-old it's ever been my pleasure to meet. She's also the stubbornest—' She broke off to smile at the old woman. 'And she's not entirely steady on her feet, while as for the stair lift—you'd swear she was taking off for Mars, the speed she roars up the stairs on it.'

'Fiddle-faddle!'

Charles ignored the interruption.

'So?'

But again it was Dottie who answered.

'Oh, she thinks I'm not safe to be out here on my own, and she knows darned well I won't move to one of those nasty places where old people rot away and die, so now she spends all her spare time here, eating me out of house and home, and leaving spies here during the week to report back to her.'

As the words were warmed by fondness, and Dottie was clinging to Jo's hand as she spoke, Charles knew it was only bluster, and understood there was a special bond between the pair.

'Dottie's right,' Jo told him. 'I don't like her being out here on her own, but I've grown to love the place almost as much as she does, so staying out here when I can is no hardship.'

She paused, looking a little rueful as she added, 'Mind

you, I didn't know about the roof. I keep asking Dottie what needs maintenance and although we've done a bit, there's been a long dry spell so the roof didn't get a mention.'

She had such an animated face the words seemed to come alive as she spoke them, but he could hardly keep staring at her, any more than he could ask her what her husband thought of this arrangement.

So he watched as she spoke quietly to Dottie, helping her to her feet.

'I usually take Dottie her supper in bed. Would you excuse us?'

For the first time, he actually took in the long Chinese robe the older woman was wearing. Had she been settled in bed when he'd arrived and thrown them both into confusion?

'Can I be of assistance?' he offered, and was rewarded with a ferocious scowl from the woman he'd come so far to meet.

'You've caused quite enough drama for one day, thank you very much. You'd best be getting back to the village and we can discuss your visit in the morning.'

'The tide, Dottie,' Jo said gently. 'He won't be able to get back to the village now. He'll have to stay the night.'

'Then put him in the front room,' Dottie said, with such malicious glee Charles knew it was either haunted or, more prosaically, lay beneath the worst of the roof damage.

Left on his own, Charles prowled around the room, aware through all his senses that his mother had once walked here, sat here, maybe helped decorate the ragged imitation tree that stood forlornly in one corner. The need to know more about her had brought him all this way.

He tried to imagine her living in this house, but his thoughts turned to Jo, and it was she he pictured in his mind, maybe on a ladder, laughing as she tried to fix a star to the pathetic tree.

He closed his eyes, replacing Jo's image with one of his mother that he had only formed from pictures, and the stories his father would tell. Would Dottie tell him more stories, the ones he'd come so far to hear? Stories of his mother as a child, her likes and dislikes, anything at all to turn her into a living person instead of a picture by his bed.

It had been close to Christmas back then, too, some annual event having brought his father to the tiny seaside town, and he knew it was a degree of silly sentimentality to have come now, to find out what he could before he married and settled down, taking some of the burden of official duties from his father.

Had his mother prowled the room as he now prowled, arguing with herself—or her parents—about leaving with the lying vagabond?

He knew that had to be his father, because neither of them had ever loved another. And a vagabond he might have been, only even then, Charles was sure, he'd have been called a backpacker. Travel had been something his father had been determined to do, the only time *he'd* ever argued with *his* parents. But although it had disturbed his relationship with them, he'd known he had to see something of the world, to mix with ordinary people, the kind of people he would one day rule.

He himself had done much the same, he realised, when he'd insisted on studying medicine in Edinburgh, with men and women from all layers of society. Eton had been all very well for an education, but he knew how his fellow students had thought and how that layer of society worked. He'd needed to know everyday people.

Even back home for holidays, he'd worked in bars and cafés in the summer, and been a ski instructor in the winter.

But getting back to his father…

A *lying* vagabond?

Jo returned before he had time to consider the word Dottie had used, bringing light into the gloomy room with her smile.

'Been looking for memories of your mother?' she said. 'I've done the same, but sadly never found a thing.'

She paused, then added, 'Though I don't pry to the extent of going through drawers. I wouldn't take advantage of Dottie that way, but I do shake out the books I borrow to read, just in case there's a photo been left to mark a page.'

Charles looked at the wall of books at the back of the room and shook his head. It would take for ever…

'Has she not spoken of her to you?' he asked.

Jo shook her head.

'Not a word, and apparently there's enough solidarity in the village that no one else ever talks about her. I know there has to be a reason because although Dottie's a bit eccentric—well, pretty eccentric—she's not irrational.'

She sighed, shook her head, and bent over to pick up a glass bauble from a box of decorations that stood by the tree, hanging it on a low branch before turning back to Charles.

'Dottie and I usually have grilled cheese on toast for supper, but if you haven't had dinner and would like something more substantial, there are lamb cutlets and plenty of salad things.'

Charles shook his head.

'Grilled cheese on toast sounds fantastic. Takes me back to student days when it was one of the few things I could cook—cheese on toast, beans on toast, eggs on toast!'

That won another smile, which was so open and honest and full of good humour that it caught at something in his chest—just a hitch, nothing more…

You *cannot* be attracted to a very pregnant stranger, he told himself as he followed her to the kitchen, narrowly missing the bucket in the entry.

But the sway of her hips mesmerised him...

It had to be abstinence. How long since he'd been with a woman? The experience of the match his father had promoted, with a young woman who had a very dubious family connection to the old Russian royalty, had been enough to put him off women for life.

Well, for several months at least!

She'd been nice enough, attractive enough, but her conversation began and ended with horses and although he quite liked horses and rode occasionally himself, as a conversational topic, they were way down his list of favourites.

He doubted the woman with the swaying hips would talk horses.

'There's the toaster, and the bread's in the cupboard underneath it. You can do the toast while I grate the cheese. I think it melts better grated. Do you like relish or chutney under the cheese? My dad used to slice up pickles under his.'

Jo only just stopped herself from explaining how her mother had liked Vegemite, and she herself didn't mind the pickles. After all, there was only so much conversational mileage you could get out of grilled cheese on toast. And it had all been a very long time ago.

The memory of that time made her shudder—so much sadness, so much despair and emptiness and loss.

Don't think about it now—concentrate on toast but don't babble on.

She was embarrassed, that was why she'd been talking so much and there were no points for guessing why!

This man's presence—or perhaps her own hyper-awareness of him—was embarrassing her. For some peculiar reason, she'd felt his eyes on her as she'd walked to the kitchen. Not casually on her, but studying her, although that was ridiculous. She'd been imagining things. Why would a man like him be studying a slightly damp, very untidy, very pregnant woman like her?

For a start, being thirty-eight weeks pregnant would announce her as unavailable!

She hauled butter and cheese out of the refrigerator, then milk for Dottie's cocoa, relish in case Charles wanted it, the bottle of pickled gherkins to slice for under *her* cheese, set it all on the scrubbed wooden table in the centre of the big kitchen, then turned to their guest.

He was waggling the handles on the doors of the toaster.

'You realise I'm touching something my mother probably touched. This toaster has to be at least fifty years old.'

Jo grinned at him.

'At least,' she agreed, 'and it doesn't flip open when the toast is done so you have to stand there and watch it and open it before it burns then turn it to do the other side.'

He gave her a 'can you believe it' look and a shake of his head before turning to watch his toast.

Setting the grill in the oven—which was probably older than the toaster—to high, Jo grabbed the grater and a wooden board and began her job.

And if she glanced at their visitor from time to time it was only to see he wasn't burning the toast.

Wasn't it?

He'd found plates and soon delivered a pile of perfectly browned toast to the table.

Toast done, she set him to buttering it—although that meant he was standing close to her, and the discomfort *that* caused had to be because he *was* a stranger...

Surely!

She was slicing gherkins when her belly tightened.

Braxton-Hicks! Her body's practice contractions. She moved a little, knowing that usually stopped them, and kept grating. Charles was now piling grated cheese on the toast he'd buttered.

'I've done two slices each, will that be enough?' he said.

Jo turned to face him, saw a smile lurking in his dark-enough-to-drown-in eyes, and hesitated, her mouth suddenly so dry she couldn't speak.

She had to be imagining whatever it was that was zapping between them.

Had to be!

'You might want more than two slices,' she finally managed, 'and I have sliced pickles under my cheese.'

'Like father, like daughter,' he teased, and she blessed the distraction of another twinge in her belly.

She would hate to think she was *anything* like her father...

Although maybe that was unfair. He'd been a good and loving father up until her mother had died and it probably hadn't been his fault he'd gone to pieces then...

Charles had turned away to put more bread in the toaster, apparently deciding he might need more than two slices, and Jo used the respite from his presence to slide the cheese-laden slices under the grill.

The extra hormones that pregnancy had sent spinning through her body—they must surely be the cause of her...

Her what?

Distraction, she decided, and said it firmly enough in her head to pretend she meant it.

Well, it could hardly be anything more than that, now, could it? She'd seen tall, dark and handsome men before and had never felt the slightest attraction, and so what if his broad shoulders curved in to a neat waist, and his jeans clung to neat buttocks?

She heated milk on the stove for Dottie's cocoa, vowing for the fiftieth time she'd buy a microwave for the house next time she was in town. She put on the kettle for tea and turned to Charles.

'Would you like tea or coffee?'

He smiled—she wished he wouldn't—and said, 'Could I please have cocoa? This has taken me back to student days and it seems right I should be drinking cocoa.'

Jo tore her eyes away from his face. What had she been waiting for, another smile? She poured more milk into the pot on the stove, told the visitor to watch the toast under the grill while she found mugs for the three of them. Even Dottie, to whom tea must be served in fine china cups, drank her cocoa from a mug, and a mug of tea was far more satisfying as far as Jo was concerned.

Charles, who was proving quite proficient in the kitchen, had found more plates and was cutting a couple of bubbling, lightly browned cheese toasts into fingers.

'Two for Dottie, two with pickles for the pregnant lady, and I'll look like a pig eating four, but it seems a very long time since breakfast.'

'You haven't eaten since breakfast?' Jo said in disbelief, but the milk was close to boiling, and she had cocoa to make, so she could hardly pursue the conversation.

Not that Charles—the name was coming more easily into her head—had replied. Instead, he was moving around the kitchen, poking into nooks and crannies, finally finding the trays, hiding in the space beside the ancient refrigerator.

'I'm assuming Dottie has the silver one,' he said, smiling so broadly Jo had to smile back.

'Yes, and slightly better china than you've found there.'

She opened a high kitchen cupboard and produced a fine china plate, bedecked with flowers and edged with gold.

'Just because she's old, she says, she doesn't have to lower her standards,' Jo quoted in explanation.

'Bless her heart!' Charles said, and the phrase must have startled him for he added, very quickly, 'As my nanny would have said.'

Bless her heart indeed!

And a nanny?

No wonder he spoke like an English toff.

Only it wasn't really like that—just beautifully pronounced words that seemed to fill the air with music.

What would it have been like to have been raised like that?

Or even in a normal household.

Another twinge reminded Jo she shouldn't be thinking about the past and definitely not about a man she'd barely met, no matter how pleasant his voice might be.

And weren't Braxton-Hicks contractions supposed to be irregular?

Still, she couldn't think about that now. She'd get the tray up to Dottie, and then...

She didn't know what.

She usually took her tray up and ate in Dottie's bedroom, but would Dottie want the stranger in her bedroom, related though he might be?

And could she, Jo, leave him alone in the kitchen no matter how inhospitable that would seem?

She'd take Dottie's tray up and see what transpired.

Dottie was sitting, propped up on pillows, in the middle of the big bed, the ornately carved bedhead a spectacular backdrop to the minute occupant. Resplendent in her colourful Chinese robe, she was every inch an empress, ready to receive her subjects.

As Jo settled the tray on the small table over Dottie's legs, she said, 'You can bring that man up here to eat his supper. You'll come, of course, so he might as well. We'll grill him, find out what he's up to!'

The last sentence would have startled Jo if she hadn't known Dottie's passion for mystery and detective fiction. Perhaps she'd always nurtured a secret desire to grill someone.

Possibly literally!

'We've been summoned,' she told Charles when she returned to the kitchen, where she found him cutting his extra toast into fingers. He'd also made a pot of tea, though where he'd found the pot she didn't know. 'Do you want sugar in your cocoa?'

'I've already helped myself, but left it to you to pour your own tea how you like it.'

Jo did just that, then lifted her tray and led the way upstairs.

CHAPTER TWO

CHARLES LOOKED AROUND the room, realising that when rain wasn't lashing the windows, Dottie would have an expansive view of the sea from her bed. Here, too, there were the early signs of Christmas decorations—a small, stained-glass decal on one window, a box of tinsel in a corner. Had someone—Jo?—started on the task before the weather turned?

But what really interested him in the room was a chest of drawers to one side of the bed, and the ranks of framed photos taking pride of place across the top of it.

Was there one of his mother?

He could hardly walk over and have a look.

Jo had pulled two chairs closer to the bed from what would be a sitting alcove by the window, and put small side tables beside each of them.

She waved him to one of them, but as she bent to set down her tray, he thought he saw her wince.

Strangers don't ask questions, he told himself, but the doctor in him had to say, 'Are you okay?'

'Practice twinges, that's all,' she said, but the pink had gone from her cheeks and she looked a little drawn.

'I'm also a doctor,' he said to her quietly, 'so if your baby decides to come early, and you can't get into the village, I *have* delivered them before.'

'This baby is *not* coming early,' was the reply, no less forceful for being whispered. 'This is to be a Christmas baby, timed to the minute!'

He considered that a bit ambitious. Would she consider having it induced on Christmas morning if it wasn't showing signs of arrival?

'What are you two whispering about?' Dottie demanded to know.

Charles smiled at her.

'I was just saying it's a coincidence, Jo being a doctor, because that's my profession.'

'Ha!' said Dottie with malicious glee. 'I knew that vagabond was lying!'

Charles shook his head—unable to make any connection.

Jo must have been equally confused, for it was she who asked the question.

'And just why, Dottie, does Charles being a doctor make his father a liar?'

'Because his father always said he was a prince, and if that was true then his son would be a princeling, or whatever a prince's sons are called, and this fellow says he's a doctor.'

She paused, smiling in malicious glee, then went on, 'Although he could be a liar, too, and the doctor thing just humbug!'

'Oh, Dottie,' Jo said, barely able to speak for laughter, 'you do come up with the most startling logic. If his dad's a prince then he's probably one, too, but he could hardly hang around waiting for his father to die so he can have a job. If the liver place is as small as he says it is, there probably aren't enough duties to keep his father busy, let alone Charles as well. He would have needed a job.'

Charles had watched Dottie while Jo was speaking—better by far than watching Jo with the laughter lingering in her eyes. The old lady didn't seem at all perturbed, eating her way through her plate of cheese toast and sipping at her cocoa.

But her eyes were on him the whole time.

Trying to make out if he was the imposter she thought him?

Or trying to see some resemblance to his mother? A family likeness of some kind...

He hoped it was the latter, but after thirty-six years would she be able to tell?

The photos up here would definitely be off limits unless Dottie agreed he could look at them. There'd been no obvious photos of his mother in the parts of the house he'd seen so far. And, like Jo, he didn't want to pry into drawers.

But he had come all this way to learn something of the mother he'd never known, so although her behaviour so far had been hardly welcoming, he had to overcome Dottie's suspicion and distrust somehow.

'Why did she call you Charles? Or did your father do that?'

The questions were so unexpected Charles swallowed some cocoa the wrong way and had to cough before he could answer.

'No, my mother named me—well, she and my father chose the names before I was born. Apparently, they both liked Charles as a name, then Edouard after my father's father and Albert after hers.'

He looked directly at Dottie.

'Your husband was called Albert, wasn't he?'

He thought the scowl she gave him might be all the answer he'd get, but then she said, 'Bertie—we called him Bertie!' in such a gruff tone Charles guessed at the emotion she was holding in check.

And why wouldn't there be emotion? How would he have felt if she'd suddenly turned up at home?

Overwhelmed, to say the least.

He set aside the rest of his toast and moved his chair a little closer to the bed.

'I know this must be a terrible shock for you, but I did write a couple of times and never received a reply so it seemed the only thing to do was to come. I'll go away again as soon as your flood goes down, if that's what you want.'

The scowl turned to a full-blown glare.

'I do *not* open letters with foreign stamps,' she said. 'You do not know what germs they might be carrying. It's how they spread anthrax, you know.'

Though slightly startled by the pronouncement, most of Charles's attention had turned to Jo, who had her eyes shut and her hand to her belly.

That, he *knew*, was a contraction!

Had his inattention drawn Dottie's eyes to Jo so that she said, 'If that was a contraction, look at your watch and start timing them.'

After which she lifted the table off her legs, set it aside on the bed, and clambered out, remarkably spry for someone who looked about a hundred.

'And don't worry,' she added, crossing the room to Jo. 'I've delivered most of the people still alive in the village, grandparents, parents and even some of the older children. I'll take care of you.'

The look of horror on Jo's face told Charles what she thought of that idea, but she rallied.

'That's very kind, Dottie, but I'm a doctor, I should be able to manage. I mean, don't women in some developing countries give birth in the fields where they are working, then wrap the baby in a sling on their back and keep working? If they can do that, I should be able to manage.'

She closed her eyes, pausing as another contraction tightened her belly.

'Anyway,' she added, 'I absolutely can*not* have the baby now. It's not Christmas Day, and Chris and Alice can't get through, and you know they want to be here.'

'You've got no choice, my girl,' Dottie told her. 'And too bad if they can't be here. I never did approve of them using you like this.'

Jo lifted her hand.

'Please, Dottie, no more of that. And I'll be glad of your help, but perhaps…'

She turned to Charles.

'You'd have a mobile, wouldn't you? If I do go properly into labour, we could start with video chat on my mobile and if it runs out of charge, could we use yours?'

'You want your labour going out on video chat?' Charles asked, totally bewildered by the speed at which things had moved from his meeting with his grandmother to possibly having to deliver a total stranger's baby in the midst of the gale that thrashed the windows and shook the house. 'With who, and why?'

'Only to Chris and Alice,' Jo said. 'You see, it's their baby.'

She spoke as if that explained everything, though from Charles's point of view it only made things more confusing.

Their baby?

'You're a surrogate?'

But even as he asked the question he watched the colour drain from Jo's face, and knew it was another contraction, a bad one. Childbirth hurt. So why would she go through it for someone else?

And how would she feel when it came time to hand over the baby she'd carried—nurtured—for nine months?

Now Dottie was issuing orders so he couldn't pursue the matter.

'Take the supper things down to the kitchen,' she was saying to him. 'Then when you get back I'll tell you where to find clean linen. There are some sheets that are washed so thin they're soft, and plenty of old towels. We'd better use this room, because the others all leak. The little chaise longue should be ideal because the back of it only comes halfway. And gloves, I suppose. There might be gloves in the kitchen!'

'Washing-up gloves?' Jo said faintly. 'You're going to deliver Lulu with washing-up gloves?'

'You just relax,' Dottie ordered. 'We'll do whatever is necessary.'

Charles carried the half-eaten meal down to the kitchen, wondering whether he should get out of this madness before he caught whatever brought it on!

Was the road really flooded?

And *that* thought horrified him!

Surely he wasn't thinking of leaving these women on their own—one to deliver her baby, the other as dotty as her name.

Of course he couldn't, flooded road or not.

So he carried his burden to the kitchen, noticed the bucket was full on the way and came back to empty it, checking there was no new stranger standing at the door before he threw the water.

Back upstairs for more orders! That part at least was a novelty. At home, and at the hospital, he was more likely to be giving them…

Jo closed her eyes and wondered if she willed it hard enough she could stop the contractions.

Forget about it!

But what about Chris and Alice? her mind protested.

Charge your mobile.

She stood up, ignored Dottie's shriek that she needed to wait for the next contraction to time it, and went to her bedroom, where, by some miracle, her mobile was already on the charger and, even more wonderful, fully charged.

The linen cupboard was her next destination. He might be willing, this Charles who'd appeared from nowhere, but she doubted he'd fathom the system in Dottie's linen cupboard.

But Dottie had been right, there were sheets washed to a softness that could be used to clean and wrap a new-born, and plenty of old towels—Dottie rarely parted with anything—on which the baby could be delivered. And she could cut up some of the old sheets to use as nappies— they'd be softer than the towels…

She pulled out an armful of each, then, because it felt good to be standing, she walked along the hall, avoiding buckets on the way, then back again.

Walking was good, until the next contraction came— far too close to the previous one—and she leant against the wall, the linen pillowed in her arms.

'Was that a contraction?' Dottie asked, peering out the bedroom door to see where her patient had gone.

Jo nodded, so bemused to discover she was thinking of herself as Dottie's patient she couldn't manage words.

The pain passed and she carried the linen through to Dottie's room, then turned back. What she really needed was a shower—and just in case this baby really was com-ing, she'd have a shower, put on a clean nightdress and—

And what?

No! The baby couldn't come. She wasn't ready! Chris and Alice weren't ready! And worst of all, there was this stupid low off the coast with wind gusts too strong for a helicopter to make it out here if anything went wrong— not with her so much, but with the baby…

She considered crying, so great was the frustration, but she wasn't the crying type—tall, well-built women couldn't get away with tears the way petite women could. Besides which, she'd never seen the point. What good did it do? *And* it made her eyes red! She'd have a shower. That way, if she did happen to cry—well, in the shower, who could tell…?

She stood under the streaming hot water for so long it began to turn cold. She knew the ancient hot-water system would take hours to heat it again and felt guilty about using it all, though Charles and Dottie had already showered.

The next contraction was strong enough for her to grab the washbasin to hold herself steady until it passed.

This *couldn't* be happening!

It was bad enough that she'd spent the last weeks of this pregnancy wondering how she could stop herself shrieking or swearing in front of Chris and Alice, but in front of Dottie and the stranger?

Dear Heaven! What *was* she to do? Didn't soldiers in bygone times bite on bullets while surgeons extracted other bullets from their wounds.

How did they not break their teeth? she wondered as she walked back to her room.

Not that Dottie would have a bullet to bite on—at least Jo hoped not, although with Dottie you couldn't be sure of anything.

Another wave of pain washed over her. This was ridiculous, she thought as she gripped the end of the bed for support. Baby was two weeks early when the obstetrician had assured her it would be late, and she was out on the bluff with the worst weather in a hundred years raging all around her, and a total stranger and an eighty-five-year-old midwife for support!

Not that she doubted Dottie's ability to do anything she set her mind to—sheer stubbornness would see to that!

As the pain ebbed, Jo pulled out a clean nightshirt, packed because it was slightly more decent than the long T-shirts she usually wore to bed, and she'd thought she might have to get up to Dottie in the night. She put cream on her face and sat on the bed, her hands on the low swell of her belly.

And images she didn't want came flooding back, sitting like this on a hospital bed at fifteen years old, a child still herself, about to have a child—a child she was going to give away.

Then Gran had been there, in her head, Gran's arms around her shoulders, telling her it would all be all right and to think how happy someone would be—the couple waiting for the baby, as Chris and Alice were waiting for this one.

And everything *had* been all right.

Another contraction brought her back to the here and now—with a vengeance! She rode the wave of pain, checked her watch, and realised she'd have to leave the sanctuary of her room.

At least if she had the baby here and now she'd be spared the indignity of a hospital gown that invariably left the wearer's backside hanging out. Should she phone Chris and Alice now, or wait until she was certain this was going to be the main event?

Unable to decide, she emptied the upstairs buckets again, then paced the corridor, up and back and up and back, not wanting to return to Dottie's room with nothing more than a purple and white striped nightshirt covering her body.

Charles appeared at some stage of her pacing, fitting his step to hers.

'I know it probably helps to keep moving but at some stage I need to check on your cervix to see how dilated it is.'

A complete stranger checking out *her* cervix?

Particularly this handsome and apparently princely stranger…

Panic welled inside her and for all she told herself that most of the doctors she saw were strangers at first, nothing eased the disturbing thought of this man looking at her most private parts.

'Dottie can do that,' she said, and the man had the hide to smile.

'I have no doubt at all about that,' he said. 'I rather imagine she can do anything she sets her mind to, but she is frail, and a little arthritic, I imagine. It would be easier for me to check.'

And as another wave of pain was clutching at Jo's body she couldn't argue. In fact, it was bad enough, she realised as it waned, that she wasn't really going to care who did what to her as long as they got Lulu safely out.

And soon!

'Do you have to do it now?' she muttered ungraciously at him.

'I think so,' he said, putting an arm around her waist to steady her as she straightened up from the wall. 'It will give us some idea of how far along you are, and if Dottie has happened to keep an old stethoscope, I should be able to hear the baby's heartbeats as well, to check it's all right.'

'*Her* heartbeats—*she's* all right!' Jo reminded him, but all he did was smile and continue to guide her towards Dottie's room with his arm around her waist.

Totally unnecessary—at least until she stiffened as her

belly tightened and another wave of pain rose inside her. She clung to him, and felt the strength in the arms that held her. Wondering how a prince might get strong arms diverted her momentarily, until keeping back the urge to yell blocked everything but the pain from her mind.

Dottie had covered the end of the low chaise longue with clean towels and was now engaged in tearing the fine old sheets into large squares.

'We can dry it with some of these then swaddle it. We'll think about nappies and such later.'

She must have caught sight of Jo's pale face.

'Coming faster, are they?' she said. 'Well, get up there so we can check your cervix. If it's not already dilated to seven or eight centimetres, you might as well go to bed in your room and try to get some sleep. It will be a long night.'

Jo, who'd managed between pains to subside onto the chaise, tried to work out Dottie's thinking. She rarely did any obstetrics work herself but *was* aware that the cervix started thinning out and dilating over the days and sometimes weeks before the active phase of labour began.

'I imagine she's been timing your contractions better than you have,' Charles said, answering her unspoken question. 'You're well into the active phase of labour, hence her guess.'

'But we'll have to get the phones ready. Mine's fully charged in my room across the passage. Would you use yours too? Please?'

'Will you stop whispering and concentrate on what you're here to do,' Dottie said in an exasperated voice, as she threw a light sheet over Jo's lower body and levered her legs up to they were bent at the knees. 'I'm quite capable of holding a phone if someone gets the number and sets the camera on go. If this bloke is a doctor, then we'll let him do the business. You're pretty low down and I don't bend as well as I once did.'

But the words were lost in a haze of pain, while Jo gripped the high side of the makeshift bed and gritted her teeth so tightly she wondered if she'd break them.

Even without the bullet, she thought grimly as the wave diminished.

'Close to ten,' she heard Charles say, but the wave returned with renewed ferocity, and she heard herself yell to someone, anyone, to get her phone.

'Chris and Alice, under C in the friends list,' she panted, now imagining Lulu's passage down the birth canal. Sliding forward with the contraction, retreating slightly as it passed.

And Chris and Alice not here to experience it…

Tears formed in her eyes and she tasted blood as she bit down on her lower lip.

'You're allowed to yell, or moan, or even swear, you know,' Charles said, squatting at the bottom of the chaise with her phone focused on her dilated cervix.

So moan she did as the next contraction seized her tortured body, although through the haze of pain she heard Charles order Dottie to take over filming, telling them the head had crowned.

Did she push now? She tried to remember her classes. No, maybe not now—let Lulu come out gently. But hadn't she pushed earlier? Pushed, puffed, panted—she'd been relying on Chris and Alice who'd attended all the antenatal classes with her to tell her what to do when, but now she was too tired to remember any of it, while her first experience had been wiped completely from her memory!

And now the contractions had stopped—well, eased at least—and Charles and Dottie were whispering at the bottom of the bed.

'What's happened?' Jo demanded, as a cold sense of dread enveloped her exhausted body.

'There, all's well,' she heard Charles say, as the small, wet mortal in his hands finally let out a cry.

'Not a Lulu, I'm afraid,' he said, coming close to reef open the buttons on Jo's nightshirt and place the baby on her chest, his head towards her breasts. 'Let's see how his instinct is.'

He was beaming down at Jo, while Dottie had come around to the side of the bed, still filming—ignoring the conversations being flung at her from the other end of the phone.

'See,' Charles said, while Jo watched in amazement as the tiny newborn wiggled his way across her body to latch onto a nipple. 'He's fine—he'll do. We've no drugs to help expel the placenta but if you let him suckle, and I massage you a bit, that should work.'

Dottie, having abandoned the phone now the main event was over, draped a soft sheet across the two of them, then glared at Charles across the bed.

'My way would have worked just as well,' she said, so much belligerence in her tone, Jo was frowning as she looked at them.

'What way? What are you talking about?' she asked when it became apparent no one was going to enlighten her.

'He was born flat,' Charles explained, 'but I cleared the mucus from his mouth and blew a breath into him and you heard his squawk.'

'In my day,' Dottie said, drawing herself up to her full five feet one and glaring at Charles across the bed, 'we flicked the sole of the foot with a finger and that made them cry—worked every time.'

Jo smiled, then looked down at the little bundle in her arms.

Letting him suckle was good.

They'd agreed, she, Alice and Chris, that the baby should take advantage of the colostrum in her breasts to help ward off infection. Had it all gone to plan, she'd have taken tablets to stop her milk coming in but the early arrival and the state of the floods had put paid to that.

She might have to feed him for a day or two, but that was okay. Right from the day she'd taken the decision to act as a surrogate she'd realised she had to stay focused on the pregnancy as a job, something she was undertaking for someone else, so although her hormones had gone all weird on her, she'd always been totally aware that this baby wasn't hers, and feeding him wouldn't change that.

Although she'd hardly have been human if she didn't feel a thrill to hold the little fellow to her breast, and she smiled up at Charles, thanking him, pleased he'd been here to help her through it all, calm and efficient—a perfect prince of a man, in fact!

She smiled again at the silly thought and, looking up, caught him smiling back, a look of such pride on his face she knew the miracle of birth had affected him as well.

Charles looked down at the mother and child, full of a feeling of pride that he'd pulled off a successful delivery, mixed with a kind of wondrous pleasure about the miracle of birth.

He saw serenity under the tiredness in Jo's face, but something else that puzzled him.

Distance?

A lack of pride?

Some kind of pain?

Because the baby wasn't hers?

Or because of something that had happened in the past?

The dread thought of rape crossed his mind, but he knew that women didn't have to proceed with an unwanted pregnancy these days.

He studied Jo again—yes, she was tired, but...detached too. That was the word he sought.

Was it not affecting her at all?

Or was she fighting whatever her hormones were telling her to stay detached from this child she had to give away?

But why were *his* emotions in such an uproar?

Was it being here in his mother's house that had made him susceptible to this sudden attraction?

Probably!

He looked around the room. Dottie had disappeared, and the phone she'd been using was ringing.

'Could you answer that?' Jo asked, gesturing to where it lay on a side table. 'It will be Chris and Alice—they'll want to see him.'

He had picked up the phone when Dottie returned to the room with a basin of water—warm, he hoped—more towels, and a hefty pair of scissors dangling from one finger.

'You're way ahead of me,' he told her, as he lifted the phone and pressed the button to answer it.

'Can we see her?'

Two excited voices rumbled in his ear and he switched the phone back to video chat mode and held it out to show the baby lying on Jo's chest.

Jo gestured for the phone.

'He's fine, although he's not a Lulu but a Louis. I'm fine, we'll see you as soon as the water goes down, but right now there's stuff we have to do, and we all need a sleep.'

She shut down the phone.

'We'll have to turn it off, they'll be ringing every ten minutes.'

'Damn silly idea, I said so all along,' Dottie was muttering as she carefully lifted the baby boy and set him on the bed to dry him off.

'Take these,' she said to Charles, producing two large stainless-steel pegs from a pocket of her Chinese robe. 'I've poured bleach over them so they should be sterile.'

Charles thought back to training days and knew exactly what was required. He clamped the cord at both ends then cut between the clamps. And with a quick twist of his fingers, the cord on the baby's end was tied, a little nub still sticking out, to dry, and fall off later.

There, baby boy, he thought as he worked, you'll have something to remember me for ever, your neat little belly button.

And as Dottie wasn't watching, he touched the baby's cheek, smiling when he opened huge eyes to check out who was near him. And the lump in his throat was probably from tiredness.

Jo had turned on her side to watch Dottie ministering to the baby, and although he guessed she'd have been happy doing that herself, she didn't want to take the fun away from her old friend.

Once satisfied he was dry and comfortable, Dottie swaddled him in a square of sheet, and handed him back to Jo.

'Try to keep him suckling, it will help with this last stage,' she said firmly, although Charles fancied he could see the glassiness of tears in her eyes.

She was as affected as he was by the birth…

By the time the placenta was delivered, Jo had drifted off to sleep, and as he helped Dottie clean up he realised that the wind had lessened and the rain no longer thundered down on the damaged roof.

'It'll be gone by tomorrow,' Dottie told him, peering out the window, a bundle of towels in her arms.

'And the road to the village?'

'It'll go down at low tide. Might flood a little more when the tide comes in again but not enough to cut us off.'

'And Jo and the baby?'

He *had* to ask.

Would the parents just turn up and take the infant?

How would Jo feel about that?

Surely it had to affect her—she'd carried the baby for nine months after all.

'Hmph!' Dottie said. 'Damn fool idea right from the start. Would you believe they'd phone poor Jo at all hours of the day and night and she'd have to put the phone on her belly while they talked to Lulu. And they sent music she had to play to her. As if a developing foetus would hear all that going on, let alone understand it.'

'They took the surrogacy thing that far?' Charles asked, wondering just how much of a trial this pregnancy must have been for Jo.

'Oh, she's told you, has she? Dottie said. 'Come down to the laundry while I get rid of this lot and I'll explain,' Dottie told him, and, sensing a slight weakening towards him on the part of his grandmother, Charles was only too willing to go along.

'Alice couldn't carry children and they longed for a baby of their own, so Jo offered to be a surrogate. Stupid idea! Worse timing! She had a perfectly good man who wanted to marry her then suddenly she's off having someone else's baby—well, he couldn't hang around nine months, could he?'

She paused, then, apparently needing to be honest, she

added, 'Not that Jo was all that keen on him. Not keen on marriage at all. I think her home life as a child put her off.'

The slight tightness in his chest as he heard Dottie's words Charles put down to tiredness. It had been a long night and he hadn't finished his grilled cheese on toast before he'd been drawn into the drama of the birth.

Down in the antiquated laundry, Dottie was running cold water into a deep stone tub.

'We'll soak all this for now,' Dottie told him, although she was doing all the work. 'Then get Jo off to her own bed for the night, not that she'll get much sleep if the baby wakes through the night, which, of course, it will. That Chris and Alice are in for some fun!'

She pushed the towels and sheet into the cold water, pressing them down so they were all covered, then headed for a door he hadn't noticed before. The place was like a rabbit warren.

'Box room,' she said, throwing open the door. 'See if you can find a decent, dry box we can pack with sheets for the baby. Having got this far, it would kill Jo if she rolled on the little fellow in the night and smothered him.'

Charles had to smile as he peered into the unlit room. It was obvious cardboard boxes had been going there to die for years, possibly decades. Which made the ones at the top of the pile the newest and most likely to be sanitary.

Pleased to have been co-opted by Dottie to help—surely it would thaw her attitude towards him, if only a smidgen— he examined the boxes with care, finally producing a clean-looking one with KURL printed in blue along the top.

He had no idea what KURL might be—tinned food, paper, linen?—but he pulled it out and held it for Dottie to inspect.

'You'll have to cut down the sides,' Dottie told him,

after a nod he took for approval. 'It wouldn't do for him to suffocate at this stage.'

She turned and led him from the room, through the kitchen where he looked a little longingly at the debris of his supper.

'The scissors are in still in my bedroom, so we'll take it up there.'

And if he manoeuvred himself into a good position he might be able to see the photos on the chest of drawers.

Clutching his box like a prize, he waited until Dottie had ascended in her lift, then followed her up to find Jo awake, sitting on the little chaise, holding the baby in her arms and looking slightly bemused.

She smiled as he and Dottie came into the room.

'I obviously didn't dream it because there's this baby here to prove it, but I can hardly believe it all happened.'

'You'll believe it soon enough when he wakes you every couple of hours during the night,' Dottie told her, going forward to lift the infant from Jo's arms. 'Now, you go to bed and try to get some sleep. We'll fix a bed for him and put him by you.'

But Charles and his box had stopped in the doorway, transfixed by the sight of this woman, her red-gold hair wild and dishevelled around her pale face, the baby resting in her arms. It was a scene worthy of the great Pre-Raphaelite paintings, and he could only stare.

She's not keen on marriage.

'Well, are you going to cut the box?'

He hoped he hadn't been standing there more than a few seconds, for all it had seemed like a lifetime. He strode forward, smiling at Jo as he passed, taking the scissors from Dottie and hacking away at the sides of the makeshift crib.

'You do that and sort through the linen for padding. You need to keep it firm. I'll take Jo to her room,' Dottie ordered, still holding the baby and occasionally smiling down at him when she thought no one was watching.

Not as tough as she made out, this grandmother of his, Charles thought, but still a very redoubtable lady.

He'd kind of accidentally moved to the far side of the bed so as he cut the cardboard he could also take in the photos.

But although he'd hoped to see at least one of a young woman, or even a girl, who might be his mother, he was disappointed. There was Dottie as a young woman, in her nurse's white uniform, clutching a rolled certificate, and a handsome young man in army uniform he assumed would be his grandfather. Unfortunately, the wide-brimmed, slouch hat of the Australian Army shadowed the man's face and before he could do more than glance at the rest he heard Dottie returning.

Hastily dropping the cut pieces on the floor, he put the scissors on the bedside table, grabbed a sheet and wadded it into the bottom of the box, then put a cut sheet, wide enough to swaddle the baby, over it.

'That should do,' Dottie told him, although she seemed reluctant to relinquish the baby into his new bed.

'You'd better get some sleep yourself,' she said instead, as Charles picked up the debris from the floor and stood there wondering what on earth to do next. 'If you turn left at the top of the stairs you'll come to the front room, though why it's always called that I don't know. But it has a view if ever it stops raining—looks south and west towards Anooka.'

He had to say *something*, Charles knew, but what?

He went with courtesy.

'Thank you,' he said. 'It's very good of you to take me in. I hadn't realised just how isolated this place would be. I had arranged accommodation—well, the hospital at

Anooka had arranged it—but having come all this way I wanted—'

'Why should the hospital have arranged accommodation for you?' Dottie demanded, definitely frosty now.

Charles shrugged. It seemed silly now, given Dottie's reaction to his arrival, but the old cliché about a person might as well being hung for a sheep as a lamb seemed appropriate here so he told her.

'I thought, when I decided to come to see you, that it wouldn't be fair to either of us if I just came for a few days. I wanted to learn something of what my mother's life would have been like growing up here, so I came in on a six-week working visa, sponsored by the Anooka and District Hospital Board. Apparently, they are only too happy to have British-trained doctors to fill in as locums, especially over Christmas.'

'You're here for six weeks?' Dottie demanded, finally placing the baby in his new bed.

'It seemed only right,' Charles said, aware it sounded a little weak.

'And you got the hospital to arrange your accommodation?'

The demand was shriller this time, as if the diminutive woman was getting more and more annoyed, though why remained a mystery.

'Did you think my home might not be good enough for you?'

Her voice cracked and he realised that she must be exhausted.

He could hardly mention the unanswered letters again, so he said, very gently, 'I thought it might be inconvenient for you, but right now we've both got a bed to go to, so maybe we should both get some sleep. I'll take the baby in to Jo's room, shall I? I'll go in quietly so she doesn't wake up. It's across the passage, isn't it, her room?'

Dottie nodded, but it was a tired nod, so Charles lifted little KURL in his box and quietly departed, pausing at the door to say, 'Sleep well!'

Would she?

He doubted it.

A grandson blown in by the storm, and a baby delivered the same night. It was a hell of a lot for an elderly woman to take in.

He pushed opened the door of Jo's bedroom, narrowly avoiding a bucket just inside it, and, checking there were no more leaks, he laid the box beside the bed, pleased the stormclouds still overhead were blotting out the stars and moon, because seeing Jo sleeping by moonlight might have been more than he could handle.

Downstairs, he found his bag, had another quick and barely lukewarm shower in the servants' quarters—at least he hadn't been banished to sleep down here—and made his way up to the room Dottie had indicated.

The three buckets with their musically tinkling drips told him his original assumption was right—this room undoubtedly had the worst leaks.

He checked the buckets—half-full, two of them. So he tipped the smallest amount into one of the others and took the two to the bathroom down the passage. He emptied them into the bath then realised he should have checked Jo's bucket.

He went back into her bedroom, but as he quietly pushed open the door he saw the bedside light was on and she was sitting up in bed, the baby at her breast.

He didn't believe in love at first sight, but of course this wasn't first sight. He'd had more to do with this woman—learned more of her—in the last twenty-four hours than most people would do in six months. And seeing her there, her vividly beautiful hair tumbling onto her shoulders, he knew what he felt was more than just attraction. It was deeper, clearer somehow—something the attraction part was clouding because it was so strong.

Or maybe he was just plain exhausted! It had been a *very* long day...

'Bucket,' he mumbled, grabbing it and backing out the door. Cursing himself for his idiotic behaviour, he emptied it, returned it, mumbled an almost inarticulate 'Goodnight' and departed, back to his own rather watery room, strung so tight there was no way he'd sleep.

CHAPTER THREE

EXCEPT HE DID, waking with sun streaming through his windows, and sounds of great joy echoing up from downstairs. He was halfway to the door, intending to lean over the bannister to see what was happening, when he realised he was naked, another hangover from student days.

He grabbed the coverlet and wrapped it around his waist, then went out quietly.

Not that he needed to be quiet, so loud was the excitement.

A couple, apparently Alice and Chris, were standing close together, both peering down at a small, tightly wrapped bundle in Alice's arms, and crowing loudly about his beauty, and his likeness to one or both of them.

Jo stood behind them, smiling broadly, while from her perch on the stair lift at the bottom of the stairs, Dottie watched the proceedings with dour disapproval.

Not one to get too excited about things, his grandmother!

He backed away into his room to dress, used the upstairs bathroom to wash and shave, then, as the noise from the bottom of the stairs showed no sign of abating, decided he'd go down, make all the right noises and disappear into the kitchen, where at least he knew how to work the toaster.

But life was never that easy. He had to be thanked, his hand pumped, his cheek kissed, the baby offered for inspection.

Jo, perhaps catching sight of his discomfort, said, 'Alice and Chris brought us supplies. They're in the kitchen.'

It was the only prompt he needed, and as Dottie leapt off her perch at these magic words, he followed her into the kitchen.

'You got children?' she asked, as she rummaged through the carrier bags piled on the kitchen table, finally coming out with a box of a dozen eggs.

'No, I'm not married,' he told her.

She looked up at him with a 'Hmph!' before adding, 'That doesn't seem to mean much these days, though I suppose being a prince it'd be a bit different. Not but what those English princes in the olden days had dozens of illegitimate children!'

As there seemed no reasonable reply to this, he asked if she'd like toast.

'Yes, but only with my eggs,' she told him. 'I like two, soft boiled, just two minutes from the time the water bubbles, mind. You'll find the eggcups in the cupboard under the toaster and the pots in the cupboard by the stove.'

Charles hid a smile. Had she once had servants at her beck and call, or had Jo been looking after her so well she'd come to expect being waited on?

Not that he minded in the least. The more time he spent with her, the more chance he had of her finally talking to him about his mother.

Jo, entering the kitchen a few minutes later, was surprised to find the table had been cleared of groceries, and from the way Dottie was sitting in her usual place with her placemat in front of her and the good china awaiting toast and tea, she'd quickly trained the visitor.

He was rescuing eggs from a pot, and presented them to Dottie, one in the pretty eggcup she always used, the other lying on the plate by its side.

'You should hit the end with a spoon so they stop cooking,' Dottie told him, quite kindly, Jo thought. 'It stops them going hard in their shell.'

She had tapped both eggs as she spoke, then, noticing Jo, she said, 'Would you like eggs, Jo?'

Charles's smile told Jo he knew exactly what the older woman was doing, but she shook her head.

'The box baby and I had breakfast at about five this morning, thank you. I told Chris and Alice I'd say goodbye for them. According to the local weather reports, we could be cut off again at high tide and they wanted to get the baby home. They've been ready for his arrival for months—for all they were sure it was a her and would arrive on Christmas Day. But they do have plentiful supplies of nappies and formula, which is all a baby really needs at this stage.'

She paused, checking her own reactions to the handover, and found she really wasn't upset. Though probably that was a lot to do with having been up with him every hour during the night. But she was pleased to find that she didn't mind—that her detachment right from the start had stood her in good stead.

And having sorted all that out in her head, she remembered her manners.

'I've got to thank you both so much for all you did last night. I'd never have managed on my own.'

'You did most of the work,' Dottie reminded her, as she lifted a spoonful of egg to her lips and tasted it, nodding in approval.

'And well done to you, young man. That's a very good

egg, though I suppose once you start work you'll be living closer to the hospital so you won't be doing my eggs in the morning.'

'I could do them on my days off, if you'll have me here,' Charles replied, not turning from where he was making more toast, presumably for himself.

Start work?

Days off?

What?

Jo looked across at him and then at Dottie. What had she missed?

'Of course you'll come here,' Dottie was saying, which was even more surprising.

Although she'd offered Jo accommodation while the locum was living in Jo's house, Dottie would soon tire of company. She liked her solitude as much as Jo did—and she'd send both of them on their way.

But she was obviously beginning to accept this man as her grandson if she'd insisted he could stay on his time off!

It was too much for Jo's tired mind to sort out...

She found out about the work thing a little later. Charles had been set the task of emptying all the buckets and returning them to a cupboard in the laundry. Jo had protested that she could do it, but Dottie had been adamant.

'You need to rest,' she told Jo, 'and don't give me any of that fiddle-faddle about women working in the fields. Just slow down a bit, get your strength back. The Prince tells me he's come here to work for a while, so he might as well stay here until he's due to start instead of paying rent in some ratty hospital flat.'

Left speechless by this turnaround in Dottie's attitude to Charles, she sneaked after him into the laundry where he was trying, without much luck, to fit all twelve buckets into the cupboard.

'You put some of them in the box room,' Jo said. 'That's where I found the extra ones.'

He turned to her and smiled.

'Do you think the fact that she's giving me orders means she's accepted me as a relative?' he asked, and Jo, who was trying to ignore the way the smile had made her feel— hormone imbalance for sure—shook her head.

'I think it's more likely that she's finding a malicious pleasure in giving orders to a prince—or to someone who *might* be a prince.'

He smiled again and she had to hope that her leftover pregnancy hormones settled down quickly before she made a fool of herself over this man. She'd just had a baby, for heaven's sake, and even though it wasn't her baby, surely she shouldn't be feeling this way.

Although maybe the baby had more to do with it than she'd realised. It *had* felt good to hold the little mortal in her arms—felt *right* somehow—as if the shadows of the past had been wiped away...

Though that didn't amount to a hill of beans as far as feeling attraction to the Prince was concerned.

'He's a *prince*, for heaven's sake, so stop reacting to a smile,' she muttered to herself as she escaped, deciding to do as Dottie said and go to her room.

Not to rest, but to calm down and attempt to find her normal, practical self, or, failing that, discover something else to occupy her mind so completely that she'd barely notice the man was there.

Or have time to think about babies!

And how likely was either of those scenarios?

Big sigh!

She could have gone home, only the locum was staying

there and she didn't want to intrude or make him feel uncomfortable. Could she put him off? Find another locum position for him and go back to work herself?

Hardly fair on him when he was supposed to be there another four weeks!

So, the only thing to do was keep busy, and she already knew there was plenty to keep her busy in Dottie's house.

So, as the low moved south in the following days, taking the howling winds and torrential rain with it, Jo moved through the old house like a whirlwind, flinging open windows to let in the sunshine, mopping up the damp floors, dusting, polishing, ordering more food to be delivered, and cooking spectacular meals.

'That's more like my Jo,' Dottie, who had taken to following Charles around the house, said to him one day. He was balancing on a rather rickety ladder—circa 1924, he rather thought—taking down curtains Jo wished to wash. 'She's always hated being idle, and while that locum she found is still there, she can't go back to work.'

Charles took this in, although more of his mind was on *his* continued presence in the house. He'd been in touch with the hospital and knew they had a job for him from next week.

But to stay here until then?

Was Dottie serious about that?

Or was she letting him stay because Jo, in her burst of frenetic activity, usually inveigled him into helping her, although most of the things he did she'd have managed on her own.

And Dottie *had* intimated that she expected him to stay...

But these days were a mixed blessing as far as he was concerned. Part of it was to do with seeing so much of Jo, getting to know more of the way she moved, and thought, and smiled—and becoming increasingly aware of the attraction he felt towards her.

On the other hand, being in the house where his mother had grown up, seeing it polished and shining as it must have been when she'd lived in it, he longed to imagine her there—to picture her in the sunny living room, the old-fashioned kitchen, the windswept garden with the thick succulent plants with huge pink flowers that apparently enjoyed blasts of salt air.

He knew coming here had probably been a mad impulse, but although he knew the time had come to marry and have children—as was his duty—something had tugged at him from the far side of the world, some need to know more about the woman who'd given birth to him, about her life, and her place in this family.

But how could he find the right image of his mother, when Dottie remained tight-lipped about her daughter?

Although he *was* learning more about this side of his family, and that, too, was important to him.

He knew his grandfather had fought the Japanese in New Guinea at the end of the Second World War and returned a hero—at least in the eyes of the locals. He'd gone on to become Mayor of Anooka, and, apparently, there was a statue of him near the town hall.

Charles knew he'd see it eventually, but statues couldn't talk.

'Dottie adored him,' Jo said to him one day, when they were in the kitchen three days after the dramatic birth, cleaning decades of baked-on food out of the old oven. 'My grandmother, who was one of Dottie's best friends, was always a bit amused by her devotion. He was older, you see, Dottie's Bertie—well, your grandfather I guess—and my Gran always said that made him easier to worship.'

Charles tucked this new titbit of his history away as Jo continued, 'And he *was* a lovely man, Gran said—kind and thoughtful and generous—but he was still a man and as far as Gran was concerned, that made him an inferior species.'

'Yet she married one,' Charles pointed out, 'or you wouldn't be here.'

Jo took her head out of the oven for long enough to smile at him.

'Purely to procreate, she maintained.'

She paused for a moment before adding, 'And that might actually be true, for she divorced him not long after her third child—my mother—was born.'

Charles, who was struggling with an urge to wipe a smudge of grease off Jo's upper lip, smiled, then bumped his head on the table as he tried to stand, brought back to earth by Dottie's sudden appearance in the kitchen.

'Shouldn't you be doing that, instead of Jo?' Dottie said to him. 'She's just had a baby.'

Charles grinned at his grandmother.

'I *have* offered,' he said, 'and she doesn't think I'll do it right, so all I'm allowed to do is rinse out the cleaning cloths and refill the sudsy bucket from time to time.

'Besides,' he added, 'I rather think it's something to do with women working in the fields, pausing to give birth and strap the baby on their back—or maybe it was front— and get on with their jobs. I think she wants to prove she's the equal of any farmhand.'

'Damn silly nonsense, but then the whole thing has been just that!'

And Dottie stumped out of the room.

'What happened to Bertie?' Charles asked, when he heard the stair lift ascending and knew it was safe to talk.

But Jo, who usually answered all his questions about

Dottie, remained silent, scrubbing away at an apparently extra-dirty spot.

Or avoiding the question?

Intrigued, Charles persisted.

Well, it was that, or imagining just how soft Jo's flesh might feel if he accidentally bumped against it. It was soft and pale, and he knew her skin would feel like silk if he ran his fingers over it.

Forget Jo!

'Did he die young?'

More silence, but that now Charles considered it, he'd seen photos of his grandfather in his mayoral robes and chain of office and he hadn't seemed all that young.

Seventyish, perhaps.

'You don't know?'

As if taking this last question as a slight on her family knowledge, Jo emerged from the oven, squatted back on her heels and stared at him.

Studying him for some reason?

Deciding whether he deserved an answer?

Or perhaps needed one…

She couldn't just keep staring at him, Jo thought to herself—not that he wasn't worth the odd stare—but seeing that darkly attractive face, those dark, dark eyes, and lips that were made for seduction—hormones still rioting—didn't provide an answer.

'It's really Dottie's place to tell you what you need to know,' she finally said.

'Except she won't,' Charles reminded her. 'She won't talk about anything personal. What's more, unless I'm very much mistaken, some of the few photos in the living room have disappeared. I'm sure there was one of a man in some kind of fancy uniform, and it's gone now.'

Jo sighed. Charles had come a long way to find his family; to learn something of the mother he never knew. And if Dottie wouldn't tell…

'He had a stroke.'

There, that bit was out. Maybe she needn't mention when, although she wasn't one hundred percent certain about the when, just had a vague feeling there was a connection.

'How long ago? How old was he? Did he die immediately or get over it or was he badly damaged by it? "He had a stroke" can't be the end of the story.'

Jo knew her lips had closed into a mutinous line, but she resisted the urge to shove her head back into the oven—and possibly clamber in after it.

'Bad,' she said. 'Bad enough that he was flown to Sydney and kept there for nearly a year—operations, rehab, OT and speech therapy—everything Dottie could think of to help him regain just a smidgen of independence. According to Gran, she was determined he'd get over it, and when nothing worked, she brought him home.'

'Hence the stair lift she really doesn't need?'

'Oh, she loves that. I think it gives her a thrill—hence the speed at which she travels—but Bertie…'

Jo paused.

'She pretended, Gran said, that he was fine. She washed and dressed him every morning, brought him downstairs and fed him breakfast, took him for a walk along the clifftop in his wheelchair, talking to him all the time, convinced he knew exactly where he was and what she was saying.'

Jo saw in Charles's eyes that he was realising just how immense this task must have been—how time-consuming—*and* how much it spoke of love.

She returned to her task, hoping she'd given him enough to think about for a while, so he'd stop asking questions.

But, really, the oven was as clean as she was going to get it, and she couldn't keep her head stuck in there for ever.

She gave the sides a final swipe with the cloth, backed out and stood up to replace the shelves she'd already cleaned—well, Charles had cleaned.

Lifting up the bucket, she chuckled as he pretended to flinch away from her, and went through to the laundry to clean up.

What a mess, she thought as she scrubbed grease from her arms. At least she'd known her mother—known, and loved, and been loved by her for fourteen years. And for all *her* upbringing had been unconventional, to say the least, the people at the commune had been an extended family.

Too close a family in the end…

But then she'd had Gran. She'd found an address in an old book of her mother's and she'd run away to find her—totally bewildered by what was happening in her body, aware women became pregnant but not believing it could possibly have happened to her.

Through Gran, she had come to know her real relations—at least, the ones that Gran spoke to…

But as she returned to the kitchen where Charles was setting out tea things on a silver tray—under Dottie's supervision—she realised she should have been thinking of ways to overcome this silly attraction she was feeling towards the visitor, not worrying about families—either his or hers.

'We're taking tea in the garden,' Dottie announced. 'If you could wait for the kettle to boil and make the tea then bring it out, Charles can organise chairs for us all.'

Charles winked at Jo over the tray before turning to follow Dottie out, for all the world like a butler following the mistress of the house.

Was it just for the sheer delight of having a prince cook her breakfast and fetch and carry for her that Dottie was treating Charles like this, or was it some kind of test she was setting him?

For the hundredth time, Jo wished she'd known Dottie's daughter. Had she been dutiful and obedient right up until the day she'd gone off with the vagabond, or had she always refused to fall into line with Dottie's wishes?

In which case, Dottie could be getting her own back through the son.

Jo shook her head. That simply didn't feel right.

She knew Dottie as a kind and generous friend. Irascible at times, certainly, and not one to suffer fools gladly, but at heart she was a good woman.

The kettle boiled and Jo made the tea, knowing by now exactly how Dottie liked it. She put the silver pot on the tray already holding a small jug of milk and a sugar bowl, and carried it out to the garden.

Obviously acting on instructions, Charles had set up the small outdoor table and chairs under the huge poinciana tree, denuded of many of its fronds of fine leaves, but still offering enough shelter from the hot December sun.

Jo set down her tray and looked around. She had a patient who did some gardening for Dottie; he wouldn't mind coming in to clean up the debris of the storm. But it was sight of the sea that disturbed Jo more than the wind-ravaged garden.

'Something wrong?' Charles asked, and she realised she must be frowning.

'It's the swell,' she said, moving back towards the table where Dottie was pouring tea. 'It'll stay up for days and it means the waves will be huge and probably choppy.'

'And they'll have to cancel the surf carnival,' Dottie announced in such delight Charles could only stare at her.

'You don't like surf carnivals? I thought they'd become part of the Australian culture. Don't some of the world's best surfers come from Australia?'

'Hmph!' from Dottie, so it was left to Jo to explain.

'The Port Anooka Carnival is one of the oldest on the east coast. It's not the biggest and it's no longer on the world surfing circuit, but it retains the old carnival atmosphere. People who've been surfing all their lives—some of them now in their eighties—turn up in their campervans and old cars and strive to relive the days when it all began.'

'Damn fool idea!' Dottie muttered. 'Place gets overrun by ageing hippies for days. Fair rides on the esplanade, and kids running wild through the village.'

'Well, I was sixteen the first time I came here on holiday with Gran, and I thought the whole thing was magical. You could sit on the cliff above North Beach and watch the surfing all day, then go to the fair at night, coming home when the fireworks finished, then do it all again the next day, and the next—magic!'

'Drink your tea,' was Dottie's response to this, and Charles had to hide a smile. Had he just seen Jo get one over the indomitable old woman?

He sat between them, looking out to sea, unable to believe he was finally here—feeling again that slightly eerie sensation that he could be walking in his mother's footsteps, sitting where she had sat.

And suddenly he knew he had to ask. Pleased that he seemed to have been accepted into Dottie's household, he'd refrained from questions, but surely...

'Did my mother go to the carnival?'

There, the words were out!

'And why would you want to know?'

The words were icy, but at least she'd spoken.

Now he had to find the right reply—he didn't want to

blow this opportunity to find out something, no matter how small it might be.

He moved his chair so he was directly across from her, and spoke quietly, gently.

'I grew up knowing so much about my father's family. I couldn't avoid it when their grim portraits stared down on me from every wall. But there was a hole where my mother should have been.'

He paused, but she was watching him.

Waiting?

'You asked me earlier if I had children and although I don't, one day I want to marry and when children come along I'd like to be able to tell them about their grand-mother who came from so far away. How she met and fell in love with a handsome prince and ran away to marry him. But what can I tell them about her as a person? About her life when she grew up here, about what she liked to do, what made her happy, and what made her sad?'

He paused, waiting perhaps, but when Dottie didn't speak, he continued. 'You've kindly asked me to stay until I start work, so I'll be able to tell them about their great-grandmother and the beautiful house she lives in high above the Pacific Ocean. Can you see how exciting that would sound to young children living in a small, rather closed-in country in Europe?'

She looked away, but hadn't hmphed or said fiddle-faddle, so he drank his tea, aware Jo was as tense as he was. Then Dottie rose to her feet and moved away, turn-ing back to say, 'Make sure you rub the silver cloth over the teapot before you put it away.'

Whether the order was for him or Jo he didn't know.

He couldn't think straight.

Then he felt Jo's hand on his arm.

'I don't know whether to laugh or cry,' she said shakily, and he covered her hand with his.

'Neither do I,' he managed, then they sat in silence, hand in hand, the tea growing cold in the cups, the silver teapot gleaming in the sun.

CHAPTER FOUR

'WAS I WRONG to ask?'

Jo and Charles were back in the kitchen, Jo washing the tea things, while Charles, having found the silver cloth in its plastic sleeve beside where the pot was kept, was polishing any suspect finger marks from the high gloss.

'Of course not,' Jo told him. 'It's the only way you're ever going to find out anything about your mother, although—'

She spun around, excitement gleaming in her blue eyes, while the echoing excitement in his body had more to do with those eyes than his search.

'I know she went away to boarding school, but that would only have been for her high school years, so there must be people in the town who knew her from primary school, and still saw her on holidays. Dottie will probably weaken to the extent she'll drop bits of information here and there, but I'm sure we can find out more.'

'We?' Charles asked, smiling at her enthusiasm.

'Of course, we,' Jo told him. 'You'd never know who to ask! How old was she when she left, do you know?'

'She must have been twenty-two or -three. She died just before her twenty-fifth birthday.'

'Far too young,' Jo said quietly, before she rallied. 'Well, come on. There's no time like the present.'

She was about to whirl out of the room but Charles caught her shoulder.

'Wait,' he said, and she turned to face him, so close he could see tiny freckles on her nose, see her chest rising and falling beneath the light T-shirt she was wearing. See the swell of her breasts, feel the warmth of her…

Whatever he'd been about to say disappeared, washed away by a great wave of…

Lust?

No, surely more than that!

Although it had been far too strong to be attraction.

'Charles?'

She was looking closely at him, and if her voice sounded a little breathy, well, that was probably nothing more than his imagination. Although the softness of her pale pink lips wasn't.

'I was going to say…'

He realised he still held her shoulder, and heat seared his hand.

'Dammit!' he muttered, stepping away from the source of his distraction, hoping that would help. 'I think I am losing my mind!'

'Going to the village?' Jo prompted kindly, and he glared at her.

Then remembered where his thoughts had been before she'd—

Cast a spell over him?

'I think it is a not good idea,' he finally managed, the words sounding stilted—foreign—even to him.

Definitely losing his mind!

'No?' Jo said, stepping back, as if she, too, wanted to avoid whatever minefield they'd blundered into.

He forced himself to think, to set aside whatever it was

between him and this woman, and be his normal, practical self.

'I think if we ask around the village, it would get back to Dottie and I think that might be hurtful to her.'

There, it was out, and his relief was such that he smiled at Jo.

She wished he wouldn't! Wouldn't smile like that, wouldn't touch her to catch her attention. She knew they meant nothing, the smiles and the touches—well, her head knew that. It was just that her body was having trouble coming to terms with it.

Her body seemed to think that, released of the burden it had carried for nine months, it could go cavorting about however it liked.

Her body, she knew, was looking for more smiles and touches—*it* was positively revelling in them.

Surely pregnancy hadn't turned her into a wanton hussy?

Or was it simply that he was unattainable—this man who admitted he wanted to marry and have children.

A prince—but not hers.

No, her life was here in Anooka, her life dedicated to her patients, marriage and children no part of it…

But a flirtation?

Would that hurt?

'Well, what do you think?'

The question, coming what seemed like hours after whatever they'd been talking about, threw her completely.

What *had* they been talking about?

'If not hurt, maybe shamed in some way? I wouldn't like that.'

Hurt?

Shamed?

Jo's brain clicked into gear, and she looked at Charles,

who had crossed the kitchen and was wiping at a spot on the window above the sink.

'Of course she would be. I'm so sorry. I just didn't think.'

And now she had her brain back on track, she added, 'Anyway, once you start work you'll probably be spending more time in Anooka than out here. Do you have a starting date?'

He stopped cleaning the window and leant against the bench, so he was silhouetted against the light.

'Monday of next week. I gave myself some time to...'

Jo smiled as his broad shoulders shrugged.

'Get to know your grandmother?' she teased, then felt a little mean. 'Anyway, that means you'll get to see the surf carnival this weekend before you start work, and maybe on Thursday—oh, that's tomorrow, isn't it? The week's just vanished! Anyway, tomorrow, if you like, I'll take you into Anooka, show you around the hospital, and introduce you to the powers-that-be. I want to go in anyway, to tell them I'm available until my locum goes, if they're short-handed.'

'Do they get short-handed?' Charles asked, and Jo found herself relaxing. She'd rattled off the suggestion because she'd remained uneasy—unsettled—and talking seemed the best route back to normal.

And hospital conversations she could do.

'Here, the carnival starts the summer holiday period. In Australia, this dread custom of "Schoolies" has developed. Young people finishing their final year in high school descend on every beach in the nation—and many places overseas—to celebrate their new-found freedom. It's chaotic, though not as bad in sleepy little places like Port Anooka as it is in the main tourist towns.'

'They party?' Charles asked, and Jo smiled.

'Like you wouldn't believe,' she said. 'But thankfully

it doesn't begin until after the carnival weekend and only lasts five days, after which many families arrive for their annual Christmas by the sea.'

'Christmas by the sea? Do you have any idea how exotic that sounds?'

'I'm afraid my main reaction to it is dread. The village trebles, or maybe quadruples, in population while, apart from casual staff in most of the shops, cafés and bars, everything else remains the same only busier.'

'Like ski season in our mountain villages—that I understand. One doctor who might normally serve three villages finds he's barely able to cope with his own, for these people don't leave their colds and flu and injuries at home.'

Jo grinned at him.

'It's all ahead of you,' she warned him. 'So, tomorrow? Do you want a lift into town to meet and greet?'

Unfortunately, as she'd been doing very well, he smiled before he replied, and her body celebrated with more of those wanton flips and tingles.

'Most certainly,' he replied, 'and I would like to hire a car as well, so I can get about.'

Had she been so preoccupied with her reactions to Charles that she'd failed to hear Dottie come up behind her?

But at the sound of her voice, Jo started, and possibly let out a little yelp, although she hoped that had been her imagination.

'I have a perfectly good car you can use,' Dottie announced, sliding past Jo into the kitchen. 'Although, if you are working in Anooka, it's best you stay there. Jo, too, if they offer her a job. But you can take the car so you can visit me on days off.'

Jo was laughing.

'I imagine, Dottie, that's your way of telling us you're

fed up with having us around. But you're right, it will be far more convenient for Charles to be closer to his work. And *so* kind to offer the car.'

Something in the words must have warned Charles what he was in for, because he frowned, then assured Dottie that it would be no trouble at all to hire a car.

'I may be based out of town for some of the time,' he said, trying to shore up his defences, but Jo knew he was lost. He was going to spend his six weeks with Port Anooka Hospital Authority driving a large, ancient, black vehicle with a rather unfortunate resemblance to a hearse.

'We're going into Anooka tomorrow, Dottie, if you'd like to come. Or if you need anything in town we could get it.'

'Anooka's too busy, too many people all bustling about the place,' Dottie replied, and although Jo raised her eyebrows, well aware how much Dottie enjoyed occasional jaunts into town, she said nothing.

'But if you've finished all your cleaning and polishing, which, I might add, pregnant women are supposed to do before they go into labour, not after, you could take me into the village now. There's no danger from the tides now, and I'd like to see if anyone has suffered or needs help.'

'That's a good idea, though I think we'd have heard if there'd been any major problems.'

'You make it sound as if this flooding is a regular event,' Charles said, as Dottie went upstairs to get ready for the outing.

'Maybe a couple of times a year,' Jo explained. 'But it must have been happening since the village was first settled because the houses and shops are built on the hills above flood level so it's only the roads in and out of the place and the sheds at the sporting fields that are really inundated.'

'So why is she keen to go?' Charles asked, and Jo grinned at him.

'She's a sticky beak! She might live out here in splendid isolation, but she likes to know everything that goes on in the village. She has a couple of cronies down there she'll genuinely want to check on, but her main hope will be that some of the buildings in the playing fields have been damaged.'

Charles stared at her in sheer disbelief.

'You're saying she wants to see them damaged?'

Jo shrugged, and smiled again, so all the symptoms of his awareness of this woman kicked in.

'Swept away more like. When her husband—when Bertie—was mayor, he arranged for the council to relocate some of the houses and businesses lower down the slopes—places that flooded regularly. Then he declared all the flood-prone land playing fields or parklands, so Dottie's been very peevish since various sporting organisations built clubhouses, *and* stands for spectators.'

'She hopes to see them washed away?" Charles asked, his disbelief so great he momentarily forgot that it was Jo in front of him.

Until she smiled again.

'Bertie wouldn't have liked it, you see.'

Charles tried to take this in, even stepping back so he wasn't quite so close to Jo and wouldn't be distracted.

Something about this new information deeply disturbed him, and he had to work out why.

'Right,' he finally said. 'She was so besotted about Bertie she hates to see any of his good works changed in any way. But surely someone with that much love and passion *must* have had some for her daughter!'

He was watching Jo as he spoke, largely to make sure Dottie wasn't coming up behind her once again, but he couldn't miss the way Jo's lips thinned as she clamped them shut, or the way her eyes darkened with something he couldn't read, just before she turned away.

'I need to get my handbag from upstairs,' she said, then fled—or perhaps escaped would be a better word.

Something had happened and that something was connected to his mother. That was all fine and good, but if he couldn't find out from Jo what it was, he'd just have to find out some other way.

He'd been the one who'd squashed the idea of tracking down any of his mother's old school friends, but that might turn out to be the way to go.

Or could he persuade Jo to tell him more?

In time, when she knew him better?

Although he already knew her loyalty was to Dottie…

Dottie and Jo returned together, and Charles was amused to notice that for a visit to a village Dottie had donned a hat and gloves, while Jo had twisted her unruly hair into a knot at the back of her head, though from the wisps already escaping Charles wondered how long it would last.

But it changed her in some way, gave her an elegance he hadn't noticed before. It added to the beauty and intensified the uproar she so unwittingly caused in his body.

'We'll take my car, the Prince can drive,' Dottie decreed.

'But he doesn't know the village, and he'd be used to driving on the wrong side of the road. I don't mind driving, and we can take my car.'

'Don't argue, Jo. If he's going to be driving my car when he goes to work, he might as well get used to it.'

Jo shook her head, her disapproval evident, although there was a small smile playing around her lips—the kind of smile that made Charles wonder just what kind of vehicle his grandmother would deem suitable for the status she obviously felt she deserved.

Reluctance dragging at his feet, he followed Jo to the garage he'd already noticed at the back of the house.

It was worse—far worse—than he'd imagined: a great black tank of a thing, about thirty feet long.

'It looks like a hearse,' he muttered to Jo.

She smiled openly now.

'I think it was, but Dottie bought it because it was the only thing she could find that fitted Bertie's wheelchair in the back. The wheelchair folded up so she could take him to appointments—doctors, and therapy, and such.'

'It seems impossible,' he said. 'She's such a tiny woman, and the photos I've managed to see of him show him as a well-built man.'

Charles had opened the driver's door and was peering cautiously into the interior of the huge vehicle.

'It probably won't start,' he said, hoping that would be true so he could hire a small, convenient vehicle for his stay.

'You're not getting out of it that easily,' Jo said, grinning at him across the top. 'Dottie says there's no point in having a car that won't go so she has it serviced regularly.'

'She still drives?'

And this time Jo laughed.

'Not any more,' she said when she'd recovered, 'but that doesn't alter her opinion about keeping it serviceable.'

Charles shook his head—it was all too much for him!

But as Jo slipped into the passenger seat beside him for the short drive to the front door, he was glad of the size of the vehicle for it left a good space between them. Sitting in a modern compact car, she'd have been so much closer and he had already come to the conclusion that being close to her was not a good thing.

He was pretty sure the attraction had been brought on by proximity, and had decided that avoiding it—at least until he could work out how he felt—was the best option.

'So, are you going to start it, or just sit there staring out the window?'

As promised, the vehicle started immediately, the engine purring in neutral beneath the big bonnet.

'Just remember the length of it when you're backing or passing another car. The few times I've driven it—decreed by you-know-who—I was a total wreck.'

He backed smoothly out of the garage and drove sedately—it was the kind of car that had to be driven sedately—to the front door. Dottie was waiting for them, a colourful, Chinese parasol raised above her head.

Jo leapt out to hold the passenger's side door for her, but Dottie shook her head.

'If I'm going to be driven by a prince, I'll do it in style, thank you. I shall sit in the back and you may sit with me, Jo.'

Jo cast an agonised look at Charles, who just smiled and nodded at her, as if to say if Dottie wanted to play games, it was fine with him.

But how much would he take?

Jo had no idea, although she was reasonably sure he'd put up with a lot in order to find out more about his mother.

And Jo knew Dottie well enough to guess she'd be impressed by his willingness to go along with her teasing.

Which was all very well for him and Dottie, Jo thought to herself. But as she had already made arrangements to spend the next four weeks with Dottie, so her locum could have the run of her house, it meant—

Unless she was needed at the hospital. That would be the answer. Okay, Charles would also be working there, but they wouldn't necessarily see each other at all.

And there were four hospital flats so they wouldn't need to share...

Share?

Nonsense—get real here!

It was pathetic to think she couldn't work in the same place as Charles, or live close by, without going all silly over him. It was a medical fact that her hormones would still be in disarray after the pregnancy, and that explained the physical manifestations of attraction she felt when she was close to him.

Or, to be honest, when she heard his voice.

Worse, if he inadvertently touched her!

Get over it!

'Are you listening?' Dottie asked, bringing Jo back to the real world.

'Sorry, Dottie, you were saying?'

'I was saying—' her voice was icy! '—that the Prince drives better than you do. The last time you drove me to the village you jammed the brakes on instead of braking gently.'

Jo didn't have to see their chauffeur's shoulders shaking to know that he was delighted with this reprimand.

'You'll keep!' she muttered at him, then turned her full attention to their hostess, who was explaining the layout of the village to Charles, and giving him directions to turn left, or right, or sometimes both at the same time when she became confused.

The road had been cleaned, but mud from the flooded creek still lay thick on the sports field and the smell of it swept through the open windows of the non-air-conditioned car.

'If you want to check on your place or the clinic, Jo, Charles can drop me at Molly's and drive you around there.'

Jo had already checked that all was well at both places,

but it was a good opportunity to show Charles something of the village.

'I'll be an hour,' Dottie decreed, once she was sure Molly was at home.

Being a perfect gentleman, Charles was out of the car as soon as it stopped, and opened the door for her, holding it open so Jo could slip out and into the front seat.

'She's certainly unique, isn't she?' Charles said, as they set off sedately up the road. 'Which way should we go when we reach the top?'

'Right will take us past the school then along the main shopping street, not that it is much to look at but it has the essentials in a general store, a baker, a butcher and hardware store.'

'And a café? Somewhere I could buy you a coffee, perhaps?

Jo was reluctant to admit to the café for all it was in a beautiful position that had views along the creek and out to sea.

And served fantastic coffee…

She was being silly, she knew. Sharing a coffee break didn't mean a thing, no matter how lovely the view.

'If you turn right again past the hardware shop, you can't miss the café.'

Now she smiled to herself, for the Seagull Café came as a shock to most visitors.

'Not the place with all the wet and miserable-looking seagulls on the roof?' Charles asked as they turned the corner.

'The very place! They're not real, although the ones that come and sit on the veranda railings and pinch your food are only too real. Kate, the proprietor, heard somewhere that if you put fake seagulls all around, the live birds would think it was the fake birds' territory and stay away.'

'It didn't work?' Charles asked as they pulled up.

'You'll see for yourself!' Jo told him, with a smile that brought goosebumps up on his skin.

Once he started work it would be all right, he was telling himself—when he realised Jo was racing down the path to the seagull-roofed café.

What had she heard?

Or seen?

He had no idea but he hurried after her, spurred on by the urgency he could read in her movement.

The reason lay just inside the back door of the café, a woman with a blood-soaked towel wrapped around her hand.

'The knife slipped,' she was whispering to Jo as he arrived on the scene.

'Dial triple zero,' Jo said to him. 'Ambulance and urgent.'

Charles dialled, pleased Jo had told him the emergency numbers, spoke, listened, thanked the person on the other end, then knelt beside the injured woman.

'Your scarf will be better than my belt,' he said, untangling the length of filmy material from around Jo's throat. 'There's so much blood it must be arterial and the person on the phone said the ambulance will have to come from Anooka so it might be a while.'

He was fastening the scarf around the woman's arm as he spoke quietly to Jo, who was, he realised, applying pressure to the wound.

But once he had the tourniquet in place and had noted the time, he went inside and found a freshly laundered towel and returned with it to their patient.

'Here, we'll use this—it will give us some idea of how much blood she's still losing.'

He spoke quietly but realised the woman was probably

beyond hearing, if the pool of blood on the floor was any indication.

Jo lifted the blood-soaked rag she'd been holding, and he heard the hiss of her breath and felt his own chest tighten as they both saw the wound for the first time. No accidental slip of the knife, but a deliberate and deep slash between the tendons on the left forearm. The classic cut of a suicide who'd checked out a 'how to' page on the internet. And the tendons standing out either side of it would make it hard to stem the flow with a pressure pad. The tourniquet would have to stay.

Jo wrapped the clean cloth around the arm, which was seeping rather than spurting blood now, watching the woman all the time, a look of deep concern, even sadness, on her face.

'We could move her inside, make her more comfortable,' Charles suggested.

'Or make her comfortable here. She lives at the back of the shop. I'll find a blanket and pillow.'

Charles watched her go, and guessed by the slump of her shoulders her worry that, as a doctor, she should have known of the woman's fragile mental state.

Silly really, the woman might not even be Jo's patient, but she was certainly upset.

Be practical! he told himself, and looked around, taking in the mess of blood.

They could move the woman, maybe into one of the low-slung chairs he could see on the veranda, then they could clean up the blood.

Or Jo could watch the woman while he cleaned up the blood—put into practice some of the household skills he'd been perfecting at Dottie's place.

He lifted the woman carefully and carried her to the front of the café. Jo had returned and followed him, drap-

ing a blanket on the chair before Charles set her down, then
covering her with a duvet, even though the day was warm.

'If you watch her I'll go and clean up some of the blood.
She won't want to come back to that kind of mess.'

'You stay and watch, I'll clean up the blood,' Charles
told her firmly. 'Just check her pulse from time to time to
ensure the tourniquet isn't too tight.'

He went back to the kitchen, found cleaning things,
and started work, and although he was meticulous, his
mind worried at the question of why a woman with what
was apparently a decent business would sit down in the
doorway of her kitchen, quite early in the morning, and
slit her wrists.

There was unhappiness everywhere, he knew that, but
if Australia was anything like his own country, mental
health services were stretched to the limit, and many people fell through the gaps.

He heard the ambulance siren and, with the kitchen
floor wet but clean, he went out to wave to it so the atten-
dants would know where to come.

They were kind and efficient, ready to whisk their patient away within minutes. But as she was carried up to the
road, she gave a cry of distress and called for Jo.

'The café!' she said. 'Who'll look after it?'

And for one frightening moment he wondered if Jo
was about to volunteer his services, for she'd certainly
looked his way.

'I'll lock it up now,' Jo told her, 'and then phone Rolf.
He'll know what to do.'

'Of course he'll know what to do,' the woman said,
bursting into tears. 'He always knows what to do.'

The crying became sobs that they no longer heard as
the stretcher was loaded into the ambulance, which then
drove quietly away.

'Rolf?' he asked Jo as she picked up the bedding and carried it back into the building.

'Ex-husband, and probably the cause of her cry for help, which was all it was, wasn't it?'

Charles nodded slowly. It was only one wrist, and at this time of the morning the woman would have been expecting customers, hence doing it at the kitchen door.

But that didn't lessen the anguish she must have been feeling to inflict that level of pain on herself.

He heard Jo on the phone, so walked around, closing and locking any open doors and windows, pausing to admire the view, regretting he hadn't sat there with Jo, enjoying a coffee.

'He'll sort out the café,' Jo told him. 'He has keys so we'll just pull the door shut so it locks, and leave it to him.'

He could hear how troubled she was, but didn't like to ask if she'd known the woman was unhappy. Maybe she'd tell him anyway.

Or maybe not, for they drove in silence back to where they'd left Dottie with her friend, and he followed her lead, saying nothing to Dottie on the drive home about the small drama they'd been part of.

'I'm going into Anooka to see how she is. I'll give her a lift home if she's okay to leave,' Jo told him when Dottie had gone upstairs to rest before lunch.

Charles knew he was frowning, but he had to ask.

'Do you really think they'll release her?'

That won him a wry smile.

'I'm almost sure of it. She'll assure whatever ED doctor she sees that she's perfectly all right, and that it was just a moment of madness, and because they really can't offer her much at the hospital, they'll send her home with a referral to see a psychologist.'

'But surely the hospital would have a psychologist or

psychiatrist who would talk to her there. The figures on people who make a second suicide attempt within days of their first are truly frightening.'

'I know,' Jo said sadly. 'And, yes, the hospital has at least two psychologists on staff but they mainly see out-patients, or give counselling to inpatients with serious conditions, and their families.'

'All of which is certainly needed,' Charles agreed, 'but still.'

'Let's go and see,' Jo said. 'If we both go then we don't need to go in tomorrow for you to meet the bosses and have a look around. I'll just let Dottie know.'

She was back within minutes, another bright scarf twisted around her neck.

'We'll take my car,' she said, leading the way back to the garage where a compact red vehicle had been all but unseen behind the hearse.

'We'll drive through the village and this time you'll get to see what sights there are,' she told him, 'then out along the river to Anooka itself. Originally, the port was to be the main town because in the early days goods came up from Sydney by boat, but after a couple of quite bad floods the town councillors realised that with such a narrow opening between the hills for the creek it would always flood in bad weather, and they shifted the town to Anooka.'

Was she talking like a tour guide to distract herself from sensations that being cooped up in the car with Charles was causing? She rather thought she was but what was the alternative?

No way could she follow the strong urges to rest her hand on his knee to feel his warmth, or touch the longer bit of hair that flopped onto his forehead! Was his hair a bit longer than he usually wore it, that he pushed it dis-tractedly away, though he must know it would flop again?

She did!

Finally arriving at the hospital was a great relief, as she'd run out of tourist guide talk when he'd touched her shoulder to ask the name of the jacaranda that was in full bloom in a suburban yard.

She'd managed the word 'jacaranda', but the effort finished her and although she'd have been happy to have the prompt of a question, she didn't really want him touching her again because his touch warmed her skin and sent shivers down her spine.

Surely they'd need an extra hand at the hospital. Work would bring her down to earth.

She sighed as she finally found a vacant parking spot and switched off the engine.

Then looked at the man who was causing all the problems.

'If I told you I feel the same way, would it help?' he said, with a smile so suggestive it should be illegal.

'I haven't the faintest idea what you're talking about,' she said crossly, and clambered out of the car.

CHAPTER FIVE

SHE LED THE way first to the ED but Kate was still in a treatment room, being stitched up, so Jo took him up to the admin offices on the top floor.

'I've always thought they should give the patients these views,' she said, as the silence between them was becoming uncomfortable.

But Charles was staring out the windows, taking in the town clustered below, then the green fields of the farmland that reached out to the rocky headlands and white sand beaches. He looked for Dottie's house, but guessed it must be further to the north.

'It *is* some view,' he said, but Jo was bent over a desk, talking to a young woman who was probably the receptionist.

'Sam Warren's in and can see us,' she called back to Charles, who was still taking in the spectacle beyond the windows. 'Sam's the general manager, and he handles a lot of the HR stuff as well, although Becky collates the staff rosters when they come up from the wards.'

Charles supposed it all made sense but as he'd had little to do with the administrative side of the hospitals where he'd worked, he really didn't know. He caught up with Jo, shook hands with Becky when he was introduced, and followed Jo into an inner sanctum.

'Jo, you're not pregnant! You've had the baby? Are you well? Please say you are because if you are, you're the answer to a fervent prayer!'

The man had leapt out from behind his desk and rushed towards Jo, arms extended, to give her a hug. And although Charles didn't know much about his own hospital's admin, he was fairly certain this wasn't normal behaviour. Although the man must be close to Jo to have known about the baby.

'What do you think, Charles?' Jo was saying, and he knew he'd missed some important bit of the conversation.

She smiled at him, which threatened to create more turmoil in his head.

'It looks like I'll be coming to work with you next week. I've still got the locum working my clinic, and Sam's desperate for staff in the emergency department. It's always the place that suffers most when something like the summer flu hits staff hard. The ED is desperately short-handed, especially with the carnival and Schoolies' Week coming up.'

Right!

The summer flu part of the conversation had given him a clue—the hospital was short-staffed—so he could understand this Sam being pleased that he, Charles, was starting on Monday, but Jo?

Sam, having shaken hands with Charles somewhere in the middle of Jo's explanation, had settled back behind his desk, and was now smiling at them in a kindly way.

'While you're in town, you might want to see the flat we have for you,' he said to Charles. 'Actually, Jo, it's a two-bedroom, if you want to share it any night you feel too tired to drive home.'

He peered at Jo for a moment, then added, 'That is, if

you've got a home. Isn't your locum living at your place? Are you still at Dottie's?'

Jo nodded, glanced at Charles, then said, 'Charles is there too. He was blown in by the storm and Dottie relented enough to let him to stay until the water went down.'

Sam laughed.

'You mean she's dragooned you into staying, Charles. She loves a bit of company for all it tires her out after a while! She's probably about to kick you out.'

Charles blinked at this very accurate description of his grandmother, but Sam was still talking.

'She delivered me, you know. Delivered half the town, and still acts as if we all belong to her—scolding us if she thinks we've done something wrong, giving orders when she needs something done.'

That sounded more like the Dottie he was getting to know!

'Even if she's happy to let you stay, you should probably use the flat—Jo will tell you how unreliable our shift times are, and you're not so far away you can't visit she-who-must-be-obeyed when you've got time off!'

Sam was smiling broadly, and Charles knew the words were spoken with great affection.

Which was all very well, but sharing a flat with Jo?

He ignored a little niggle of what seemed like excitement and turned his mind firmly back to the conversation, which had moved on to practical matters.

He found, when he considered it, he would very much like to work with Jo, to see her in another setting.

But sharing a flat?

He tuned in to what Sam was saying—something about rosters…

'…try to get you both on at the same time. If Dottie does decide she'd like you to visit, you might as well travel together. And it will save you hiring a car, Charles, at least for the moment, as Jo can give you a lift.'

Charles's mind flashed back to the hearse and he hurried to say that would be most convenient, super, in fact!

And if the twitch of Jo's lips and the twinkle in her eyes were anything to go on, she knew exactly why he was so excited at the prospect of travelling in her car.

Sam had stood up to come around the desk and shake his hand once again, fervent in his thanks, suggesting, if they had the time, Jo could show him around the ED while they were there.

'We're heading that way anyway,' Jo told him. 'We sent you a patient earlier and wanted to check up on her.'

'Well, see Becky on your way out for a key to the flat. It's the one with the green door. We're slowly doing them all up, thinking we might rent them out as most of the staff have homes in town.'

Jo thanked him, and they said goodbye.

But Sam was already dictating a note to his secretary— no doubt about new rosters and the extra doctor who had fallen, so fortuitously, into his lap.

While Charles's thoughts were on the flat… Bad enough to be working with Jo, but sharing a flat?

The idea shocked and excited him in equal measure.

Was she mad? Jo asked herself, as the sudden jolt told them the elevator had reached the ground floor. Arranging to work with this man, who was already causing her no end of physical trouble?

And what on earth had he meant earlier—that bit about feeling the same way.

Of course it didn't help!

If anything, it threw her into even more confusion. How

could he possibly know what she was feeling, let alone feel it himself?

How could a handsome, intelligent, worldly man like Charles—a man who probably called half the crowned heads of Europe by their first names—possibly feel attraction to a flabby, post-pregnant redhead?

The questions were hammering in her head as she left the building, a key with a green tag clutched in her hand. She headed across the car park, while the idea of sharing the green-doored flat with Charles made her walk even faster.

Until she was brought up short by a deep, beautifully modulated voice from behind her.

'Weren't we going to the ED to see your friend, and so you could show me around?'

'Oh, damn, of course we were. Come on.'

She spun around and walked quickly back towards the ED.

She felt Charles following her, her heightened awareness of him making her back feel uncomfortably...

Twitchy!

He caught up with her, which wasn't much better as now his arm brushed against hers.

'I think I should let you visit her, while I have a look around. She was obviously deeply upset about something and will talk more easily to a friend than a stranger.'

Jo glanced at him. He was right, of course, she should have thought of that herself. So why did it niggle at her?

Him being right, or the whole silly situation, which, in fact, she was probably imagining?

They walked into the huge room together, seeing patients scattered on chairs that were set in groups, rather than lined up along walls as they'd been when Jo was training.

'Looks comfortable,' Charles remarked, and Jo smiled.

To hell with whatever was going on with her body, the man was an acquaintance, passing through her life. And in this case, their thoughts were on the same wavelength.

'I think the same thing every time I walk in here,' she said. 'I don't know where the idea came from but I'm sure the people waiting to be seen get less impatient because the wait is more comfortable than at a lot of places.'

She led him to the reception desk and introduced him, explaining he'd be starting here on Monday.

'Just have a look around,' the nurse on duty told him. 'We're so short-staffed I can't offer you a guided tour, but poke your head in wherever you want to and introduce yourself.'

'And I'd like to see Kate Atkins,' Jo said. 'She was brought in from Port about an hour ago.'

The nurse checked her computer.

'Doctor's hoping to admit her, but we've got one ward closed so it's hard to find a bed. She's in that kind of holding bay out the back. You know the way?"

Jo smiled at her.

'Should do,' she said. 'I've filled in here often enough and I'll be back on Monday too.'

She made her way out to the big room behind the ED, then peered through the curtains into the cubicles until she found a drowsy Kate, lying on her narrow stretcher, tears still damp on her cheeks.

'You okay?' Jo asked, and won a watery smile.

'For now, I suppose,' Kate told her.

'Well, that's the main thing,' Jo said. 'Go with "for now" and we'll sort out the rest later.'

She paused then gently touched Kate's cheek.

'We *will* sort it out, I promise you,' she said quietly, and Kate's smile improved.

'I know that,' she finally said. 'It was stupid. I felt lost—

trapped—the busy season starting… Could I manage on my own? But now I know nothing's ever that bad. Thank you for finding me. I knew by the time you got there, I really, really didn't want to die.'

Jo grinned.

'You hold onto that thought,' she said. 'That's a huge first step towards getting to wherever you want to go. Now, is there anyone else I can phone? Rolf said he'd manage the café, but would you like your mother to come and stay for a while?'

Kate shook her head.

'Rolf will look after me when I go home. We've been best friends for ever. It was just the marriage part that didn't work out.'

'I understand,' Jo said. 'Now, what you need is sleep. You've got my mobile number if you need it, and I'll call in over the weekend, or come and get you if they decide to send you home.'

She bent and brushed a kiss against Kate's cheek, unprofessional for a doctor but definitely okay for a friend…

Back in the ED, Charles was waiting by the desk, chatting to the nurse.

'See you Monday,' he called to her, as he joined Jo near the door.

'It's a well set-up ED,' he said, as they walked out. 'I gather the hospital is fairly new.'

'Only opened eighteen months ago. The old one hadn't kept up with the population growth of the district, but this one's a beauty.'

She was reaching in her handbag for her car keys when she felt the other key, the one with the green tag, colour coded to the door.

They *should* have a look at the flat; check out what it contained in the way of home comforts if they were mov-

ing in next week. Yet the blithe way Sam had explained it
was a two-bedroom so they could share had sent shivers
down her spine.

She was having enough trouble with her reactions to
Charles with Dottie around as chaperone. Heaven only
knew where things might lead if they were sharing the
flat, even occasionally...

'Aren't we going to see the flat?'

Trust him not to have forgotten it!

'Of course,' she said, clasping the key more tightly in
her hand and striding out towards the back of the building.
She'd done some time in this hospital before going into
private practice and had lived in one of the flats, which
had been behind the old building. As a very junior registrar her days had often been long, and night duty a regular occurrence.

They hadn't improved!

That was her first thought when she saw the rather ram-
shackle line of flats tucked away beneath some spreading
poinciana trees, brilliant red and orange flowers just beginning to appear among the new leaves.

'Poincianas,' she said, before Charles could ask, but he
seemed uninterested in the trees, focused instead on the
end flat—the one with the green door.

Jo handed over the key, happy for him to lead the way
inside, but of course, gentleman that he was, he opened
the door and stood back so she had to go through first,
passing very close to him, into a space that was neatly
furnished with a three-piece suite, television, coffee table
and a kitchenette at the far end. Two bedrooms, beds already made up, with fluffy towels folded on them, separated by a bathroom, led off a small hall, all in all a neat
little place.

But not one Jo would want to spend time in—not if it

meant sharing with Charles. The way her wanton hormones were behaving, she needed distance, not togetherness.

'Much better than some hospital accommodation I've lived in,' he was saying as he prowled around, opening cupboards in the kitchen and peering out the window that overlooked the paddocks behind the hospital.

'I assume we're to keep the key?' Jo said. 'Although, really, we'll need two—we won't both be coming off duty at the same time, even if we're rostered on the same shifts—no shifts ever end on time.'

Charles smiled at her.

'We'll be working in the same department. How hard will it be to get the key from whoever's got it—or even leave it in the tea room for whoever finishes first to take?'

It was the smile that did it!

No way could she spend her off-duty time in the close company of this man. She'd have to visit friends, or shop, or—

Something!

She was being silly. Yes, there was attraction there, so what harm would a little flirtation between them do? It couldn't go very far, and it might be fun!

Fun?

Was she out of her mind?

We'll need two keys,' she said firmly. 'I'll get another one cut.'

'That's fine,' he said. 'It's really no big deal and, who knows, this might be fun!'

'Fun!' Jo echoed, hardly able to believe he'd just voiced her thoughts. '*What* might just be fun?'

He grinned at her.

'Might take us both back to carefree, student days.'

Jo was about to say 'Hmph' but knew she'd sound just like Dottie, so she muttered at him instead.

'I can't remember too much that was carefree about my student days—more lectures and assignments and exams and always worrying whether I was going to faint dissecting a formaldehyde-laden body.'

'So you never considered pathology?' Charles teased, and Jo had to smile, which confirmed her strong belief that sharing a flat with this man was *not* a good idea.

The days continued warm and sunny, and it was Charles, who'd been out for an early morning walk, who announced that the surf carnival people were arriving.

'At least,' he said, as he delivered two perfectly boiled eggs to Dottie, 'I suppose that's what all the cars and tents and caravans are doing on the far headland. Shall we all go?'

'Seen one, seen them all,' Dottie said. 'But Jo should take you, show you around. There'll be fireworks at night so you might as well stay all day.'

Disconcerted by what was really a dismissal, Jo was about to protest when Dottie added, 'Oh, don't fuss about me, Jo. You know perfectly well I can look after myself—even cook my own eggs when I don't have someone to do them for me—and Molly's going to look in later.'

'So?' Charles said.

And Jo, although every instinct was warning her against it, sighed and said, 'I suppose it's something you should see. We'll take our swimmers and towels so we can swim when it gets too hot, and hats, plenty of sunscreen, and the parking will be a nightmare so we'll walk.'

'Walk? But isn't it the other side of the village?'

'There's a foot bridge,' Dottie informed him, 'so people can get from one side to the other in a flood. Besides' she gave him a slightly hesitant look '...your mother always walked.'

Jo, who was quietly eating her breakfast, looked up in time to see the brief look of shock on Charles's face, and knew that this—Dottie's first unasked-for mention of his mother—must have struck deep. But he rallied, and smiled at Dottie.

'Then I shall certainly walk.'

He cleared his and Dottie's breakfast things off the table, and began to rinse the dishes.

'Leave those,' his grandmother ordered. 'I can still handle a little washing up. You get ready, and, as Jo said, don't forget the sunscreen.'

Jo stood up as he departed, cleared her breakfast things and, ignoring Dottie's protest, quickly washed and dried the dishes.

'I'm all ready to go,' she said. 'As soon as I woke up to the bright sunny day I knew we'd have to make the most of it. Are you sure you wouldn't like to come? We could take the car, and deck chairs to sit on, even a beach umbrella for shade.'

Dottie shook her head.

'No, you and the Prince go,' she said, 'and, for goodness' sake, have some fun. He looks as if he might be fun to be with and it's a long time since you've let your hair down.'

Jo had trouble processing this command, and she studied Dottie's face for a few moments, wondering just what the old woman was up to, but a rock would have given more away.

Dottie had been right in one thing. The Prince did look as if he might be fun to be with, and perhaps she could forget all the attraction stuff and just enjoy being with him.

Having fun!

They said goodbye to Dottie, who was in the living room, pulling dead flowers from a big arrangement and replacing them with others she must have collected earlier. Setting off along the clifftop, they dropped down as they came to where the creek ran out into the ocean and followed it along towards a small footbridge that was high above the now quiet water.

And walking along, with the sun warming her skin and the air redolent of the sea, Jo felt a surge of joy.

Joy?

The word that had come into her head surprised her but, considering it, she knew that it was the right one, for it was more than pleasure she was feeling. It was the bubbling happiness of joy!

'You look radiant!' Charles said, and she turned to him, stunned by *his* choice of word.

'I feel great!' she told him with a smile she knew was still in joyful mode. 'Just relaxed, and free, and utterly at peace with the world. I suppose the pregnancy might have taken more of a toll on my resilience than I'd realised, but right now I'd like to skip and dance and laugh and probably go a little mad. We're in a beautiful place, on a beautiful day, so why not go mad?'

They were under a shady tree at the approach to the bridge, and she felt Charles's hand on her shoulder—the hand that made the flesh beneath her skin feel warm.

'Just how mad?' he asked, a smile on his face but a distinct huskiness in his voice.

She stared at him, aware her words had been a little crazy, but as his head moved closer, and his lips met hers—just a brush at first, like a breath it was so light—then the madness took them and Jo hoped the kiss would never end, that the madness would go on for ever...

'Madness!' she said, when they finally broke apart and she looked hastily around to make sure none of her patients were viewing this erratic behaviour.

'Madness?' he echoed, and she knew it wasn't. It was far more than that to her—something she had never felt before, not with anyone. Not that there'd been many 'anyones'…

But she couldn't tell him that, so she just smiled and said, 'What else could it be?'

What else indeed? She was seriously attracted to this man who'd just kissed her, but nothing could come of it—he was a prince, for heaven's sake—*and* he'd want children, which she believed, deep down and with utter conviction, that it would be unfair of her to have.

So, on her first holiday here, she'd settled on Port Anooka as the perfect place to spend her life. As the local GP she'd have a position in the town and plenty of acquaintances, and wouldn't need a label like wife or mother because she already had one—doctor!

They crossed the bridge while these thoughts tumbled in her head. Reminding her, reassuring her…

They climbed the far headland, while she considered whether having a light flirtation with someone passing through would fit into this life-plan and had almost decided it wouldn't when she tripped.

Charles caught her arm, held her until she was steady on her feet, and maybe just a little bit longer.

'You okay? You were walking blindly there.'

She looked at him and smiled, having done a complete backflip as he'd caught her arm and come down on the side of the flirtation being okay—providing she kept it light!

Maybe!

They walked on, dodging between the many small camps set up on its lush and still very damp grass. And when Charles took her hand to steady her as she stepped over another taut tent rope, she let it stay there, enjoying the connection to another human being—enjoying, if she was honest, the connection to him.

'Oh, my word!'

Charles's exclamation said it all. From the clifftop it looked as if the sea was alive with people. Lon boards, smaller modern surfboards and bodyboards, all were out, their riders taking advantage of the high curling breakers that swept in to the beach, while on the shore children played in the shallows, and the bright beach umbrellas looked like some newly sprung-up tent city.

'Quite something, huh?' Jo said to him, proud of the spectacle her little village had turned on.

'Quite something,' he repeated, although he was looking at her as he said it, and she felt heat rush through her body.

She should have brought the car—*and* the key to the green door! They could have this day—this one day out of time—and then forget about the whole attraction thing. It would be easier to forget after just one day, but after six weeks?

Impossible?

She didn't know…

Although even thinking about the flat with the green door was foolish, when one considered that she had given birth so recently. The baby might not have been hers, but her body still needed to get back to normal. Oxytocin might be helping her uterus contract, but it would take months of exercise to get her flabby stomach into shape.

She glanced at Charles, pleased to see he was caught up in the spectacle before them so wouldn't have seen the lascivious thoughts she'd been having reflected on her face.

They made their way down to the grassy dunes above the beach and found a space large enough for her to spread her big beach towel.

Locals close by called out hello, enquiring about the baby and how it was doing, and asking how she was.

Answering their questions was good, normal, and right

now she needed as much normality as she could get. Some stopped to chat, and she introduced Charles, which was a bit of a dilemma as she wasn't certain Dottie would want him introduced as her grandson, so she went with the doctor who was starting at the Anooka Hospital on Monday and she was showing him the sights.

'They like you, your patients?' he said when they were on their own.

She laughed.

'I think all patients like their doctors, or at least pretend to. If they get stroppy with us we might retaliate by jabbing the needle in too far.'

But Charles was no longer listening. He was on his feet, looking down towards the beach, and, standing up, Jo could see a lifesaver on a jet-ski, trying to herd a group of swimmers back towards the shore.

'There is something wrong?' he asked.

'It's probably a rip, and it's taking the swimmers into the area where the surfers come in on their boards. With so many boards in the water, there could easily be an accident.'

'But, look, they have missed one.'

Most of the people on the dune were pointing now to where the head of a swimmer bobbed up and down, right in the path of a surfer on a longboard.

'There's a lifesaver in a tower on the beach, he will have seen that person and someone will be on their way to get him or her.'

Even as she spoke Jo saw the familiar red and yellow cap of a lifesaver in the water, no doubt heading towards the person in trouble.

'See the orange float he has over his shoulder? That will keep the swimmer afloat on the journey back to the beach. On the bigger beaches they are using drones to patrol the area, which also have the capability of carrying one of those floats and dropping it close to anyone in trouble. It's amazing what they can do.'

'That board-rider has gone into the curl of the wave, he won't see them,' Charles said, and before Jo realised it, he'd taken off, racing down the dune and across the beach and into the water.

Jo followed, more so she could yell at him for putting himself in danger than with any thought of giving help. The lifesavers who patrolled the beaches were well trained, and most clubs had at least one paramedic among their members.

Beside which an ambulance was parked beside the club—a necessity at any sporting event.

'They know their job,' she said, rather breathlessly, when she caught up with Charles. 'People drown trying to save someone else.'

She'd grabbed his arm and was holding onto him before she realised he was only in knee-deep water and probably hadn't intended going further in.

'I would not be so foolish,' he said. 'But that board was coming right at the swimmer and the lifesaver. See, that's the board coming in to shore now, but all three of them are somewhere under the waves.'

Four lifesavers were now at the scene and the jet-ski rider had gone out to stop the surfers until the accident was sorted. Now they could only wait.

The board-rider was the first to appear from the tumbling waves, followed by the lifesaver, helped by one of his mates, while another of the lifesavers now had the swimmer, holding him on the float as she headed for the beach.

The swimmer, a man, they discovered, was lifted from the water and laid on the sand, two of the lifesavers immediately beginning CPR while another arrived with the pack containing the resuscitation kit, the ambos following behind with a stretcher.

'They know their jobs and we will only get in the way,' Jo said to Charles, taking his arm as he made to step toward the drama.

He watched for a moment, then nodded.

'Like our ski patrols,' he said. 'This is what they train for. I—'

Whatever he was going to add was lost in an urgent cry of 'Hey, Doc!' and Jo turned to see one of the lifesavers waving towards her.

She hurried towards him, Charles on her heels.

'Can you look at Susie's leg? I think the board caught her.'

A young woman was sitting on a towel, holding one end of it to her calf. Her swimsuit told them she was one of the lifesavers on duty, although she looked very young.

Jo knelt beside her, and lifted the towel. The fin on the back of the board had sliced her calf open, leaving a six-inch gash, deep enough to need absorbable sutures on the muscle before skin closure.

'She'll need to go to the hospital to have it cleaned and stitched,' she told the lad who'd called them over. 'Can you bring the first-aid box? We'll put a pressure pad and bandage on it then, rather than wait for the ambulance and the other patient, I'm sure you'll find a volunteer to take her to the hospital.'

'I'll take her,' the lad said, before running swiftly back to the clubhouse to get what was needed, while another club member sat down beside Susie to comfort her.

'Would you have repaired it at your surgery if you were working?' Charles asked as they stood and waited. And something in the way Jo looked at him made him add, 'I am wondering from the point of what GPs do—how far their duties might range.'

She grinned.

'So it wasn't a test of what I'm capable of?'

She was beautiful in his eyes all the time, but something in that impish grin stirred up all kinds of responses in his body.

Stick to the conversation, he warned himself, aware they'd already strayed into dangerous waters.

'Of course not, but would you?'

She shook her head.

'Something less deep—a clean cut even—but you need to think of the person. A surgeon at the hospital will do a much better job and leave barely a scar. For a young woman—for anyone—that might be important.'

He liked the way she thought, this woman, Charles decided, but surely this liking, this attraction was happening because this was his sentimental journey, and the romantic elopement of his mother with his father was ever-present in his mind.

And for all he imagined the attraction was mutual, immediately after having a baby was really not the best time to be considering any kind of romantic relationship, now, was it?

CHAPTER SIX

'I THINK THAT excitement was enough to put me off a swim this morning,' Charles said, as they returned to their belongings.

Jo nodded.

'Especially as the rip could get worse as the tide comes in. And given the crowds already packing the beach, a walk along it isn't too enticing.'

'So let's go back to the house and put up the Christmas decorations. I have noticed boxes of them in many of the rooms, and that Christmas tree looks sad with only one bauble on it!'

She had to smile.

'And what would you know about putting up Christmas decorations?' she asked, certain an array of servants would have done any decoration in a palace—not that she knew much of how he lived but surely there'd be a palace…

'Nothing,' he admitted with a grin so full of cheek it made her head spin. 'But if I am to learn of my Australian roots then I must learn this custom, too, no?'

'Of course, and that's a great idea. I was about to start when the water began coming through the roof,' Jo said, gathering up her belongings. 'And if we get finished in time, we can go to the coffee shop for lunch—Rolf serves the most fantastic avocado smash on toast and he'll still be in charge.'

She was folding her big beach towel to put into her backpack when Charles reached out and took it from her hands. His fingers brushed hers, startling her so she glanced up at his face and saw he, too, had felt that flash of something—almost like recognition.

He half smiled, shrugged, then bent to put the towel in his backpack—a gentlemanly act to lighten her load.

It wasn't the weight of her backpack worrying her as they set off but her physical reactions to what had been nothing more than an accidental touch. She had just given birth so, hormones or not, she was hardly in a position to plunge into an affair.

In fact, it was out of the question.

But a flirtation, that was different, surely. A few kisses now and then, touching, teasing, flirting. And if he made her feel more alive than she'd ever felt before, and sent fire racing through her body with a smile, then surely that was just, well, an added benefit—a reminder that she was, in fact, a woman...

She hitched her backpack onto her shoulder and led the way back through the crowds of spectators and campers, the carnival going on without much more than a slight delay.

But the light flirtation idea didn't seem so good as they headed back to the house. Walking beside him, aware of him in every cell of her body, was torture and she felt her tension building and building as they approached the tree where he had kissed her.

'I think perhaps we should kiss again, don't you?' he asked as they grew inevitably closer. 'Establish a little custom that is just for us?'

And although her nerves were screaming with frustration, her body demanding at least a kiss, she hesitated, suddenly aware that no flirtation with this man would ever be light.

But before she could process this, his hand slid around her waist and he drew her into the deep, hidden shadow beneath the tree, and, unable to resist, she let him. She let him turn her towards him, press her body against his, and claim her lips with a kiss that burned through any doubts and melted her bones so she slumped against him, replete for the moment, although she knew she'd want more.

Need more…

They resumed their walk in silence as crossed the bridge, and as they climbed back towards the house on the bluff Jo finally found enough breath to form words.

'We can watch the fireworks tonight from up here,' she said.

'Coward!'

The word made her turn to look at him and his teasing smile made her blush even before he spoke. 'You don't want to walk past the tree again! And what if I want to see the fun fair—I saw they have rides and bumper cars?'

'It will be getting dark and we'll drive,' Jo said firmly, and she stalked on ahead of him, although in two strides he was back by her side.

She'd thought hanging Christmas decorations would provide respite from the bombardment of sensations her body had been suffering, but no. The contents of the boxes had to be sorted, so hands inevitably brushed, and handing tinsel up to someone on a ladder meant fingers tangling—tingling!

They'd barely started in the living room when Dottie appeared.

'Do you have a special way you like things hung?' Jo

asked her, and she shook her head, settled into a chair and watched the proceedings in silence.

Most un-Dottie-like!

With the windows swathed in tinsel and festive streamers, Jo declared they would start on the tree.

'That tree's no good,' Dottie declared suddenly enough to have them both turn and stare at her. 'It's too old, too worn and, anyway, Bertie always liked a live tree.'

'A live tree?' Jo echoed faintly. 'Does anyone in Anooka sell live trees? I can't remember seeing them anywhere.'

'Bertie always cut one down,' Dottie informed them. 'You know the kind, Jo, those dark green native pines. There are always some in that bushland at the back of the house. They grow in sandy soil all along the east coast.'

'I know the ones you mean. And you say there are some out the back? I must say I've never ventured far out there, but if there's a hatchet in the garage I'm sure Charles and I can find one.'

'Thank you,' Dottie said, and the words were such a surprise Jo could only stare at their host, who was looking out the window with a look of such sorrow on her face Jo wanted to hug her.

Charles had already picked up the old tree and was carrying it out of the room, so Jo followed, pausing only long enough to ask Dottie if she wanted anything before they left.

But the older woman remained silent, so lost in thought she probably hadn't heard Jo's voice.

'The poor dear,' Charles said. 'I suppose after Bertie had his stroke, she had to buy an artificial tree.'

Jo nodded, then shook her head.

'But she wasn't going to *not* have a tree! It's as my Gran said, she carried on as if nothing had ever changed despite Bertie being in a wheelchair.'

'*And* my mother being gone,' Charles reminded her as he dumped the old tree in a rubbish bin by the garage. He paused, his hand still holding the lid of the bin. 'I wonder if concentrating all her energies on Bertie helped her get over my mother's defection?'

'You're probably right,' Jo said with a sigh. 'It would explain why she looked so sad talking about the trees—your mother had probably decorated the ones that Bertie cut. She probably went with him to find the perfect one.'

'So why can't she tell me that?' Charles asked, and Jo, hearing the pain in his voice, took the bin lid gently from his hand, set it down in place and put her arms around him, offering a comforting hug.

'Was it very hard, growing up without your mother?' she murmured against his shoulder.

He eased her far enough away that he could look into her face.

'I can't honestly say it was. I had a nanny, of course, and I think most of the children I knew were the same. We were often brought out to be paraded before guests, or I'd be taken to dine with my father from time to time, and he would talk about the things I would have to do when I took his place. But it was Nanny Pat who brought me up, and when I went to school, so many of the other boys had grown up in a similar way that to us it was normal.'

Having delivered the hug she'd thought he needed, Jo had dropped her arms and moved a little away, but now it was her turn to feel sorrow, sorrow for a little boy—for all the children who had never really known their mothers.

Did her own child feel that way? Did she feel let down by the mother who had given her away? Did she carry a hidden sorrow for all she had loving parents?

At least Jo hoped to hell she had loving parents...

She thrust the thought away as she'd been doing now

for nearly sixteen years and returned to the conversation with a question.

'So why the interest in your mother now?'

He smiled.

'For a start, I went to university where I learned that other people had real relationships with their parents. Would my mother have been equally interested in me both as her son and as a person in my own right? Would I have known her as my friends know their mothers? Or would she have been someone I ate with once a week, who checked my manners, and questioned whether I knew the order of precedence for seating at state dinners?'

Jo shook her head. She'd thought she'd had it tough, having only known her mother for fourteen years, but after a brief hiatus she'd had Gran.

But Charles!

'I'm sorry! We'll work this out, I'm sure we will. It's easy to see why you want to know more about your mother as a person, and you've come all this way and found a grandmother who refuses to mention her. But there has to be a reason, because Dottie, while gruff and forthright, is a kind person at heart.'

They'd moved into the garage as they were talking, and although Jo felt he needed at least one more hug, she turned her attention to the task at hand and found a small hatchet on the shelves, which the gardener kept meticulously tidy!

She handed it to Charles.

'Let's go find a tree,' she said. 'Maybe a real live Christmas tree will mellow Dottie into talking.'

Charles followed Jo out into the wild tangle of reeds and trees beyond the mown edge of the garden. They ducked under a branch of a particularly ugly tree with spiky, grey-green leaves, and large grey and bristly misshapen things that he imagined could give children nightmares.

'Banksias,' Jo said, right on cue. 'The flowers you might know as bottlebrush because they are exported as cut flowers to many parts of the world, but when they die they turn into one of these with those fluffy, beak-like seed pods.'

She snapped one off to show him.

'As children many of us were read stories about gum nut blossom fairies, and these featured as the big bad banksia men.'

Charles took the strange object, and could see how it had developed from a bottlebrush flower.

'It would have scared me,' he said.

But he'd lost Jo's attention. She was staring fixedly ahead, and as he finished speaking she murmured, 'Look!' in awed tones.

For there, right in front of them, was a small green tree, a perfect tree, about five feet in height, with its branches beautifully proportioned, and soft green foliage making it the ideal Christmas tree.

'It's beautiful,' Charles agreed. 'But should we take it? Is this public land? Or might it be a protected species?'

Jo turned to him, some of the excitement fading from her expressive face.

'Not public land,' she said, 'because I know Dottie's property extends right back towards Anooka itself. Apparently, Bertie wanted the land preserved as nature intended it so future generations could see the natural coastal scrub that grew in these parts before development took over.'

'It's certainly fascinating,' Charles said, moving a little away to a tree with strips of its bark hanging off it. 'See this?' he said, pulling at a strip of bark and admiring the soft pink colour of the inner layer. 'My mother didn't take much when she ran away, but she did have a small, framed scene of mountains and a creek and I'd swear it was made out of different colours of this bark.'

'Bark pictures!' Jo said. 'They were all the rage at one time. My gran used to collect bark when we were here on holiday and take it home to make a picture.'

Charles touched the tree, feeling the layers of paper-fine bark, wondering if this was the tree that had given its bark for his mother's scene.

'They're coastal tea trees but their common name is paper bark,' Jo was saying, but his mind had conjured up an image of his mother—not hard when his father had dozens of photographs—and now Charles pictured her by the tree, her hand where his was resting, and he knew with certainty that he'd done the right thing in coming here. He was learning about her, getting to know her, even without Dottie's help.

'Christmas tree!' Jo prompted, and he came back to earth to smile at her.

'It's perfect,' he said, 'and, better still, now I look around, there are plenty more of them, big and small, so they obviously regenerate well and we're not doing too much environmental damage to the…scrub? Is that what you called it?'

'Coastal scrub,' Jo confirmed, 'but you weren't thinking about that as you stood there.'

He smiled again.

'No, I was realising that even without Dottie's help I am learning so much about my mother. Looking at the young people at the beach this morning, from children upwards, they were all having fun, living such obviously free lives in the sunshine that I know she must have been like that. She would have swum there, played in the waves, maybe she rode a surfboard, then walked home along the path, sandy and tired, a little sunburnt maybe. She is coming to life for me now!'

With a lump almost too big to swallow in her throat, Jo

reached out and took his hand, holding it tightly between hers, squeezing his fingers and hoping he'd hear the words she was too moved to say.

He used the hand she held to draw her closer, and took her in his arms, kissing her more gently this time, a long, exploratory kiss that started out as thanks that she was helping him along this journey of discovery and ended up, he hoped, saying much more.

For as he held her, kissed her, the vague suspicion that she was special to him—very special—firmed into knowledge and he found himself wanting her as he'd never wanted anyone before.

Was this what love felt like?

'We're here for the tree,' she whispered against his lips, and slowly he released her, looking into her face and seeing the shadows in her eyes, as if she too had felt a shift in their relationship.

'Cut it low,' she said, now totally in control while his head battled with the word 'relationship'. Really, it was hardly that!

He cut the tree and carried it back in triumph, going straight to the house while Jo replaced the hatchet.

Had Dottie watched them return that she was at the door to open it as he arrived?

'I've got a bucket of sand ready for it,' she said, leading him back into the decorated living room, then sitting again, watching.

To check if he was up to this?

To measure him against her beloved Bertie?

Jo returned in time to hold it steady while he packed sand around the trunk, but when it was done and she'd moved away towards Dottie to check it was upright, and he'd squatted on his haunches, pleased with his efforts, Dottie's voice broke the silence.

'You look like him, you know,' she said, and Charles turned slowly to look at her. 'Especially from side on, when he was young, when I first knew him.'

Her voice wavered on the final words and he saw Jo move to rest her hand on Dottie's shoulder, but the sight of the pair of them was blurry and he could find no words to speak.

Jo broke the still, taut silence.

'Perhaps you've some photos of Bertie when he was Charles's age that we could all look at sometime,' she said.

But Dottie had moved on—regained her composure and shut the door she'd so tantalisingly begun to open.

'It's lunchtime,' she said. 'Molly brought some avocados and we've Turkish bread in the freezer.' She turned to Charles. 'Do you like avocado?'

Unable to shift mental gears as swiftly as his grandmother, Charles nodded.

'Then Jo can make us avocado smash for lunch,' Dottie continued. 'In my day we called it avocado on toast but the smash thing seems to be all the go in cafés these days. And it is better on that Turkish bread, which we didn't have in my day. Just bread, brown or white, and now there are at least two dozen different breads in every supermarket.'

Was she talking to hide what she might have thought was a moment of weakness?

And was she a witch that she'd suggested the lunch Jo had spoken of them having at the café?

Charles sighed. How would he ever know? He was beginning to think if she lived to be a hundred he still wouldn't be able to work her out. But as Jo had left the room, no doubt to smash a few avocados, he should get rid of the bucket of leftover sand and tidy up around the tree.

They ate lunch under the poinciana tree. He'd been drafted in to move the chairs and table once again, but as he sat there, looking out to sea, biting into the crisp toast and creamy avocado, generously sprinkled with lemon, salt and pepper, a feeling of great well-being swept through him, and all the muddle of thoughts and questions in his head disappeared so he could simply sit and enjoy the company and the lunch, *and* the spectacular view out over the Pacific Ocean.

Pacific—peaceful! That was how he felt.

It was so pleasant—so peaceful—sitting there beneath the tree, that even though lunch had been finished for a while and the desultory conversation had stopped altogether, Jo was reluctant to leave.

In the end it was Dottie who moved first.

'You can't be hanging around here all afternoon,' she announced. 'You've that tree to decorate.'

She stood up and headed for the house, while Charles, housetrained in spite of having grown up with servants, stacked the dirty dishes on the tray and followed her.

Left alone, Jo would have liked to stay—to sit and think a bit more—but Charles was a guest and although she was quite happy for him to wash and dry the dishes and generally clean up the kitchen, she felt duty bound to do something about decorating the tree.

She walked into the house as Dottie zoomed up on the stair lift, surely at more than her usual breakneck speed.

Was she all right?

Jo hesitated in the entry, but as she wondered if she should go up and check, Dottie reappeared with a battered old cardboard box held in her arms.

This time she sat carefully on the lift's chair and came down decorously.

Once at the bottom, she stayed seated, calling Jo over to her.

'Use these decorations,' she said. 'There's an angel for the top.'

She passed the box to Jo and up she shot again.

Jo stood there for a moment, wondering what all this was about, then shrugged and took the box through to the living room, setting it down on a chair near the tree.

'Thanks for your help with the washing up,' Charles said to her as he walked into the room.

'Hey, I cooked,' Jo reminded him, and he laughed.

'Smashed the avocados at least!' he said. 'What have you got there?'

She told him about Dottie's behaviour.

'I hardly like to open the box,' she said, feeling again the apprehension she'd experienced as Dottie had handed her the box.

'Let me,' Charles offered, and he came to stand beside her.

'Be careful,' Jo warned, and he turned, grinning at her.

'You think it might be booby-trapped?'

'Don't be silly!' Her reactions to that damn grin of his made her speak more sharply than she'd intended. 'But the contents might be fragile.'

And fragile they were! Beautiful, delicate, crystal objects—balls, and bells, and birds, even butterflies.

Carefully they lifted them from their tissue paper wrappings, admiring each one before hanging it carefully on the tree. Light from the windows caught the baubles and made a million tiny rainbows around the pair of them as they worked.

'It's as if the tree knows where it wants each one,' Jo said quietly, as they neared the bottom of the box and the tree was evenly covered with the fragile objects.

'You're right,' Charles murmured. 'I've barely had to think before placing each one.'

And at the bottom, doubly wrapped, Jo found the angel, small and perfectly formed, with an inner ring of wire beneath the skirt so it could be fitted upright on the very top of the tree.

They stood back, shoulder to shoulder, ignoring the box of crumpled tissue on the chair.

'It's beautiful,' Jo said, shaking her head in wonder at the magic the crystal objects had wrought.

'Stunning,' Charles agreed.

'They were your mother's, yours now, I guess, if you want them.'

They turned to see Dottie right behind them, as if she'd just materialised there for they'd been too absorbed to hear the stair lift.

'I wouldn't use them on that artificial tree,' she continued. 'It didn't deserve such beauty—so I bought coloured ones from the shops and used them instead.'

Jo found herself swallowing hard yet again and turned to see how Charles was taking it.

But he had stepped behind her and crossed to Dottie, taking both her hands in his.

'Thank you,' he said, 'they are really beautiful. But I think they should remain here, and when I have children and come to visit, they can see them for themselves.'

Jo saw the brightness of tears in Dottie's eyes and waited, wondering how she would react.

'Well,' she said, 'they do need a small tree and you probably have an enormous one in your palace. But for myself, I've always wanted to see snow, especially at Christmas, with snowmen, and carol singers, and sleigh rides.'

'And so you shall!' Charles said, his face alight with happiness as he lifted Dottie off the floor and swung her round. 'You'll have it all and more besides. We can alternate our Christmases, one here so the children, when they come, know their Australian heritage, and one at home, so their great-grandmother can see snow.'

CHAPTER SEVEN

THEY'D WATCHED THE fireworks from the bluff, Dottie sitting between them in the deckchairs Charles had set up, eating fish and chips from cardboard boxes at Jo's insistence that it was a summer carnival must.

The fish, freshly caught by one of the trawlers moored on the harbour wall at the mouth of the creek, was delicious, the chips hot and crispy.

Charles leant back in his chair and watched the rockets shoot into the sky, bursting into brilliant bouquets of light that reflected on the water below so the whole world seemed to glow with colour.

He watched Jo's face, too, from time to time, surprising a child-like wonder in the gaze of this seemingly practical woman.

But he couldn't sit and stare at Jo. Dottie would be sure to notice and right now whatever it was they had between them was too new and fragile to be put under Dottie's blunt scrutiny.

He turned his thoughts back to his grandmother.

Her talk of seeing snow at Christmas had come as such a surprise he could barely take it in, but she'd said it, and it could only mean she'd accepted him as her grandson.

It might only be a small crack in the wall of silence she'd built around his mother, but it was there.

And was he thinking of Dottie so he didn't have to think about too much about Jo—another woman he knew but really didn't know? He was reasonably sure the attraction he felt ran deep—but for a virtual stranger?

He'd picked up snippets about her life here and there, and seeing her around the house, watching the consideration with which she treated Dottie, he knew she was kind, thoughtful and very caring.

But why the surrogacy?

Because she was kind and caring?

And what kind of life had she led before it?

Hadn't Dottie mentioned a man?

A woman as beautiful as Jo would attract most men.

'...no work clothes here, and I don't want to disturb my locum and his family, so I might go into Anooka tomorrow and get some basic mix and match things there. The stores are all open seven days a week right through the holiday period.'

He'd missed the first part of the conversation. Had she asked if he wanted to go along?

The question lost relevance when Dottie said, 'And while you're away, Charles can take me down to the harbour, and we'll walk along the jetty, and I can show him where the big boats used to come in when the town was first settled.'

'Do you think she's mellowing?' he asked Jo when he'd put the deck chairs away and found her in the kitchen, making Dottie's night-time cocoa.

'Definitely,' Jo said.

'That was a "definitely" with a "but" hovering above it,' Charles told her.

'The "but" is your mother, isn't it? You're learning more about Bertie but, apart from the crystal ornaments, she's still tight-lipped about your mother, though it's hard to fathom why. Okay, so she ran off with someone Dottie didn't approve of—or maybe it was Bertie who disapproved. Maybe it was he who determined she cut herself off from their daughter, for all my gran said he was a lovely man.'

She sighed, which made Charles smile.

'There's no point in our speculating, is there? Let us just hope she continues to mellow, and drop tiny pearls of information that will one day give me a picture of my mother.'

'I think pearls make necklaces, not pictures,' Jo said to him. 'I'm taking this cocoa up to Dottie then going to bed myself. I'll see you in the morning.'

He watched her walk away, his mother forgotten as a new worry struck him. Had Jo been doing too much? Surrogate or not, she was a woman who'd just had a baby, and yet she'd barely stopped since the baby was born. First in her frenzy of housework, then showing him around the place, and now she was due to go back to work on Monday. Had *volunteered* to go back to work!

Was she keeping busy so she didn't have to think about the baby? Was she feeling loss, although she'd always known he wasn't hers?

Why hadn't he thought about it before, maybe talked to her about it—let her just talk…

He followed her up the stairs.

'You should be resting more,' he said, as she was about to disappear into Dottie's room.

'I'll rest tomorrow,' she said over her shoulder, and then she was gone.

Sunday dawned bright and clear and over breakfast Jo explained the hospital's shift system.

'Sam should have told you this but in most regional hospitals the day is divided into two shifts, eight to eight, though the day staff are lucky if they get away at eight, which is why staying at the flat makes sense. Becky emailed that we're on at eight tomorrow morning, and while I'm in town today I'm going to pick up some basic foodstuffs for the flat and a few spare clothes and toiletry items to leave there.

She spoke so matter-of-factly Charles had to wonder if she hadn't felt that shiver of excitement he'd felt at the flat—and did again now as she spoke about it.

He knew there wouldn't be a full-blown affair, not right now, but with such a strong attraction between them there'd certainly more kisses—mind-numbing kisses like the last one beneath the tree...

His brain was stuck on mind-numbing kisses so it wasn't until Jo had finished clearing the table and washing the dishes, and was about to leave the room, that she brought him back to the present with strict instructions to use plenty of sunscreen.

'Down by the harbour with the sun reflecting off the water, you can get very burnt.'

And she was gone.

Taking her neat compact car!

He was stuck with the hearse, although this time Dottie condescended to sit in the front so she could give a running commentary on the residents of the houses they passed— *drinks too much...lets her children run wild...has a lovely wolfhound...that dog bites.*

But he had to admit that the little harbour was lovely. Fishing boats, brightly painted and hung with nets, lay moored beside each other.

'We'll buy some fresh prawns and eat them at the end of the jetty,' Dottie suggested, and they did.

Charles was astonished at the nimble way this new-found grandmother of his got down so she could sit with her thin legs dangling over the water. He settled beside her—the ever-present 'Did she do with this with my mother?' question hovering in his head, but he wasn't going to spoil the pleasure of either of them by mentioning it.

The prawns were fresh and sweet, the sun spread warmth right through his body, and as he wiped his hands on some wet wipes Dottie had produced from one of her capacious pockets and watched tiny fish swirling in the water below them, feeding off the discarded prawn shells, he knew he'd done the right thing in coming to this place.

'We came here most weekends,' Dottie said, 'Bertie, Maggie and me. Bertie said a few hours in the fresh air—even with the smell of fish—would keep us all alive for ever!'

Maggie! His father had always called her Margaret, so this pet name was like a gift. He waited, wanting to hear more but afraid to ask—afraid to push Dottie into talking.

'You'll have to help me up,' she finally announced. 'I can get down, but attempting to get up would probably land me in the water.'

'I'll lift you, that's the easiest way,' Charles suggested, and his grandmother turned and looked up at where he now stood beside her.

'Think you can?' she said, her smile a challenge, but there was nothing of her and he lifted her gently to her feet, steadied her with his hands on her shoulders, then offered her his arm.

He was inordinately pleased when she took it...

And the signs of truce were strengthened in the afternoon when he returned from a long walk south along the headland and back through the bushland Jo called scrub. Dottie met him in the entry.

'Jo's staying in town for dinner with some friends, so

will I make cheese on toast for you for supper, or will you make it for me?'

Another challenge, but he gauged her mood was still amenable and suggested, 'Couldn't we make it together? You can grate the cheese and I'll do the toast.'

'Pah to grated cheese, sliced is just as good.'

But she followed him into the kitchen and pulled out what they'd need, handed him the bread and set to work, slicing cheese.

But his hope that she might talk more about his mother came to nought, for she worked in silence until they'd grilled the toast and made her cocoa—Charles making tea for himself.

It was then she said, 'I'm a little tired. I'll take mine up to bed. Help yourself to some books from the library. Bertie had some good ones on Australian history, and Maggie's head was always stuck in a book.'

She picked up her tray, ready to depart, but he took it from her.

'The least I can do is carry it up for you. The way you go flying up the stairs on that death machine, you'd probably spill the lot.'

There was no reply, but as he took the tray from her unresisting hands he saw the faraway look in her eyes and he knew she was back in the past, perhaps sitting in the library with his grandfather and his mother, both lost in books.

'Make the most of my last day as egg cooker,' Charles told Dottie next morning, setting her place at the table and pulling out her chair, while Jo fussed around, making lists of phone numbers and checking there was plenty of food in the cupboards and fridge.

'Stop that now, Jo. You know I've looked after myself

perfectly well for years and will continue to do so until they carry me out of here in a box.'

'Which might be sooner than later if you don't slow down on the chair lift,' Jo warned her.

'Fiddle-faddle! Now, have your breakfast and leave me in peace. You're both welcome back when you've days off, but it will be nice to have my house to myself.'

Which mustn't have made Jo feel any easier about leaving her friend, Charles decided as they drove into town. Or was the tension he could feel radiating off Jo more to do with work?

Or the flat?

Sharing the flat?

As Jo parked in the staff area behind the hospital, he couldn't help glancing towards the row of flats, particularly the one with the green door.

'It's called plunging right in,' Jo said to him, as they walked into the emergency department. They'd come into the hospital through a side door, and Jo had shown him the lockers, the tearoom, and stock cupboard, where a supply of crisp, white coats was kept. He pulled one on over his T-shirt and jeans, adjusted his stethoscope around his neck, and followed her into mayhem.

The waiting room was packed, and nurses flashed from one curtained cubicle to the next.

'Accident out on the highway, mini-bus and two cars,' Fiona, who was at the triage desk, told them.

'The most severely injured have been airlifted to major hospitals, but we've got six here, plus all the people who don't want to spoil their weekend with a hospital visit so come on a Monday morning.'

She was checking her computer as she spoke, and looked up to say, 'Jo, if you could take Cubicle Three, suspected appendicitis, and Charles—may we call you

Charles?—take Cubicle Five, one of the RTA victims with serious cuts and abrasions, query damage to left arm and shoulder but X-rays should be back to the cubicle by now.'

Charles introduced himself to the patient, Ken, who was obviously in pain, his face grey and sweaty. He had an IV port open on the back of his right hand.

'Hook him up to a monitor, we need an ECG,' Charles told the nurse who'd been picking bits of gravel out of the patient's leg. 'Have you taken blood?'

The nurse shook his head.

'Then I'll finish what you're doing, you take a sample and get a rush test on troponin levels.'

'You think the shoulder pain could be his heart?'

Charles nodded, but as he attached the last lead and started the monitor for an ECG, the man stiffened and the monitor showed erratic rhythms then a flat line as the patient went into cardiac arrest.

Charles hit the emergency button, which had been the first thing he'd looked for as he'd entered the cubicle. He'd seen a resuscitation room on his tour with Jo, but there was no time to move the patient.

Jo came in with the crash-cart team and it was she who found the adrenalin they needed to get into the man as soon as possible to increase blood supply to the heart. Charles checked the syringe and used the open port on the man's hand to administer it, Jo already drawing up another dose for when it was needed.

The crash team had the paddles of the defibrillator set up, and the 'Clear' command had them all standing back, eyes on the monitor, waiting for the black lines to appear—hoping, praying for a regular rhythm.

Lines appeared then disappeared and the operator cranked up the machine and shocked the man again, and this time the lines came up and stayed there.

'More adrenalin, then we'll move him to the resus room,' a woman Charles now learned was Lauren, the ED registrar, said. 'If he's stable, we'll move him to the coronary ICU later this morning.'

She turned to Charles and introduced herself.

'You took blood?' she asked, and he nodded.

'Mainly to check his troponin levels when X-ray failed to show damage to his shoulder.'

Lauren nodded, then followed the patient as he was wheeled out of the room.

'Well, you don't waste any time getting noticed,' Jo said. 'All I've had is a suspected appendicitis who has gone to Theatre, and one of the RTA victims who's gone for X-rays—possible fractured pelvis.'

Charles caught up with Lauren as the patient was hooked up to the equipment in the resus room.

'I'll leave a nurse here but keep an eye on him myself, so check with Fiona who's next on the list. Hopefully it will be the child who's been wailing since he got here. The noise is beginning to sound like a drill in my head.'

Charles smiled, although he hadn't noticed the noise until she mentioned it, too caught up in the drama of his first Australian patient.

The child had earache, he discovered when he met Peter and his mum in a cubicle.

'Have you given him anything for it?' he asked the mother as they settled Peter on the examination couch so Charles could examine the ear.

'Paracetamol this morning at about four,' she said. 'He went back to sleep after that but woke up with it still sore so I brought him in.'

'So we'll have to have a look, won't we, Peter? How old are you?'

'Seven,' Peter told him, stopping his wailing so he could speak. 'You talk funny!'

'Peter!' from his mother, but Charles only smiled.

'I did all my studying in England and over there they do speak a bit differently. But they have the same instruments and this one's called an otoscope.'

'Like a telescope?' Peter asked, checking out the instrument the nurse had handed Charles. 'Only it's got like a little TV on the end.'

He pointed to the screen that would give Charles a magnified picture of the inner ear.

'That's where I look to see what's wrong,' Charles told him. 'Now, I have to move your ear a bit and it will hurt but not for long, then we'll give you something to help the pain and you can have the day off school. How's that?'

'Silly, there's no school, 'cos it's holidays.'

'Ah,' Charles said, pleased that the conversation had allowed him to pull Peter's ear gently up and back, and insert the otoscope.

'Maybe your mother will think of another treat because you're being so good.'

'Ice cream, Mum?' Peter asked and Charles smiled. Young Peter was obviously a child who didn't miss any opportunities that came his way.

'Your ear is infected,' he told the lad. 'We'll give you something now to stop the pain and some antibiotics to take. They will clear it up in a couple of days, but no swimming until it's better.'

'But it's the holidays,' Peter complained as his mother helped him sit up on the couch.

'Then you'll have to find some other fun, like riding your bicycle maybe.'

'Or my new skateboard—it's awesome,' Peter told him. 'It's red with a white stripe and the best wheels!'

'Sounds great,' Charles said, while behind him the nurse was asking Peter's mother about allergies.

'You really didn't have much of an induction into this place.' Charles looked around to see Jo standing just inside the cubicle. 'Lauren was going to do it when you arrived, but with the RTA and usual Monday-itis you were thrown in at the deep end. For antibiotics, we write out a script—there'll be a pad on the trolley—and the patient, or in this case…' she smiled at Peter '…the patient's mother takes it to the hospital pharmacy.'

She turned from Charles to Peter's mother.

'Do you know where that is?'

The woman nodded.

Charles wrote out the script and signed it, shook hands with Peter as he left, then turned to Jo.

'You were good with him,' she said. 'Do you like working with kids?'

'I suppose I do,' Charles told her, 'but what are you doing? Checking up on me or just skiving off?'

'I'm actually your supervisor,' she told him with a grin. 'Apparently, you foreign blokes can't just walk in here and start practising willy-nilly. You have to be supervised for a few weeks, or maybe it's a month, Lauren did explain. And because I'm just filling in as well, I've been appointed to keep an eye on you.'

'That *will* be nice!' Charles teased, and was surprised to see colour creep into Jo's cheeks.

Surprised, or pleased?

The question flitted through his head, but this was not the time for introspection…

'Right now I'd better report to triage again or you'll be giving me a bad report.'

Jo should have followed him, been given a patient for herself, but she felt unsettled. Had it had something to do with seeing Charles and the little boy that her arms began to ache and for a moment she felt the loss of the child that hadn't ever been hers to lose.

'Silly sentimentality!' she muttered to herself, as she made her own way to triage to find Charles had already been given a new patient.

'He's in Cubicle Seven, if you want to check,' Fiona told her. 'Elderly woman with acute diarrhoea. I told him we should probably admit her.'

Jo laughed.

'I don't know what we doctors would do without the nurses in the ED. We'd certainly never manage.'

'Of course you wouldn't,' Fiona said. 'But right now, if you think the new bloke is okay with diarrhoea, you can see Mr Bell in One. His daughter brought him in, says he's got dementia.'

'Of course she does,' Jo replied, far too harshly. 'It's the holiday season and she'd like him put in hospital so she can have his house to herself.'

Fiona nodded, 'But we still have to see him,' she said, and Jo agreed.

She made her way to Cubicle One, knowing she could pull up the basic test for dementia on the screen in the cubicle but more worried about Allan Bell.

'Hello!' she said, as she walked in, hoping she sounded brighter than she felt. 'Did you not like the locum that you've come to see me here?'

She spoke to Allan, not his daughter, who was staring at her with disbelief.

'But you're on leave,' she said to Jo.

'And filling in here,' Jo said, as she took Allan's hand and gave it a squeeze.

'So what's the problem?' she asked him, but he couldn't

speak, the glassiness in his eyes revealing how emotionally upset he was.

'He's got Alzheimer's,' the daughter announced, and Allan shook his head.

'The locum at my practice could have done a test,' Jo told her. 'Why bring him here?'

Silence!

'I'll do a test,' Jo said. 'Would you like to wait outside? We won't be long.'

The daughter looked as if she was about to argue but eventually she flounced out.

Jo smiled at her old friend and patient.

'Well, now you're here I'll have to check you out.' She wound a blood-pressure cuff around his arm as she spoke. 'But you know this situation isn't going to get any better, don't you?'

Allan nodded, his face drawn with worry.

'You like Rosemary House and you've friends there, we've talked about it before.'

'But I'd have to sell the cottage,' he murmured, while the nurse wrote down his blood-pressure reading and swiped a thermometer across his forehead.

'It's *your* house,' Jo reminded him gently.

'But Barb lives there too now and where would she go?'

'She can find a nice flat somewhere at Port, or here in Anooka, or she could go back to Sydney and be closer to her grandchildren. She has plenty of options, Allan.'

'But she wants *my* house! If I sell it, she won't get it when I die.'

'No, but she'd get plenty of money when your place at Rosemary House is sold.'

Jo realised they'd had this conversation many times before but she persevered.

'Or if you're determined to keep the house, we can put

in support services for you to make it easier to manage on your own, and Barb can go back to her family.'

'She won't!' Allan said dolefully.

'No!' Jo said, then dutifully pulled up the early dementia test on the screen, handed Allan a notepad and pen and ran through the test, altering it slightly as he knew it almost by heart.

'Is there someone else in the family who might come and stay with you, even just for a few weeks?' she asked.

Allan shook his head.

'Only one of Barb's kids and that's really what she wants, to have them all there over the holidays, but if one comes, they all come and that's five adults and seven kids and there's just not enough room. They have to sleep on the floor in the living room and in the garage. Barb says they don't mind, but it's too much for me to have them there for the whole six weeks of the holidays. I love them—well, most of them—but all of them at once, it's—'

'Hard,' Jo finished for him, although considering the size of Allan's cottage she thought impossible would be a more apt word, while the thought of an elderly man stepping his way over sleeping bodies to get to his own kitchen made her fearful for his safety.

'I'll talk to Barb now, if you don't mind waiting outside.'

Allan looked a little apprehensive, but stood up, such a neat man, well shaven, hair brushed back, wearing belted shorts with his shirt tucked in, leather sandals on his feet.

'So?' Barb said to Jo as she walked back in. 'I suppose you're going to tell me there's nothing wrong with him.'

'Not that I can find,' Jo said quietly. 'But I wonder if *you* need a break, Barb. We can organise support services for your father so you'd know he was being looked after, even put a carer in his house if you think he needs one there full time, and you could go down to Sydney and have Christmas with your family.'

'He's my family and we're his, and all the grandkids want to have Christmas at the beach. They want to come here.'

'Then they should rent a house—I know you probably won't get one now, but plan for next year. Allan's cottage is too small, and he finds it difficult when everyone is there, you must know that. So why not go to Sydney this year, then organise something up at Port for next Christmas?'

Barb's glare told her what she thought of that idea.

'So you're saying there's nothing wrong with him?' she demanded, and Jo nodded.

'Well, thanks for nothing!'

Jo watched her storm out, concern for Allan twisting her gut.

She could try to get a respite placement for Allan for few weeks, but when she'd done that once before, he'd returned home to his find his house like a deserted squat, and had been more distressed than angry.

In fact, having seen it, Jo had sent him back to respite for a week, while she and her fortnightly cleaning lady cleaned the place, even repainting a couple of walls the smaller children had drawn all over.

But right now she had to think about Barb.

She was muddling the situation around in her head as she entered the tearoom to find Charles standing by the urn, filling a mug with the steaming water.

'Would you like a cup? There are teabags and instant coffee but at least the milk is fresh.'

'Coffee, please, one sugar, no milk,' she said, absent-mindedly, although she did walk over to the cupboard and pull out the biscuit tin, hoping the night staff hadn't scoffed the lot.

There were four left, so she took them out, sharing them with Charles, who had set her coffee down on the table.

'If you're going out later for a spare toothbrush, you might buy a couple of packets of biscuits as well. There used to be a bottle for staff to put money into for snacks but they gave up on that and now whoever finds the tin empty usually buys new ones.'

'I'll do that,' he said, sitting down across the table from her. 'In fact, Lauren said to take a break now, because the worst of the morning rush has cleared. But I think there's more than biscuits on your mind.'

So as she drank her tea she told him about Allan, fit and spry in his late eighties and well able to take care of himself.

'His daughter used his age as an excuse to come and live with him—to look after him, she said, but she's never home, visiting friends or down at the club playing the pokies, so Allan not only looks after himself but her as well.'

'Is he managing that?' Charles asked, and Jo saw the empathy in his eyes.

'Just about,' she said. 'He's really very self-sufficient but come holiday time, she wants to bring all her family up to stay. Allan's cottage really isn't big enough and he hates having them all there at once, so she'd like him hospitalised—"for tests", she says. But it's mainly so her lot can have the run of the house, leaving their mess behind for Allan to clear up.'

Charles nodded.

'I imagine the mess isn't as bad as what he must feel when he sees how little respect the family has for the house he loves.'

'Exactly!' Jo said, and felt her frown deepening.

'So?' Charles prompted.

'I worry that she'll nag and nag and nag at him about it

and it will wear him down—or wear him out so he does end up in hospital.'

'A subtle form of elder abuse,' Charles said quietly, and Jo nodded.

'Well, we'll just have to see that doesn't happen,' he continued. 'They don't know me, so I can turn up there from time to time, telling his daughter that because she had concerns about his mental health, I've been asked by the hospital to keep an eye on him. Tell her I have to make sure he's safe, and comfortable, and coping well.'

'Charles, that's brilliant,' Jo told him, smiling broadly as relief for Allan washed through her. 'I might even get my locum to do the same so she's never really sure when someone will come.'

'That's settled, then,' Charles said. 'So, moving on, do you have the key to the flat? I'll get some spare toiletries and things and drop them off before I come back to work.'

It's work, nothing more, and anyway the state you're in, what could happen? Jo thought as she handed over the key to the green door.

But inside she still felt a little thrill, so her hope that once they got to work the silly attraction thing would go away was well and truly dashed.

She'd spent the previous day keeping out of his way, telling herself it would be good for him and Dottie to spend some time together—just the two of them—but deep inside she'd been avoiding Charles, thinking a whole day out of his company might cool the heat he could generate so easily within her.

It hadn't worked.

Wouldn't ever work, she suspected, but at least she'd tried…

CHAPTER EIGHT

BY LATE AFTERNOON the place was so quiet Jo began to hope they'd get off duty on time. She thought of the basic provisions she'd left in the flat, then blanched at the thought of cooking after a twelve-hour shift.

Somewhere in the tearoom there'd be a pile of takeaway menus, there for staff who knew they wouldn't make it home in time to cook dinner.

'Are those takeaway menus you're perusing?'

She spun around to see Charles right behind her, and as her heart thumped and her nerves jangled she wondered how she'd get through the next two weeks, not only living in the same small flat but working in the same place as the man who was causing her so much confusion.

'For us to share in the flat?'

There was something so suggestive in his tone of voice she felt a blush creeping up her cheeks.

Ridiculous that a thirty-two-year-old woman should be blushing!

'Well, I certainly won't be cooking when we finally get off duty!' she said, more snappishly than necessary. 'Do you like Thai?'

She was saved from further embarrassment by a nurse poking her head around the door to announce that the first of the Schoolie patients was on the way in.

'He was crowd surfing on the beach at last night's con-
cert but they dropped him and he landed on an ice-box
someone had there. He was probably excited enough to
feel no pain last night but it's got progressively worse during the day. The ambos suspect cracked ribs.'

'At the very least,' Jo said, thinking aloud while the
nurse explained what an ice-box was to the man who didn't
frequent Australian beaches in summer.

They greeted the patient together, speaking to the
ambos as they transferred him onto an ED trolley.

'He's not entirely sober and not feeling well so I'd have
a basin handy,' one of the ambos said quietly to Charles.

'I'll get one,' the nurse who'd called them said, and she
disappeared from the cubicle.

'Let's check him over before we send him to X-Ray,'
Jo said. She turned to the young man to ask his name and
date of birth.

He gazed at her through bleary eyes but confirmed what
the ambos had already filled in on the admittance form.

'And where's it hurting?' Jo asked, and the young man
tried a rather twisted smile.

'All over right now, but I fell on my back, right onto
the damn box. The lid was open and I got twisted up in
it somehow.'

Jo was calmly removing his shirt as he spoke, and motioning to Charles to pull down his shorts so they could
check his hips and pelvis.

Bruises were already beginning to spread up his body
from the lumbar region to the upper ribs.

'F—!' the patient yelled as Jo touched his ribs. 'Sorry,
but that hurt.'

'We'll ease your shirt off and a nurse will take you
through to Radiology to have the area X-rayed. But if your

rib hurt that much it's probably cracked or broken, so it will be very sore for some time to come.'

'But I'm only here five days!' he wailed, and Charles knew Jo was hiding a smile. Not because the young man was in pain but because of his priorities—having fun would come before any concern for his aches and pains.

'Will you see him when he comes back?' Jo asked, and it was Charles's turn to smile, but he didn't hide it.

'More checking up on me?' he asked, and to his surprise she looked embarrassed.

'It's just something we have to do with overseas trained doctors, apparently,' she said, looking so uncomfortable he touched her on the shoulder.

'Hey, I was only teasing.'

She turned towards him, said something he didn't hear—or didn't take in—because suddenly he was back on the walk home from the creek, thinking of the kiss they'd shared beneath the tree, thinking about how she'd felt in his arms, how his body had felt against hers.

He shook his head. Talk about inappropriate workplace behaviour! And he on probation!

He spoke to Fiona, hoping for another patient, but she told him to stay with Jo while they checked the X-rays.

Not a job for two doctors, but it *was* quiet!

Back in the cubicle he read what little there was on the young man's chart, finding out, at least, his name was Stewart, usually known as Stewie.

The trolley returned, Jo with it, and together they found the hairline crack in the eleventh rib, the first of the floating ribs.

'There's really not much we can do for you,' Charles explained. 'At one time the ribs were bound but patients then ran the risk of pneumonia as they weren't breathing as deeply as they should. The very best thing is ice—not on your skin but either using an ice-pack from the chemist or a packet of frozen peas, wrapped in a cloth and rested against the painful part for twenty minutes at a time. By tomorrow any swelling should have gone down, and you can use a heat pack—one of those you heat in the microwave for two minutes—thirty minutes on, thirty minutes off.'

'But I'll be missing all the fun,' Stewie complained. 'I can't sit around the apartment with hot and cold things on my back, we're all going rock climbing this afternoon and to the carnival tonight. Can't I just take drugs?'

'Paracetamol four-hourly,' Charles told him, and Stewie groaned.

'That won't help. What about something stronger, something with codeine or an opioid in it?'

Out of the corner of his eye Charles saw Jo give a minimal shake her head.

'We can give you an injection of painkiller that will get you home, after which I suggest you rest with the ice and then the heat as the doctor recommended,' Jo told their patient, with enough bite in her voice to prevent any further argument. 'You'll feel sore because your back is bruised, but that will settle down. The rib will hurt for weeks so be a bit careful about bumping into things.'

After he'd left, Jo explained.

'I'm not suspicious of that particular young man, but at this time of the year we get young people looking for opioid drugs they can sell in the pubs for up to twenty dollars a pill. The Schoolie kids are pretty innocent, but we also get those we call "Toolies", who are older young men and some women who come back year after year. They hang around and take advantage of the largely innocent young school-leavers.'

'With drugs?' Charles asked, intrigued by this end-of-school ritual.

'Some!' Jo said.

'So how on earth can a place as small as Port Anooka handle this?'

Jo grinned at him.

'Did you see Stewie's plastic armband? As soon as they've unpacked, the Schoolies all report to a tent on the beach where their ID is checked and they are issued with a numbered and coloured armband. Over eighteens, who can legally go into a hotel or club, get a green band, while those underage have a red one. Because the bands are all numbered, the organisers have details of name, address, parents' contact details, etcetera to hand should anything go wrong. They know where each person is staying, and they give out information, particularly about a "buddy" system, where everyone has someone they are responsible for and who is responsible for them.'

'So you don't leave your drunk friend on the street corner to find her own way home to go off with a boy or girl you fancy without telling your buddy and making sure he has someone to see him home.'

Jo nodded.

'In the beginning it was chaotic, but now, thanks mainly to volunteers, it's a really safe environment.'

'Can we go and check it out?' Charles asked, and Jo smiled.

'If you can stand music that could burst your eardrums!' she said, while Charles battled his reactions to that smile.

'The council closes off a section of the beach and puts on live concerts every night, and only those in red or blue armbands can get in.'

'It's starting to sound like a good old-fashioned orgy but with rules,' Charles told her, hoping to win another smile.

But a buzzing in his pocket—he'd now been trusted with a pager—sent him back to the triage desk.

Schoolie number two, a young woman this time, red armband, vomiting and diarrhoea so severe her heart was racing from extreme dehydration.

Charles ordered fluids and carefully inserted a cannula into an almost flat vein on the back of her hand.

One of the ambos who'd been finishing the hand-over moved his head to indicate Charles follow him out the door.

'We asked if she'd taken anything and she denied it, but I'd run full bloods on her just in case.'

Charles nodded and as his nurse assistant was still setting up the fluid bag, he poked his head out of the cubicle in search of Jo.

She was nowhere to be seen, so he asked the nurse, aware pathology departments had dozens of different tubes for blood collection, usually colour-coded for particular tests.

He was still hesitating when Jo materialised by his side once again.

'We have a pathology nurse, just ask the desk to page her,' Jo told him. 'They like to do it, and we let them. That way, we don't get the blame if things go wrong.'

He was about to leave when he realised he hadn't checked the fluid bag. He'd asked for something with electrolytes in it to replace some of those lost. The bag was the right one, so he titrated it to run slowly and steadily into the patient's body.

And now he could check her over more carefully, finding bruises on her arms and legs that were more easily explained by stumbling and falling than by being attacked. But why was she here on her own?

Wouldn't her buddy have travelled with her in the ambulance, if only to see that she arrived safely at the hospital?

He'd no sooner thought about it than Jo returned, this time with another young woman in tow.

'I lost her,' the teenager said. 'I knew she was feeling sick and I should have stayed with her.'

'Well, you're here with her now,' Jo said. 'Do you know if she ate or drank anything out of the ordinary?'

'She wouldn't! We both agreed no drugs. Although when she started feeling sick and we were on our way to the first-aid tent, someone handed her a bottle of some red drink—said it would help with nausea. Could it have had something in it?'

'Possibly,' Jo told her, while Charles explained to the pathology nurse what tests he'd like to have done.

'And a general tox screen,' Jo added. 'Someone gave her something to drink—there's no knowing what was in it.'

'Would someone deliberately spike a drink with drugs?' Charles asked. 'The poor kid was already as sick as a dog—she wouldn't have been up to any fun and games.'

Jo shook her head.

'Some people don't care whether their victim is conscious or not.'

She sounded so upset he'd have liked to put his arm around her and give her a hug. Actually, even if she hadn't sounded upset he'd have liked to give her a hug!

And *that* thought sent him striding away towards the tearoom—no, it could be busy. Maybe the bathroom, somewhere quiet where he could try to sort out what was going on in his head.

He'd dated nurses and doctors he'd worked with, but had never even imagined giving any of them a hug during working hours. Talk about inappropriate behaviour—and if it was bad here, how would things be at the flat?

It wasn't only Jo's physical beauty that attracted him, but some kind of inner serenity that seemed to him to shine from her. And here, seeing her at work, it was doubly obvious.

He stuck his head under the cold tap and rubbed his face vigorously, before scrubbing his head dry on paper towels.

Then, confident he'd managed to put a stop to his inappropriate thoughts before they got out of hand, he headed back to check on his patients.

'Snowing outside?' Jo asked, reaching up to pick a scrap of paper towel out of his hair and undoing all the good work the cold water had done.

'At home it would be,' he growled, and strode back to his patient.

She was sleeping, her buddy also asleep, sitting on a chair with her head resting on arms she'd folded on the bed.

The nurse brought up the results of the blood test on the monitor screen and swivelled it towards Charles.

Jo wasn't sure whether she was being diligent in her supervision of the new doctor or simply liked being near him. She went with the former, because she didn't want to believe she was pathetic enough to be following him around like a teenager in the first throes of love.

Well, how she imagined such a teenager might behave. She'd kind of missed those years, what with her mother dying and the drama that had followed.

But surely she couldn't be making up for it now…

Whatever!

She found herself back in the cubicle with the sick young woman, and as the nurse had brought up the path results on the screen, it was only sensible that Jo move closer so she and Charles could read them together.

She'd done it hundreds of times with colleagues—read notes together—but all the other times she hadn't wanted to sidle closer so her arm could brush against his, and perhaps their hips would touch and she'd feel his body, his warmth…

'Nothing there?' she said.

Charles shook his head.

'Not even alcohol,' he pointed out. He left Jo staring at the screen and turned his attention back to his patient.

'Something she ate?' Jo said, being careful not to stand too close as she, too, studied the sleeping young women.

Charles shrugged and shook his head.

'It was a pretty extreme reaction. And if we don't know what caused it, it could happen again.'

He sounded worried enough for Jo to consider touching his arm—just as a colleague-to-colleague show of support—but the remaining shred of common sense in her brain told her to stop being stupid and to concentrate on the problem in front of them.

'What's your gut instinct about it?' she asked instead, and he turned and smiled at her.

'I was just about to ask you that but as you asked first, I'd like to let her sleep, and see how she is when she wakes up. I imagine as this is one of the first major events in her...' He paused. 'Would you call it her grown-up life?'

He was so earnest, so caring Jo had to smile.

'I suppose so,' she said. 'It's certainly considered a rite of passage.'

'Well, given that, she's not going to want to miss out on any more of it than she can help. So see how she is when she wakes up, ask her what she thinks, ask the buddy if she can manage, and take it from there.'

Jo nodded.

'And suggest she buys some electrolyte ice-blocks and drinks plenty of fluid.'

The words, though softly spoken, brought the buddy awake.

'They give out bottles of water all the time on the beach and on the streets and we keep drinking that, but I've just remembered she had one of those caffeine drinks last night. Could that have done it?'

Jo pictured the scene—the throng of young people on the beach dancing to the music, sculling a caffeinated drink to keep going.

'Maybe more than one?' she asked the buddy, who shrugged.

'We aren't joined at the hip,' she said, then began to cry.

'Most likely just exhaustion,' Charles said. 'I imagine they push themselves so they don't miss anything that's happening, particularly early in their stay. We'll keep an eye on her, let her sleep. We might even be able to find a bed for her buddy.'

He smiled at the still weeping young woman, and Jo read empathy and compassion in the smile. It was true the ED wasn't busy, but he took the time to care for his patients as if they mattered as people, not just cases, and she believed that was the most important thing a doctor could offer.

But as she walked back to check on her own patients she wondered if she was seeing him this way because of the attraction.

That would be really daft!

She forced her mind back into work mode. If she just did her job, kept a purely supervisory eye on Charles, she could get through the day without making a fool of herself.

Probably!

In the end, they both got through the day, finishing with all Charles's patients being discharged and only one of hers—a burst appendix—admitted. But it was eight-thirty by the time they'd finished, and a quick phone call to check on Dottie told Jo the older woman had already had her supper and intended having an early night.

'You don't have to be checking on me every day,' she

told Jo, 'and, anyway, Molly is coming to stay for a few days tomorrow. You and Charles just do your jobs, and I'll see you when you have time off.'

'She called you Charles,' Jo said to him, and he smiled at her.

'Do we take that as a sign she's warming to me, or does she consider it more formal than "the Prince"?'

Jo shrugged.

'I was wondering that myself, but I guess only time will tell. But right now we need to eat—well, I definitely need to eat—so what do you like? Indian? Thai? Chinese?'

She smiled, before adding, 'I don't think Anooka rises to Livarochean cuisine, but it does have a Spanish tapas bar.'

'Let's go there,' Charles suggested. 'I'd be fascinated to see what Australians do with tapas.'

'Ha! You forget we're a multicultural nation,' Jo told him. 'It's not far, and a lovely evening for a walk.'

They walked through the balmy night to where a tall stone wall hid a courtyard lit by soft lanterns amid potted palms and bushy shrubs, already glinting with coloured Christmas lights. Tables were scattered here and there, and along a bar that ran the length of the building behind the terrace were wooden stools, many of them already occupied.

'We can eat at the bar or choose a selection of food and bring it over to a table.'

'Who would have known?' Charles said as he looked around. 'It's delightful. Let's eat in the courtyard.'

Big mistake, Jo realised a little later when they were sharing a plate piled high with different tapas and sharing a small carafe of Spanish rosé.

The lanterns, the palms—it was far too intimate—the table small enough for their knees to brush together, and as they selected little delicacies on their forks and lifted them to their mouths, their spare hands seem to have taken hold of each other, fingers tangling in some kind of silent language.

His thumb brushed across her palm and the shiver that ran down her spine was so extreme she wondered he hadn't noticed her stiffen.

'This is very good,' Charles said. 'I must come back and speak to the chef. He must be Spanish to get the little delicacies just right.'

'If Alejandro is a Spanish name then he certainly is, although he has been here for a long time.'

They finished the meal, with Charles insisting he pay the bill, then wandered back to the hospital hand in hand, although Jo wasn't sure how that had happened.

And as they drew closer to the flat, in the shadow of the poinciana tree, he put his arm around her shoulder, and when she didn't object, he drew her closer, wanting to feel her body pressed to his, to feed off her warmth, to pick up the scent of her, arousing excitement through his body.

And through hers?

He had no idea, although he suspected this attraction wasn't all one-sided, especially not if her reaction to his kisses were any guide.

But just to make sure, as they reached the door of the flat he turned her in his arms and brushed his lips across hers. Her response was immediate, a kiss that numbed his lips and set his groin on fire. Her arms were tight around his shoulders, fingers pushing into his hair, her body pressed to his as if seeking to fill every crevice with his warmth.

At length, she slumped against him, arms still around his neck as if she needed to hold onto him for support.

'You have no idea how much I needed that,' she muttered against his neck. 'All day at work, sitting in the restaurant, walking back, and every moment wanting to kiss you, to feel your body against mine, to touch your arm, your cheek—I can't believe it's all so desperate. It *has* to be the pregnancy—the hormones it released.'

He tipped her head back and smiled into her flushed face.

'Because the alternative is that you're a sex-crazed woman who'd leap on any available man?'

He felt the sigh that filled her chest before slithering from her lips.

'I'm not sure that they'd even have to be available,' she said, looking so downhearted he had to kiss her again.

'Best we go in before someone comes into the car park and sees two doctors carrying on in public,' she said when they broke apart again.

But when they entered the flat he knew that something had changed—that Jo had drawn back from him.

Regretting her admission that she'd needed the kiss so badly?

Now she was talking about Dottie, about the house, and the roof and how she'd have to ask around at the hospital to see if they could get someone who would fix it.

The words—the suggestions—all made sense, but he knew beneath them she was lost in some dark or maybe far-off place. He felt a sense of frustration that he didn't know her better, hadn't known her longer, couldn't even guess at her thoughts and feelings.

Except when she was kissing him!

CHAPTER NINE

SHE SHOULDN'T KEEP on kissing him, Jo thought as Charles wandered around the flat, touching surfaces, opening cupboards.

She knew she'd cut him off when they'd come in, but the kiss, and her confession that she'd wanted it all day, had made her feel very uncomfortable.

It wasn't that she was initiating the kisses, which would be a very forward thing to do, as her gran would have said, but she'd definitely been responding, although responding barely covered the passion with which she'd met his kiss.

And kissed him back...

The kisses had left her hot and flustered, and slightly wobbly at the knees, yet Charles seemed unaffected. Hadn't he simply taken the key from her unresisting hand and opened the flat door?

As if he'd guessed at the emotional storm inside her.

Heaven help her if that was the case—if he was perceptive enough to realise the effect he had on her...

She'd be like putty in his hands, and if he stayed six more weeks, and her body had returned to more or less normal, there'd be no way she wouldn't end up in his bed.

Maybe he wouldn't stay and, anyway, would he really want her in that way? It was one thing to exchange a couple of almost chaste kisses—well, not very chaste...actually quite hot—but he had a position to uphold and was probably very wary about whom he took to bed, and when, and she doubted a flabby, post-delivery woman would be his first choice.

So maybe she'd just consider it kissing practice, like getting back on a horse after a fall—yes, that was how she'd look at it.

In the meantime, they had to settle into their temporary quarters—and how awkward was that likely to be?

Perhaps it would be best to get it out into the open.

Well, anything would be better than the tension she was feeling, alone in the flat with Charles.

'I'm sure it's only proximity,' she said, aware her voice sounded as strained as she felt. 'We've been thrown together, first by the weather and now with work and the flat. Proximity, that's all this is.'

Even to herself it didn't make sense so when Charles crossed the room towards her, cupped her cheek in his hand and said, 'What "this"?' she had no idea how to answer him.

She stood, rooted to the spot, the warmth of his hand on her cheek sending sparks of agitation through her body. And short of throwing herself into his arms to show him what 'this' she meant, she had no idea.

But the wretched the man was waiting for an answer, and making matters worse by smiling at her.

Or at her confusion!

'The attraction thing!'

She all but spat the words at him, annoyed at being put on the spot, although she'd brought his question on herself.

She stepped away, forcing him back, and crossed to the kitchen window that looked out over the scrub. She felt him come up behind her, not touching, just being there…

'I think you know as well as I do that it's not proximity,

this attraction between us, but something real and strong and, to me, quite shocking in its intensity, given how quickly it sprang into being.'

He touched her shoulder, turned her, kissed her gently on the lips—a quiet kiss, no pressure, but saying so much more than words ever could.

Or was she imagining it?

'I'm lost!' she admitted, needing to get this almost-relationship out into the open. 'I've no idea where this can go. If I hadn't just had a baby, making it unfeasible for us to go to bed together, we could have had a short affair, you'd go back to Livaroche, and I'd get on with my life. Do you think it's *because* we can't go to bed together right now that the attraction seems so strong?'

Charles drew her close, his arms around her back, holding her to him, as he said quietly, 'Could it not be more complicated than attraction?'

'More complicated than attraction?' Jo echoed. 'I would have thought attraction was complicated enough.'

'And love?'

Jo stepped back, breaking the loose hold he'd had on her body.

'Love?' Another echo! 'How could it possibly be love? You're a prince, you need a princess, or someone close to princess status at least. You can't go falling in love with a redheaded nobody from a village so small it's not on most maps. Besides which you barely know me, *and* I threw a bucket of water over you.'

He'd taken her hands so she couldn't back away further.

'I think it was the bucket of water that did it for me,' he said, laughter gleaming in his eyes.

Jo shook her head.

Love?

He *had* to be joking!

'I have to go to bed. It's after midnight and we've work tomorrow. I put my things in the front room, so you can have the back. I'll just have a quick shower and get out of your way.'

She could hear the words tumbling over each other as they left her lips, and hoped they were making sense.

Charles watched her go then turned back to look out the window, over the dark shadows of trees and bushes that made up the scrub, and tried to think.

To make sense of his emotions…

To separate them from his reason for being here, his search for knowledge of his mother.

Was his attraction to Jo something to do with that? A romantic hangover from his father's tales of love…?

Was he subconsciously trying to replicate those stories?

He didn't know, although deep down he doubted the answer was so simple.

Deep down, there was a sureness that Jo was something special—something special to him and for him.

Love?

He shook his head, heard her soft, 'Goodnight,' as she flitted from bathroom to bedroom, determined not to turn and look, to catch one last glimpse before she went to bed.

And he certainly wasn't going to think about beds in conjunction with Jo Wainwright—that way lay madness…

But she would soon be gone. The baby was supposed to have been born on Christmas Day and probably she'd booked the locum for a week or two after that, which left four days to Christmas, and another, maybe ten, then she'd no longer be working at the hospital, or living at Dottie's, and he needn't see her again.

But far from cheering him up, that idea left him feeling slightly ill, so he pushed it all out of his head and headed for his bedroom to collect a pair of boxers as he was pretty sure his habit of sleeping in the nude would *not* be a good idea in this small flat.

Work was the answer!

He'd throw himself into work, and when he had no patients to see, he'd explore the hospital, talk to the nurses and doctors, learn how the system worked.

They'd still be sharing the flat, but he could handle that.

Or so he thought until he entered the bathroom and a scent that was probably no more than soap, yet was quintessentially Jo, lingered there, and his body responded immediately.

At least he was in the right place for a cold shower...

Had their thinking been along the same lines that the first thing she said to him next morning was, 'I've phoned the hospital to tell them I'll be late—I have to go out to Port and sign some papers at the surgery.'

He'd been up for some time, taken a walk along a track behind the flats and been surprised to find the ocean at the end of it. Somehow he'd imagined they were further inland.

Now he was at the kitchen table, spreading marmalade on his toast, when she'd poked her head out the door and spoken to him.

'No worries,' he said, using the expression he had heard so often at the hospital the previous day.

Empty the bedpan—no worries. Do an extra shift—no worries. Crash cart? No worries!

They definitely weren't lackadaisical people, for they performed all their duties with swift efficiency, but it seemed to him, on such short acquaintance, that no one ever got flustered.

Laid-back! That was the word.

Well, he was pretty sure he could do laid-back as well as the next person.

Until Jo came out of the bedroom wearing a lemon dress that emphasised her still considerably lush breasts, trim waist and long slim legs.

Definitely not laid-back—more gobsmacked.

Because he'd never seen her in a dress?

And here she was, all woman in sunshiny yellow, stirring every nerve in his body into a kind of longing he'd never felt before.

He couldn't have felt it before or he'd have remembered.

Had he gone pale that the vision in yellow said, 'I won't be too late,' in a kind, reassuring, doctor-to-patient voice, and before he found his own voice she'd disappeared.

Well, that was one night in the flat he'd survived, he thought gloomily as he made his way over to the hospital, aware he should be glad Jo wouldn't be there for a while, and yet already—

Missing her?

Ridiculous!

Fiona's smile was enough to bring him back to earth and cheer him up, because she was obviously delighted to see him.

'Would you mind seeing Mr Bell? He's Fiona's patient really, but she's not in until later, and he's really not very well. Cubicle Two.'

Mr Bell?

Was this the elderly man Jo had been concerned about?'

He'd no more than set one foot inside the cubicle than the woman sitting by the patient began to talk.

'I told Jo he was no good—but, oh, no, she knew best. She sent him home and now look at him.'

Mr Ball did indeed look bad. He had a huge bruise on one side of his face, older than his other contusions for it was already turning yellow. And the smell emanating from him suggested he'd urinated on himself.

Charles introduced himself and explained that Jo wasn't in.

'Thank heaven!' muttered the woman Charles took to be the daughter.

'Would you mind waiting outside while I examine your—father, is it?'

'Yes, and I'm his only daughter and closest relative, not to mention having to be his full-time carer.'

'Yes, well, if you could wait outside I'll come and get you when I've finished.

The nurse was carefully peeling back Mr Bell's shirt, revealing yet more bruises.

'Barb says I fell,' the old man said. 'But I've never fallen before, not in all the time I've lived by myself.'

Jo had suspected elder abuse, but what to do? It had obviously got out of hand this time. Very gently he palpated the old man's ribs, feeling for any movement as a broken rib could damage the lungs and cause a multitude of problems. Everything seemed intact but an X-ray would confirm it.

Moving down the body, he found a vivid red abrasion across the lower abdomen. Could the old man have been tied up? Tied to a chair perhaps?

Feeling quite ill as he continued to examine the injuries, he was relieved when Jo walked in.

'Oh, Allan, what has happened to you?' Jo asked, taking one of the old man's hands in hers.

'I'm sure Barb didn't mean it,' he said. 'I must have fallen and hit my cheek' he pressed a gnarled hand to where a clear handprint was visible '...and she decided I'd be safer if she tied me in my chair, not tight, mind you, but she went out and I had to—well, you know my bladder isn't very strong—and when she came home she was so angry, and said I couldn't live at home any more and brought me here.'

Jo shook her head and looked at Charles, who had no idea what to suggest, except they couldn't send him home with that harridan.

'We'll sort it,' Jo said gently to the older man, and Charles knew from the determined glint in her eyes that it didn't bode well for Barb! 'We'll get you X-rayed to make sure there's nothing broken, then how about I find a carer to move in with you? Just till after Christmas. Those ten days people get off around Christmastime is when Barb wants all her family there, and if a carer is around to keep an eye on you, she can go down south to them for a change.'

'Oh, Jo, could you really fix that for me?' Mr Bell asked.

'Of course I can, I'll get straight onto it. Now, I'll hand you back to Dr Charles to organise some X-rays and I'll talk to Barb—tell her you need medical attention for a few weeks and a carer can give it to you. I'll tell her that if a trained carer is living there, her reports will make it easier for me to tell if you're losing your marbles—that should go down a treat!'

Jo was smiling but Charles could see the anger in her eyes, sheer fury that anyone could treat an old man like this.

He organised an orderly to take Mr Bell to X-Ray, then went back to Fiona for a new patient, pausing only briefly on the way to eavesdrop on Jo's conversation with the implacable Barb.

But Jo was standing no nonsense.

'You know there are only two bedrooms in the cottage and I'll need the other one for the carer. Why not take the opportunity to have Christmas with your family?'

'I could have Christmas with my family right here if

that old man wasn't so stubborn.' Barb spat the words at Jo, but she remained calm, although Charles guessed she was reining in her temper with difficulty.

'Did you win?' he asked Jo later.

'*And* got her a seat on this afternoon's flight,' Jo said, but there was little triumph in her tone.

'It just shouldn't happen, Charles,' she said. 'Allan's been nothing but kind and generous to Barb and she treats him like that.'

'Should we keep him in hospital overnight?'

She nodded.

'I think so. Just in case there's some kidney damage or something else we don't know about. And it will give me a chance to get someone in to clean his cottage and find a carer who'll feed him decently. He's practically skin and bone.'

Jo left Charles to check Allan's X-rays, clean up his wounds, and admit him overnight for observation, and reported to the triage desk

But the usual steady stream of patients failed to materialise, and the regular staff decided to pull out their Christmas decorations, so Jo was struggling to attach a lot of disparate branches to a plastic Christmas tree in such a way it looked approximately the right shape when Charles appeared, having personally delivered Allan Bell to a ward for observation.

'Are you sure that's how it's supposed to look?' he asked Jo as he walked around the battered tree to get the full three-sixty-degree experience.

'No, of course I'm not,' she snapped at him, thrusting a bunch of branches into his hands. 'You have a go!'

'Huffy, huh?' a passing nurse said, and Jo sent her a glare that would have melted ice.

'I volunteered to help out with patients,' she muttered. 'I shouldn't have to be doing this!'

'Then leave it to me,' Charles told her. 'You might be better at hanging tinsel, although the person currently doing that is about to be decapitated by the ceiling fan.'

By the end of the day, between patients, the staff had filled the ED with Christmas spirit, from the tree Charles had managed to assemble perfectly to fake pine branches along the window sills.

Jo met Charles in the staffroom.

'I've just been visiting Allan,' she said. 'I was feeling bad because I'd threatened getting the police if Barb didn't get on the Sydney flight, but when he told me a little more of what had happened, I was almost sorry I hadn't put in a complaint.'

'Did she hit him?' Charles asked, and Jo shook her head.

'Allan's too loyal to say so, but that's a palm print across his face—a palm complete with fingers—and it must have had some force to cause so much bruising.'

'Is there respite care available to give them a break away from each other?'

Jo shook her head.

'It's quite expensive and she hates spending money—his money, mind you. That's why she's been bringing him here. She knows we do it on a short-term basis and it costs nothing. The ideal would be for him to sell his cottage and move into an assisted living place called Rosemary House. He'd have his own small studio apartment, all meals provided and his laundry and cleaning done once a week'

'But it's a place you have to buy into?' Charles guessed, and Jo nodded.

'He doesn't want to sell the house, he wants it to go to Barb and her family, but while he's still alive, he insists it's his house, not hers.'

'So Jo to the rescue!' Charles teased.

'Not really,' she said. 'I just happen to know someone who could do with the work and wouldn't mind filling in. It's a small place, Port Anooka.'

Charles was laughing as a white-faced nurse appeared in the doorway,

'It's Schoolies, three of them, drug-affected, hyper-thermic—I've put them in the quiet room, although they're none too quiet.'

Charles glanced at his watch. Nearly seven, but surely too early for these youngsters to be drug-affected.

'Do we know what drugs are most commonly taken?' he asked Jo as they hurried to the treatment room.

'Ice is in epidemic proportions, but younger ones tend to stick with MDMA. They call it Molly and it makes them feel they can dance for ever—which is where the hyper-thermia comes in. They'll have been treated at the first-aid tent with cooling packs, and been washed down. The ambos could have started a cold crystalloid infusion, but they are still likely to be excitable.'

'Which means?' Charles asked.

'Sedation, just until we get their core temperatures down. Ketamine is useful, or benzodiazepines can help.'

The youngsters, all women, had arrived in two ambulances, so the room appeared to be full of ambos.

Jo quickly checked the handover details, all three already having been treated with cold packs and had drips running into them.

'Didn't want to go the sedation route until you'd seen them,' one of the ambos said.

The nurses were exchanging the cooling pads for fresh ones from the freezer. Two of the patients were pale and quiet while one kicked and struggled against the restraints that still held her secure on the ambulance stretcher.

'I suggest we sedate her before we move her to our bed,' Charles said. 'If she gets her hand on the drip she'll rip it out for sure.'

The young woman was cursing and swearing at them, refusing to admit there was anything wrong with her and wanting to get back to the party.

But all three needed cardiac and blood oximetry monitoring, at least until their temperatures returned to normal.'

'Ketamine?' Charles said to Jo.

'I think so,' she said, looking up from the patient she was tending but leaving it to Charles to work out the dose.

Once sedated they moved the third young woman easily, and within minutes they were all hooked up to monitoring equipment and peace was restored.

But although Jo had left him to it, Charles knew there was a lot more to do. He ordered blood tests for all three. With free bottles of water being readily available, all three of his patients could have been drinking copious amounts to cool down before a seizure in one case and a complete collapse with the other two had meant they'd been taken to the first-aid tent.

So their sodium levels could be well down, and that in itself could cause heart arrhythmias, coagulation factors and multi-organ shutdown.

He waited until the blood-test results came through, gave orders to the nurse he was leaving to watch them, and aware from the increased noise levels that the ED was now very busy he went out to discover where he could be most useful.

'I'm beginning to think there was a bad batch of MDMA out there at Port.' Lauren had caught him before he got as far as the triage desk. 'Are your three calm?'

Charles nodded.

'Good. I'll send someone to shift them to cubicles because there's a very distraught patient on his way in. Seizures, hallucinations, the lot! You'll manage?'

'Of course,' Charles said, although it hadn't really been a question, more of a statement of her confidence in his ability.

CHAPTER TEN

'Do you need a hand?' Jo asked, when she met him outside the calm room at ten. 'Things have settled down somewhat and I'm no longer needed.'

'I've only my patient in the quiet room, but I'll stick around until someone's available to take him over.'

'Takeaway tonight?'

'Sounds like a great idea, you choose the menu,' he said. 'I should be through here before too long.'

'I got a spare flat key today so we can each have one. I'll go across and open the place up to let some fresh air in, then get us something nice for dinner.'

Discussion of the day and their various patients was the conversational focus during the meal.

Nice, safe conversation, Jo thought. And sitting opposite Charles at the small dining table was distracting, but not as distracting as if they'd been touching.

Since they didn't have a cat, she was reasonably sure it was his foot that rubbed gently up her calf from time to time and sent shivers down her spine.

But Charles had mentioned Dottie earlier, and Jo knew he had questions, so when they took their coffee into the sitting area of the small flat she knew she'd have to answer them.

Still, it was better than the conversations about attraction and lust and love…

'Is she struggling for money?' Charles asked, and Jo knew who he meant.

'She has a pension,' Jo explained, 'but I imagine the rates and land tax eat up most of it. Bertie loved the place, and she's been determined to keep it, although the house is falling to pieces and the roof leaks—as you know.'

'But there must have been money in the first place for them to own the house and all the land around it.'

Jo nodded.

'Then Bertie had the stroke,' she said, 'and Dottie wanted only the best of care and attention for him, and that's expensive.'

'So you stay with her from time to time not because it suits you but to see she's not starving to death! This is ridiculous. I can give her money—only I doubt she'd take it. And if she'd read the letters she'd know there was money from my mother for her.'

Charles was so agitated he'd stood up and was pacing the room, disbelief vying with concern on his strong face.

Jo stood, and stopped his pacing with a hand on his shoulder.

'She's a very proud woman.'

'Very stubborn more like!' Charles said, resting his forehead on Jo's as he let out a long sigh.

And although they were still discussing Dottie, somehow his arms were around her waist and he was drawing her body close to his.

'You've had more practice with her,' he said against her cheek. 'How do you get away with doing things around the house and providing food?'

Jo eased back a little so she could smile at him.

'I tell her I'm going to buy it—the house—when she's gone so I need to keep it liveable.'

'And are you?'

His dark eyes, looking into hers, were serious and she knew there was more going on behind this conversation than Dottie and the house on the bluff.

'Never in a million years,' Jo admitted. 'I'd never be able to afford it, but Dottie doesn't need to know that.'

'I thought as much,' Charles said, as he drew her close again. 'You are one very remarkable woman.'

The kiss seemed to emphasise his words, as if a remarkable woman needed a remarkable kiss, but no sooner had his lips touched hers than Jo was lost—abandoned to the delight of his mouth on hers, his body pressed against her, his hands in her hair, fingers trailing down her neck.

It was a kiss that fired up every nerve in her body, so her skin and the flesh beneath it came vibrantly alive. His lips explored her face—temple, eyelids, ear—while hers slid down his neck, tasting the maleness of him, wanting him, although she knew it couldn't be.

But this kiss had altered their relationship because now she wanted only to be near him and as he dragged her down onto the couch and put an arm around her shoulder, snuggling her closer, she knew he'd felt it too.

Just to touch, explore, with fingertips and kisses—to be one, bodies merging.

'I'm here for another five weeks,' he said, when they were both so tired they'd been drifting in and out of sleep right there on the couch.

'And I'll still have baby flab,' Jo told him gently.

'Which will not worry me,' he declared. 'Not one iota!'

'But then you'll be gone,' Jo reminded him.

'You could come,' he said, holding her tightly again. 'I'd show you Europe!'

Jo shook her head.

'I rather doubt it's seemly for a prince to be dragging his mistress around Europe with him.'

'I wouldn't be the first,' Charles told her, but Jo shook her head.

'I don't think it's quite me,' she said, kissing him as she spoke, then easing back to look deep into his eyes. 'I'm not that person, well dressed and worldly, able to find enjoyment in doing nothing more than smiling at photographers. Besides, it just isn't practical. I've got to get Allan Bell sorted out and Dottie's roof fixed, and my locum's due to finish, so, thanks, but I don't think so.'

She kissed him again, stopping the protest she could see on his lips, then stood up.

'I'm off to bed,' she said. 'If you thought today was busy, there's always the knowledge that tomorrow could be worse.'

Tomorrow *was* worse, as were the tomorrows after it. For a start, the woman Jo thought would be happy to spend time at Allan Bell's wasn't well and needed care herself.

She thought of moving in herself—a cowardly thought that would remove her from Charles's presence in the flat and the chaos *that* was causing in her body. But with work, she'd hardly ever be there, and Barb had enough cronies among the neighbours to know.

It was Allan himself who solved the problem, popping in to the ED to talk to her.

'I've been talking to a friend whose son's a builder and he says he can have a bathroom installed at the back of my garage by New Year. Then I buy a fridge and microwave for out there, and tell Barb her family can come, but only one family at a time, and they have to camp in the garage.

Mostly they go out for meals but they can eat with me, just not be under my feet all the time.'

'That's brilliant, Allan. That way you get back on good terms with Barb, and her family will all get their holiday. There are four more weeks of summer holidays after Christmas so they can take turns to come.'

'And better still I'll have the builders here until New Year to keep an eye on me, so you needn't be worried. And my friend's wife says I'm to have Christmas dinner with them.'

Jo beamed at him, pleased because he'd sorted this out by himself, which certainly disproved Barb's contention that he was losing it.

'It's a great solution,' she said to Charles that evening as they walked home from the tapas bar that was fast becoming their regular eating place.

'And this friend of Allan's can really get it done in such a short time?'

'Apparently,' Jo said, feeling his hand take hers and hers actually nestle into his palm.

Damn it all! She was trying to stay aloof from Charles's not-so-subtle influence over her body and here was her own hand nestling, of all things.

Not that she removed it...

But was he feeling the strain of this not quite real relationship that he suggested a walk before they turned in?

'Have you followed the path out the back?' he asked, and she smiled in the darkness.

'Not for a very long time,' she said.

'Then let's go.'

He led her around their flat to where the path began and, hand in hand, they wandered down towards the sea, hearing it long before they saw it.

'It's so beautiful,' she murmured as they stood on the

clifftop where they could listen to the soft shush of the small waves washing against the cliff and look out across the shining ocean.

'It's a magic place!' Charles replied, then turned her in his arms and looked into her face.

Not kissing her, just looking—sighing—then turning to the ocean once again.

Could it be that his mother had implanted a love of the sea deep within him that he was so drawn to it in all its moods—marvelling at its power and strength and beauty?

But what had drawn him to the woman who watched it with him?

Surely not some part of a romantic hangover from his father's tales of love.

Was he subconsciously trying to replicate those stories?

Not that there was anything subconscious in his attraction to Jo!

He put his arms around her and held her close, aware that what he felt for this woman grew stronger every day, and certain that the feeling wasn't one-sided.

But something held her back!

Oh, she joked about pregnancy flab, and he knew now was the not the time for a physical affair, but her response to his kisses told him one thing, while the distance she could put between them left him puzzled.

And not knowing the answer, he made do with a kiss, just to confirm he was right about her response, which, when they finally broke apart, left him breathless and aching for her.

The walk back to the flat was much slower than the walk out to the ocean, both needing to touch and be touched, both needing—no, both greedy for—the sensations their kisses produced.

'You can use the bathroom first,' Jo whispered to him

as they reached the flats. 'I need to pop over to the hospital to check on something.'

By which she meant, *You cool down first and I'll just stay out of the way so we can go off to our separate bedrooms as if those kisses never happened.*

He smiled at her in the glow from the security light above their flat, and brushed her lips with one last kiss, then headed inside to contemplate celibacy, and wonder how some men managed it.

Christmas was fast approaching and by chance—or perhaps because they weren't regular staff—both she and Charles had three days off for the festivities.

'So back to Dottie's this afternoon,' Jo announced at breakfast. 'Hopefully we'll get off work on time so we're not too late getting out there. I've let her know we'll be back and I could almost hear a little excitement in her voice so maybe she's missed us.'

'Missed you, I'm sure,' Charles said, coming out of a little daydream where he and Jo breakfasted together every day—if possible for ever.

For all she responded to his kisses, and often was the instigator of them, she cut off from him if he talked of the future.

And knowing by now how open and honest Jo was, he knew there was some deep reason for her stepping back—for drawing a line between now and whatever lay ahead.

But he had a little time to think for Christmas was upon them.

'So, Christmas Eve, that's tomorrow, we shop,' Jo said as they drove back to Dottie's place, Charles looking forward to seeing his grandmother and feeling the warmth of the old house after the sterility of the flat.

'Christmas Day we cook and eat and sleep it all off,' Jo continued, 'then Boxing Day is a day of rest.'

Jo was talking so she didn't have to think about Charles in the seat beside her—too close by half—as whatever it was between them seemed to intensify by the minute, or perhaps by the second...

'Cook?' he said, resting a hand lightly on her knee and sending her heart into palpitations.

'Turkey, ham, crispy potatoes done in duck fat. I have it all ordered, we just have to collect it tomorrow and get the pudding, fruit and vegetables.'

'You're going to cook a turkey in weather that's just about touching one hundred degrees? In Dottie's ancient range?'

'And a ham and vegetables,' Jo corrected him. 'It's tradition.'

'It's tradition in Europe where there's probably a foot of snow outside the door, but here? Why don't we just have a salad?'

'Because it's Christmas!' Jo told him, pleased he'd moved his hand to wave it around in the air to show his disbelief.

He shook his head then rested his hand on her shoulder—which sent her heart fluttering again.

She did wish they would stop, all these reactions to this man.

Or did she?

Weren't they both enjoying their attraction, and what harm could it do?

Apart from leaving her a mess when he departed...

Charles tried to imagine a traditional Christmas dinner served in the Australian summer, and decided he'd just have to wait and see, and in the meantime he had a little shopping of his own to do.

Like his father with Margaret, he hadn't spent long with Jo, but the more he saw of her, the more convinced he was that she was the woman for him. She was intelligent, outspoken when she needed to be, fiercely loyal and protective of those she cared for, and so beautiful she still took his breath away when he caught sight of her unexpectedly around the house or hospital.

While the attraction between them, which he spent a lot of time trying *not* to think about, would enrich their union enormously.

So he'd slip away from discussions on the turkey that were sure to take place in the butcher's to see what the shops of Anooka could provide for him.

The day arrived, and although Charles baulked at shelling peas in the stiflingly hot kitchen then peeling mounds of potatoes—'There are only three of us!' he'd protested—he began to enjoy the preparations taking place.

Dottie herself had cooked the morning eggs, telling both her visitors not to eat too much toast as they had to keep room for lunch, but she'd then departed, muttering something about wrapping presents, which he'd already been told would be unwrapped after lunch.

'And after that,' Jo said, 'we lie around in a soporific stupor, due mainly to over-indulgence in sub-tropical temperatures.'

Charles had smiled at the image, although he understood they would probably do just that.

It was two in the afternoon before they sat down, by which time a south-easterly sea breeze was blowing through the windows, bringing much-needed relief from the heat.

The table was set with silver cutlery, and shining silver vegetable dishes overflowing with goodness were placed around a beautiful arrangement of vivid red poinsettia.

'Charles can carve,' Dottie decreed, adding, 'That's always assuming you know how to carve a turkey.'

He winked at her, his years following the housekeeper around coming in handy.

Jo passed him plates, and he placed slices of both turkey and ham on them, Dottie complaining that there was no roast pork.

'For just three of us, Dottie,' Jo said, 'I think I've already over-catered.'

But once they'd laden their plates with vegetables, gravy and cranberry jelly, even Dottie conceded there'd have been no room for the pork as well.

They pulled the white and gold crackers set in front of each place, donned party hats, and read silly jokes, sipping ice-cold French champagne Dottie had unearthed from somewhere.

As they ate the delicious meal, Dottie reminisced about Christmases past, Jo made sure everyone had enough to eat, and Charles felt he'd found a place where he belonged— that this was family.

Had Dottie guessed at his thinking that she said, 'Tell us about Christmas at your place.' He did, starting with the enormous tree the staff erected in the front entrance, the fresh pine smell of it and the branches that decorated the banisters rising on either side of it.

Of the formal red and gold dining room, and the international visitors and relatives from other countries who usually graced the dinner table.

'But we eat as we ate today, although our dessert is the traditional pudding, carried in wreathed in flaming brandy, but I think for here, the ice cream one was fantastic. As full of Christmas flavours as the ones we have at home, but without the heaviness.'

He paused for a minute, then added, heart in mouth, 'But you will see, for you will come next Christmas, no? To see the snow and ice and people skating instead of surfing. Come earlier, in fact, Dottie, to see the magic of our autumn leaves, come sooner even, whenever you are free.'

Had he said the wrong thing?

For long moments he waited, then finally Dottie said, 'And Jo? Is she invited?'

His turn to hesitate. He knew he wanted to say that by that time he hoped Jo would be there, because the thought of being separated from her for a full year was more than he could bear.

But that was between him and Jo, so he settled for, 'Of course!'

And the conversation ceased.

'Why don't you two move to the living room while I clear the dishes away?' Jo suggested. 'Then it will be present time.'

Charles felt as if a giant fist had grabbed his gut and was squeezing hard.

Had he chosen wrong?

Would she be embarrassed?

He held Dottie's chair for her and carried her champagne into the front room, where he discovered stacks of presents set beneath the crystal baubles on the tree.

Jo returned and began proceedings by handing him an enormous parcel.

He opened it to find a beach towel like an Australian flag, and rubber slip-slops also emblazoned with the flag—underwear, board shorts, a T-shirt and even a hat—all Australian souvenirs.

'That's so when *you* come back, you'll have the right

gear,' she teased, although he'd never seen such a blatant display of Australiana at the beach.

He parcelled it up.

'I shall treasure it,' he said, catching her gaze and holding it, so she knew he meant it, because even in fun it came from her.

He was watching the blush creep up her cheeks when Dottie handed Jo a present—a small box, wrapped and tied with ribbon. Jo opened it cautiously, then gasped, and said, 'Oh, no, Dottie, that's far too good for you to be giving to me.'

Her fingers trembled as she drew the object from the box, revealing a delicate gold necklace, set with sparkling sapphires the exact blue of her eyes.

'Put it on,' Dottie ordered, but Jo shook her head.

'It's far too precious and I'm all hot and sweaty from the kitchen.'

'Fiddle-faddle. Jewellery is made to be worn,' Dottie told her. 'They were my mother's and should have gone to Maggie, but maybe they'll go to Maggie's granddaughter someday!'

'Dottie, I can't—we can't—I won't—'

Her old friend smiled knowingly at her, and as he was closest, Charles took the necklace from Jo's trembling fingers and fastened the clasp at the back of her neck, his fingers trailing on the pale skin beneath her upheld hair.

'My turn,' she said, one hand on the jewels, her voice still shaky from surprise. 'Mine to you pales in comparison, but I couldn't decide between buying you another dozen buckets or getting someone in to do the roof.' She smiled as she spoke. 'A patient of mine owes me a favour, and he's starting on the second of January.'

She handed Dottie a card that probably held the written promise.

'Busybody!' Dottie said, but even Charles could see she was pleased.

'My turn,' he said, and they both turned to him.

'But you're a guest, you don't have to give us presents,' Jo protested, but he'd already passed across his presents.

Dottie opened hers, admired the snow scene and red robin on the card, then opened it.

'It's an open plane ticket so you can come whenever you like,' he said. 'Whenever you like, and as often as you like, and stay for as long as you like.'

'Is yours the same, Jo?' Dottie asked, but Jo's hands were shaking too much to open it.

'Later,' she said, and left the room.

Dottie and Charles watched her go, then Dottie turned to him.

'I have something for you,' she said. 'An apology for one thing, to you and your father and most especially to your mother. But you came here looking for her and this is the best I can do.'

She pulled an old red box out from behind the couch, pushed it across the floor towards him, then stood up.

'There's your mother,' she said, her voice thick with tears as she beat a hasty retreat towards the door.

Jo, the unopened card thrust into her pocket, cleaned up the kitchen then returned to find them gone.

'In here,' Charles called, and she found him in the dining room, sitting at the table with piles of papers spread out in front of him.

'My mother's letters,' he said, his voice charged with emotion. 'Right from when she went away to boarding school. Dottie kept every one of them. And look, see

these, date stamps on them—from when she went away—
unopened but still kept.'

He had spread out the envelopes along the table.

'Count them. She must have written every week, although Dottie never replied, and here, that must have been
when she died, because that's my father's handwriting.'

Jo looked at the unopened letters sorted by date on the
table, and put her hand on Charles's shoulder.

'Can you handle this?' she asked, and he nodded—
looked up at her and smiled.

'Don't you see, through this gift my mother will come
to life for me.'

It was Jo's turn to nod, although those unopened letters
bothered her, seeing them set out like that.

'There has to be a reason,' she muttered. 'It can't only
be her running away!'

But Charles didn't hear her, so engrossed was he in the
rather untidy letter that had been his mother's first one
from her boarding school.

Aware he needed to be alone with these treasures, Jo
went up to her room, intending to rest, but those letters
had been kept—treasured, even if left unopened. Why?

She slipped downstairs as the faintest glimmer of an
idea began to take shape in her head. Dottie was resting,
Charles discovering his mother—neither would miss her.

She drove swiftly to the hospital and walked into the
administration area, greeting the few people she saw but
heading for the archives. She'd been here before, seeking
information on the parents and grandparents of one or
two of her patients, working out whether their problems
could be genetic.

Bertie had had a stroke—he would have been admitted here before being transferred to Sydney, so somewhere
here she'd find a date.

* * *

Supper was a casual meal, out on the bluff beneath the shady tree—leftovers and salad spread on the table for the three of them to pick at.

'And where did you scoot off to in your little car?' Dottie asked as Jo threw a cover over the remaining food and they all lay back in their chairs to enjoy the colours of the sunset reflected on the ocean and watch the first stars show their gleams.

'I went to the hospital, Dottie, and confirmed something I'd been thinking.'

She reached out and took Dottie's small hand in hers. 'Since Charles arrived, the puzzle of Maggie's disappearance from your life began to drive me mad. I knew it wasn't in your nature to turn your back on anyone, let alone a beloved daughter, and, no, don't shush me, because I think it has to be said.'

'Not if Dottie doesn't want to talk about it,' Charles said, firing up in defence of the grandmother he was still coming to know.

But Jo ignored him, waiting, watching the older woman, who was looking out to sea.

And caught the faintest of nods!

Jo turned to Charles this time.

'I went back through the hospital records and checked the date of Bertie's admission after his stroke. It was the day after your mother left.'

'And you blamed my mother?' Charles asked, but gently, without any hint of judgement.

Dottie shook her head and Jo squeezed her fingers.

'Knowing Dottie as I do, I believe she was more afraid that your mother would blame herself—that Maggie would think the argument they'd had and her leaving home had caused her father's stroke, and Dottie didn't want her carrying that burden.'

'Of course I didn't!' Even softly spoken, the words were vehement! 'How would she have felt? And how could she carry such a burden into whatever new life she'd found?'

'But she'd have come back—helped you, I'm sure,' Charles said, and Dottie turned to Jo.

'It's your story, you tell it.'

'I think,' Jo began, uncertain now about her theory but determined to get it out, 'that with Bertie close to death and the flight to emergency care in Sydney and the long battle to keep him alive that followed, he *had* to become Dottie's priority. She had to be strong for him and if she started thinking about the loss of Maggie it would undermine that strength. Even reading a letter would open up the wound in her heart that was Maggie, and weaken her resolve. Answering a letter—that would be impossible without telling Maggie about her father's illness and causing Maggie distress.'

Charles nodded slowly, then got out of his chair to kneel by Dottie's side.

'I cannot even imagine the pain you must have felt,' he said, 'but I've read the letters—my mother's letters—and in every one she said she loved you and her father and regretted the pain she'd caused you. But she also said she understood there'd be a reason why you couldn't write, because she could never doubt your love for her.'

Silence stretched between them until Dottie was the first to swipe at the tears on her face.

'Well, I hope you're happy, Jo, making us all cry like this on Christmas Day!'

Charles stood up from where he'd stayed kneeling, his arm around his grandmother's thin shoulders.

'Shall I make you some cocoa before bed?' he asked, helping her as she began to stand up.

She nodded, and allowed him to hold her elbow all the way back to the house.

'You can bring it up,' she said, as she climbed onto her own private rocket.

And, thus dismissed, he went through to the kitchen to fix the nightly drink.

Jo had stayed out on the bluff—deliberately, he thought—and although his heart was filled with love for her and what she'd done, he knew his first duty, right now, was to Dottie.

Upstairs in her bedroom, she was already in bed, the Chinese robe like an empress's gown around her shoulders.

He set the small table over her knees and handed her the cocoa, then hesitated, aware there was more to be said, but also aware that she must be emotionally exhausted.

'Sit a minute,' she said—a plea rather than an order this time.

He sat.

'So?' she asked.

'Do I believe that's what happened?'

She nodded.

'It makes sense to me, Dottie, and nothing else did. I've been around you long enough to know you're kind and caring for all your gruffness, and I know you're loyal to a fault. At the time of my grandfather's stroke, you knew your first duty was to him. And if you'd thought about my mother going off you'd have been torn in two and so not able to give him what he needed from you right then.'

'It broke my heart,' she said, 'but I just didn't have the strength to worry about both of them. I chose Bertie and hurt your mother.'

'But I think Jo was right. Telling her would have hurt her even more—she would have blamed herself.'

Dottie sipped at her coffee, nodding slowly.

'It hurt me more than you can ever know,' she said quietly, then she handed the empty mug to Charles and said goodnight.

CHAPTER ELEVEN

Emotionally drained, Charles walked back onto the bluff. He put out his hands to grasp Jo's and pull her out of her chair.

'You are the kindest, most amazing, perceptive and wonderful person I have ever met. I love you, Jo. It's not just attraction, I know that, and I think you do too.'

And almost without conscious thought, he dropped to his knees, her hands still in his, and said, 'Marry me!'

'Silly!' the woman he'd just proposed to said, tugging at his hands to get him back on his feet. 'That's just silly! You're in an emotional whirl after all that stuff came out and it's gone to your head. I've told you already I'm not who you need. You need a princess at the very least, not a country doctor from a very small village in Australia. There must be dozens of spare princesses roaming Europe—beautiful, sophisticated young women who speak half a dozen languages and will do you proud.'

He was on his feet now, his arms around her, looking down into her lovely face as she spoke this nonsense.

'I don't want them, I want you,' he said, and then he kissed her.

'And I think you want me too,' he murmured, when he'd recovered a little breath after the fervour of her response.

He felt her body tremble and the shake of her head against his.

'No, Charles,' she said, and a cold certainty crept through him.

'You mean it?'

She nodded this time.

'I do, Charles, I really do.'

But there was a deep sadness in her voice, and when he tilted her head he saw the tears glistening in her eyes.

'Tell me you don't love me,' he said, speaking gently because he knew there was something very wrong about all of this.

She shook her head, then gave a little huff of cynical laughter.

'I can't do that either,' she said. 'You are the most re-markable man I've ever met. You can bring my body to life with a touch or even a look. You have made me happy in a way I've never felt before and, yes, I love you, but I can't marry you.'

She tried to edge away but his arms tightened around her, holding her against his body, not kissing her but want-ing her close to him, in his arms, as if through the contact he would work out what was wrong.

Finally, by some unspoken agreement, they both turned and walked in silence along the cliff, then into the scrubland where they'd cut the Christmas tree.

Back at the chairs, as he prepared to fold them and re-turn them to the garage, he had to ask.

'Will you tell me why?'

Jo looked at him for a long moment, then subsided into a chair, pulling his close so she could hold his hand for strength to tell her story, as well as gain comfort from its warmth.

And there in the moonlight, with the sea splashing

on the rocks beneath the clifftop, she began. She owed him that.

'I don't know how much you know about surrogacy but here very few IVF programmes will accept a surrogate who hasn't had at least one child.'

'You'd had another child?' he asked, and she could hear the other questions in his voice—where is he or she now, did the child die, did you give him, or her away too…?

That last bit was the clincher. What kind of woman gave away her own child? But it was also the nub of the story.

'I grew up in a kind of commune. There are still many of them here and probably everywhere, but it was a place where several nuclear families all lived on a particular parcel of land and worked it, farmed it, living as closely as possible to self-sufficiency. It was great—other kids to play with, dozens of aunts and uncles, as well as Mum and Dad.'

She paused, aware Charles must be wondering where all this was leading.

'Mum died when I was fourteen. My father took it badly. He shut himself away in his grief, isolated himself from everyone, including me.'

'The person he should most have cared for,' Charles said quietly, and Jo nodded.

'Except that Mum's death finished him in some way—he died five years later, but as far as I was concerned everyone was kind. The women made sure we had food to eat, but it was Leon, a relative newcomer to the commune, who understood that what I really needed was someone to comfort me; to hold me and let me cry and tell me everything would be all right. He made me happy and—well, you can guess the rest. I thought it right, when he asked, that I should make him happy too. Looking back, it was stupid, of course. I knew all about procreation—we had every variety of animal around to learn from, but never in my wildest dreams did I consider that what was happening would lead to pregnancy.'

Had her voice broken that Charles stood up and lifted her so he could sit down again with her in his arms, holding her as she told a story she'd only ever told to Gran.

'I thought I was getting fat because I was eating properly again, then Leon left and I was totally lost. I found Gran's address in an old notebook of Mum's and headed off to Sydney. She was wonderful. She took me in and gave me all the real love that I needed. I was going to be fifteen when the baby was born, a child with a child. We talked about options but it always came back to what I could possibly offer a child. I hadn't finished even high school education, had no job prospects and could hardly depend on Gran to support me and a baby.'

She paused, needing to get it said.

'But the worst thing was, Charles, that I really, really, didn't want that baby. I felt it had been foisted on me, and I hated Leon with all the passion an immature teenager can muster. So I gave the baby away. I hope and pray she has a happy life—I have to believe she does. There, it's out!'

Charles held her close, rocking her slightly on his knee, pressing kisses in the little hollow behind her ear, silently telling her of his understanding.

'But,' he finally said, 'I know you felt you had to tell me, and apart from wanting to find and kill some bastard called Leon who took advantage of you when you were at your most vulnerable, I cannot see what it has to do with marrying me.'

'Oh, Charles,' Jo whispered, sinking deeper into his warmth and comfort, 'of course I can't. You have to marry and have children, it's your duty to do that to protect the family line, and I've known for quite a while that I don't want children of my own. How fair would it be to that child

I gave away for me to have more children—half-siblings she would never know? How would she feel about it if she found out?'

'Can't we ask her?' Charles said gently. 'I know most countries have agencies that help birth mothers find their children, and adopted children find their birth parents.'

She looked at him, hoping the despair she felt wasn't clear to read in her eyes.

'I've tried, Charles, registered with all of them, because I've felt so bad—so guilty—about my feelings at the time. It wasn't her fault she was born.'

'And you've never heard from her or her parents? Never discovered if she's looking for you?'

Jo shook her head.

'I've read a lot about it and most adopted children don't look until they're older, and usually independent of their parents. But I wrote to her on her sixteenth birthday two months ago. I tried to explain, and sent the letter through the government agency, who would have sent it on to her parents and left it for them to decide whether or not to give it to her.'

'Oh, Jo,' he said, and wrapped his arms around her, feeling the pain she held in every cell of her body. 'I just don't know what to say—how to help—what I can do.'

'Just love me for a little longer,' Jo whispered to him, snuggling into his arms.

They were sitting under the poinciana tree the following day when Jo's phone rang. She glanced at the number, hoping it might be something she needn't answer, because the previous evening's conversation, though cathartic, had left her exhausted.

'My locum,' she said. 'I do hope there's not a problem.'

'Hi Jo,' her cheerful stand-in said, 'there are some people who've just called at the house, looking for you. Should I send them up to Dottie's?'

'Did they say who they are?' Jo asked, totally mystified, and hoping they weren't reinforcements from Barb ready to storm Allan's house.

'A Mr and Mrs Grey, and their daughter Caitlin. They say they'd don't know you but you sent them a letter.'

Jo shook her head.

'I haven't written to anyone,' she said, 'but best you send them up.'

She closed the phone, and stood up.

'Some people coming to see me,' she explained to Dottie and Charles. I'll go down to the house and find out what they want—I shouldn't be long.'

Charles watched her walk away, his heart aching for this stubborn woman he loved so much.

Then something in Jo's side of the phone conversation—'I haven't written to anyone'—struck him like a bolt of lightning, and he was out of his chair and striding across the lawn to catch up with her as a vehicle pulled up outside Dottie's front door.

Three visitors tumbled out, an older couple and a teenager with vivid red hair.

He saw Jo's face lose all its colour and was close enough to hook his hand around her waist to steady her.

The couple introduced themselves, and then the redhead—Caitlin—the mother crying now as she thanked Jo for the gift she had given them sixteen years ago.

Then Jo was crying and the girl was in her arms, Jo muttering, 'Please don't hate me,' through her sobs.

The girl stepped back so she could look up into Jo's face.

'How could I hate you when you've given me such wonderful parents?'

Then she grinned and added, 'The red hair I could have done without!'

Then Dottie appeared and took in the situation at a glance, obviously having known the backstory of the adoption. She took over what was usually Jo's role in the house and ushered everyone inside, settling them in the living room where the crystals on the tree threw rainbows around the room.

'You all talk,' she said. 'Charles and I will forage for food.'

And with a look that told Charles he had to follow, she left the room.

The Greys had departed, and Dottie was tucked up in bed before Jo and Charles finally had some time alone.

'Well?' he said, and watched her shake her head.

'I can't think straight,' she said, and seeing the pallor of her skin and the exhaustion in her eyes, he knew this wasn't the time to be demanding an answer to his proposal.

'Go to bed,' he said, taking her gently in his arms and dropping soft kisses on her hair. 'Would you like some cocoa to help you sleep?'

She shook her head and smiled at him.

'There's just so much to take in that I might never sleep again, but I'm so tired, Charles, I'm sorry.'

'Don't be silly,' he said gruffly. 'We've plenty of time to talk.'

And he walked her to her bedroom door, opened it, kissed her goodnight and closed the door.

But for all that nothing had been said, his heart beat with a new happiness. Meeting Caitlin would surely put Jo's mind at rest over having children in the future, and he took himself to bed, to dream of little redheaded children cavorting around the palace.

The ringing phone woke the household at three in the morning, and Jo, used to emergency calls at odd hours of the night, was the first out of bed to answer it. She'd barely worked out what the accented voice was asking when Charles appeared beside her.

'I think it has to be for you,' she said, and passed him the receiver, although she stayed close beside him, holding his free hand, as he answered.

She recognised the words he spoke as French, but it was his voice that told her the matter was urgent.

'What is it?' Dottie called from the top of the stairs, as Charles replaced the receiver.

'My father,' he said. 'He has had a heart attack. They have done a triple bypass, using stents to open up his blood vessels, but although he is recovering well, I must go home.'

A faint sigh came from the top of the stairs, then a bump as Dottie slid to the floor.

Jo raced towards her, beating Charles by inches, but Dottie was sitting by the time they reached her, shaking her head.

'So silly,' she muttered. 'I never faint.'

There was a pause before she added, 'But it was like history repeating itself. You must go home, Charles, of course you must. Go with Jo and make the arrangements.'

'Not until you're safely in bed,' Jo told her, as Charles lifted Dottie to her feet, then swept her up to carry her to her bedroom.

'And the arrangements are already made,' he said. 'The consul here will organise a plane to fly me back to Sydney first thing in the morning, and they have booked flights home for me from there.'

Jo was checking Dottie's pulse, satisfying herself that her old friend was all right.

'I'll sit with her a while. You go and do whatever you have to do. If that was someone official calling, you might get more information from someone closer to your family.'

'I might have heard it from them if I'd actually charged my phone. I spoke to my father only twenty-four hours ago, phoning him to wish him a merry Christmas, then left my phone by the bed and didn't charge it.'

'Well, do it now,' Jo said. 'Presumably someone local will ring you to let you know when the plane will be here.'

Charles nodded, bent to kiss Dottie's cheek and left the room.

'You could go with him,' Dottie said to her. 'Your locum's booked for another two weeks.'

Jo shook her head, although her whole being longed to be with him on that journey, offering whatever comfort he would accept.

'It's not my place, Dottie,' she said. 'And if his father's had a bypass there should be no risk of another problem at the moment.'

Then Jo bent and kissed her old friend's cheek.

'Try to sleep,' she said, 'and keep in mind that now Charles has found you, you'll be seeing him again. You have the ticket—you could be off to Livaroche next week!'

'You have a ticket too,' Dottie said sleepily, as Jo went quietly out the door.

Charles was waiting for her at the bottom of the stairs.

'This is not how it should be,' he said quietly. 'There is so much we need to talk about, I hate to leave like this.'

Jo put her arms around him.

'But you have to go. Your father needs to know you're there, ready to take care of things until he is well again, and you need to reassure yourself he is recovering, so there's no more to be said.'

'There is much to be said—*so* much—but surely now there is no reason we can't marry.'

'Maybe,' Jo conceded, giving him the lightest of kisses on the thinned line of his lips. 'Let me know when you hear about the plane. I'll take you to the airport.'

His lips had softened so she dropped another kiss on them.

'And say goodbye?' he asked.

But she couldn't answer. Too many things were happening too quickly.

'We'll see,' she managed as he wrapped his arms around her body so they were melded into one.

In the end, Jo broke away, easing herself out of the arms she could have stayed in for ever.

'Go and pack, contact whoever you need to contact, then get some sleep if you can.'

He stood stock still in front of her, his head bowed, until she put her arms around him in a fierce hug.

One last kiss and she walked away, feeling so bereft she wondered if they did marry, would she feel like this whenever he was called away?

If she *did* marry?

She hadn't allowed herself to think of this for a single instant, but since Caitlin's arrival in her life she knew Charles would see it as the end to any impediment.

But how could she be a princess in a foreign land—learn about protocol and how to speak the languages they spoke and…?

The list grew and grew until finally she fell asleep, totally wiped out by the revelations of the day.

Jo had been back at work four weeks, long enough for the Christmas idyll to be little more than a dream.

Well, a dream and an ache in her heart, made worse

every time she spoke to Charles, heard his voice from so far away, and worried for him as he took on his father's duties—for all he assured her it was what he'd been brought up to do!

But he sounded tired and downhearted, and though he spoke of love and missing her, there'd been no talk of marriage.

Dottie had given her a going-away present when she'd left the big house—two language CDs—one French and one Spanish.

'Just in case he does come back sometime,' she'd said to Jo, 'you'll be able to surprise him. Besides which, I can hardly travel all that way on my own, so you can use that plane ticket and come with me when I go at Christmas to see the snow.'

As if! Jo thought, but didn't say.

Let Dottie have her dream—and Molly could have Jo's plane ticket!

The summer heat departed and on the balmy autumn evenings Jo walked the beach and headlands, reciting the foreign words she'd learned.

Not for Charles, of course, or because she ever intended to visit Livaroche, but it had become a challenge to the extent that once a week she went to the tapas bar in Anooka to practise with real people.

It occupied her mind and gave her little time to brood, so even in the dark of the night when sleep couldn't come, she could run through French verbs or talk to herself in halting Spanish.

She was nearing the end of her afternoon appointments when her receptionist came in.

'Gary Cavill has cancelled but that gorgeous man is here,' the woman whispered.

'What gorgeous man?' Jo asked crossly, pleased she didn't need to have her weekly argument with Gary about wanting heavier opioid painkillers, which she knew he sold for cash in the local pub, but not wanting a new patient.

'The gorgeous man from Dottie's house at Christmas! The one everyone says is her grandson.'

Jo's heart gave an excited little flip, then plummeted to her boots. Did he *have* to come back at the end of a very long day, when she was feeling grubby and tired and probably looked a right mess?

'Send him away,' Jo told her. 'He'll be staying at Dottie's. I can go up and see him later.'

But as the door closed on her receptionist, she wondered if she would.

Her heart still ached but surely the ache had grown less painful? Did she really want to open up that wound?

The door opened to let her flustered receptionist back in.

'He won't go!' she whispered, and Jo shook her head.

'You go,' Jo told her. 'I'll see him in a minute.'

She propped her elbows on the desk and held her head in her hands, aware that hair was escaping from the once neat roll with which she'd started the day, and she must look totally wrecked.

Not that it mattered, the sensible part of her said, but...

She stood up, washed her face and hands, tidied the wildest bits of hair with a splash of water, and marched out into the waiting room.

She was angry now!

What right had he to just walk back into her life like this?

And how pathetic was it that she was practically paralysed with excitement to be seeing him again.

He stood up as she entered, and somehow she ended up in his arms, tears streaming down her face as he patted her back and made soothing noises.

He eased her back a little, produced a spotless handkerchief—probably monogrammed and with a crown over the initials—and mopped her face then smiled at her, and she felt her heart breaking.

'You see,' he said, so gently she wanted to cry again, 'I didn't want to do it over the phone. I wanted to be there, with you, to see your face, touch your hair.'

She frowned at him.

He was definitely speaking English but she didn't seem to understand the words.

'To propose to you!' he added.

Jo felt her legs give way and prayed there was a chair behind her because she couldn't stand up any longer.

Subsiding none too gracefully, she closed her eyes and tried to think—to sort out what Charles had been telling her. Her eyes were closed because thinking was impossible if she could see him.

Then he was beside her, holding her hand, and it didn't seem to matter what he said because he was here, he'd come back, and somehow everything would be all right.

It was an hour before they got to Dottie's, to meet the housekeeper Charles had brought from his home—the one who'd been his surrogate mother.

And somehow it all got sorted.

Jo would find someone to take over her practice and go back to Livaroche with Charles. And then, come Christmas, when Caitlin had long summer holidays, she and her parents would fly over with Dottie, who had insisted that, first, she would be the one to give Jo away and, second, the wedding could only be held at Christmas because she wanted snow and Christmas lights and—'Would you have a sleigh we could ride in, Charles?'

But Dottie wasn't done with organising.

'You go home with Jo, Charles,' she said, as the evening finally wound down. 'There's really not enough room here for you.'

'That was telling us,' Charles said as Jo drove him back to her place.

'In no uncertain manner,' Jo said, and knew her voice was shaking. Why wouldn't it? Every bit of her was shaking, and in some distant part of her brain she was glad she'd done so much walking in an effort to forget this man, because at least it had trimmed her body right down.

But as they kissed and held each other, talked and went to bed, it was as if there'd never been any other ending possible for the two of them, as if love always found a way...

EPILOGUE

JO MET THE Australian contingent of wedding guests at the airport, and drove them—no sleigh today—to the palace, where Charles and his father waited.

If the oohs and aahs had been significant as they drove through the snowy landscape with the streets garlanded with Christmas decorations, it was nothing to the delight with which the enormous Christmas tree in the front hall of the palace was greeted.

But up in the apartment that had been set aside for Dottie—hers for whenever she visited, Charles had promised—there was a small, unadorned Christmas tree.

'Did you bring them?' Charles asked, and Dottie dug into her enormous handbag, producing a carefully wrapped parcel.

'I'll just get my father,' Charles said, and when he came they knelt, just the four of them, and hung the crystal ornaments on the little tree.

For Jo it was the perfect prelude to her wedding—a private time before the very public day that would follow the Christmas festivities. They'd chosen New Year's Eve so the bells that would ring out at midnight would ring in their married life as well as the new year.

The day dawned bright, the sun reflecting off the snow so the whole world seemed to sparkle.

In Jo's bedroom, the clamour of female voices outdid the cooing of the white doves that had magically appeared around the castle, fluttering past doorways and pecking at the windows.

Caitlin and her mother had joined Dottie in helping Jo get dressed—Caitlin already in her bridesmaid's dress of rich blue velvet, a soft white muff dangling from one hand, while Dottie was keeping to the colour scheme in a soft blue-grey dress with a sweeping train.

But it was Jo they were all focused on as she slipped into the simple white velvet gown she'd chosen for the occasion—Jo with her hair swept up in a tangle of bright curls on the top of her head and Dottie's sapphires sparkling around her neck.

'Stand still,' Caitlin's mother ordered, as she climbed on a chair, the better to set a pearl and sapphire comb in the curls, so Jo stood, surrounded by what she considered her family, and fingered the sapphire ring the man she loved had given her. Soon she'd take it off so he could put another ring on her finger, a ring that would bind them together—for ever!

'Sleighs are here!' Caitlin called from the window, where she'd been watching the excitement in the court-yard below.

'Real sleighs?' Dottie asked, and Jo laughed.

'I do hope they're what you wanted, Dottie,' she said, 'because Charles had them especially made.'

She slipped the earrings Charles had given her into her ears and led the troupe out the door, along the portrait-hung corridor and down the winding staircase to where the pal-ace staff had gathered in the entrance hall to wish her well.

Then, holding tightly to Dottie's hand, she walked out to the sleigh, Caitlin and her mother climbing in behind them, while up in front a red-coated driver flicked his whip and six white horses with red plumes on their heads stepped out, drawing the sleigh smoothly over the icy road—especially iced by Charles's decree so Dottie could have her sleigh ride.

They drew up outside the cathedral, and Dottie, as regal as a queen, alighted, then reached out to take Jo's hand. And together they went through the great arched doors, and with the rich, flaring music of 'The Prince of Denmark's March' rising all around them they walked towards the altar, where Charles was waiting, turned towards them, smiling at the pair of them, his grandmother and his bride.

He greeted Dottie first, bending to kiss her cheek before leading her to her seat beside his father, then he turned and took Jo's hand in his, clasping it so tightly she realised he was as nervous as she was.

Until she looked at him and smiled, and saw his eyes light up with love—nerves forgotten in the certainty of the love they had for each other, the love they were about to pledge that would unite them for ever…

* * * * *

FIREFIGHTER'S CHRISTMAS BABY

ANNIE CLAYDON

MILLS & BOON

To Sareeta.
With grateful thanks for steering me
through my last four books
with such grace and aplomb.

CHAPTER ONE

AFTER TWO WEEKS of feeling the sun on his skin, and not having to bother with a razor, Ben Matthews had cut himself shaving. His uniform had felt unfamiliar and a little too crisp when he'd put it on this morning, but it was good to be back in a routine. The thing about holidays was that they gave him far too much time to think, and he was ready to get back to work now.

'Good holiday?' The fire station commander smiled across his desk, and Ben nodded.

'Has anything been happening here that I should know about?'

'I imagine you've already read the station reports?' Ben nodded in response. 'The only other thing is our visitor this morning.'

'Yes?' As the watch manager, Ben always liked to have a little warning if an inspection was taking place, but he had no concerns. It was a matter of both principle and pride that he and his crew were constantly ready for anything.

'She's a photographer. This is just a preliminary visit, she'll be back again in a month to take photographs over Christmas. It's partly her own project, to widen her portfolio, but we have an option to use any of the photographs she takes in our publicity campaigns and there's also going to be a calendar, which we'll be issuing at the end of next year.'

This all seemed very rushed. Ben wished he'd known about it when it had been in the planning stage, rather than being presented with a fait accompli. 'And this has all been agreed?'

'There wasn't much time to set it up. Ms Walsh specifically requested that she take the photographs over Christmas to add authenticity to the calendar shots. She's hoping to include some off-duty moments.'

Ben frowned. The only calendar he'd seen that had featured firefighters had involved underwear and Santa hats. And that was just the men...

'This is going to be...done sensitively, I imagine?'

'Of course. It's a bit of fun but there's a serious message, too. We want to raise public awareness about what we do, as well as raise money.'

'Right.' Ben was all for the serious message. Just as long as this photographer understood that too. 'The crew knows about this?'

'Yes, they're all for it. Ms Walsh came in last week with her portfolio and showed us some of her work. I thought it was excellent, and there was some disappointment amongst the other crews when she chose to shadow Blue Watch.'

This photographer seemed to be calling all the shots. Not with *his* crew...

'And you've given her a free hand?'

The station commander smiled. 'I haven't imposed any restrictions on her, if that's what you mean. I know I can count on you to ensure the smooth running of the operation.'

'In that case...' Ben needed to get back to his crew. Now. Before this photographer started to think she *did* have a free hand and anyone persuaded anyone else that taking their shirts off was a good idea. 'I'll be getting on if there's nothing else.'

'No, nothing else.' The station commander picked up a file from his desk, and Ben rose, heading for the door.

Ben opened the door of the ready room and found it empty. Of course it was. Gleaming red and chrome was sure to appeal as the backdrop for the calendar photographs. Walking downstairs into the garage, he heard voices and laughter.

'No, I don't think that's going to work.' A woman's voice, clear and brimming with humour. 'I'm after something a bit more spontaneous…'

'*Spontaneous, my eye.*' Ben muttered the words to himself, marching through the narrow gap between the two fire engines and almost bumping into a woman who was standing by the front one of them.

At least she was good at getting out of the way. That was exactly the kind of aptitude she'd need. Ben caught a trace of her scent before she stepped quickly to one side and he came face to face with Eve and Pete, in full protective gear, standing beside the chrome fender, both with fixed smiles on their faces. That looked absolutely fine to him but, then, he wasn't in the business of art photography.

'Okay…let's break it up.' It seemed that the rest of the crew had decided that the taking of a few photographs required them to stand around watching. 'Give us a minute, will you?'

'Good to see you back, boss.' Eve grinned at him, taking her helmet off and unbuttoning her jacket. Ben heard the click of a camera shutter beside him and turned to the woman standing next to him as the crew dispersed quickly.

'Hi. I'm Callie Walsh.' She was holding the camera loosely in one hand, the other stretched out towards him. 'You must be Ben Matthews.'

'Yes.' Ben shook her hand briskly, omitting to say that he was pleased to meet her. 'The station commander told me you'd be here.'

She nodded, looking up at him. She had green eyes, the kind that seemed wholly dedicated to making a man stare into them, and the prettiest face he'd seen in a long while. The softness stopped there. Her short, corn-blonde hair was streaked with highlights and slicked back from her face. Spray-on jeans, a fitted leather jacket with more zips than seemed entirely necessary, and a look of determination on her face gave the overall impression of a woman who knew how to steamroller her way over pretty much anything.

Instinctively, Ben stepped back, leaning against the chrome on the front of the fire engine. When she raised her camera, pointing the bulky lens in his direction, he frowned.

'Before you take any more photographs, I think there are a few ground rules we need to have in place.'

'Of course.' Her face was impassive, and Ben wondered what she was thinking. That didn't matter. It didn't matter what he thought either. What mattered was the well-being and effectiveness of his crew.

'This is a working fire station…'

'I understand that. I know how to keep out of the way.'

That had only been his first concern. There were many more. 'As Watch Manager I'm responsible for the safety of everyone connected with Blue Watch…' His gaze drifted to the high heels of her boots. What she was wearing didn't come close to practical, if she was reckoning on venturing anywhere other than the ready room.

She seemed to read his thoughts. 'I'm hoping to just get everyone used to the idea of me being here today. I won't be accompanying you to any calls…'

'You won't be doing anything, at any time, unless I allow it.'

Perhaps he should qualify that. She could do whatever she liked, as long as she didn't mess with him or his crew. Callie was regarding him thoughtfully, as if she was assessing her next move.

'I can handle myself in emergency situations and I know how to follow operational and safety guidelines.' She unzipped her jacket, pulling a sheet of folded paper from an inside pocket. 'You probably haven't had a chance to look at my CV yet, but when you do you'll see that I'm a paramedic.'

If she'd been trying to surprise him, she'd pulled off a master stroke. When he took the paper, it seemed warm to the touch. Ben put that down to his imagination, rather than the heat of her body.

'When did you change jobs?' He unfolded the paper, scanning it.

'I didn't. I did an evening course in photography when I was at school and found that I can take a decent portrait. The income from that helped put me through my training as a paramedic, but now I want to extend my range a little. I think my first-hand experience of working with the emergency services gives me something unique to bring to this project.'

It was either a canny career move or some kind of personal crusade. It was difficult to tell what sparked the passion that shone in her eyes, and it really wasn't Ben's job to decide. All he needed to concern himself with was the practicalities, not whatever made Callie Walsh tick.

'All the same, I'd like to have first sight of all the photographs you take…'

Callie shook her head. 'That's not the way I work.'

'It's the way *I* intend to work.'

The edges of her mouth curved slightly, as if she already had her answer ready and had been waiting for the right time to slap him down.

'Then you'll have to adapt. I decide which of my photographs goes forward, and they go to the individuals concerned first, so they can review them and choose whether they want to sign a release. After that they go to the station commander. It's all agreed and I'm sure he'll show them to you if you ask nicely.'

Ben ignored the jibe. The procedure sounded reasonable enough but he would have no hesitation in circumnavigating it if he saw any threat to the welfare of the firefighters on his watch.

'All right. But if I feel that any of the photographs are inappropriate, I won't hesitate to block them.'

She folded her arms. 'You want to give me some artistic direction? What do you mean by "inappropriate"?'

He shouldn't feel embarrassed about this, even if her green eyes did seem to rob him of his capacity to stay dispassionate. It was simply an observation.

'I won't have any of my crew treated as...eye candy.'

Ben had expected she might protest. But her gaze travelled from his face, looking him up and down slowly. He tried to suppress the shiver that ran up his spine.

'You think you'd be good eye candy?'

Ben had a healthy regard for disdain, particularly when it emanated from a beautiful woman. It was almost refreshing.

'No, that's just my point.'

'Good. We're in agreement, then. Anything else?' Callie smiled. Her face became softer when she did that, and the temptation to enjoy this confrontation became almost overwhelming.

'Don't leave any of your equipment around. I don't want anyone tripping over anything.'

'I'm looking for spontaneity, not posed shots, and my camera is all I need. I never leave it around.'

'Okay. And if the alarm sounds, I need you out of the way. Quickly.'

'Understood. I'll flatten myself against the nearest wall.' Her gaze met his, and the thought of crowding her against a wall and kissing her burst into Ben's head. Maybe he'd muss her hair a little first and find out whether the soft centre that her lustrous eyes hinted at really did exist.

He dismissed the idea. If the alarm sounded, that would be the last thing he should be thinking about. And if it didn't then it was still the last thing he should be thinking about.

'That's great. Thank you.'

'My pleasure. May I get on and take a few shots now?'

'Yes, please do.' Ben turned, and walked away from her. Maybe...

There was no maybe about it. Callie took his breath away. He'd aired his concerns less tactfully than usual because her mesmerising gaze had the power to make him forget all his reservations about her presence here. Even now, he was so preoccupied by the temptation to look back and catch another glimpse of her that he almost forgot he'd intended to go back his office and found himself heading on autopilot towards the ready room.

He didn't need this kind of complication. He'd been burned once, and if he allowed himself to be burned again, that would be entirely his fault. This was a professional relationship, and that was where it began and ended.

Callie watched his back as he walked away. Gorgeous. One hundred percent, knee-shakingly gorgeous. Dark, brooding looks, golden skin and bright blue eyes that the camera was sure to fall in love with. It was a shame about the attitude.

But he'd only said the things she'd known already. Stay out of the way. Treat the people she photographed with respect. Maybe he'd loosen up a bit when he saw that she knew how to handle herself.

Callie almost hoped that he wouldn't. If this guy ever actually got around to smiling at her, she'd be tempted to throw herself at him. If she wanted to avoid all the woman-traps that her mother had fallen into over the years, it would be a great deal easier if Ben Matthews didn't smile. Ever.

Ben had watched her all morning, and had hardly got a thing done. His crew, on the other hand, had been subtly persuaded to get on with their jobs, while Callie observed. She asked questions, laughed at everyone's jokes, and made a few self-deprecating ones of her own. It was all designed to put them at their ease, wipe the fixed smiles from their faces and get them to act naturally.

He saw her quietly lining up a few shots from the corner of the garage, and Ben had puzzled over why she should want them. Then the alarm sounded and she was suddenly back in that spot. He realised that it was the optimum out-of-the-way location to catch the movement of men and women, and then the noisy rush as the fire engine started up and swept out of the garage. She was good.

Maybe the professional thing to do was to try giving her the benefit of the doubt. He'd assumed that Callie was all about the cliché, but everything she'd done so far told him that she was all about the reality. Ben waited for a lull in the morning's activity and saw her heading for the ready room. He followed her, pouring himself a cup of coffee.

'Would you like one?' He gestured towards his own

cup and Callie shot him a suspicious look. He probably deserved that.

'No, thanks. A glass of water…' She pursed her lips and something in her eyes told him that one of the quiet, dry jokes he'd heard her share with the crew was coming. 'If you trust me not to throw it all over you, that is.'

'You're thinking about it?'

'I'm told that wet fireman shots are very popular.' She smiled suddenly, and Ben reconsidered the dilemma that had been bugging him all morning. The best thing about Callie wasn't the way she moved, or her long legs, or even her bright green eyes. It was her smile.

'I guess I deserve that.'

'I guess you do.'

The sound of ice breaking crackled in his ears as he filled a glass from the water dispenser. Ben walked over to the table, leaving an empty seat between his and hers when he sat down.

Callie was watching him thoughtfully. 'Your concerns are reasonable. Everyone wonders what a photographer is going to make of them, and one of the issues that was raised when I visited last week was that I didn't glamorise your work.'

Ben had missed that. Maybe that was why his crew all seemed so relaxed around her. She'd already talked about the kind of photos she intended to take, and they knew what he hadn't stopped to find out. Perhaps he should try asking questions before he jumped to conclusions.

'Why did you choose Blue Watch?'

'Because you're the only ones on duty over the whole of the Christmas period.'

Of course. Ben felt suddenly foolish.

'If there's anything else you want to ask me…' Her gaze

dropped from his face suddenly and she started to fiddle with her camera.

There was something. 'You say you're just an observer. But you frame your shots. I saw you scoping out the best place to stand when the alarm rang.'

This time she thought about her answer. 'Sometimes you have to be in the right place to see things clearly.'

Callie reached for the tablet on the table in front of her. Switching it on, she flipped through the photographs. 'What do you think of this one? Is it an accurate representation?'

Ben caught his breath. It wasn't just a photograph of a fire engine leaving the station, she'd caught the movement and urgency, hinting somehow at the noise and the touch of adrenaline that accompanied it. Ben hadn't thought that would be possible unless you'd lived those moments.

'That's really good.' *Really good* didn't sum it up. But, then, he was no art critic. 'I'd say it was accurate.'

'Thanks.' She stood up suddenly. 'I'd better get on.'

Ben watched her walk away from him. Perhaps *that* was the attraction. A beautiful woman who could walk away without looking back.

But maybe that was just the last eighteen months talking. He and Isabel had never really been right for each other, but he'd been intoxicated by her soft beauty. When he'd realised that it wasn't going to work between them, he'd tried to break things off gently, but Isabel wouldn't have it. Texts, phone calls. Looking out of his window to see her car parked outside at all hours of the day or night. And then the *real* craziness had started…

That was over now, and he didn't want to think about it. He wasn't particularly proud of the way he'd handled things and Isabel hadn't contacted him in months. A woman walking away from him was just that—not some sign that there was someone out there who could make him feel the things that had come so easily before he'd met Isabel.

He studiously ignored Callie for the rest of the day. She was making a good job of keeping out of the way, and that suited Ben just fine.

CHAPTER TWO

'THE PHOTOGRAPHS ARE IN, BOSS.' Ben found Eve hovering at the door of his office.

'Photographs?' He wondered whether his expression of surprise cut any ice. He'd been thinking about Callie a lot more than was strictly necessary over the last two weeks.

Eve rolled her eyes. 'There's a parcel on your desk. It came by courier.'

'Okay, thanks.' It seemed that Eve wasn't going to leave him alone to open it. 'Let's take a look then.'

Eve followed him into his office, looking over his shoulder as Ben carefully ran a knife around the tape that bound the box on his desk. Inside was a brief letter from Callie, stating that she'd enclosed a few photographs for review. And underneath that a stack of sealed manila envelopes, each of which carried a name and a *Private and Confidential* sticker.

'Where are mine...?'

'Hold on a minute.' Ben sorted through the envelopes, handing over the one that bore Eve's name.

'You can show them to me...if you want to.'

Eve was the one member of his crew that he wanted most to protect. Ben hadn't been there when she'd sustained the burns on her shoulder, but he'd been told how much courage she'd shown that day. And he'd seen the pain in her face when he'd visited her at the hospital. Eve had cried, just the once, saying that the burns were so ugly, and when she'd finally returned to work, Ben had noticed that she never wore anything that exposed her upper arms, even on the hottest day.

'I might...' Eve sat down on the chair next to his desk, running her finger under the seal of the envelope and taking the A4 photographs out. She flipped through them carefully and Ben saw her cheeks burn red. Then a tear rolled down her cheek.

If Callie had upset Eve in any way, if she'd made her feel anything less than beautiful, she wouldn't be coming back here. No more photographs, no more talking to his crew to gain their trust.

'What's up, Eve?' He tried to banish the anger from his voice, speaking as gently and quietly as he could. Eve tipped her face up towards him and suddenly smiled.

'Look at me, boss.'

As she handed the photos over, her hand shook. Ben took them, forcing himself to look.

There was one of Eve running, buttoning up her jacket as she went. Another of her climbing into the cabin of the fire engine. Eve's frame seemed somehow diminutive next to her crewmates, but she was clearly one of a team and the angle from which the photographs had been shot showed her ahead of the men, not following on behind.

'These are... Do you like them?' Maybe Eve saw something in them that he didn't.

'Yes, I like them. I *really* like them.'

'Me too.' Ben looked at the next photograph, and saw what had prompted Eve's tears.

'Callie took this at your home?'

'Yes, we made an arrangement for her to come and see

me. What…do you think?' Eve wiped the tears from her face with her sleeve.

She was sitting on the floor with her four-year-old son in her lap. Isaac was clutching a toy fire engine and Eve's dark hair was styled softly around her face. She was wearing a sleeveless summer dress that showed the scars on her shoulder.

'I think… It's a lovely photograph of you and Isaac.' Ben decided to concentrate on the mother and son aspect, and the love that shone in Eve's face.

'It is, isn't it? I didn't think…' Eve shrugged.

'Didn't think what?' Ben was still ready to spring to Eve's defence, but perhaps he didn't need to. Maybe she saw what he did, and that was what her tears were all about.

'I didn't think I'd ever wear that dress again. Callie and I talked about it for a while, she said that we could stop if I felt uncomfortable and that these photos were just for me, not anyone else.'

'You should be proud of yourself, Eve.' Somehow Callie had captured everything in the image. Eve's love for her son, her strength and her vulnerability. The scars looked like badges of courage and they brought a lump to Ben's throat.

'Yes.' Eve took the photographs back, hugging them to her chest as if they were something precious. 'I'm going to show the guys.'

Ben put his own envelope to one side, slightly surprised that there was one, and stacked the rest back into the box. 'Will you take these out with you? Make sure everyone gets just their own envelope.'

'Yep.' Eve paused, grinning. 'So you're not going to show me yours?'

His could hardly be as moving, or mean so much. He tore at the envelope, taking out the glossy prints.

'Go on. Take a look.' He handed them straight over to Eve. He didn't much want to look himself, and find out how Callie saw him.

'Nice… Very action hero.' Eve laid the first photo down on his desk and Ben saw himself caught in the act of loading equipment onto the fire engine. A second showed him climbing into the cabin.

There was one more to go. And Eve was grinning suddenly.

'Wow, boss. Never knew you were a pin-up.'

'Neither did I.' Ben reached for the photograph, snatching it from her.

Oh. He remembered that now. He'd been sitting in the ready room, after returning from the fire they'd been called to that afternoon. Watching as Callie had talked to a couple of the other firefighters. Suddenly she'd turned and pointed the camera at him.

Perhaps it was Ben's imagination, but he thought he saw the subtle winding-down process after a call where there had been no casualties and the fire had been successfully contained. And there was something else. His eyes looked almost startlingly blue under tousled hair that was still wet from the shower.

'Do I really look like that?' For the first time in his life it occurred to Ben that he looked handsome.

'Yeah, on a good day. Sometimes you look a bit rough…' Eve laughed at his protests, narrowing her eyes to squint at the photograph. 'Maybe she's turned up the blue tones a bit. She explained to me how you do that. She said that she could turn down the red of my scars a bit but when we'd talked about it I decided that she shouldn't. All or nothing, eh?'

'Good decision. You can be very proud of your photos, Eve.' Ben looked at his own photograph again. None of the other blues seemed to be so prominent. Maybe it was a trick of the light…

He decided not to think about it. Gathering up the photographs, he put them back into the envelope and threw it back into the box.

'Here. If anyone wants to see these, you can show them.' He led by example. If anyone on the crew wanted to see what Callie had made of him, they could have a good laugh over it.

'Right, boss. Thanks.' Eve put her envelope in the box with his and shot him a grin before she left him alone.

What Callie had made of him. It was a thought that wouldn't go away, because the photograph had hinted at the smouldering heat that invaded his thoughts whenever he looked at her.

He shook the thoughts from his head. Christmas was only a week away and Callie would be back to take the photos for the calendar. He would be sure to thank her for her sensitivity with Eve and then he'd keep his distance. Ben didn't trust himself to do anything else.

Callie had stared at Ben's photograph for a long time before deciding to include it in his envelope. Perhaps it looked a like a come-on, betraying the way she saw him a little too clearly. But it was really just the way that the lens saw him. The camera was indifferent to him and incapable of lying. That image was all about Ben and nothing about her.

Her friends would have taken one look at the picture and told her that capturing Ben's smile for real should be her number one priority over Christmas. But anyone who seriously thought she'd take that advice didn't know much about her. Callie was all about avoiding risk.

It was one of the reasons she'd wanted this job so much. She'd wanted to understand what made the firefighters tick, what allowed them to do a dangerous job and then go home to their families afterwards. She'd been too young to understand when her father had failed to come home from work one day, but she'd understood her mother's tears and in time she'd come to understand that he'd never be coming home.

She'd learned afterwards that her father had been a hero. A police officer, called to an armed robbery that had gone bad. He'd saved two of his fellow officers but he had been unable to save his own wife and child from the mistakes and hardships that had resulted from his death.

It was the best reason in the world not to get involved with Ben, a man who took risks for a living, like her father had. He might be mouth-wateringly handsome and Callie had always had a soft spot for men with a hard exterior and warm eyes. But he was very definitely on her not-to-do list this Christmas. It was okay for the camera to register his smouldering eyes but she wasn't going to think about them.

One of the firefighters let her into the station on a crisp, cold Christmas Eve morning. Callie made her way to the ready room, adding the two dozen mince pies she'd made last night to the pile of boxes of Christmas fare in the kitchenette. Then she sat down, her camera ready, waiting for something to happen.

No sprayed-on jeans this morning. If he'd known in advance, Ben might have thought that Callie in a pair of serviceable trousers, heavy boots and a thick red hoodie would be an easier prospect. But that would have been a mistake because she still looked quite terrifyingly gorgeous.

He'd made sure that the photo of himself, captioned 'Hunk of the Month', had been taken down from the ready room notice-board. Everyone had taken their chance to have a good laugh, and there was no need for Callie to see it.

She was sitting quietly in the ready room. Blending in, as he'd seen her do before. Watchful, observing everything. He'd bet the silver sixpence from the Christmas pudding that she'd already sized up the decorations and the small tree in the corner of the room, deciding how best they might be put to use in her photographs.

'You're here.' He suddenly couldn't think of anything else to say.

'Yes.' She turned her green eyes up towards him thoughtfully. 'So are you.'

That got the patently obvious out of the way. Ben sat down.

'Eve showed me her pictures.'

She reddened a little, seeming to know exactly which of the pictures he was referring to. 'You know that she called the shots?'

'Yes, Eve told me that you'd talked about it all at some length, and that she was happy with what you'd done.' Ben liked it that Callie was unsure what his reaction might be, and that she actually seemed to care what it was.

She nodded slowly, obviously pleased. 'She rang me and said she'd be happy for them to be included in the pictures for the calendar.'

'And what do you think?'

'I think they're exactly the kind of thing we want. But I'm going to leave it until after Christmas and give Eve some time to think about it. Sometimes people say yes to a proposal and then change their minds when it becomes a reality.'

'I'll leave you to sort that out with her.' Two weeks ago it had been unthinkable that he could leave Callie to negotiate directly with his team, but now… Maybe her photographs had worked a little magic on him as well.

'You're expecting to be busy today?' She asked the question with an air of innocence and Ben smiled.

'Yes, we're often busy over Christmas.'

'I'm hoping that you'll agree to my going with the crew on a call-out. The station commander gave me the go-ahead and I've signed the waiver. But the final decision's down to you.'

He'd been half expecting this. For someone who was so invested in how things looked, it was impossible that her own appearance didn't mean something. She'd even ditched the bulky camera, replacing it with a smaller one that might easily be stowed away inside a jacket.

'Can you earn it?' The words slipped out before he could stop them. He usually put things a little more tactfully than that, wrapping it all up in talk about basic fitness and health and safety procedures.

If it was the little tilt of her chin that he'd wanted to see, she didn't disappoint him. Neither did the defiance in her eyes.

'Just watch me.'

CHAPTER THREE

CALLIE WOULD HAVE thought that four years working as a first response paramedic might have allowed some of the more basic procedures to go without saying. But it appeared that Ben took nothing for granted.

'Don't forget to stand where he tells you.' Eve's eyes flashed with humour as she whispered the words to Callie.

'Sorry about this…' The yard wasn't the place to be in this freezing weather, and everyone looked as if they'd rather be in the ready room, making inroads into the stack of Christmas food.

Eve grinned. 'It's not you. He does it with everyone. Everyone he likes, that is…'

Right. This was obviously the hurdle that she had to jump to gain entry to the team. She could respect that, there was no such thing as being too careful when your job involved the kinds of risks that the crew faced every day.

'Callie! Over there…' Ben shouted, and she started. She was already standing well out of the way of the fire crew, and the point he'd indicated precluded any good photographic shots of the imaginary conflagration.

She ran obediently to her allotted spot and he nodded, seeming to be fighting back a grin. 'All right. Thanks, everyone.'

The crew followed his lead, at ease now as they left

their positions and started to meander back inside. Ben was suddenly one of them again, just another member of the crew, but Callie was under no illusions that as soon as the alert bell rang, he'd be their leader again.

'Did I pass?' She murmured the words to him as he strolled back across the yard towards her.

'Yeah. Full marks.' This time he allowed himself to smile. 'Make sure you do the same when this is for real.'

This wasn't for real? Full marks meant that she had a chance of going with the crew on their next call-out. That made it real enough.

They didn't have long to wait. When the alarm sounded, Callie was on her feet with the others, pulling on the high-vis protective jacket with 'Observer' written across the back of it.

She was familiar with the sound of a siren but it usually emanated from her own rapid response vehicle. The fire engine made more noise and she wasn't used to the sway of the vehicle or to being squashed between Eve and one of the other firefighters while someone else did the driving. Neither was she accustomed to feeling like a parcel, only there for the ride.

But she did as she'd been told, waiting for the firefighters to get out of the vehicle before she did. Smoke and flame plumed upwards from what looked like a storage yard behind a brick wall.

'Callie, stay right back. There are gas canisters in there.' There was a popping sound as one of the canisters exploded in the heat of the conflagration. Ben didn't look back to make sure that she complied with the instruction as he hurried towards the back of the fire truck, where the crew was already deploying two long hoses.

Water played over the top of the wall, another jet aimed at a gate to one side. Callie knew that the angles were carefully chosen to maximise the effect of the hoses, but it seemed that no one had actually made that decision. It was just a team, working together apparently seamlessly.

Photographs. That was what she was here for. She'd almost forgotten the camera in her hand in favour of watching Ben. In charge, ever watchful and yet allowing his crew to do their jobs without unnecessary orders from him. It was a kind of trust that she wished he might bestow on her.

He turned, waving her further back, pointing to a spot beside the police cordon. At least she was out of his line of sight now, and she could remove the heavy gloves that made it practically impossible to take photographs. Not that it mattered all that much. She was standing so far back that the people behind the cordon probably had as good a chance of taking a meaningful shot as she did.

I hate this. She was used to working on her own and making her own decisions. But if she proved she could comply with Ben's orders, he might ease up on her a bit.

In the meantime, she'd do what she could. Callie turned for a shot of the cordon, people lined up behind it watching anxiously. Some were passers-by who'd stopped, while others in bright-coloured sweaters and dresses rather than coats had obviously been evacuated from the houses closest to the blaze. Over the steady thrum of the fire engine and the roar of the flames she could hear a child crying and another babbling in excitement.

Panning back towards the firefighters, a movement caught her eye. A twitch of the curtains in one of the houses in the row next to the yard. When Callie pressed the zoom, she saw a head at the front window.

'Ben…!' She ran towards the fire engine, screaming above the noise, and he glanced back towards her. 'Over there, look.' She pointed to the window and he turned suddenly, making for the house. He'd seen what she had, that the police evacuation had left someone behind.

It appeared that since he'd given Callie no indication that she should move, he expected her to stay where she was. Forget that. Callie tucked the camera into her jacket and followed Ben.

'Go back. We've got it...' They met on the doorstep. The woman had disappeared from the window and without a second glance at Callie he bent down, flipping open the letterbox to look through it and then calling out.

'That's right, my love. Open the door. No... No, don't sit down. You need to open the door for me.'

Suddenly he puffed out a breath and straightened, turning to Eve, who had arrived at his side. 'We have an elderly woman sitting on the floor, leaning against the front door. We'll go in through the window.'

Eve nodded and Ben reached into his pocket, pulling out a window punch. It took one practised movement to break one of the small glass panes in the windows at the front of the house.

'Callie, I won't say it again. You're in the way...' He didn't look round as he reached in, slipping the catch and swinging the window open.

'Since when was a paramedic *in the way* when you have a possible trauma? You should be getting out of *my* way.' Callie resisted the temptation to kick him. Playing along with Ben at the fire station was one thing, but this wasn't the time or the place.

He turned quickly, a look of shock on his face. Then he took the helmet from Callie's hand, securing the strap under her chin and snapping down the visor. 'Put your gloves on. Stay behind me at all times. Eve, stay here and let me know if the fire looks as if it's coming our way.'

He pushed the net curtains to one side and climbed in,

turning to help Callie through the window. She ignored his outstretched hand and followed him. When he led the way through to the hallway, Callie saw an elderly woman sitting on the floor behind the door. Her eyes were closed but her head was upright so she was probably conscious. Callie tapped Ben's arm to get his attention.

'Did she fall?'

'I don't think so. She just seemed to slide down the wall.'

'Okay.' Standing back wasn't an option now and neither was staying behind him. The house wasn't on fire and Ben's skills were of secondary use to her. Callie pushed past him and knelt down beside the woman, taking off her helmet and gloves. She wasn't used to working with these kinds of constrictions.

'Hi, I'm Callie, I'm a paramedic from the London Ambulance Service.'

The woman looked up at her with placid blue eyes. It seemed that the urgency of the situation had escaped her, and Callie saw a hearing aid, caught in the white hair that wisped around her face, with the ear mould hanging loose. She was clutching a pair of glasses that looked so grimy that they could only serve to obscure her sight.

Great. No wonder she hadn't responded when Ben had called through the letter box. Callie gently disentangled the hearing aid, putting it in her pocket. There was no time now to do anything other than make do with what the woman could hear and see.

'Are you hurt?' She tipped the woman's face around, speaking clearly.

'No, dear.'

'Have you fallen?'

The woman stared at her, her hand fluttering to her chest. Callie heard Ben close the sitting-room door so that more smoke didn't blow through the house from the broken window. The smell of burning was everywhere, filtering through every tiny opening from the outside, and Callie knew that the air quality in here wasn't good.

She felt a light touch on her shoulder. 'You're happy to move her?'

Suddenly Ben was deferring to her. Callie's quick examination had shown no sign of injury and the woman's debility and confusion might well be as a result of smoke inhalation. On balance, the first priority was to get her into the fresh air.

'Yes.'

Thankfully, he didn't waste any time questioning her decision. Ben used his shortwave radio to check with Eve that their exit was still clear and helped Callie get the woman to her feet. Her legs were jerking unsteadily and it was clear that she couldn't walk.

'Can you take her?' She'd be safe in Ben's strong arms. He nodded, lifting the woman carefully, and Callie scooted out of the way, opening the front door.

Outside, the fire in the yard was almost out, quantities of black smoke replacing the flames. Ben didn't slacken his pace until he'd reached the cordon, and as a police officer shepherded them through, a woman ran up to them.

'Mae... Mae, it's Elaine. Elaine Jacobs...' The older woman didn't respond, and the younger one turned to Ben. 'Bring her to my house. Over there...'

'Thanks.' Ben shot a glance at Callie and she nodded. There was nowhere else other than the police car to set Mae down and examine her.

Ben carefully carried his precious burden into the small, neat sitting room, and Mrs Jacobs motioned him towards a long sofa that stretched almost the length of one wall. He put Mae down carefully and turned to Callie.

'Ambulance?'

'Yes, thanks.'

'Okay, I'll see to it.' He turned to Mae, giving her a smile, and her gaze followed him out of the room.

'I'm all right.' Mae seemed to be addressing no one in particular, and Callie guessed that she was trying to reassure herself as much as anyone else. She touched her hand to catch her attention.

'I know you are. Just let me make sure, eh?'

CHAPTER FOUR

HOWEVER HARD HE tried to put Callie into a box, she just seemed to spring straight out again. He'd thought her capable of steamrolling over him and his crew if he allowed her to, and then she'd shown herself to be sensitive enough to make a difference to the way Eve saw herself. Ben had tried to limit her to the role of observer, and she'd shown him that she wasn't just that either.

Perhaps he had trust issues. It made no difference what Callie did, he couldn't bring himself to trust the warmth that her mere presence sparked in his chest. Maybe he never would truly trust a woman that he was attracted to ever again.

When he knocked on Mrs Jacobs's front door, he meant to stay on the doorstep, but she wouldn't have any of it, ushering him inside and telling him that he couldn't possibly compete with the mess that her two teenagers were capable of making. Callie was kneeling beside Mae, chatting to her, and looked up when he entered the sitting room.

'Everything all right?'

'Yes. The fire's out and we're making everything safe.' He trusted his crew. He'd trusted Callie, back at the house, when she'd snapped suddenly into the role of paramedic. Maybe that was what he should remember, rather than the way her smile seemed to plunge his whole world into chaos.

'The ambulance is on its way?'

'Yes.'

Mae had turned her gaze up toward them, obviously following their conversation. By the simple expediency of cleaning her glasses and making sure that her hearing aids were seated correctly, Callie had wrought an amazing change in the elderly lady. Ben bent down, smiling at Mae.

'How are you feeling now?'

'Callie says I have to go to the hospital…' Her voice was cracked and hoarse, but it was difficult to tell whether that was the effect of emotion or smoke inhalation. 'On Christmas Eve…'

'It's best to be on the safe side. If it were me, I'd take her advice.'

He heard a sharp intake of breath behind him. Mae's presence in the room had probably saved him from the humiliation of one of Callie's put-downs.

Mae's questioning gaze focussed somewhere to his left, and he turned. Callie's smile was almost certainly for Mae's benefit, but still it made Ben's heart thump.

'I'll come to the hospital with you, Mae. We'll find ourselves a handsome doctor in a Santa hat, eh?'

'Thank you dear. You're very kind.' Mae managed a smile. 'I'll pick a nice doctor for you.'

Callie chuckled. 'Make sure you do. I don't want just any old one.'

He couldn't do anything to help with the journey to the hospital but he could make things a bit better for Mae's return. 'I know someone who'll board up the window for you. I'll write their number down…'

Mrs Jacobs rummaged in a drawer and produced a pen and paper. Ben scribbled the number on it and handed it to Callie. 'Tell them I gave you their details. They'll liaise with the insurance company and help get things moving.'

Mae shot him a worried look. 'How much will it cost?'

'It won't cost you anything. All part of the service, Mae.' It wasn't officially part of the service. The number was for a local charity. It had been Ben's idea to contact them and set up a task force to help vulnerable people clean up after a fire, and he and a number of the station staff volunteered with them.

'And when you get back from the hospital, you'll stay here over Christmas.' Mrs Jacobs sat down on the sofa next to Mae. 'No arguments, now. Stan and the boys will go over to your place and help sort things out there.'

'But…it's Christmas.' Despite her neighbour's firm tone, Mae argued anyway.

'Exactly. It'll do them good to go and do something, instead of sitting around watching TV and eating. I'm sure Stan's put on a couple of pounds already so he can do with the exercise.'

'You're very kind.' A tear dribbled down Mae's cheek. 'All of you.'

'It's Christmas. We'll all pull together, eh?' Mrs Jacobs put her arm around Mae and the old lady smiled, nodding quietly.

Ben beckoned to Callie and she frowned. He glared back, beckoning again more forcefully, and she rolled her eyes and followed him into the hallway.

'What? I'm busy.'

The tight-lipped implication that she was just trying to do her job and that he was getting in the way wasn't lost on Ben.

'I just wanted to know… How *is* Mae? Really?'

Callie's angry glare softened slightly and she puffed out a breath. 'I've checked her over the best I can, and she doesn't seem to be having any difficulty with her breathing. But she has a headache and she seemed very confused earlier, and you can hear she's a bit hoarse. She needs to be seen by a doctor. I'm going to stay with her.'

The thought that Callie might not come back to the fire station once she had finished here filled Ben with unexpected dismay. He had no one but himself to blame if she made that decision.

'I shouldn't have said that you were in the way earlier. It won't happen again.'

'I can take care of myself in these situations. I do it all the time.'

'Got it. I apologise.' Ben saw her eyebrows shoot up in surprise. Was that what she thought of him? He was perfectly capable of saying sorry when the situation warranted it.

But prolonging the conversation now while she was still angry with him probably wasn't a good idea. He'd said his piece and he should go.

'I'll see you later?' Ben tried not to make a question out of it, but his own doubts leaked through into his words. Callie gave a nod and he turned, making for the front door. He guessed he'd just have to wait and see about that.

The wait at the hospital hadn't been too protracted, and after X-rays and lung capacity tests had been carried out, Mae was discharged. They arrived back at Mrs Jacobs's house to find that the charity task force that Ben had put her in touch with had already boarded up Mae's window.

She had no qualms about leaving Mae here. Two cups of tea and a plate of mince pies appeared, and a yelled exhortation brought Mrs Jacobs's son tumbling down the stairs, a board game in his hand. He and Mae began to sort through the pieces together, and Mae finally smiled.

Mae's Christmas would be just fine. Callie's was a little more uncertain. The success of her project at the fire station depended on clearing the air with Ben, and there was no time to sit quietly and wait for him to let her in. She had to do something.

She took a taxi back to the fire station. He wasn't with the others in the ready room and Callie found him alone in the small office with the door wide open. She tapped on the doorframe and he looked up.

Blue eyes. The most photogenic eyes she'd ever seen, flickering with warmth and the hint of steel. The kind of eyes that the camera loved and... That was all. The camera loved them but Callie was just an impartial observer.

'Everything okay?'

'Yes. Mae was discharged from the hospital and she'll be staying with Mrs Jacobs over Christmas. The charity task force has been great.'

'Good.' His gaze was fixed on her face. 'I've been thinking about what you might be wanting to say to me.'

Perhaps he was trying out a management technique. Put yourself in the other person's shoes. Callie sat down.

'Okay, I'll play. What might I be wanting to say to you?'

'That I'm not giving you credit for the experience that you have. You need access to be able to work and I'm being unreasonable in withholding it.'

Actually, that pretty much summed it up. Callie dismissed the rather queasy feeling that accompanied the idea that he'd been reading her thoughts.

'And... I guess that you'd say in return that you and the others rely on teamwork. That kind of trust isn't made over a matter of days and you're not sure of me yet.'

The look on Ben's face told her that she was right. More than that, he found it just as disconcerting as she did to hear someone else voice his thoughts.

'I'll…um… I'll be honest. I wasn't much in favour of you being here when the station commander first told me about it.'

'Really? You hid that well.' Callie risked a joke. Somehow she knew that he wouldn't take it the wrong way.

He narrowed his eyes. Maybe he *was* taking it the wrong way. Then suddenly Ben smiled. 'So we see eye to eye, then.'

Rather too much so. If he really could see what was going on in her head… Callie gulped down the sudden feeling of panic. Of course he couldn't.

The awkward silence was broken by the alarm bell. Ben rose from his seat, making hurriedly for the door, and Callie followed him.

She took her turn climbing up into the fire engine and found Ben sitting opposite her. As the sirens went on and they started to move out of the fire station, he leaned forward, bracing his foot against the lurching of the vehicle and checking her helmet.

Callie frowned. He'd been the one to say it and he hadn't even listened to himself. He was still double-checking everything she did.

'If I get the chance, I'll take you in as close as I think we can safely go.' The light in his blue eyes kindled suddenly.

'Thanks for that, boss.'

Ben's eyebrows shot up as he realised that Callie was using the word 'boss' to make a point. Then he grinned. Maybe this *was* going to work after all.

The word 'boss' on Callie's lips could hardly be anything other than a challenge. But they'd both risen to it. Ben had motioned her to stand next to him as he directed the firefighters in extinguishing a small blaze at the back of a shop. Callie had become like a shadow, never giving him a moment's concern for her safety, and adroitly stepping out of the way of both equipment and firefighters.

'I got some good shots. They'll do you all justice.' She waited until he was about to tell her that they were leaving now, catching his attention for the first time since they'd been there.

'Good. Thank you.' He smiled, and she smiled back. Then she turned to join the rest of the crew climbing back into the fire engine, leaving Ben with the distinct impression that his legs were about to give way under him.

It took some time to persuade himself that this evening would be nothing to do with wanting to spend more time with Callie but simply a matter of showing her another side of the job. But for once she made things easy for him. As the night shift arrived she hung back in the ready room, flipping almost disinterestedly through the photos she'd taken that day, as if she were waiting for something.

Ben dismissed the thought that it might be him. But then he found himself caught in her clear gaze.

'I wanted to catch you before I left. To say thank you for this afternoon.'

'My pleasure. You have plans for tonight?' Ben tried to make the question sound innocent. He'd already heard Callie's answer when Eve had asked earlier.

'No, not really. It's an hour's drive home and I'll probably just curl up with some hot soup and decide what I want to try and shoot tomorrow. You?'

'I'm going carol singing. We have a decommissioned fire engine, which is kept at one of the other stations. It's used for charity and public awareness events and this evening it's parked up in town. You should join me.'

She gave a little shake of her head. 'Are you ever entirely off duty?'

These days...no. Ben had always been immersed in

his job but he'd known where to draw the line between work and home. But in the last year his work had been a welcome relief from worrying about what Isabel might do next.

He reached inside his jacket, laying two hats on the table. 'Can't really be *on* duty when you're wearing one of these.'

Callie's hand drifted forward, her fingers brushing the white 'fur' around the edge of the Santa hat and then moving to the bells around the edge of the green elf hat. A sudden vision of texture and movement and the feel of Callie's fingers on his skin drifted into his head. He could tell she was tempted to accept his offer.

'You get to pick. Elf or Santa.'

She smiled. 'I'll be Santa.'

Of course she would. He was beginning to understand that this was something they shared, and that she too never felt entirely comfortable unless she was holding the reins.

'Okay.' He handed her the Santa hat. 'Play your cards right and you might get to drive the sleigh.'

Green suited Ben. No doubt red would have done too, but Callie had to admit that he made a very handsome elf. No doubt he'd be the one who got presents wrapped twice as fast, without even breaking a sweat.

After the bustle of the fire station and the cheery good-byes of the crew she'd suddenly felt very alone. She'd had to remind herself that returning to her cold, dark flat was exactly the way she wanted it. No one to welcome her home meant that there was no one to pull the carpet out from under her feet.

She pulled on a down gilet for warmth and put on her coat and gloves, attaching her camera to a lanyard around her neck, ready for use. Tonight was about photos and not Christmas cheer, she told herself stubbornly.

The quickest and easiest way to get to the centre of London was by the Underground. They left their cars at the fire station and twenty minutes later they were in the heart of the city.

The fire engine was parked on the edge of a small square, flanked by bars and shops, and there were still plenty of people on the street. As they walked towards it through the crowds, Callie could see that one side of the vehicle had been decorated to turn it into Santa's sleigh. There were carol singers and people were crowding around a warmly clad man in a Santa costume, who was helping children up into the driving seat.

Ben greeted the men already there and introduced Callie. Their names were lost in the music and chatter, but there were smiles and suddenly it didn't much matter who she was or why she was here. She was just one of the team.

A bundle of leaflets was pressed into Ben's hands and he set to work, wishing everyone a happy Christmas, in between singing along with the carols in a deep baritone. He placed leaflets in everyone's hands with a smiling exhortation to read them on the way home.

Callie picked up a leaflet that had fluttered to the ground. On one side were wishes for a safe and happy Christmas from the London Fire Brigade. On the other side was some basic fire safety advice that was easy to read and follow.

'So all this has an ulterior motive?' She saw Ben looking at her and she smiled.

'You could call it that. Although I reckon that having a house fire is one of the unhappier things that can happen to anyone, so it's really just a practical extension of us telling everyone to have a happy Christmas...'

He turned for a moment as a woman tapped his arm, responding to her question. 'Yes, that's the British Standards safety sign. Always make sure your tree lights carry it.'

'Okay. I'll check mine when I get home.'

'Great.' Ben gifted her with the kind of smile that would persuade the angels themselves to switch off their heavenly lights if they weren't up to safety standards and wished her a happy Christmas.

'Can I take some of those?' Callie pointed to the leaflets in his hand.

'Yes, of course. Don't you want to take some photographs?'

That was what she was there for but her camera was zipped under her coat and taking it out seemed like taking a step back from the circle of warmth and light around the fire engine. Realistically it was impossible to reduce the children's delight as they were lifted up into the driving seat to just one frame, so instead she took the opportunity to just feel the joy.

'Later maybe. I've got an interest in this, too.' As a paramedic, Callie didn't fight fires but she'd seen some of the of the injuries they caused.

He handed half his stack of leaflets to Callie. Ben didn't say a word but his grin spoke volumes. No more fighting each other. The season of peace and joy seemed to be working its magic.

CHAPTER FIVE

SUDDENLY IT FELT like Christmas. Callie was animated and smiling, approaching people on the edge of the crowd that had gathered around them and giving them leaflets. She seemed softer, warmer somehow. As if she'd dropped her defences and with them the hard edges that didn't quite suit her.

'Getting cold?' Even though she was never still, she couldn't disguise her red fingers. Gloves made it difficult to separate the leaflets and hand them out, and she'd taken hers off and stuffed them in her pocket.

'Yes, a little.' She smiled up at him, clearly not of a mind to let frozen fingers stop her.

'There are flasks with hot coffee...' He motioned up towards the cabin of the fire engine, which was now closed and dark. The families had all gone home now, and the crowd mainly consisted of revellers, wanting to squeeze the last moments from their pre-Christmas celebrations.

'So that's why everyone's been nipping up there every now and then? Why didn't you tell me sooner? I'd love some.'

'You have to give out at least a hundred leaflets before you get coffee.'

'Well, I've given out three handfuls. That must be a hundred so...' She gripped the front of his jacket in a mock threat. *'Give me my coffee, elf. Or else...'*

However much he wanted to warm up, standing his ground now seemed like a delicious moment that couldn't be missed. 'Or else what?'

'Or... I'll make you collect up all the old wrapping paper, peel the sticky tape off it and smooth it flat to use next year.' She grinned.

'In that case...' Submitting to the threat was another delicious moment that made the hairs on the back of Ben's neck stand to attention. 'This way, Santa.'

He led her over to the fire engine, opening the door for her, and Callie climbed up into the cockpit, sliding across to sit behind the wheel. Ben followed her, reaching for the three large flasks in the footwell. Two were already empty, but the third was heavy when he picked it up.

As he poured the coffee, he saw Callie's fingers touch the bottom of the steering wheel lightly, as if she was yearning to take hold of it and pretend to drive, the way kids did when you sat them in that seat. She was looking ahead of her, the bright Christmas lights reflecting in her face, softening her features. Or maybe it was just the look on her face.

'Thanks.' She wrapped her fingers around the cup, clearly wanting to warm them before she drank. Ben poured a second cup for himself and propped it on the dashboard. The only heat he wanted right now was the heat of her smile.

'You can try it out for size if you want.' He nodded towards the steering wheel. 'I won't tell anyone.'

The thought seemed tempting to her, but she shook her head. 'Bit late for that now.'

'It's never too late...' Ben let the thought roll in his

head. It was an odd one, since he'd privately reckoned that it *was* too late for him.

And Callie seemed to think that too. She shook her head, turning to him with a smile. 'Did you sit in a fire engine when you were a kid?'

'All the time. My dad was a firefighter and he used to lift me up into the driving seat of the engines whenever my Mum took me to the fire station.'

'So you knew all along what you wanted to be when you grew up.'

'Yeah.' Ben wondered which side of her life had been a childhood dream. Photographer or paramedic. 'What did you want to be?'

'Safe…' The word had obviously escaped her lips before she had a chance to stop it, and Callie reddened a little.

'Safe is a good ambition.'

Her gaze met his, a trace of mockery in it. *Do you even know what safe is?* Ben realised that it was the last thing he'd have thought about wanting when he'd been a child. He always *had* been safe.

For a moment the questions he wanted to ask hung in the cold air. Then Callie shrugged, grinning. 'My dad died when I was six. He was a police officer and he was killed in the line of duty. That was when I found out that…anything can be taken away.'

'I'm sorry. I can't imagine how that must have felt.'

She shrugged. 'I'm not entirely sure how I feel about it either. How did *you* deal with the risks of your father's job?'

'I guess… I never had to think about them. He always came home.'

'And now? You must have thought about them when *you* joined the fire service.'

The question seemed important to her, and Ben thought

carefully about his answer. 'There are some things that are important enough to take risks to achieve. Without that, a life can become meaningless. And we don't take risks for their own sake, you know that we're all about safety.'

Callie nodded silently. She didn't seem much convinced by his answer and Ben had the feeling he hadn't heard the whole story.

'But you never felt safe? As a child?'

'I did for a while. Mum remarried and I thought that we'd go back to being a family.' She shrugged. 'Her new husband ran up a pile of debts and then disappeared. We lost our house and pretty much everything we owned. After that it was horrible. Mum worked all the time and I was scared to be in our bedsit on my own. We got back on our feet but it was a struggle for her.'

Callie spoke almost dispassionately, as if she didn't care that she'd lost her father and then her home. In Ben's experience that meant she cared a great deal.

Nothing he could say felt enough. He reached for her hand, feeling a deep thankfulness when she didn't snatch it away.

'Here...' He guided her hand to the steering wheel, wrapping his over it. 'How does that feel?'

She gave a nervous laugh. 'That feels pretty good.'

'Try the other one.' He reached across, taking her coffee from the other hand, and Callie took hold of the steering wheel and gazed out ahead of her. Suddenly she laughed.

'Okay. You've made your point. I'm sitting on top of... how many horsepower?'

'About two hundred and fifty.'

'That much? And I'm looking over everyone's heads. It feels good.'

'Is powerful the word you're looking for?' Ben remembered the feeling of sitting behind the wheel when he was a child. Of being able to do anything, meet any challenge. That seemed to be the ultimate safety.

'That'll do.'

Suddenly he wanted very badly to kiss her. If he really could meet any challenge then perhaps he could meet this one? But Callie took her hands from the steering wheel and the spell was broken. She reached for her cup, wrapping her fingers around it again, and sipped the hot coffee.

Large snowflakes began to fall from the night sky, drifting down and melting as soon as they touched the pavement. Ben ignored them in favour of watching her face. It tipped upwards as the snowfall became heavier, a sudden taste of the magic of Christmas. Callie wasn't as unreachable as she tried to make out.

'There's always one, isn't there?' She quirked her lips down suddenly, and Ben could almost see the real world taking over from the imaginary. He followed her gaze, looking towards a couple of men in business suits and heavy overcoats, clearly involved in a drunken argument.

'Yep.' He wanted to tell her to disregard them. To come back with him to the world where it always snowed at Christmas, and where it was still possible to make up for all the things Callie hadn't had during her childhood. But one of the men suddenly took a swing at the other.

A space opened up around them as people moved out of the way. The argument seemed to become hotter and the carol singers faltered as the men's shouts reached their ears.

'So much for comfort and joy...' Ben muttered the words angrily, pulling the door of the fire engine open and getting out. A couple of the other firefighters were already on their way over to break up the fight.

But the brawlers were determined. One broke away from the firefighter who was crowding him back and threw a punch. The other slipped and fell, rolling on the icy pavement and cursing loudly. He tried to get unsteadily to his feet, and Ben could see blood running down the side of his face.

The men were separated quickly, with a minimum of fuss, and Ben made for the one who'd been hurt. He was standing unsteadily now, half supported and half held back by two of the firefighters. Then Callie pushed past him, her head bare, the Santa hat protruding from her jacket pocket. She'd snapped back into paramedic mode.

'Let me see... Bring him over to the fire engine.'

Ben walked the man over to the truck, opening the door of the cabin and helping him inside. Callie climbed in on the other side and the man relaxed back into the seat, seeming to want to go to sleep.

'You're carrying a first-aid kit?'

'Yep.' It was about the only piece of working equipment that the fire engine still carried. He went to collect it, adding a flashlight, and handed both to Callie.

She carefully examined the man, trying to elicit a sensible answer to some simple questions, but he was too drunk to even tell her his name. Or he had a concussion. Ben knew that it was impossible for even Callie to tell.

The stench of sweat and alcohol filled the cabin but she seemed not to notice. She cleaned the blood from his face carefully, and it appeared that the cut on his forehead was deep but relatively minor.

Finally, she blew out a breath. 'He's probably just drunk, but he's hit his head and it looked as if he was unconscious for a few moments. He should go to the hospital. Is there anyone here with a car who can take him? I'd call an ambulance but on Christmas Eve...'

The ambulance service would be busy and there would be a wait. It was quicker to have someone take him.

'I think so. I'll ask…' Ben didn't want to leave her alone with the man. He was unpredictable, and at any moment he could lash out at her. He wound down the window and called to one of the men standing next to the fire engine.

'Hey…! Close it.' The cold air blowing into the cabin seemed to wake the man for a moment and he shivered.

'All right. We're going to take you to the hospital, so they can make sure you're okay.' Callie's voice betrayed a note of caring that the man almost certainly didn't deserve.

'No! Going home…' The man tried to climb over her to get out of the cabin, and Ben caught his arm before he elbowed Callie in the face.

'Stay put. And be quiet. You do what the lady tells you.' The threatening note that he injected into his tone was enough to subdue the man.

'My hero…' Callie rewarded him with a flashed smile and the murmured words, and he felt his chest swell in response.

Outside, the discussion amongst the other firefighters seemed to have come to some conclusion, and Ben saw one of them signal that he'd take the man when they were ready. Callie made one last examination and then opened the man's coat, looking for an inside pocket. Finding the man's phone, she switched it on and scrolled through the contacts list.

'This is your home number?'

The man reached out to snatch the phone from her, and Ben caught his arm before he could touch her. If he laid one finger on Callie, Ben might forget his training and be tempted to hurt him.

'Don't even think about it,' he growled at the man, opening the door to get him out of the cabin. Callie shot him a smile and dialled the number, speaking quietly into the phone.

The car drew up and he propelled the man into the back seat. Two of the other firefighters got in and, seeing that he was outnumbered, the man sat quietly, seeming to fall back into a drowse.

'Wait a minute. Callie's got his phone.' Ben looked round and saw that Callie had ended the call and was walking towards him.

'Shall I go with them? To the hospital?'

'No. The guys all have basic medical training, they can handle it. Jim will give them a lift home once they've taken him to the hospital.'

Callie hesitated, turning the corners of her mouth down. 'I spoke to his girlfriend and she said that he was meant to be home hours ago, and that we could leave him in a gutter for all she cared. She gave me his brother's number, though, and he says he'll pick him up from the hospital.'

'Fine. Just give the guys his number and they'll deal with it.'

Callie still looked unconvinced, but she handed over the phone to Jim, bending down to look into the back seat of the car to check on the man one last time. It seemed that she was repeating her offer to go with them and Jim was repeating what Ben had told her. The car started and Callie shrugged, turning her attention to the other man, who was sitting on a nearby bench, his elbows propped on his knees, staring at his feet.

'Are you okay?'

'No, not really. They're taking Carl to hospital?'

'It's just a precaution. We don't think he's hurt, but he's drunk and he's hit his head. He needs to be checked over.'

'My sister's going to kill me. Carl's girlfriend…'

Ben saw Callie's lips press together momentarily. 'I dare say that everything will work out.' She'd clearly decided not to share what Carl's girlfriend had said to her on the phone.

'Yeah, right. She'll start talking to my wife...' The man shook his head. 'She wanted me to be home before the kids went to bed. I said we were just going out for a quick drink...'

'We'll get a taxi for you.' Ben decided it was time to step in. 'You're sure you feel okay?'

'Dead man walking, mate. You know how it is.' The man grinned at Ben, as if he was in league with him.

He could almost feel Callie's anger. She took a step forward and he reached out automatically, touching her arm. She heeded the silent warning and turned suddenly, walking away.

She looked so alone suddenly, standing with the fire-fighters, who were still giving out leaflets to the last of the passers-by. It was getting late, and there were few enough of them now, and Callie seemed silent and preoccupied. Common sense told him that he should leave her alone for a moment and she'd cool down, but Ben couldn't do it.

'Forget it.'

She was staring at her feet now, shivering with cold. 'I just... It's Christmas, for crying out loud. Couldn't they have just taken one night off and gone home? Been where they ought to be?'

'I know. But you can't let it get to you. No one can change what happened to you when you were a kid, but you can take *this* Christmas back. Wrestle it to the ground if you have to, beat it into submission and show it who's boss.' He reached for the Santa hat, pulling it out of her pocket and putting it firmly back onto her head, pulling it down over her ears.

She looked up at him suddenly. For a moment he thought he saw the magic again, reflected in her troubled eyes, but it was probably only the lights strung along the side of the fire engine. Suddenly she smiled, adjusting the hat to a jauntier angle on her head.

'All right. Are there any leaflets left?'

'A few...' Ben picked up the last of them and split the pile into two, giving her half. 'You want to see who can get rid of theirs first?'

She rose to the challenge. Of course she did, she didn't know what else to do with a challenge other than meet it headlong. But when Ben turned to watch her, she seemed suddenly so very alone in a crowd where everyone seemed to have someone.

CHAPTER SIX

CHRISTMAS DAY DAWNED bright and clear. Callie was up early and on the road almost before she was properly awake. The fire station was thrumming with noise and light when she arrived, but the noise was that of sirens, and the lights flashed blue in the morning mist.

It wasn't just another working day, though. Everyone smiled and wished each other a happy Christmas, and between calls there were mince pies and a roast dinner, eaten in haste before the next call came in. But peace and joy brought oven fires, wrapping-paper fires and even a patio fire, where one brave soul had thought it a good idea to finish the turkey off on the barbeque.

Ben had been relaxed and jocular—there was nothing that Blue Watch couldn't deal with easily and the arrival of a fire engine brought extra interest, people coming from their houses with Christmas fare and good wishes for the firefighters. A young boy was cut from where he'd got lodged in the park railings, with the minimum of fuss, and seemed none the worse for the experience.

Callie photographed it all, working side by side with the crew. It seemed that Christmas Day was going to end with no serious damage to life and limb, but just as darkness was beginning to fall, the call came.

There was no room for her in the disciplined scramble.

Ben took a moment to call an address to her and then Callie was left to her own devices. She waited until the fire engine was out of the garage, the sirens retreating into the distance, and then got into her car.

When she arrived, Blue Watch was already in action, along with three other teams that were in attendance. Fire was spurting from the windows on one side of a large, two-storey block of flats. Callie didn't need to be told to stay back out of the way. She knew that her presence would only hamper the men and women who were struggling to get the fire under control. She could see the firefighters of Blue Watch donning breathing equipment, ready to go inside.

She raised her camera and then lowered it. This wasn't a scene for calendar shots. Maybe afterwards, once it was clear that there had been no casualties.

All the same, she watched. Counting the firefighters of Blue Watch in and hearing her heart beat out the seconds and minutes before she could count them back out again. Ben had been the first in and she hadn't seen him come out yet.

Then he appeared in the doorway, a small bundle wrapped in his arms, protected from the smoke that curled around him. Behind him came a woman, supported by two firefighters.

The ambulance crew ran forward and Ben delivered the bundle to them. The woman was being helped to the waiting ambulance, reaching towards the child that Ben had brought out of the building. Tears blurred Callie's vision and she felt a lump rise at the back of her throat.

He tore the mask from his face and bent over in a movement of sudden weariness. Callie knew that the heavy equipment and the difficult conditions inside the building could exhaust even the fittest man quickly. But Ben took only a moment to catch his breath, walking over to the tender and gulping down water from a bottle. Then he turned, motioning to another two of the firefighters, including Eve. He was going back in again.

Callie turned away. She couldn't watch this. But she couldn't not watch either. The thought that little Isaac might not see his mother tonight... Or that she might not see Ben again.

She had to get a grip. Ben was doing what he had to and he was part of a team. No one would be hurt and no one would be left behind. Callie had attended plenty of scenes like this and she'd done her job, tending to those who'd been hurt. It was not having any job to do that was killing her.

Looking around, she saw a small family group sitting huddled together on a bench. Holding each other tight as they watched silently. No one seemed to be taking much notice of them and Callie walked over.

'Hello. Have you been seen by anyone? I'm a paramedic.'

The man looked up at her and Callie saw tears in his eyes. 'Yes. Thanks. We got out as soon as we heard the alarms go off.'

'You must be cold.' The woman had a baby in her arms, which she was holding inside her coat. There was a little girl of about six, who was swathed in a coat that was obviously her father's and the man wore just a sweater.

He looked up at her as if the idea of warmth or cold didn't really register. Just shock, and concern for his family.

'Do you have somewhere to go?' Callie sat down on the end of the bench. If she could be of no help to the fire and ambulance crews, maybe she could do something here.

'Yeah. My wife's brother...'

'He's coming to collect us.' The woman spoke quietly. 'He's driving down from Bedford.'

'It'll be a little while before he arrives, then. My car's over there. Why don't you come with me and get warm?'

The whole family had piled into the back seat, seeming unable to let go of each other. Callie had got behind the wheel and started the engine so she could put the heaters on full for a while, and as the windows started to mist up, the woman told her that her name was Claire and her husband was Mike. Then the little girl spoke up.

'What's your name?'

'I'm Callie. What's yours?'

'Anna.' Now that she'd emerged from the wrappings of her father's coat, Callie could see blonde hair tied up in a ponytail with a red and green ribbon, and a red pinafore dress over a green sweater. Anna was looking around her, adapting to her new situation with the kind of resilience that only a child could muster.

'Are you taking pictures?' Anna's eye lit on the camera in Callie's lap.

'Not at the moment. But I've been at the fire station today, taking photographs.'

Anna frowned, and her mother reached out to her, smoothing a stray lock of hair from her face. 'There's always someone at the fire station, even on Christmas Day, sweetie. When they hear that there's a fire, they come quickly and put it out.'

'But…' Anna rubbed the condensation from the window with her hand, staring outside. 'It's not out yet.'

'Sometimes it takes a little while. But they won't leave until the fire's out.' Callie tried to sound reassuring.

'I left my presents behind…in my room.' Tears began to form in Anna's eyes. Her parents had clearly tried to shield her from the gravity of the situation, and she didn't know how much she'd lost yet, but she was beginning to work it out for herself.

Mike held his daughter tight. 'Everything's going to be all right, button. We're going to Uncle Joe's and we'll stay there for a little while. All that matters is that we're safe and we're together, and when we come back again I'll make sure everything's as good as new.'

'You…promise?'

'Yes, darling. I promise.'

Callie swallowed down the lump that formed in her throat. Opening the glove compartment, she found the bar of chocolate that was usually stowed away in there. It was all she had to comfort the child.

'Hey, Anna. Would you like to share this with your mum and dad?' She tore the wrapper open and broke the chocolate into squares.

Anna took the chocolate, holding a square up to her mother's lips. Claire smiled and opened her mouth. The little girl solemnly fed her father a square and then picked the biggest one for herself.

As the flames subsided, it became possible for the fire-fighters to rest a little longer than just the time it took them to get back on their feet. Ben had waited until each of his crew had taken their turn to have a ten-minute break, and then his chance came. He stood alone, scanning the people who stood beyond the police line.

She wasn't there. Somehow Callie had opened up a hole in his life that hadn't existed before. Something missing, which he'd never thought about until now.

He should turn away and find something else to do. Taking his break, sitting down and getting his breath would be a good idea because he suddenly felt very weary. But when he looked again, he saw Callie's car parked some way up the street, shadows on the rear window indicating that it wasn't empty. Before he knew what he was doing, Ben had started to walk towards it, drawn by the inescapable urge to just see her.

As he passed through the police cordon he removed his helmet and gloves, finding that he was wiping his face with one hand. He hadn't bothered before, and there was no way he could wipe away the grime and soot, but still he ran his fingers through his hair to flatten it a bit, feeling it rough and caked with sweat and dirt.

As he approached, the car door opened and she got out, smiling breathlessly in a good imitation of the way that Ben himself felt.

'You're…okay?'

Warmth swelled in his heart. He was okay now.

'Yes.'

She took a step forward as if to hug him and Ben stepped back. The filth on his jacket would spoil everything. He wanted her just as she was now, untouched by the ravages of fire, a bright, gleaming reminder that life would go on. Now he understood why the parents in his crew went home and just stared at their sleeping kids.

He pointed to the car, searching for something to say that didn't betray his joy at seeing her. 'They escaped from the fire? Are they all okay?'

'Yes, they got out as soon as they heard the alarm. Their flat's on the ground floor…' She pointed to the left-hand side of the building in an obvious question. How bad was it? Ben could see a small head bobbing between the two adults who sat in the back seat and felt his heart bang in his chest.

'The fire damage isn't as bad on that side. But everywhere… It's all going to be waterlogged, Callie. Do they have somewhere to go?'

'Yes, they have family coming to collect them from Bedford. They'll be here soon.' Callie's look of disappointment couldn't have been more acute if it had been her own home.

There was nothing he could say. All Ben could do was wonder whether Callie was reliving the time when she'd lost her home as a child. The back door of the car opened and a man got out, holding a little girl in his arms. Instantly, the loss and the heartbreak on Callie's face was replaced by a smile.

'I want to thank you.' The man held out his hand to Ben and he shook it, muttering his regrets that they hadn't been able to save their home.

'That doesn't matter. My wife and my kids are safe. Everyone else got out?'

Ben nodded an assent. Then the little girl called his name.

How did she know? Perhaps Callie had seen him walking over and had told the family. Then Callie grinned. 'I've been showing Anna some of the pictures I took back at the fire station. I'm not sure *I* would have recognised you with all that grime on your face.'

Suddenly he felt self-conscious, as if he'd turned up for a date with a piece of broccoli caught in his teeth. Ben shook off the feeling. He'd just been fighting a fire, for goodness' sake, and Callie was no stranger to people not looking their best in an emergency situation.

'Daddy, I want to take a picture...'

The man laughed. It was an incongruous sound amongst the noise of destruction, but when he looked at his daughter the stress lines on his face disappeared for a moment. 'I'm sure that Ben has better things to do, sweetie...'

'That's okay. Everything's under control and I've got a

short break.' Ben glanced behind him to check again that he wasn't needed for a few minutes.

'Why don't I take the picture? You can be in it.' Callie addressed the child and she nodded.

Her camera was on a lanyard around her neck, but she turned back briefly to the car, fetching something from the front seat. It was a small compact camera, and Ben wondered why she would choose that one. Anna was lowered from her father's arms and Callie took the warm coat, which was far too big for her, from her shoulders to reveal a red and green Christmas outfit.

'Go and stand next to Ben, Anna. Try not to touch him, you'll get yourself all dirty.'

Ben sank to his knees next to the child. She was fresh and clean and, above all, safe. *This*. This was why he'd chosen his job and why he continued to do it.

'This is what we do at the fire station.' He folded his arms, smiling into the camera. 'Comrades...'

Anna glanced at Callie and she grinned. 'Comrades means friends. Everyone stands in a straight line, folding their arms.' She clearly understood Ben's reticence to leave a smudge on the child's hand by holding it.

Anna got the idea. Standing to attention, as straight as she could, she folded her arms. Through a daze of fatigue Ben heard Callie laugh, and new strength began to surge through him.

She seemed to be taking her time, which was unusual for Callie, who saw a shot and took it almost as naturally as breathing. When she was done, and Anna ran back into her father's arms, he realised why. She'd used both cameras.

Anna's father called out a thank-you, wrapping the coat around his daughter again. Callie motioned them back into the car, giving them the compact camera in response to

Anna's demands to see her pictures. He and Callie were alone again for a precious few moments.

'Where did she get the camera from?' Ben reckoned he knew. It seemed unlikely that the family, who hadn't stopped to pick up their child's own coat, would have chosen a camera as the one thing to save from their home.

Callie shrugged it off. 'I keep a back-up camera in the boot.'

'Looks brand new to me.' The camera still had some of the manufacturer's stickers on it. Ben shot her a glance, which said she couldn't get away with this act of kindness without someone noticing, and she reddened a little.

'So it's new. My old one was on its last legs, so I bought a new one and happened to have it in the boot of my car. Knock it off, Ben. It's Christmas Day...' Callie's steel resurfaced, all the more captivating because he knew that it concealed a heart of gold, which knew what it was like to be a child with no presents on Christmas Day.

He lost the chance to tell her that she'd made a generous gesture. A shout behind him turned her attention to a man running up the road towards them and Anna's father got out of the car, waving in response.

'That must be their lift...'

And she would want to say goodbye to Anna. Maybe hug her. The thought didn't seem so outrageous as it would have a few days ago, now he'd seen the evidence of Callie's softer side. 'I've got to get on. You're going straight home from here?'

The thought that he wouldn't get to touch her tore at his heart. Maybe he wouldn't need to so badly after he'd had a shower and changed his clothes, but now it was all that Ben could think about.

'No, I thought I'd see them off and then go back to the fire station...' She shot him an agonised look, which effortlessly penetrated the layers of protective clothing that shielded his heart. Maybe Callie wanted to be close to him as much as he wanted to be close to her. The idea fanned the flames that flickered in his chest.

'I'll see you there, then.' With an effort, he turned his attention to Anna, who was sitting in the back seat of the car, cuddled up close to her mother. The little girl seemed tearful now, and perhaps the reality of leaving her home behind, which Callie had somehow managed to hold back, was dawning on her.

Anna managed a smile and a wave, and her father shook his hand again. Then Ben turned, not daring to take another look at Callie before he walked back to his crew.

CHAPTER SEVEN

IT WAS LONG past the time when his shift had ended, but Ben seemed in no hurry. He'd made time to exchange a few words with every member of his crew, trading jokes and casual goodbyes, which had somewhat covered the fact that he was clearly checking on everyone.

Callie had reckoned that seeing him showered and dressed in clean clothes might dispel the image of him walking towards her car, clearly exhausted and caked in grime. She hadn't been in any danger but he'd seemed like a hero, coming to carry her away and save her.

But it didn't. He seemed just as handsome, just as much the kind of man who might buck the trend and show her that it was possible to rely on someone and not get hurt. Callie dismissed the thought, reminding herself that she'd needed saving a long time ago. Her life was on track now and she was just fine on her own. If seeing Ben smile at Anna had awakened the thought that Christmas could bring unexpected presents, then this one had arrived far too late to change anything.

'Did you take any photographs?' She was sitting in the ready room, fiddling with her camera, trying to pretend that she wasn't waiting her turn for Ben to speak to her. She wasn't a part of his crew so maybe he didn't reckon that was necessary.

'A big fire like that isn't really the kind of thing to put on a calendar. People get hurt...' She felt herself redden.

'Yeah. You came anyway.'

'Well, it turned out that I could make myself useful.'

He grinned, as if this was exactly the thing he'd wanted her to say. 'That little girl's going to remember the person who gave her a camera when she had nothing else on Christmas Day. Maybe it'll make another little girl feel a bit better, too.'

The other little girl being Callie. The fearful child who knew that life was quite capable of taking everything she had, if she wasn't careful.

'Enough, Ben. I'm not in the mood for deep and meaningful at the moment.' Callie picked up her camera. 'Can I have one last shot? You by the Christmas tree?'

'Now I'm a little cleaner?' He got the point immediately. It was all about the contrasts, the rigour of his work and the winding-down process afterwards. He went and stood by the tree in the corner of the room, folding his arms.

Callie raised the camera, took a couple of shots in the hope that might make him relax a bit, and then lowered it. 'That's not quite right. Perhaps you could try looking a bit more awkward?'

Ben laughed uneasily. Some people smiled when they looked into a lens and some people froze. He was a freezer. The only really good posed shot she'd been able to get of him had been the one she'd taken with Anna, when Ben had been too exhausted to think about feeling self-conscious.

He uncrossed his arms, shifted from one foot to the other and then crossed his arms again. 'What do you want me to do with my hands?'

There was an answer to that but Callie wasn't going to give it. 'Try... No, not like that. You look like my sixth form biology teacher.'

He shook his head. 'I have *no* idea what that means…' For a moment Callie thought that she was going to get the relaxed shot that she was looking for, and then he stiffened up again. If all his smiles were that cardboard, she'd have no problem resisting them.

She took another couple of pictures and then gave up. She'd have to sneak up on him later. 'Okay, that's good. Thanks.'

Ben relaxed and walked back towards her. *That* was the shot she wanted but she'd already put her camera down and it was too late.

'Are you ready to go? I'll walk you to your car.' He picked up his jacket from the back of the chair. Callie nodded, picking her coat up and following him out of the building.

The car park was deserted. Just him and her, and a biting wind. Ben stopped next to Callie's car, as if that was the most natural thing in the world.

'I'm glad you're safe.' She was closer to him now, the sleeve of her coat almost touching his.

'Me too. It's…' He shrugged. 'We balance the risks and eliminate them…'

'Yes, I know. I'm still glad you're safe.' Leaving now without touching him might just trigger another emergency situation. One where she'd have to be hauled clear and revived. Because Callie felt that she wouldn't be able to breathe without Ben.

He didn't want her to make a fuss. He did this kind of thing all the time and so did the other firefighters.

Who are you trying to kid, Ben? He wanted Callie to make as much fuss as possible. He wanted to comfort her and then have her make a fuss all over again.

She was so close and yet not close enough. His hand

drifted to hers, his fingers brushing the back of her hand. And then suddenly she flung her arms around his shoulders.

'This doesn't mean…' She buried her face in his shoulder, holding him tight.

'Anything…' Ben used the same excuse as she did to wind his arms around her waist. The cool-down after an emergency, when everything seemed so much simpler. The adrenaline still coursing in his veins and the feeling that everyday concerns didn't matter so much.

But it *did* mean something. He brushed his lips across her forehead, knowing that was never going to be enough, and felt her body move against his as she stretched up.

When he kissed her lips, it felt like all the Christmases he'd ever had rolled up in one big, beautiful parcel. It felt like a summer breeze, an autumn chill and the raging heat of an open fire, crackling and spitting as the flames blew hot and hard. Callie responded to him with just the right measure of softness and passion.

And then the fire subsided. They'd reminded themselves what it was like to be alive and safe this Christmas, and now it was time to let her go. But Ben couldn't.

'When you get home…' he linked his hands loosely behind her back '…and you switch on the lights on your Christmas tree…'

She shook her head. 'No Christmas tree this year.'

'What?' The image of Callie sitting next to her Christmas tree, drinking a toast to him at the same moment that he drank one to her, dissolved. It had been his last chance of walking away from her.

'What kind of person are you?'

She smiled up at him. 'One who's working over Christmas?'

No. Callie was the kind of person who knew exactly

what a bleak Christmas was like. The kind of person who could prove to herself that she was strong enough for it not to matter by not caring about Christmas now. He wouldn't allow it.

'I have a tree. With lights. And I have sherry, and turkey sandwiches, and Christmas cake…'

'No! What are you, the Christmas mafia?'

He bent, whispering in her ear, 'I have red and green paper napkins. And board games. They're quite old, though, they're the ones I used to play when I was a kid.'

She laughed, nudging at his shoulder with her hand. 'Enough! I could drop in for an hour, I suppose. Since we're not back on shift again until Boxing Day evening.'

'My thoughts exactly.' The watch rota was two days and then two nights, separated by a twenty-four-hour break. Ben usually stayed up as late as he could after the second day, sleeping in, so he'd be fresh for his first night's work.

He took her car keys from her hand, unlocking it, and opened the driver's door. 'You'll follow me?'

'Yes, I'll follow you.'

Ben had given her the address and watched her punch it into the satnav, but even so Callie had stayed behind him, following him into the east end of London. Two cars, almost alone on the dark streets, winding through the hodge-podge of old buildings, most of which had been refurbished and given a new lease of life, making the area a vibrant and exciting place to live. He drew up outside a pair of iron gates, and they swung open, allowing them into a small parking area.

'What is this place?' Callie looked around at the massive building, which seemed to once have housed something industrial.

'It's an old warehouse.' Ben punched a combination into a keypad and swung the heavy entrance doors open, leading the way through a small lobby. A staircase ran around a large, commercial-sized lift and he pulled back the old-fashioned gates.

'It's got a lot of character.' Callie looked around her as she stepped into the lift. The lobby was bright and clean, paint having been applied directly onto the exposed brick-work to preserve the industrial feel.

'That's the nice way of putting it. When we bought this place we didn't have the funds to do more than just clean up and get everything working properly.'

'You did this?'

'A group of us. A friend of mine is an architect, and the company that owned this place was one of his clients. They were going to convert it into luxury apartments, but they only got as far as stripping it out and adding the internal walls to form separate living spaces before they ran out of money. They were selling the building at a bargain price, so my friend got a group together and we bought it.'

They stood on opposite sides of the lift as it ascended slowly. The drive, and this talk about home improvements hadn't diminished Callie's desire to touch him again, but she was handling it. Callie cleared her throat.

'How many apartments here?' She tried to make the question sound as if the information was vital to her.

Ben's smile made her shiver. He knew that this was all just a delicious game, that they'd play for an hour and then she'd go. And he seemed okay with that.

'Twelve. They were just shells when we bought the place, and each of us had a lot of work to do. It helped a lot having an architect on the team, because he knew how to undertake a big building project, what we could do ourselves and what we needed a contractor and a project manager for.'

The lift drifted to a halt on the third floor, and Ben drew back the gates, turning right to one of the two doors at either side of the hallway.

Callie was expecting something unusual, but when he opened the door to his apartment, ushering her inside, she was still surprised. A large, open space, the vaulted ceiling supported by round pillars and heavy metal beams. At the far end, a mezzanine had what seemed to be a sleeping area above it and a kitchen and dining area below. And in here it was most definitely Christmas.

Ben flipped a switch and the tree standing by the tall windows lit up. Fairy lights from top to bottom glimmered against gold baubles and frosted-glass icicles. Swags of greenery, mixed with tinsel and fairy lights ran along the length of the metal railings that edged the mezzanine. He walked over to a large brick fireplace surrounded by easy chairs and a sofa and turned the gas fire on, the leaping flames making the ornaments on the tree sparkle.

'This is… It's like something out of a magazine. I couldn't do it.'

Ben laughed, stowing her coat away in one of the built-in cupboards by the door and making for the kitchen. 'You're the photographer. I think you could do a lot better.'

Maybe with the small things. But the grand plan was beyond anything that Callie could conceive of doing. 'I wouldn't have the courage to put everything into a project like this. I'd think about it and then decide to play it safe and stick with what I had.'

Ben lost interest in the contents of the fridge, looking round suddenly. 'That's a bit of a recurring theme for you, isn't it? Playing things safe. I'd guess it's something you've learned and it doesn't come naturally to you.'

He was breaking the rules. This game of dropping round on Christmas night for sandwiches and board games shouldn't include anything more personal than whether she wanted cranberry sauce with her turkey. She walked over to the breakfast bar and sat down on one of the high stools that faced into the kitchen.

'Okay, I'll play. Why don't you think it comes naturally to me?'

'Because... Most people with a talent for something would stay in the nine-to-five and think, *If only.* You've gone out and made a success of your photography, and that takes a bit of self-belief and a lot of guts.'

Callie hadn't thought of it that way. 'It's nice of you to say that. But I never really thought of my photography as a decision.'

'Don't you think that everything's a decision? Even if we don't really think about it?' Ben took a cold turkey breast from the fridge and started to cut slices from it.

'It didn't look as if you were stopping to make any decisions today when you went into that building.' She'd resolved not to ask Ben about that but she couldn't help herself.

He laid the knife down. 'I made that decision a long time ago, when I joined the fire service. I don't want to be the person who stands by and watches, not able to do anything to change things.'

'Despite the risk?'

'I take a calculated risk, which is always minimised by training and preparedness. You're a paramedic. How many of your patients walked out of their homes, assuming they were safe without even thinking about it, and then something happened to them?'

He had a point. 'Most of them.' Callie snagged a piece of turkey from the pile. She didn't usually talk about any of this. Correction. She *never* talked about any of this. But, then, she didn't do Christmas either, and here she was, eating cold turkey and admiring a tree.

'So what made you make the decision to put up a tree, cook a turkey breast for sandwiches, and then spend Christmas alone?'

'I was working. In case you hadn't noticed.'

'That's no excuse. And you're not working now.'

'I'm not on my own either. You're here.' Callie raised her eyebrows and he shrugged. 'I had a bad break-up just after Christmas last year. I decided to go this one alone.'

So there it was. Two people who wanted to be alone had ended up together. This Christmas just wasn't going to give up.

Ben finished making the sandwiches and took the mince pies from the oven, sliding them onto a plate. Everything went onto a tray, along with forks and side plates, and he carried it over to the easy chairs, which were grouped around a coffee table in front of the hearth.

'I have juice and ginger beer...' He walked back to the kitchen, taking two glasses from the cupboard and flipping the door closed. Callie remembered that she was intending to drive tonight.

'Ginger beer's fine. Don't let me stop you if you want a drink, though.'

He thought for a moment, obviously tempted, and then shook his head. 'No. I think I'll join you.'

CHAPTER EIGHT

CALLIE HAD WOLFED down her sandwiches, slowing a little for the mince pies, and now she was relaxed, slipping off her boots and tucking her feet up under her. Ben reached for the bottle of ginger beer and refilled her glass.

'Thanks. Cheers.' She stretched across the table, clinking her glass against his, and took a sip. 'So, were you serious about the board games?'

'Deadly serious.' Ben gestured towards the cabinet that held games he'd played practically every Christmas since he'd been a child. 'You get to choose which one, and I get to beat you at it.'

'You wish.' She got to her feet, making a thorough inspection of the contents of the cabinet. 'Snakes and Ladders. I haven't played that in years...'

'Good choice. I always win at Snakes and Ladders.' Ben grinned at her, and she carried the box over, opening it and laying out the board and pieces on the table.

'I always win too. So watch out.' She dropped the dice into the plastic cup and pushed it towards him. Delicious, competitive tension suddenly zinged in the air between them, like the promise of something forbidden.

His first throw took him to an empty square and Callie's took her to a short ladder. Ben picked up the dice, blowing on his fingers, and threw a six, which took him to the foot of a long ladder stretching halfway up the board.

'It's like that, is it?' Her gaze was on his face as she threw the dice again, and when she looked down at the board she wailed in frustration. 'No! A snake!'

'Admit it now. You're going to lose…'

She made a face at him, sliding her piece down the snake's body before taking a sip of her drink and taking her sweater off.

Ben looked back into her face and saw a smile that was beyond mischief.

If she was trying to make him so befuddled that he couldn't even count the squares, she was making a good job of it. Ben shook the dice and moved his piece. Two more moves each, which proved beyond any doubt that when snakes became suddenly interesting, ladders and empty squares were all you got.

'Ha!' Callie exclaimed in triumph as his next move took him right into the mouth of a long red and green snake, which wound its way almost to the bottom of the board.

'It *is* getting warm in here.' He pulled his sweater over his head. One look at Callie told him that he hadn't needed to voice the disclaimer. They both knew exactly where this was headed.

She landed on a snake. Her hand drifted to the buttons of her shirt, and Ben felt a bead of sweat trickle down his spine before he realised that no gentleman would allow her to do this. 'You could… A sock would be just fine, you know.'

'Where's the fun in that?'

Right now a mere inch of bare flesh, even if it was just an ankle, was likely to drive him crazy. Buttons would be a point of no return.

'I didn't… This isn't why I asked you here…'

'It's not why I came.' She turned the corners of her mouth down. 'Should I go?'

'No…' If she went now, she'd tear away the greater part of him. 'I really want you to stay.'

'A little Christmas madness?' She regarded him with a clear-eyed gaze. Such beautiful eyes, which seemed to see right through him.

'Just because it's not for keeps, it doesn't make it madness.' When she'd kissed him, it had been sheer magic.

Maybe she felt the same as he did, that *not for keeps* gave them both the freedom to do whatever they wanted tonight. Callie unbuttoned her shirt slowly, seeming to know that he wanted to watch every movement she made.

Even though she was wearing a sleeveless vest underneath, her bare arms and the curve of her breasts beneath the thin cotton were almost more than he could bear. It was an effort to tear his gaze from her, but somehow he managed to throw the dice and count the squares, knowing that this game was far too good not to be pushed to the point where neither of them could stand it any more.

They played in silence, smiling at each other across the board. A ladder each, and then Callie landed on another snake.

'Just my luck!' She puffed out a breath, sliding her piece back down the board.

'Why don't you let me take this one for you…?' Ben unbuttoned his shirt, feeling suddenly self-conscious. He wanted more than anything for her to like what she saw.

She did. He could see it in her face. The muscles across his shoulders tightened as the temperature climbed steadily higher.

He worked out. Of course he did, he had to be fit for his job. But right now it seemed as if someone were unwrapping the best Christmas present she could think of right in front of her eyes. Callie wanted to jump across the table and tear at his clothes.

But she didn't. Their initial hesitancy had set the pace. Slow and so deliciously tantalising.

She watched as he cupped the dice in his hands, blowing on them for luck, while he grinned wickedly. Ben was unafraid of his own body, not bothering to suck his stomach in or square his shoulders. He didn't need to, he was perfect, and his lack of self-consciousness just made him even more so.

He landed on a ladder. Callie grinned.

'Winning move…' His smile was deliciously wicked. 'What have you got to divert my attention from that?'

'A sock?' She teased him.

'I'll take a sock. As long as I can be the one to take it off…'

'Yes…'

Suddenly he was all movement, pushing the board to one side and stepping across the table. Then he fell to his knees in front of her and Callie shivered. It was all she could do not to reach out and touch him.

Ben propped her foot on his leg, slowly pulling her sock off. And then the other one…

'Hey! Are you cheating?'

'Yep. Are you arguing?'

'No.'

Callie slid to the edge of the chair, winding her legs around his back and pulling him close. His skin was smooth and warm, brute strength rippling beneath its surface. In one bold, swift movement he pulled her vest over her head, kissing her as if she was the one thing in the world that he truly possessed.

Right now she was. When his movements slowed, tender now, she began to tremble. His hand lingered for a moment over the catch at the back of her bra in an implied question, and Callie reached behind her, undoing it for him. She felt his lips curve into a smile against hers as he gently pulled the straps from her shoulders.

'Your skin… *So* soft…' His fingers were exploring her back, her breasts crushed against his chest. Callie moved against him, desperate for a little friction, groaning in frustrated impatience when it wasn't enough.

'Look sharp…' She whispered the words that Ben called when he wanted to hurry the crew along, and he chuckled. 'Is this an emergency?'

'Yeah. I'm calling a Code Red…' she gasped into his ear, clinging to his shoulders.

He didn't let her down. Getting to his feet, he lifted her up in his arms, striding to the curved staircase. The mezzanine was dark, but in the fairy lights strung along the railings Callie could see a bed. That was all they needed.

He laid her down, pushing her hands away when she reached for the button on the waistband of his jeans. He was going to let her watch.

As he stripped off the rest of his clothes, the power in his body seemed to seep through her veins. She *had* to have him inside her. Callie wriggled on the bed, pulling at the zip of her trousers, but she was too slow. Ben had it, and was slowly drawing them down over her hips, kissing her burning skin as he went.

'One minute…' When she was finally naked, he backed away suddenly, grinning.

'What? Where are you going?'

He disappeared through a door leading to a walled-in space at the side of the open balcony. Bathroom? Callie heard the sound of glass crashing and breaking on a tiled surface, but Ben was clearly in too much of a hurry to stop and clear it up, because he appeared in the doorway moments later.

'You didn't forget these, did you?' He was holding a packet of condoms in his hand.

'You remembered for me...' Callie felt suddenly foolish. She never relied on a partner to take care of things like this.

'Only just.' He slung the condoms onto the bed, crawling towards her and covering her body with his. 'All I can think about is what I want to do with you.'

'And what I'll do with you?' She liked it that he was just as lost in this as she was.

'Yeah. Particularly that...' He guided her hand between her legs. Waiting for the clues she gave about exactly where and how she wanted to be touched, and when he had them his fingers took over from hers. *So* much better.

'Where else...?' He whispered the words against her ear, chuckling when Callie moved her hand to her breast. 'Of course...'

No more words now, because his tongue and lips were busy with an altogether more pleasurable exercise. Ben took her gasps as a challenge, pinning her down and turning them into moans. When he slipped one finger inside her, everything suddenly focussed on that one spot.

She fought the overwhelming urge to be taken, now, because there was something she wanted to do much more. Somewhere she found the strength to push him off her, over onto his back.

Her gaze held his as she planted kisses on his chest, moving downwards. His hands moved to her shoulders, his fingers trembling lightly on her skin. Callie watched the anticipation build in his face, and then his head snapped back suddenly, his body arching.

'Do that again...' It was practically a command.

'Do *what* again?' This time she used her tongue to caress him instead of her fingers. His groan told Callie that he was heading right to the place she wanted him. Joining her, on the edge of madness.

They pushed each other further. With each caress she wanted him more, until finally there was no resisting it. Ben held her down on the bed, fumbling with the condom with one hand. And then he was inside her, moving with all the urgency of a man with only one thought in his head.

She could feel herself beginning to come, and there was nothing she could do to stop it. Nothing she wanted to do. Pinned down by his weight, she could only respond to his driving rhythm. Callie choked out his name, digging her fingernails into his back, and then let go. She let go of everything she'd ever cared about, everything she'd ever wanted, turning herself over completely to Ben.

CHAPTER NINE

SHE WAS SO SWEET. So incredibly sexy. And physically they were a perfect match. She liked hot and hard, crazy desire that had blown Ben's mind to smithereens.

She liked lazy, tender lovemaking as much as he did, too. Feeling himself harden again inside her, and feeling her soften as he whispered in her ear. He told her she was beautiful and felt her cheek flush with pleasure against his. Callie's smile filled him with the kind of warmth that Ben knew he could only take for a little while. But that little while was now.

They made love until they were exhausted and then slept. Got out of bed to eat something and then made love again, and slept until the Boxing Day sun was low on the horizon.

'Do you know the way back to the fire station?' He swallowed down the hope that they might take just his car, leaving hers here so she'd have to return with him to pick it up.

She nodded. 'I'll find it. Maximum deniability, right?'

She had a point. Ben took the toast from the toaster and put two pieces on a plate, pushing it across the kitchen counter towards her. She nodded a thank-you and set about layering it with butter and apricot conserve.

'I like your hair...like that.' After they'd showered, her

hair had dried in curls. It made her look soft and sexy, and Ben ventured the compliment even though he guessed that straight hair went a little better with the image that she wanted to project to the world.

'Do you?' She rubbed her hand across her head. 'I always think it makes me look a bit ditzy.'

Ben snorted in laughing disbelief. 'No. A little softer but definitely not ditzy.'

She grinned. 'Maybe I'll leave it for today, then. Where are my clothes?' She was wearing his towelling robe, which Ben privately thought looked a great deal better on Callie than it did on him.

'I put them in the washer-dryer while you were asleep. They'll be dry now.'

'You are a dream. You buy apricot conserve, you have a full fridge and you do my washing. Any chance I might kidnap you?'

Something tugged hard in Ben's chest. The voice of reason had been strangely silent up till now, but it was back in full force, reminding him that he couldn't take even the slightest suggestion that he was ready for a full-time relationship.

'Not really...' He shook his head, and heard her laugh as he turned away from her, pretending that the coffee machine needed his immediate attention.

'I know. Only joking. I'm not looking to keep you for much longer.'

If he were in any other place in his life, the sudden reappearance of the other side to Callie's nature, the hard shell that kept everyone at arm's length, would have been disappointing. The fact that it was strangely comforting reminded Ben that he was in no position to deal with anything other than temporary. He turned, leaning across the kitchen counter to kiss her forehead.

'That doesn't mean… Last night was everything, Callie. You are so much more than beautiful.'

She smiled, as if that was just what she'd wanted to hear. 'I couldn't get enough of you.'

That was what *he* wanted to hear. Despite the feeling that the world had spun a little slower over the last twenty-four hours, he couldn't help wanting more.

'We have an hour before we need to leave. Ten minutes to finish our coffee, and then twenty minutes to shower and dress….'

'Which means we'd have to be quick…' She grinned at him, taking a condom out of the pocket of his robe and holding it up. It was disconcerting the way she thought so much like him.

'That's thirty seconds you've saved already.' He rounded the kitchen counter swiftly, taking her toast out of her hand and putting it down on the plate. Picking her up off the stool, he carried her over to the sofa.

She was shrieking with laughter, wriggling in his arms, and when he tipped her down onto the cushions she made a lunge for him, pulling him down. This was how it had been all night, a heady give and take that they'd both revelled in.

'Not this time.' He pinned her down, grasping at her wrists with one hand and undoing the tie of the dressing gown with the other. 'This time's all for you…'

She stared into his gaze, suddenly still. The smile she gave, when she knew he was about to make love to her, had the power to break him. But having more of Callie, feeling her break him, was the one and only thing he wanted right now.

It wasn't just that every minute with Ben seemed like ten. Last night he actually *had* spent hours making love to her. And his idea of a quickie before they went to work was thirty minutes, dedicated to giving her an orgasm so devastating that she would have fallen off the sofa if she hadn't been safe in his arms.

It felt as if his scent were on her. Swirling around her in her car as she drove the longest route she could think of to the fire station, so that there would be no possibility of them arriving together. No one seemed to notice it when she joined the rest of the crew at the ready room table, making sure she sat with her back to Ben, but when she pulled her sweater over her head, draping it over the back of her chair, she shivered, sure that her shirt smelled of him.

It was just his washing powder. His soap on her skin. But still there was that indefinable extra element to it, which reminded her of Ben alone.

Perhaps she should go and do something useful, instead of awkwardly trying to pretend that he wasn't in the room. She grabbed her camera, standing up suddenly and almost cannoning into a wall of hard muscle.

'Oh… Sorry…' She jumped back in alarm, and Ben grabbed her arm to steady her.

'My fault. Are you okay?'

She glanced around the table, suddenly terrified that it would be obvious that they'd been making love less than two hours ago. If it was, no one seemed to care.

'Yes, I'm fine.'

He nodded, grinning. Then the pressure of his fingers tightened on her arm for a moment, before letting go. His lips formed a silent word, just for her, and then he turned away.

Later…

Later. Ben had kept himself busy tonight, and Callie had done the same, but that one word made all the difference.

An acknowledgement that the last twenty-four hours couldn't just be forgotten now they were back at work. She wanted there to be a *later* too, even if it only meant half an hour alone to talk to him.

'Not another one…' Eve threw a half-eaten piece of stollen in the bin as the bell rang and Ben called out that this was their second abandoned car fire of the night. 'What is it with Boxing Day and joyriders? Haven't they ever heard of "Silent Night"?'

'That was supposed to be last night, wasn't it?' The night after Christmas Day.

'Is it? I suppose we're making up for it now, then.' Eve was already collecting her gear, ready to go. 'Good shot at four o'clock.'

The crew had taken to pointing out what they reckoned were good camera shots. Mostly Callie smiled and took the picture anyway, knowing she could delete it later, but Eve had a good eye. When she looked in the direction that Eve had indicated, she saw Ben, working with one of the other men to heave some heavy equipment onto the tender.

It was a great shot, full of movement and urgency. Callie raised her camera and then lowered it. She hadn't taken a picture of Ben all day, feeling that somehow it crossed the line between professional and personal.

He glanced over, catching her watching him, and grinned. And then he was back at work, making sure that the crew had everything they would need and calling out to Callie to get on the truck *now* if she was coming with them.

The night shift was finally over. Callie had looked for Ben in the small office and bumped into Eve her way back to the ready room.

'Have you seen Ben?'

'You wanted him? He's gone.'

'Gone...?' The news hit Callie with an uncomfortable force.

'Yes, he got a text and then dashed off. Said he had to see to something.' It seemed that some of the shock of realisation had shown on Callie's face, because Eve was looking at her questioningly. 'He'll be back here tonight. Or call him if it can't wait.'

'It can wait.' Callie forced herself to smile. 'Sleep well. I'll see you tonight.'

Callie collected up her gear, walking alone to her car. She'd been so sure that *later* had meant the end of their shift. Maybe she'd been mistaken. But Ben could have given her just one smile before rushing away. Just one sign that he hadn't come to regret what had happened between them. Callie grimly shook her head as she got into her car. It wasn't as if they'd promised each other anything.

All the same, Ben's scent seemed to follow her all the way home. She showered, throwing her clothes into the washing basket, and still it stayed with her like a ghost of Christmas, curling around her senses when she closed the curtains against the morning light and got into bed.

Callie had tried to sleep and found it impossible. Cocoa hadn't helped, and neither had sitting in front of the television, watching daytime TV. In the end, she had eventually fallen asleep for a short stretch on the sofa, and woken with a stiff neck. She considered staying at home tonight, but thought better of it. If Ben didn't want to say goodbye that was fine. She still had to say her goodbyes to the rest of the crew.

She was late, missing roll-call and Ben's briefing. She popped her head around the ready room door, letting the firefighters know that she was there, and then made for the locker room.

'You made it...' Ben's voice behind her made her jump.

'Yes. Sorry, I was a bit delayed.' She turned to him, trying not to look into his face.

Keep it professional. Get through tonight and then walk away.

'Since you're not officially on the roster, you're at liberty to come and go as you please.' He took a step closer, his voice quieter. 'I want to apologise. For last night.'

Callie's mouth felt suddenly dry. 'That's all right. You're at liberty to come and go as you please as well.'

'You've every right to be angry...'

'I'm *not* angry, Ben.

'Let me explain—'

Oh, no. Explanations weren't something that either of them had signed up for. Explanations made everything complicated.

'There's no need to explain anything. We're not...' She felt herself redden as the words she wanted wouldn't come.

'Not what?' He raised his arm, planting it against one of the locker doors. It was an unequivocal sign that if she wanted to end this conversation, she was going to have to push past him, and that would involve touching him.

'I'm nothing to you. You're nothing to me.'

The look he gave her made her into a liar. She wanted him so badly that he could be everything to her if he would just reach out and touch her.

'That's not true—' He broke off as the bell rang, cursing quietly under his breath.

'Go. You have to go.' She'd been saved. By an actual bell, of all things.

He turned, and relief flooded through her as Ben began to hurry away. But it took more than a bell to dissuade Ben.

'We're not done, Callie. Not yet...' He shot the words over his shoulder.

CHAPTER TEN

THEY *WERE* DONE. They had to be. They'd made love, and Callie had been hoping they might be friends. Maybe even lovers again, for a little while. But he'd walked away without a word, and that was something she couldn't deal with. Not when she'd been beginning to feel that she might just be able to depend on him.

It was a busy night again. There wasn't much time for photographs at the fire station, and when they were called out, Callie made sure that she took up the vantage point that Ben indicated, without looking at him. The crew's mood became silent and dogged, as if they were all wishing for the end of the shift as much as Callie was. This morning they could all go home and celebrate what was left of Christmas with their families.

When she said her goodbyes, trading hugs and promising not to be a stranger, Ben was nowhere to be seen. Callie emptied her locker and made for the car park.

He was leaning against her car, hands in the pockets of his jacket in the morning chill. Callie took a breath, trying not to alter her pace as she walked towards him.

'I'm off now. I'll see you around.' Callie had regretted her bitter words in the locker room earlier. There was no reason to be uncivilised about this.

'No, you won't. Not if you can help it, anyway.'

Right. So this was how he wanted it. 'Step aside, Ben. I'm going home.'

He moved silently away from the back door of the car, letting her open it and put her bag inside. Then suddenly he was there again, blocking her path to the driver's door.

'Ben!' Callie tried to inject as much warning as she could into her voice.

'Trust me, Callie. Just enough to come with me and let me explain.'

He knew that was impossible. He knew she couldn't trust.

But the look on his face told her that he wasn't going to give up. Callie puffed out a breath.

'All right. We'll go to the café on the corner and you can buy me a cup of tea.'

Ben had messed up. Big time. He'd been longing to see Callie alone, knowing from their quiet, exchanged smiles that she wanted to see him. And then his phone had pinged, and the text had sent him running for the hills. Scared and confused.

He owed her an apology, and an explanation. After that, she was at liberty to throw her tea in his face and tell him that he needed to get his act together, and that he couldn't treat people the way he'd just treated her. It was no less than he'd been telling himself all night.

She followed him wordlessly to the café. One of the few small cafés left in London, where just one kind of coffee was served, and you could get a traditional breakfast. The morning rush was over, and they could sit in one of the booths that were arranged along the side wall and get a little privacy.

He ordered tea, and coffee and a bacon sandwich for himself. Callie's beautiful eyes were studying him solemnly and they gave him the courage to broach a subject that he suddenly realised he'd kept secret from even his closest friends.

'I rushed off yesterday morning, because I had a text...' When he said it out loud the reason sounded even more flimsy.

'I know. Eve said.' She brushed it off as if it meant nothing, but the hurt in her eyes gave the lie to that. If he was going to make her understand, he had to tell her everything.

Show her everything. Ben took his phone from his pocket, tapping the icon for messages and then displaying the four texts that had come in moments apart yesterday from an unrecognised number. When he laid the phone on the table in front of her, Callie ignored it.

'They all say the same thing. They're from my ex-partner.'

She puffed out a breath and looked at the phone, frowning when she saw the texts.

Happy Christmas. Love Isabel x

'Ben, if you wanted to be with someone else then you could have just said. The only promise we made to each other was that...there were no promises.'

'I didn't want to be with her—' He broke off as the waitress chose that moment to put their cups down in front of them, adding a plate of bacon sandwiches for Ben. He managed to get a 'Thank you' in before she turned her back on them, and then they were alone again.

Ben pushed the bacon sandwiches to one side. There was something he needed to do more than eat. More than breathe, if he was honest. 'It's a long story...'

'Not too long, I hope.' She glanced at her tea in a clear indication that when she'd drunk it she would be gone.

'I'll keep it as short as I can. Isabel and I met eighteen months ago, I know her brother slightly. We went out a few times, it was a pretty casual thing…'

'Because you don't do anything other than casual.' She shot him a cool glance.

'Things were different then. She was a lot of fun to be with, but it was never going to work between us. I said I'd like to see her again but just as a friend. Then I got this long rambling letter, saying that she knew I didn't mean it, and that she'd decided to take me back.'

'*Did* you mean it?'

'Yeah, I meant it. But the more I tried to step back, the more she seemed to cling to me. She said that it was only my shift patterns that were keeping us apart, and that she'd give up her job so we could be together.'

Callie took a gulp of her tea, concern registering in her face. Maybe she could already see the danger that Ben had failed to recognise at the time. 'I know shift work is hard on relationships but…most people find a way to work that out.'

She didn't know the half of it yet. 'I told her that neither of us were giving up our jobs, but she wouldn't take no for an answer. She started to write to me, cards and letters, two or three times a day. She called and texted me at work all the time, and in the end I had to block her number. I reckoned she'd get tired of me soon enough if I didn't respond…'

Just talking about it was making Ben feel sick with self-loathing, but when he looked into Callie's face he saw a warmth he didn't deserve.

'In my experience, when a woman acts like that, they generally don't get tired of it. It's more likely to be a result of what's going on with her, not anything you did.'

It was good of her to make excuses for him, but Ben

knew exactly what he'd done. When she heard everything, Callie would too, and she'd see that what had happened between them had been *his* fault, and maybe stop telling herself that the world had it in for her.

'When Isabel started calling on the landline at work, I realised that I had to do something. So I went to see her and told her that it couldn't go on. No more calls and no more letters. The next evening I came home from work to find a bunch of flowers and a note, saying that she wouldn't call again.'

'That's…' Callie shrugged. 'I'm guessing it wasn't a sign that she was beginning to find some boundaries?'

'The flowers were in a vase, sitting on the kitchen counter. She'd let herself in with a key I didn't know she had.'

The sick feeling, that had overwhelmed Ben when he'd looked at the flowers returned. In that moment he'd begun to understand violation. He'd thrown the flowers away, looking around the apartment for signs of Isabel, and he'd found them. Dismay had turned to despair as he'd slowly begun to realise that someone had been through everything he owned.

'You changed the locks. Please tell me you changed the locks.'

'It was late and I was working the following morning. I didn't have a chance. I texted Isabel to tell her that she wasn't to let herself in again and…the following evening I got home and found her in my bed. Naked. I told her that she had to get dressed and go, and she told me she was pregnant.'

Callie put her head in her hands, rubbing her face in a gesture of helplessness. Ben thought that he'd probably done exactly the same thing himself.

'I always wanted kids but I knew this wasn't an ideal

situation to bring a child into. I told her that I'd take care of them both but that we couldn't go back to being a couple. Then, a couple of weeks later, Isabel told me she'd made a mistake and she never had been pregnant. I didn't know how to feel...'

It had been a mixture of relief and sorrow. Concern for Isabel, although in truth she hadn't seemed to mind all that much, and guilt. Ben had never felt so deeply flawed, and so incapable of doing anything about it.

'Ben...don't take this the wrong way, but did it occur to you that she was just trying to make you stay with her?'

Callie had asked the question that Ben hadn't dared to even think. 'When a woman tells you she's pregnant and the baby's yours, disbelieving her isn't the best way to respond.'

'Yes, I know, but...' She puffed out a breath. 'You had to know that this wasn't normal.'

'I tried to get her some help, but she wouldn't take it. The next thing I knew I had a call from her brother, saying she'd locked herself in her flat and was threatening to take a full packet of paracetamol.'

Callie was shaking her head slowly. 'She needed professional help. Lots of it... He didn't call the emergency services?'

'Isabel was asking for me. I went round and broke the door down. As far as I could see, she hadn't taken anything, but we took her to A and E just to be sure. She fought me and said she wanted to die...' Ben closed his eyes. Isabel had kicked and screamed, blackening his eye. In the end, that had turned out to be the only physical injury in a night that had taken a heavy emotional toll on everyone.

'She got the help she needed, though?'

'Yes. Her brother and I both stayed the night to keep an eye on her, and the counsellor I'd contacted agreed to see her the next day. He told me that it was best if I didn't have any further involvement, and that I should let him and her family give her the support she needed.'

'So that was it?'

'I speak to her brother regularly. He says she's doing well.'

'And these texts…' Callie nudged his phone with one finger. 'I imagine it was really hard to see them.'

Somehow Ben managed to smile. 'Yes. I called her brother and he says they're dealing with it.'

'But you can't help.' Callie turned the corners of her mouth down. 'That's pretty tough for someone like you, who's used to making a difference.'

She made him realise what really hurt. The helplessness, and his complete inability to make things right.

'It's the best way. Maybe she really did just want to wish me a happy Christmas…' Ben shrugged. 'But that doesn't matter. I want to tell you that the way I acted yesterday morning had nothing to do with you. And that I'm sorry.'

'I imagine it was a knee-jerk reaction.' She was looking straight into his eyes now. 'A bit like the one I had.'

'You had every right to be upset.'

'Don't make excuses for me.' She reached forward, picking up one of the bacon sandwiches from his plate. 'Have you talked about this with anyone?'

Ben shook his head. If he had then maybe he'd have found the perspective and understanding that Callie was so ready to give. Or maybe that wouldn't have made such a difference if it hadn't come from her.

'Maybe you should.' She reached out, taking his hand. 'Stop trying to pack it away in a box and forget about it.'

How did she know him so well, after so little time? Callie seemed to get the parts of him that even he didn't get.

He picked up the other half of the sandwich and they

ate in silence. There was something about the silence between him and Callie. Warm and companionable, it was allowing them both to heal.

'Are we done, Callie?' Finally he found it in himself to speak.

'I…' She looked up at him, and he saw all the warmth in her eyes that he'd found when he'd made love to her. 'No. We're not done yet.'

CHAPTER ELEVEN

CALLIE HAD FOLLOWED Ben's car back to his apartment, and they stood quietly together in the old, creaking lift. Her heart had gone out to him when she'd seen the pain and guilt in his face when he'd talked about Isabel. He'd been damaged…

But, then, she was damaged too. And somehow that meant that they fitted together well. There was no danger that either of them would take this relationship beyond what the other could handle.

Ben opened the door to his apartment, ushering her inside. Light was streaming through the high windows, making the ornaments on the tree glisten and gleam. Christmas wasn't over yet.

Neither were they. Callie reached for him, and he moved suddenly, taking her into his arms, his warmth flooding through her and making her gasp. His keys clattered unheeded on the floor and he backed her against the wall, his hand behind her head to cushion it from the exposed bricks.

'I have the next four days off. Will you spend them with me?' He kissed the soft skin behind her ear, and Callie shivered.

'That would be…wonderful.'

* * *

Tired from the night's work, they'd spent the rest of the day and the following night sleeping and making love. And when dawn had broken, Ben had got out of bed, promising her breakfast. Sausages, bacon, eggs…the works.

'That smells great.' Callie had put on her clothes, fresh from the washer-dryer, and had gone downstairs to find him standing at the cooker, wearing a towelling robe. 'You know the good thing about you is that you always have a full fridge.'

He leaned over, kissing her. 'The only good thing?'

'You know the others. I'm not going to repeat myself.'

'Okay. Will you watch the pan while I go and take a shower? I might be a while, I'll be needing to revive my broken ego.' He flashed her an irresistible grin and Callie laughed.

'Your ego's just fine….' She called after him.

He reappeared in a pair of worn jeans and a crisp white T-shirt. Crisp and white suited him. It accentuated his dark hair and the softly smouldering look in his eyes.

'Why don't we go to the zoo this afternoon? I haven't been to Regent's Park in ages.' He crowded her away from the pan and Callie took two mugs from the cupboard to make the coffee.

'Sounds like a plan. I like the zoo. I'd like to pop home this morning and get a change of clothes.' Something a bit nicer than work boots and trousers perhaps.

'Okay. Leave your camera behind so that I know you'll come back.'

Callie laughed, winding her arms around his waist. 'I'll be back. I'll leave my tablet as well, so you can have a look through the photos if you like.'

He turned away from the pan to face her. 'Really? You

told me that I was the last person on the list to get a look at them.'

'I was making a point. Everyone has to approve the photographs that feature them, but it doesn't matter if you take a look. I'd really like to hear your thoughts, actually.' They'd come so far since that first day.

'Ah. So you were putting me in my place, were you?'

'Only because you didn't want me around.'

He bent down, kissing her. 'I can't imagine what I was thinking. I must have been crazy.'

'I thought you were nice looking with a bit of an attitude.'

'I thought you were gorgeous. But very scary.' Ben wound one of her curls around his finger. She knew he liked it better when she left it to curl naturally, and letting her defences down with Ben was becoming surprisingly easy.

They tramped all the way round Regent's Park, working up an appetite for lunch, before going to the zoo. They then spent the evening curled up on the sofa together, watching an old film, and then another night together. Ben was sure that there must be something in his life that had made him as happy as Callie did, but he couldn't call it to mind.

They got up early and went out for breakfast, then took a stroll through the buzzing network of streets of the East End to do a little window shopping. Now Callie was sitting cross-legged on the sofa, wearing an oversized sweater and a flowered skirt, which draped around her legs. She was busy with a pad and pencil, listing and ticking off photographs. And Ben was busy watching her.

'So…you have a thing about fire engines, then? Or is it firefighters?'

She looked up at him, grinning. 'You're the one with the

thing for shiny red and chrome. And I only have a thing for *one* firefighter.'

Ben chuckled. Callie had a way of making him feel good without really trying. 'What made you propose this project at the fire station, then? I imagine you could get much better rates elsewhere, and you're putting a lot of work into it.'

'Actually, I'm doing it free.' Her cheeks reddened, as if she'd been caught in a good deed and was slightly embarrassed about it.

'Really? So what made you do it?'

In the last two days they'd talked about everything, felt everything together. It seemed so natural to ask questions but this one made Callie hesitate for a moment.

'I want to make a difference with my photography, not just take good pictures. I think it's important to show the realities of the work the emergency services do.'

Ben suspected there was a little more to it than that. 'I would have thought the ambulance service would be closer to your heart.'

'I particularly wanted to come to a fire station because… of my dad. You take risks every day in the course of your work, and I wanted to understand that a little better.'

Something prickled at the back of Ben's neck. As if a door had just swung open, and he wasn't sure whether he wanted to go through it.

'And do you?'

She shrugged. 'Maybe. I heard everything you said about the choices you made, and I understand it. It's a bit soon to be feeling it, though.'

It was almost a relief to imagine the door swinging shut again. The possibilities behind it, what might happen if Callie found a place where she could contemplate a long-term relationship with a certain firefighter, weren't something that Ben had thought about.

Callie had gone back to her list now, clearly not inclined to say any more. Ben should concentrate on the here and now and make the most of that, not worry about an impossible future.

'You fancy some lunch? I'd really like to see the photographs you've chosen, and perhaps we could do that afterwards over a glass of wine.'

She nodded. Risk averted. 'Yes, thanks. That would be nice.'

Callie was happy with her choice. Two or three photographs for each month, featuring different aspects of the work. Some formal and others informal, with a flavour of the Christmas festivities at the fire station on the December page.

'I like these especially.' Ben pointed to the choice for November. 'Putting the one of Eve with Isaac right next to the one of her on duty makes them both stronger.'

He'd picked the ones she was most pleased with. 'I like them too.'

'You know, if you want to make a difference, you could think about doing more of this. You have a way of showing strength and beauty that could change lives.'

Callie hadn't thought of it that way before. 'Portraiture as therapy, you mean? That would be...amazing.'

'I think so too.' He grinned, putting his hand to his chest in a gesture of mock distress. 'Although I'm mortified to find that you no longer see me as either strong *or* beautiful.'

He'd noticed. Out of the hundreds of photographs she'd taken during the last two shifts at the fire station, there wasn't a single one of Ben. Callie tried to laugh it off.

'Sleeping with you and then taking photos… It didn't seem right somehow.' Callie had never *wanted* to take photographs of anyone she'd slept with. Giving that much of herself and then having the photograph to prove it after it was over didn't much appeal to her.

Ben nodded, not seeming to want to push the subject. But she could see that he was a little disappointed with her answer. And so was Callie. They'd been talking about giving her heart to her photography, and she'd shied away from the first opportunity.

She looked around the apartment. Ben was so perfect, so handsome that she wanted something imperfect to photograph him against.

'Do you have any more exposed brickwork? Like that?' Callie pointed up at the roof space, spanned by heavy metal beams and flanked on either side by bare bricks.

'I have plenty of exposed brickwork, if that's what you want.' He laid the tablet down on the sofa between them, reaching for the soft sheepskin boots that she'd slipped off and left by the sofa. 'You'll have to put those on, though.'

'Where are we going?' Callie pulled the boots on, reaching for her camera and a folding tripod from her bag. He didn't answer, getting to his feet and leading the way to the doorway under the stairs. It led to a small corridor where the spare bedroom was situated, and then another door that Callie had assumed must be a cupboard. When he unlocked it and swung it open, the chill of a large, unheated space brushed her cheek.

Ben flipped a switch and lights came on, pooling under metal shades. The floor area was almost as much again as that of the apartment, and the space was clearly a continuation of it, double height with a cavernous roof supported by the same metal beams. But it was entirely untouched, bare brick walls and metal window frames, caked with many layers of paint.

'What's this, Ben?'

'When I chose the space I wanted I thought that it would be good to have room to grow, if I ever needed it.' He shrugged diffidently, as if he didn't know now why *room to grow* had ever been a factor in his thinking.

Callie swallowed hard. This was the family home that Ben had once wanted but now couldn't contemplate having. If she'd crossed a line, by taking her camera out and trying to capture what he meant to her, then he'd crossed one too, by bringing her here.

Ben hadn't brought anyone else in here for over a year. He no longer had any need of the space that he'd once thought might accommodate the needs of a family.

He loved his apartment. Even if he didn't grow old here, he'd reckoned on growing a good bit older. But however old he got, he reckoned that this space would remain the same, ready for the next owner to make something of it.

Watching Callie taking photographs of the walls and windows calmed him a little. She saw it in terms of light and shade, texture and colour. It was just bricks and mortar to her.

'Over there…' She'd set the camera onto the tripod she'd brought with her and suddenly turned her attention to him, pointing to a stretch of wall by one of the high windows.

'Here?' Ben walked over to the wall, feeling suddenly awkward and under scrutiny.

'No, a couple of yards to your left. Closer to the window… That's good. Maybe just rest your hand on the windowsill.'

Every time Callie pointed the camera at him, his hands became suddenly clumsy and felt twice their usual size.

At least he knew what to do with one of them now and he complied, feeling the chill of the tiled sill under his fingers.

She bent to adjust the lens, and he smiled in response. Being photographed was far easier when Callie just crept up on you and you weren't aware of it.

'Okay… You're a little wooden…' She wrinkled her nose, inspecting her camera as if adjusting the settings might make him feel more at ease. Ben waited and saw her face light up as she looked towards him again. 'Oh. Look.'

She pointed at the window and he turned. It was snowing, large flakes blowing against the window and already gathering at the bottom of the small panes of glass. He heard her boots, padding softly on the concrete floor, and felt her body next to his.

'It's lovely, isn't it?' She stared up into the dark sky. This was clearly one of those things that Callie just wanted to experience, rather than photograph.

'Yes, it is.' He took her in his arms. It would be…interesting…to make love with her here. Feel the cold of her hands on his skin, while heat exploded between them. It wouldn't be comfortable, but feeling the rough brickwork against his back, protecting her against it with his own body, seemed only to heighten the pleasure of the fantasy.

It *was* just a fantasy. Callie wasn't his to protect, and even doing it for a while would make him want what he was too afraid to take. Her presence made him realise that a few of his old dreams still lingered here, not yet banished with the ruthlessness that he'd swept them out of the other parts of his life.

She walked away from him, clearly set on the idea of photographing him and not the snow. Ben resumed his awkward-feeling pose, looking at the camera.

'Don't smile.' Her voice floated out from behind the

lens and he pulled his face straight. She took a couple of photographs, but seemed unhappy with them.

'Look at me, Ben. Think about…the wall behind your back. How does it feel?'

'It feels…like a wall.'

'Okay. That's a start. How does the window feel?'

'It feels a little draughty.' Ben grinned at her. 'I don't have your ability to give walls and windows any more meaning than just…'

He broke off. Callie had stepped forward again, standing on her toes to kiss him. When he moved his hand to wind it around her waist she stopped him.

'Don't move…. Don't move.'

'You do this with all your portraits?'

'It's a new technique. Just for you.'

Ben liked that a lot. And he liked the way it was difficult to keep still while Callie planted her palms on his chest, kissing him. The way she pressed herself against his body, seeming to know that he was suddenly aching for her.

Hot and cold. The rough surface of the wall against his back and the softness of her skin. It was almost unbearable.

'Stay still.' She backed away from him, her gaze still locked with his. Her fingers moved to her lips, grazing them as if she was trying to recreate the feel of his mouth. 'Still…'

He felt it. The way that Callie brought emotion and meaning into everyday actions and things. The way she wove a fantasy into the hard facts of reality. As he gazed into her eyes, he was aware of nothing other than her.

She must have stretched out her hand and touched the camera, because suddenly she walked back towards him. 'I think I've got the shots I want.'

He wound his arms around her. Ben was still trembling slightly from an emotion that he couldn't quite describe. Whatever shot she'd taken, he imagined that it must show both their hearts, and he wasn't sure whether he could bear to see it. He'd told her that he liked the rawness of her photographs, but maybe this was a little too raw.

'It's cold in here.' It was the only excuse he could think of to move. Callie nodded, breaking away from him, collecting the camera and tripod as he ushered her back into the apartment, closing the door behind them and locking it. The lines that they'd promised not to cross had somehow been crossed, and the feeling that maybe they'd gone too far nagged at him.

'You want to see?' Callie had fitted the lead from her tablet to the camera, and the photographs had already downloaded.

'I'm…not sure.'

'I can delete them.' She turned her mouth down, seeming to sense his discomfiture.

'No…' Ben held out his hand. How bad could it be? A regular guy, standing against a wall.

She walked over to the hearth, warming herself, while Ben looked through the photos. It was all there. His face, his eyes were just the same as the ones he saw in the mirror every morning, but there was a raw undertone of passion.

The shadows, the texture of the brickwork and the smooth white of his T-shirt. Snow falling at the window and warmth in his face. It was a mass of inconsistencies, which felt rather too uncomfortably like the truth.

He laid the tablet down on the sofa and walked across to the fire. 'They're great. You have a talent, Callie. Don't let it go to waste.'

She snuggled into his arms. The screen on the tablet dimmed and then shut down, but Ben couldn't shake the image in his head.

That night, Ben made love to her tenderly, almost regretfully. Callie woke in the early hours to find him lying on his back, staring at the ceiling, and when he realised that she was awake he turned over, curling his body around hers and whispering to her to go back to sleep.

In the morning, she woke to the sounds of him moving around downstairs. She stumbled into the shower, rubbing her face hard in the stream of water, trying to gather her splintered thoughts.

They'd stepped out of the bounds that they'd both set themselves and tried to touch the impossible. And the bond that had formed so naturally between them couldn't withstand that.

Callie closed her eyes, turning her face up into the stream of water. If they called it a day now, they could keep everything that was special. Carrying on would only destroy that, because at some point they'd find that their deeply held fears were stronger than their desire to be together.

She blow-dried her hair, tugging it straight. Then she dressed and packed her things away in her overnight bag.

He had coffee ready for her, along with toast and apricot preserve. The silence grew heavier by the minute.

'I think…' He broke off, realising that Callie had opened her mouth to speak at the same time as he had. Even in this, they seemed in perfect synchronicity. 'You first.'

'I should go home. I have some more work to do on the photos, and I need my computer and printer.'

He nodded. 'Yeah. There are a few things I need to do today too. Call into the fire station maybe…'

This was the final acknowledgement that it was over between them. Irretrievably broken. Callie didn't have to go home any more than he needed to go to the station. After all the honesty they'd shared, they'd started to make excuses to each other.

'Right, then. It's been…'

'It's been too good to last.' The sudden flash of warmth

in his eyes was too much to bear, and Callie looked away. She gulped the rest of her coffee down and put her mug in the sink, then collected up her camera and tablet, stowing them away in her camera bag.

'I'll walk you to your car.' Ben picked up his keys, shoving them into the pocket of his jeans.

'No, thank you. I'd rather you didn't.' Callie pulled on her coat and turned to face him. 'Time to get back to our real lives. Live yours well, Ben.'

'You too, Callie.'

She was aware that he stayed in the doorway after the lift had creaked its way up to collect her and she'd got in. As it crept slowly downwards, she heard his front door close. Callie took a deep breath, trying to stop herself from trembling.

It was done. They'd both lived up to their side of the bargain and the whole of the rest of her life was waiting for her. Somehow the rest of her life seemed an awfully long time to contemplate at the moment.

Ben was sure that this was the right thing to do. There was no way forward, he'd understood that last night when he'd showed Callie the other side of the apartment.

Christmas had been a fantasy bubble, where neither of them had needed to think about the difficulties and complications of real life. They'd been able to live for the moment, and that was why it had all tasted so intoxicatingly good. But if every day of the year was Christmas Day, the novelty of it would soon wear thin.

He watched her go for as long as he dared. Until the lift began to move downwards and he could no longer see her behind the metal trellis of the gates. Then he kept the promise he'd made and turned away. He would miss her, but this was what they both needed.

CHAPTER TWELVE

THE DULL THROB of missing Ben hadn't eased off in over six weeks. Callie knew that she couldn't contemplate anything other than a parting, and neither could he, but that didn't seem to make things any better. But if she thought *that* was bad, there was worse to follow.

'How was your day?' Sophie, her best friend at the hospital, was sitting in the canteen, a cup of tea in front of her. They'd followed this routine for years, meeting up for half an hour after work every Thursday, whenever their shifts allowed. This Thursday the normality of it was comforting.

'Busy. Have you seen a red-haired boy? Acid burns to his stomach?'

Sophie nodded. 'Yes, he came up onto the ward at lunchtime. You brought him in?'

'Yes. How is he?'

'The burns are second degree. The doctor had a look at him and said that he doesn't need a skin graft. It'll be a while but he'll heal. How did a five-year-old manage to get burns like that?'

'Bottle of bleach under the sink. His mother said that she never screwed the lid back on properly because she couldn't get it open again when she wanted to use it.'

Sophie rolled her eyes. 'Great. Because the whole point

of child-proof containers is for so-called adults to leave them open.'

'Something like that. I don't think she'll be doing it again.'

'Bit bloody late now…' Sophie's blue eyes flashed with anger and Callie nodded.

'Yeah. Keep an eye on him for me, won't you? He's a brave kid.'

Sophie nodded. This was what they did. Talked a little and got the frustrations of a day's work out of their systems. Then Sophie went home to her husband, and Callie went home to…

Another worried, sleepless night. It was about time she grasped the nettle and found out, one way or the other.

'You want one of these?' Sophie pulled a packet of blueberry muffins out of her bag, and offered one to Callie.

'No, thanks. Feeling a bit sick.'

'Oh. Stomach bug?'

'No, I don't think so. I've been feeling like this for more than a week.'

'Probably not something you've eaten, then.' Sophie frowned. 'You're a bit young to be getting an ulcer, but it might be stress…'

'It's not stress.'

Sophie rolled her eyes. 'You don't always know it, these things creep up on you. So what do *you* think it is, then?'

'It's…worse in the mornings.' That should be enough of a clue. By now Callie's mother would have been on her way to the shops to buy wool to knit a pair of bootees.

'Worse in the mornings? If it's acid reflux, you really should go and see someone about that.' Sophie took a sip of tea.

Maybe it was a bit much to expect of Sophie. Callie had been like a rabbit caught in the headlights, immobilised and too afraid to do anything to either confirm or deny her increasing suspicions. Wanting her friend to step in and sweep her off on a tide of common sense when she didn't have all the facts wasn't entirely fair.

'I have amenorrhoea, nausea in the mornings and my breasts are a little swollen and tender.'

Sophie stared at her, her teacup suspended at a precarious angle in mid-air. 'You're pregnant?'

Finally! 'Well, I don't know for sure… Don't spill your tea.'

Callie grabbed the cup and set it down on the table. Sophie was still wide-eyed, obviously trying to decide which question to ask first.

'You haven't taken a test?' Her friend came through for her, asking just the question that Callie wanted her to ask.

'No, I… I was too afraid.'

Sophie's nursing training kicked in. Grabbing her coat and bag from the back of her chair and taking hold of Callie's hand, she marched her to the door of the canteen. 'You're coming with me. Now.'

They drove to Sophie's house, stopping on the way for a visit to the chemist. Jeff, Sophie's husband, greeted Callie warmly, asking if she was staying for dinner, and Sophie bundled him into the kitchen while Callie sat miserably on the sofa. Then she heard the front door bang shut.

'Jeff's gone to the pub.' Sophie appeared in the doorway of the sitting room, the paper bag from the chemist in her hand.

'Soph, I'm sorry. I didn't mean…'

'That's all right. It's quiz night, and his mates will be down there. Do you want a glass of water?'

'No, thanks. I think I'm good.'

'Right.' Sophie jerked her thumb towards the stairs. 'Come on.'

* * *

Callie handed the wand from the pregnancy test kit around
the bathroom door without even looking at it. She heard
Sophie walking downstairs and filled the basin, splashing
water on her face, before following her back to the sitting
room. Sophie waited for her to sit down and then glanced
at the wand again, as if to confirm what she'd seen.

'You're pregnant. It says more than three weeks.' Sophie's voice was calm. That was good, Callie needed some
calm.

'Right. Thanks.'

'Do you know when it happened? Was there a contra-
ceptive failure?'

'I don't remember there being one. We used condoms…
I left it to him.' She'd let herself rely on Ben. 'I'm so stupid.'

'Let's get one thing straight here, Callie. These things
happen. Not often, but abstinence is the only thing that's
one hundred percent and beating yourself up about it isn't
going to help.'

Callie shrugged. 'Oh, so tempting, though.'

'I know. But only you would give yourself a hard time
over finding a reliable guy and leaving it to him to take
care of things. You're still with him?'

'No, it's over. We were together between Christmas
and the New Year.'

'When you were doing the shoot for the calendar?' Sophie's eyebrows shot up. 'He's a fireman?'

'Firefighter's the correct term…' Callie felt numb. She
was pregnant by a man who didn't want to see her again.

'Not in this case. It's clearly a fire*man*.' Sophie stood,
plumping herself down next to Callie on the sofa, putting
her arms around her shoulders. 'I'm reckoning you haven't
told anyone yet. Not your mum?'

'No. You know what Mum's like, she'll think it's all a case of cherubs and wedding bells.'

'You've got a point.' Sophie pressed her lips together. 'You need to tell him.'

Callie shook her head. 'I can do this by myself.'

'Yes, you can. Doesn't mean you should.' Sophie pulled Callie into a tight hug. 'You have choices here, Callie.'

'Thanks, Soph.' Callie could feel tears pricking at the corners of her eyes.

'No problem. You've always got me, you know that, don't you?'

Callie cried a little, clinging to Sophie. Then Sophie made a cup of tea, putting an unnecessary amount of sugar into Callie's cup. Callie appreciated the gesture, even though despair was a more accurate description of her reaction than shock.

'So…have you thought about what you'll do?' Sophie finally asked the question, her tone gentle.

'I'm keeping it.' There had never been any question in Callie's mind about that.

'Good. What about work?'

'I don't want to give up medicine. But I've been thinking about developing my photography, maybe specialising in hospital settings or using it therapeutically.'

Sophie nodded. 'It would be good to have the option to work from home. And it's a great idea. What made you think of it?'

'Someone suggested it to me.' It had been Ben. It seemed that during their few days together he'd touched almost every part of her life. 'I don't know if it's viable.'

'If that's what you want to do then we'll find out. We'll read up on it, and I bet that Dr Lawrence, in the burns unit, would be able to advise you.'

'Thanks Soph. I don't know what I would have done without you.'

Sophie chuckled. 'You're usually the one who knows what to do in any given situation. You've seen me through a few scary times in my life, and I'm glad to return the favour.'

Callie sighed. 'I have to do this right. I'm the one responsible for this baby, and it's going to have a stable, secure childhood.'

'Not like yours, you mean.' Sophie pressed her lips together. 'Callie I know you don't want to hear this, but it is possible to find a man who'll step up and take care of you.'

'That's...complicated.'

'I've got time. I'd say I had a bottle of red in the kitchen but that's not much use at the moment.'

'Don't let me stop you. Have you got anything to eat?'

'You're hungry?' Sophie grinned. 'That's good. I've got some pasta and I'll make a Bolognese sauce. I'll drink for both of us while I'm cooking.'

'So...he's as much of a commitment-phobe as you are.' Sophie paused to stir the sauce and take a swig from her glass. 'Who knew that there were two of you?'

Callie smiled. Sophie had a way of making everything seem better, and she was beginning to feel that she might be equal to whatever was coming next.

'Well, it seemed a perfect fit at the time.'

'I'm sure it did. Which month is he in the calendar?' Sophie had already seen the photographs that Callie had taken, and her choices for the various months.

'He's one of the September ones.'

'September... September...' Sophie clicked her fingers, obviously trying to remember which photos Callie had selected for September. 'September! Mr Blue Eyes?'

'Yes.'

'You never said you slept with Mr Blue Eyes! Is he as gorgeous as the photo, or did you do something to it?'

'I don't airbrush my photos. He's…' More gorgeous. Callie swallowed down the thought, because that was only going to lead to heartbreak.

Sophie shook her head. 'All right, that's probably a bit too much information. Is he someone you'd want to be a father to your baby?'

'I can't tell him…' Callie felt a new, different panic start to overwhelm her.

'Don't you think he *should* know? At least give him the chance…'

'It's not that simple, Soph. His ex-girlfriend told him she was pregnant after they split up.'

'The one you said stalked him? He has a child with her?'

'After Ben told her that he'd look after her and the baby, but they couldn't be a couple, she said she'd made a mistake and that she wasn't pregnant after all.' Sophie's eyebrows shot up and Callie shrugged in answer to her unspoken question.

'I don't know, Soph. It didn't sound all that believable to me, but he's too honourable to say so. He said he knew the situation wasn't ideal, but he'd always wanted children and he was really upset when she told him she wasn't pregnant.'

Sophie thought for a moment. 'To be honest with you, Callie, if you were going to choose a father for your child, he doesn't sound like a bad bet. I know you grew up without your dad, but at least you know who he was. And this guy's honourable, and he wants kids…'

'That's just the problem, though. Suppose he does all the right things, and we get back together for the baby's sake. It didn't last at Christmas, and there's no reason why it should be any different next time around.' The only thing

worse than not having Ben would be having him again and
then losing him.

'Well…maybe make it clear that a relationship between
you two isn't on the table. Tell him that it's just a matter
of him knowing his child.'

'I suppose so.' It would be hard, but Callie could do it.
For the sake of her child, she could do almost anything. 'I
think… I'm going to leave it a little while, though. Until
I'm more sure.'

'You mean until you're showing? So there's no question
in his mind that you actually *are* pregnant?'

Callie nodded. It would remove one of the difficulties,
and it would give her plenty of time to think about what
she was going to say to Ben.

CHAPTER THIRTEEN

Six months later

BEN HAD THOUGHT he'd caught a glimpse Callie. The woman had been sitting in the passenger seat of a car that had parked across the road to the entrance to his apartment building. He'd cursed himself roundly as he'd thought he'd stopped seeing her face in crowds and catching her scent when no one was there.

Maybe he shouldn't have ignored the text Callie had sent last month. Maybe he should have agreed to see her again, just once more, to lay the ghosts to rest. But Ben knew that it wasn't going to work that way. Seeing Callie again would just re-set the clock on the process of trying to forget her. Nothing had changed, and their ending would be exactly the same.

He entered his apartment, slinging his jacket onto the back of the nearest chair and opening a few windows so that a breeze would begin to circulate. It had been a long night, and this morning all he wanted to do was take a shower, then eat something and go to bed.

Ben heard the tap on his door as he walked back downstairs to the kitchen. Wondering who it was, he ran his hand through his wet hair to tidy it a bit and opened the door.

For a moment he wondered whether he *was* seeing

ghosts. Her corn-blonde hair was curling softly around her face now, instead of being blow-dried straight. The image of the woman he'd slept with kicked him hard in the gut, only to be followed a split second later with a blow that almost brought him to his knees. She wasn't just pregnant. She was *very* pregnant.

'Callie…!'

'Hi. I rang the bell downstairs and someone let me in.' Her hand fluttered nervously to her stomach.

'I was in the shower.' As if it mattered. But the conversation seemed to be continuing under its own steam, while Ben's mind screamed in disbelief.

'I'm sorry if this isn't a convenient time.' Her gaze was clear-eyed and determined. A stab of guilt accompanied the thought that he really should have answered her text.

'It's…it's fine. I'm off shift now for three days.'

She nodded. 'I know. I looked up the rota on the fire station's website.'

Ben hadn't been aware that the watch rotas were even published on the website. But, then, he never had much occasion to visit it. Callie had obviously carefully picked her time to come here, perhaps reckoning that he might need a couple of days off work to get over the shock.

Shock. That was it. That was why he was standing there gawping at her and thinking about websites when there were far more important things to consider. It was why his limbs felt that they'd lost the power of movement. He needed to pull himself together.

'Please. Come in.' He stepped back from the doorway, watching her as she walked inside. She wore leggings and a pair of trainers, with a light summer top that fell loose over her stomach, reaching down to her hips. Pretty and practical. Less guarded somehow than the image she'd clung to when…

When he'd had sex with her. *He'd had sex with her and now she was pregnant.* The idea that the latter might well be a direct consequence of the former screamed in his head.

'How are you?' She looked up at him. Her gaze was less guarded too.

'Fine. Good.' The thoughts crowding his head seemed to have left him unable to frame a longer sentence. Ben took a breath, making an effort to at least say something.

'Come and sit down. Would you like a cup of tea or some juice?'

'Some juice would be great, if you have it.' Callie walked over to the breakfast bar and clambered up onto a high stool, exerting a little more effort in doing so that he remembered. Before he turned away from her to open the fridge door, he caught a glimpse of her drawing something out of her handbag. Ben poured two glasses of juice and when he turned back to face her she pushed a folded sheet of paper across the counter towards him.

'Since there's an elephant in the room, and I appear to be it...' She gave him a smile, as if she understood that he was struggling. 'As you can probably see, I'm going to have a baby. It was conceived in late December, here's my due date from the prenatal clinic.'

'Just tell me, Callie. Is the baby mine? Ours...' Finally. He'd managed to say something that sounded vaguely like the right thing.

'Yes. There's no doubt. But I want you to be sure too. There's no question you can't ask me.'

Where to start? 'Why...did you wait this long? Before you told me?'

She pressed her lips together. Clearly some questions were harder to answer than others. 'At first I wanted to be sure. Then I wanted to think things through a little. Time got away from me…'

She'd been afraid. Afraid to tell him, in case he didn't believe her. Or he told her he wanted nothing to do with the baby. Ben didn't quite know what he wanted at the moment, but he was sure of two things. If Callie said that this was his baby, he believed her. And if it was his baby, he wanted to be a father to it.

'We should—'

'Don't!' Her tone was almost sharp, and she gave a nervous smile. 'There's no *we*, Ben. I came to tell you this because you have a right to know. I don't expect anything from you, and I know it's a shock so I don't want you to say anything before you've thought about it.'

Yes, it was a shock. And the greatest shock of all was the way that his heart was pounding with joy at the thought that Callie was pregnant with *his* child. The way he wanted to take her in his arms and protect her. Now. From whatever threat he could think of.

He took a gulp of juice from his glass. It didn't surprise him all that much that Callie had a plan, and right now he wanted to know what that was. Needed to know whether he had some part in it.

'It's the last thing I thought would happen, but…that doesn't mean that I'm not here for you, Callie.'

She nodded. 'It's your choice, Ben. I won't stop you from being involved with your child if that's what you want.'

Callie had clearly already ruled out the possibility of a relationship between them, and he could live with that. He had done for the last eight months. But this… This changed everything.

She drained her glass and started to wriggle uncertainly

towards the edge of the stool. Ben rounded the counter, taking her arm and helping her down.

'Thanks.' She accepted his help but as soon as her feet were on the floor she moved away from him, delving into her bag and withdrawing another sheet of paper. 'This is my address and my phone number. When you've thought about things a bit, you can give me a call.'

'You're going?'

'It's probably best to leave you to think about this.'

She was right. He should marshal his thoughts before he said anything else, but the one thing he wanted her to know was that he'd be there for her.

'Tomorrow afternoon. May I come and see you then?'

'Tomorrow afternoon's fine. Does about two o'clock suit you?'

'Two it is. I'll be there.'

She nodded, making her way to the door. The sudden feeling that she couldn't—mustn't—go just yet seized Ben. 'How are you getting home now?'

'I came with a friend. She's waiting outside in the car.'

'Right. Well…be safe, Callie.'

She grinned at him. 'I always am. I'll see you tomorrow.'

'Wait…' She'd got almost to the door before Ben realised that there was one more piece of information that he had to know. 'Do you know whether it's a boy or a girl?'

'Yes. You'd like to know?'

'It doesn't make any difference to the way I feel but… Yes, I'd like to know.'

'It's a girl.'

She refused to allow him to see her downstairs and almost glared at him when he stood at the doorway, watching her into the lift. Ben waited until she'd disappeared from view before closing the door. Walking over to the sofa, he threw himself down on the cushions before his legs decided to give way.

He had a little more than twenty-four hours to get his act together. Ben stared up at the ceiling, too shell-shocked for anything other than one thought.

Callie was having *his* child. His daughter.

Callie was shaking. She'd made the step. *I'll do it tomorrow* had finally turned into *I'll do it today* and it hadn't been as bad as she'd expected it to be. She'd made her intentions clear, and Ben hadn't questioned whether he was the father of her baby. Maybe that would come later, after he'd thought about it a bit.

His car drew up outside her house at exactly two o'clock. It was something of a relief that he wasn't late. Callie had been sitting watching the road for the last half-hour, and she didn't think she could take much more of this. She watched him get out, and to her horror he reached back into the car, bringing out a bunch of flowers.

He didn't get it. This wasn't about flowers or promises. It was all about working out something that they could both live with long term, and having the gumption to stick with it. You didn't bring flowers to a business meeting, and Callie was determined to take the emotion out and be businesslike about this. She could think more clearly when she wasn't fantasising about his touch.

She took a deep breath as she walked to the door. Ben looked like a nervous suitor on a first date. He was wearing a tie and holding the flowers as if they were some kind of defensive measure.

At least they weren't roses. He proffered the bright yellow and orange blooms and she took them. She supposed that putting them in water would give her something to do with her hands, rather than clasping them together, her nails digging into her palms.

'How are you?' he enquired solicitously.

'Good, thank you.' If you didn't count the light-headedness and the constant feeling that she was about to be sick. That had been bugging her for a day or so now, and was probably more to do with Ben than her pregnancy.

'Have you just moved in here?' He was looking around the freshly painted hallway, and his gaze lit on the stack of mover's crates under the stairs.

'Yes, I…was thinking of selling my flat and getting a small house, and this place came up. It didn't seem quite the right time to be moving but it was too good to miss.'

'And you've been decorating?' There was a trace of reproach in his tone.

'I haven't been doing it myself. The last owner had a penchant for primary colours, which is probably why he had a problem selling it. I got the painters in and they did the whole place in cream. That'll be fine for the time being.'

'If you need any help…'

'Thanks, but no. The sitting room and bedroom are both sorted, and the kitchen and bathroom aren't my choice of colour but they're both pretty much new. I have all that I need.'

He nodded and followed her through into the kitchen, still looking around as if he was assessing the house to see if it was fit for purpose. Callie ignored him, fetching a vase from under the sink and dumping the flowers into it.

'Coffee?'

He shook his head. 'I've had too much coffee already this morning. Do you have tea?'

'About twenty different kinds. My mother's been bombarding me with tea for months.' She opened the cupboard to reveal the stack of boxes.

'Regular tea will be fine, thanks. Your mother... She knows about this clearly.'

'Yes, she and Paul have been great...' Callie bit her tongue. She deserved the look of reproach in Ben's eyes. Other people had known about this for months when he hadn't.

'Paul's her partner. They've been seeing each other since last year and... I think she's found someone at last...' Callie saw her hand shake as she reached for the teabags.

'I'm glad you have their support.' His face softened suddenly. 'You have mine too.'

He carried the tea into the sitting room, and Callie let him do it. If he wanted to help, he could do the things that didn't matter so much, the things that she wouldn't miss if he left. Then he produced a piece of paper from his pocket.

'I've written this down. What I'd like...' He handed the paper to her and Callie took it, unfolding the single sheet. There were just two sentences and numbering them seemed a little over the top.

'Number one... No. I don't need you to help support me and my baby.'

'*Our* baby,' he corrected her quietly.

He could say that when his ankles started to swell and he couldn't get comfortable in bed at night. When tying his shoelaces started to become an exercise in balance and reach, and he'd been prodded and pummelled by what seemed like a whole army of doctors and nurses. Callie let that point go in favour of the greater principle.

'My photography's going well and... I'm sure I can manage.' *Sure* was a little bit of an overstatement, *hope* was a bit more like it. But she'd explored her options and the photographs she'd taken at the fire station had added a different slant to her portfolio, which had helped a lot.

'My offer isn't negotiable.'

'Neither is my refusal.'

They'd fallen at the first fence. Quiet words, which showed how diametrically they were opposed in their approach to this. Callie stared at him and he stared back.

Ben was the first to break the impasse. 'Okay. I'll set up an account and pay the money into it monthly. If you need it, it's there. If not, it's there to cover her university tuition fees.'

'She's going to university?' Callie hadn't thought that far ahead. That was the difference between them, she was focussed on getting through the next few months and he didn't have to worry about that. He could afford a few big dreams.

'When she's eighteen she can do whatever she wants. The money will be there for her.'

'Okay. I...guess that's between you and her.' If it happened then it happened. If Ben lost interest, she could provide for her daughter.

'We're in agreement, then?'

'Yes.'

'And number two?' He was doing it gently, but he was pushing her.

'Yes. You can have regular access to her, that's not a problem. We can sort something out...'

'Can we do that now?'

'No. We have to see what works and...' She felt dizzy, and Ben was going too fast. Sudden pain shot across her belly.

'Callie...? Are you all right?'

'Yes!' She took a breath to steady herself. 'Yes, I'm fine. I dare say something's hit a nerve somewhere...' If this was a new pain, to add to the other nagging aches and pains, it was one that Callie could do without. Particularly when she was engaged in negotiating with Ben over her daughter's future.

She shifted on the sofa, feeling a sudden warmth between her legs. Before she could check to see what it was, Ben's face told her that something really *was* the matter.

CHAPTER FOURTEEN

HE'D EXPECTED HER to agree to number one straight away, and then fight him on number two. It was just like Callie to do the opposite. She might look a little softer but she was still determined to do things her way.

And determined not to take his help. Her face had contorted in pain, but she'd just kept on insisting that she was all right and it was just one of those things.

Then she'd moved, and he'd seen the blood soaking into the pale fabric of the sofa cushions. That definitely wasn't one of those things, and she wasn't all right.

She knew it too. She looked at him with frightened eyes, perhaps realising that even her carefully primed defences couldn't stop this.

But she was still trying to deal with it alone. Callie tried to get to her feet, her hand reaching for her phone, and he gently sat her back down again. 'Stay still, Callie. I'm calling for an ambulance.'

'Yes.' There was no compliance in her eyes but there *was* fear. He'd take fear. Whatever allowed him to help her. Ben took his own phone from his pocket, dialling quickly.

'Tell them... I don't think I'm in labour yet. I feel light-headed and sick, and...' She looked miserably at the spreading stain on the sofa. 'Severe vaginal bleeding... Possibility of *placenta abruptio*.'

Ben relayed the information, adding that Callie was a paramedic to justify the attempt at self-diagnosis. The woman on the other end of the line told him that someone would be there in ten minutes, and Ben begged her to ask them to hurry. He wasn't exactly sure what *placenta abruptio* was, but he knew enough to understand that it wasn't good.

'I'm just going to breathe and stay calm.' Callie took the words right out of his mouth. 'They'll be here soon.'

'That's exactly right. Do you want to lie down?'

'Yes… I think so.'

He gently helped her to lie down on the sofa. Then knelt down beside her and held out his hand.

'Go on. Take it. We can forget it ever happened.'

She quirked her lips downwards, and then she took his hand. 'Our secret, eh?'

'Yes. Our secret.'

For a moment the old understanding flashed between them. If Callie would accept this temporary truce, that was a beginning. Temporary could be stretched until it resembled permanent.

'I need to call my mum.' She gestured towards her phone again. Ben picked it up and switched it on, scrolling through the contacts and dialling the number before giving it to her.

It seemed almost wrong to listen to her conversation, but Ben wasn't going to leave her side. Callie was making an effort to downplay the situation, but when she handed the phone over to him so he could take her mother's number, the woman on the other end of the line sounded worried.

'Text me when you know which hospital they're taking her to. And don't you leave her alone for one second until I arrive.'

'I won't.' He wasn't even sure whether Callie's mother

knew who he was, and she rang off before he could tell her. He should have let her know that he would do anything, if only Callie and the baby were all right.

He held her tightly when her face contorted with pain and didn't let go when it passed. Ben was used to waiting for medical help, he'd done it many times before, but this time… It had never felt that he was so inextricably linked with someone that his own survival was entirely dependent on theirs.

'They're here…' Blue flashing lights reflected through the windows and across the room. Ben hurried to the front door, wishing that the two men would walk a little faster up the front path.

He ushered them through to the sitting room and the older of the two knelt beside Callie. Their exchanged smiles made it clear that this was one of Callie's colleagues.

'All right, lass. Symptoms…'

Callie rattled her symptoms off, seeming to rally a little now that the ambulance was here. Someone she knew. And trusted. Ben stood back, out of the way, fighting the urge to be the one that she clung to.

'I think there's a possibility of *placenta*—'

'Give it a rest, Callie. I can't abide patients who tell me what's wrong with them, you know that.'

'So what do *you* think?'

'Possibility of *placenta abruptio*.' The paramedic gave her a reassuring smile. 'We'll get you to the hospital now, and they'll confirm it.'

Callie puffed out a sigh. 'That's a hospital stay at best. Or they may have to do a Caesarean…'

'We'll see. One thing at a time, eh? You know the doctors don't much like it when we tell them what to do, even if we do know better than them.'

'Tell me about it.'

Ben was at a loss. He couldn't walk away and leave the medics to do their job, the way he usually did. He had to *know*. 'Please…what's wrong with her?'

The man flipped a querying look at Callie and she nodded. He turned to Ben. 'It's possible that Callie is suffering from *placenta abruptio*, which is where the placenta separates from the wall of the uterus. It's something we take very seriously.'

'What does that mean?'

'It means that I might have to have the baby by Caesarean section. Now, before it becomes distressed or I bleed to death.' Callie was obviously in no mood to beat about the bush.

'Right. Thanks. We'll go now?'

'Yes, my partner's gone to get a wheelchair. We'll get her there as quickly as we can.'

'I'd like to go with her.' The desperate feeling that he had no right to insist on anything, but every reason to, gripped Ben.

The paramedic's gaze flipped once more to Callie in an unspoken question and Ben held his breath.

'Let him come. He's the father.'

Callie was surrounded by nurses and a doctor as soon as she reached the hospital. The ambulance crew stayed for ten minutes before they had to leave for another call, leaving Ben standing alone in the corner of the cubicle.

'She'll be all right. She's in good hands.' A nurse patted his arm. She was obviously the one who'd been assigned to calm the nervous father.

'Thank you.' Ben craned his neck, trying to hear and see as much as he could of what was going on. If there were decisions to be made, he at least wanted to know what they were, even if it was unlikely that Callie would give him any say in them.

Finally, the doctor turned and explained to him that Callie was bleeding heavily and that a Caesarean section was needed. He added that it was a straightforward procedure and that Ben could look forward to welcoming his baby a little earlier than he'd thought.

Ben nodded his thanks, omitting to say that he hadn't had a chance to think anything yet. The doctor hurried out of the cubicle, and finally Ben could take his place at Callie's side.

'Hey, there.'

'You're still here?' She looked up at him a little blearily.

'No, I'm just a figment of your imagination.'

'Okay. That's fair enough.' She smiled at him, squeezing his hand, and Ben felt his overworked heart in danger of bursting.

A nurse arrived to take Callie down to the operating theatre, and hard on her heels came a woman who bore a marked physical resemblance to Callie.

'Mum…' Callie called for her, holding out her hand, and Ben stepped back again, wondering what he was supposed to do now.

There was no chance to do anything. The nurse released the brakes on the trolley that Callie was lying on, and before Ben could tell her any of the things he wanted to say, the trolley was manoeuvred out of the cubicle. Callie's mother ran a few steps to catch up, taking Callie's hand as she was wheeled away.

He should be glad that her mother had arrived in time. Callie had clearly arranged that her mother should be there at the birth, and she needed her right now. But all Ben could see was that Callie was being taken from him.

A neatly dressed man of about sixty approached him. 'You're Ben?'

Ben nodded, keeping his eyes on the trolley and the retreating figures of the nurse and Callie's mother.

'I'm Paul. Callie's mother's partner. Shall we wait together?'

Ben followed Paul to the waiting room in a daze, glad that at least someone seemed to know what to do next. Stopping to drop a few coins in the vending machine, Paul brought two cups of tea over and sat down next to Ben.

'The waiting's the worst part. It'll all be worth it, though.'

'You have children?' Ben took a sip of his tea, thankful that this kindly man was here. Without someone to talk to he'd probably be banging his head against the wall.

'Two girls. My wife died when they were teenagers.'

'So you brought them up on your own?'

Paul nodded. 'I didn't think I'd find anyone else. But then I met Kate, Callie's mother. Just goes to show…'

'Goes to show what?'

'That you never know what's around the corner, waiting for you.'

Ben allowed himself a smile. Callie had said that her mother had finally found the right man, and he was willing to grab at any slender proof that life might allow second chances. He had to believe that was the case, that Callie and their daughter would be all right, and that somehow they could find a way through this.

After what seemed an age, a nurse popped her head around the door of the waiting room, calling out Ben's name. He stared at her for a moment, almost afraid to hear what she'd come to tell him.

'Go on. What are you waiting for?' Paul spoke quietly.

Ben got to his feet and hurried over. The nurse smiled at him.

'Mother and baby are both doing well. Callie's had a Caesarean section, and she'll be very drowsy for a little while. Her mother's with her and they'll be taking her back to the maternity ward soon. You can go and see her there.'

'Thank you. And the baby?'

'It's a beautiful, healthy girl. She's a little premature, so she'll be looked after in the high dependency care unit for a few days, but that's just a precaution.'

'Can we see her?' Ben heard Paul's voice behind him. 'I'm sure Ben would like to see his daughter.'

'Yes. Very much.' He was feeling a little unsteady on his feet, but he shot a grateful look in Paul's direction.

'I'll take you there now.' The nurse began to walk briskly along the corridor, leaving Ben and Paul to follow.

The high dependency unit was a large, quiet ward, all gleaming surfaces and technology. The nurse guided Ben to an incubator, and he looked at the tiny baby inside, willing her to open her eyes.

'She doesn't need any help breathing, and she's a good weight for being a month premature. Six pounds exactly.'

Ben couldn't stop staring at his daughter. *His* daughter.

'Kate said that you were going to call her Emily.' The nurse spoke again.

'Emily?' Ben could feel tears forming in his eyes.

The nurse laughed quietly. The fact that Ben didn't even know his daughter's name didn't seem to bother her. Maybe all new fathers were this dumbfounded, or maybe she'd just seen everything. 'I'll leave you here to get acquainted.'

'May I take a picture?' Something to take away with him, to remind him that this was real.

'Yes, of course. Callie got to hold Emily for a little while in the recovery room, but I'm sure she'd like a photograph.'

Ben took his phone from his pocket. At last, there was something he *could* do.

Paul accompanied him back to the maternity ward and they waited outside Callie's room for a moment before Kate appeared, her face shining.

'I won't stay, she's still groggy. But she'd like to see you for a couple of minutes, Ben.'

'Thank you.' Ben wondered whether the suggestion had come from Kate or from Callie, but right now that didn't matter. He had his entry pass and he wasn't going to argue.

'I think we should be going. We can come back in the morning.' Paul put his arm around Kate. 'We'll see you then?'

Wild horses wouldn't keep him away. He shook Paul's hand, thanking him, and opened the door to Callie's room quietly. She was lying still on the bed but her eyes were open, following him as he moved towards her. He smiled and suddenly a broad grin lit up her tired face.

'You did it, then.'

'Yes. I did it.'

Their connection, which had seemed so remote over the last two days, seemed forged anew. Ben sat down beside the bed.

'And you made a great job of it. She's beautiful.'

Callie chuckled quietly. 'Yes, she is. She's got blue eyes...'

'Most newborn Caucasian babies have blue eyes.' It was one of the few things that Ben knew about babies. He was committed to knowing more as soon as he possibly could.

'She has a little bit of dark hair as well.'

Like her daddy. The thought made the world swim

around Ben slightly. He wondered whether Callie would ever say them.

'I didn't see her hair, she had one of those little hats on.'

'She has a tiny birthmark on one of her fingers and she weighs six pounds. That's good for a late pre-term baby.' Tears formed in her eyes. 'I know I'll be able to see her in the morning but I just want to hold her now.'

'Of course you do…' There was no point in saying that this was for the best, and that their baby was being well looked after. Callie already knew that.

He reached into his pocket and brought out his phone. 'Here…' He'd taken a video of the tiny baby, keeping it running until the memory on his phone gave out. Holding it in front of Callie, he saw her immediately transfixed by the small screen, her face mirroring each movement and each of the tiny grimaces on her daughter's face.

'She knows how to pull a face already.' He reached for Callie's hand, squeezing it, and she squeezed back. The regulator on the transfusion lead attached to her arm dripped a little faster.

Tears formed in Callie's eyes. 'Yes, she does. Thank you, Ben. Thank you so much.'

'Keep watching. And keep squeezing my hand.'

She glanced at the regulator and nodded, then her gaze was fixed back on the small screen. When the tiny baby sneezed, her own face scrunched up, as if she was trying not to.

'How are you feeling?'

'Very numb still.' She tried for a laugh and then thought better of it. 'The bits of me that aren't numb are starting to hurt.'

'You'll feel better soon.' Ben had no idea whether or not that was correct, but it sounded like the right thing to say. 'You're strong. Like her.' *That* he knew.

'Play it again.' She nodded towards his phone.

'Okay.' Ben wanted to watch it again, too. 'Keep squeezing my hand.'

The nurse brought in a milky drink for her, and Callie took one taste and scrunched her face up. Ben laughingly encouraged her to drink, helping her hold the cup. She was weak and shaky still, and if she was going to be able to hold her baby, she needed to build up her strength.

She was fighting sleep, wanting to see the video a third time, but Ben switched it off and made her close her eyes. As they talked quietly, Callie's voice became slower, more slurred, and finally she drifted off to sleep.

Ben settled in the easy chair, watching her. He imagined Callie wouldn't like the idea of his standing guard over her while she slept, but since she *was* asleep, she didn't have much say in the matter.

He was beginning to relax, soothed by the sounds of Callie's regular breathing, when the door opened quietly and a dark-haired nurse entered. She smiled at Ben and walked over to Callie's bedside, reaching out to brush her forehead with her fingertips.

'I'm Sophie, Callie's friend. You must be Ben.' She spoke in a whisper.

Ben nodded. When Callie's family and friends were around, his claim to her seemed to grow more tenuous. If Sophie wanted to throw him out, she probably had the authority to do so.

'How is she?'

'The doctor said she's doing well. She's very tired…'

'Yeah, I'll bet she is. I came as soon as my shift ended.' Sophie sat down in an upright chair next to the bedside. 'How are you?'

'Me?' Ben wondered how much Sophie knew.

She grinned at him. 'I was in the car outside your apartment yesterday, waiting for Callie. She left it a bit too long before she told you so this must all be a shock.'

The impulse to defend Callie tightened in his chest. 'It's okay. She had her reasons.'

'All the same…' Sophie subjected him to a steady, en-quiring look, and when Ben didn't reply, she let the matter drop. 'You've seen your daughter?'

'Yes. She's beautiful… Perfect.'

Sophie looked at him thoughtfully. 'You want to stay?'

Ben had nowhere else to go. The only home he had was with Callie and his little girl. And whatever Callie had told her friend about him, it couldn't be all that bad, because she seemed willing to let him remain here.

'Yes. I…' He shrugged. 'If the staff tell me to leave, I'll sit outside.'

'Okay, I'll have a word. They won't kick you out.' Sophie rose, stopping for one last look at her friend. 'I'll see you again?'

'Yes, you will. Quite a lot, I imagine.'

'Good.'

When the door closed quietly behind Sophie and Ben had settled back in his chair, it occurred to him that he'd passed some kind of test. There would be more to come, a lot more, but at least this was a start.

CHAPTER FIFTEEN

BEN HAD BEEN there for her. He'd done more than possibly could have been expected of him over the last few days, coming to the hospital every morning and spending the day there. The joy and indignity of being a new mother had made Callie forget for a while that she'd promised herself that she could do this on her own.

When he'd told her that he was taking two weeks' emergency leave from work, she'd protested. But he hadn't listened, insisting that he wanted to be there. He clearly wasn't sleeping much and even though he smiled every time he looked at their little girl, there were dark rings under his eyes.

Callie watched him as he sat rocking their baby. She'd be released from the high dependency unit in a few days, and then Callie could take her home.

'I've been thinking. About her name.' Callie hadn't once called her daughter Emily, it didn't seem to suit her.

'Yeah?' Ben had steered clear of the decision-making. He was there, always listening, but he always deferred to Callie's opinion.

'Do you think that she really looks like an Emily?'

Ben considered the thought carefully. 'Most of the babies here don't really *look* like their given names. I dare say they'll grow into them.'

That was about as close as Ben was going to get to speaking his mind. Callie pursed her lips. 'Only... I just can't get used to Emily. I love the name, but...it just doesn't seem to fit.'

Ben chuckled. He obviously thought the same. 'So what did you have in mind?'

'I don't know really.' Callie had thought of a few names she liked better, but she wanted to hear what Ben thought as well. 'Any ideas?'

He smiled and shook his head, answering too quickly to have thought about it at all. 'No, not really.'

'Go on. Don't you have any favourite names?'

Ben sat for a moment, holding the tiny baby. Then he drew in a breath. 'What about Riley? You probably don't like it...'

Callie said the name a couple of times, trying it out for size. She liked it a lot. 'What made you come up with that?' Perhaps one of the guys at the fire station had a kid named Riley.

'When my sister was pregnant, she wanted my brother-in-law to come up with a few names...he was a bit stuck and we went to the pub to brainstorm it. I liked Riley but he didn't, so it never made it onto the shortlist. It means *valiant*.'

That was exactly what Callie was going to teach her daughter to be. Valiant. 'I really like it.'

Ben looked shocked. 'Do you?'

'Yes, I do.' She cooed the name a couple of times, and the little girl opened her eyes. 'She likes it too...'

'She's probably just hungry.'

Callie ignored him. She knew what her daughter liked and didn't like. 'I think Riley's a great name. Let's call her that.'

He gave her a smile so bright and enchanting that there

was no question about Ben's approval. And no question that he appreciated having been asked in the first place. 'If that's what you want, I think it really suits her.'

Callie had brought Riley home when she was five days old. Her mother had moved in for a while to help with the baby and Ben had visited every day, busying himself with helping to unpack crates and finding jobs to do around the house when he hadn't been spending time with his daughter.

It had been time well spent. He and Callie had talked about access to Riley on an ongoing basis, and it seemed she was committed to making it easy for him and working around his shift patterns. And he'd fallen in love with his daughter.

All the same, the idea of going back to work was a relief. Helping make Callie's house into a home had been a little too much like having someone to build a home and family with. They were lost dreams, and he needed to get back to the realities.

But even the reality of going back to work had changed. When he walked into the ready room he found that Blue Watch had embraced the unexpected news that he was a father. A loud bang produced a shower of sparks and streamers and everyone crowded around to shake his hand.

Ben endured the jokes and friendly advice and managed to ignore the words 'dark horse' when he heard them. Eve had waited until he was alone again and proffered a brightly wrapped package that she'd been holding behind her back.

'Eve…thank you.' Ben didn't know what to say. This was an aspect of parenthood that he hadn't quite counted on.

'It's just a little something…for the baby.' Eve seemed as embarrassed as he was.

'I...' Ben stared at the package. 'Should I open it now?'

'No, boss! You're supposed to give it to Callie and let her open it.' Eve grinned suddenly. 'You haven't got the hang of this yet, have you?'

'No, I haven't. It was all a bit of a shock.' Ben wondered whether Eve would ask. He almost wished that she would. 'I didn't expect anyone to make a fuss...'

Eve shrugged. 'A baby's something special. It doesn't matter how it happens.'

All the same, Ben felt like a fraud. His only real contribution to Callie's pregnancy had been the obvious one at the very start. And now people were slapping him on the back and giving him presents.

'I don't know... How do you do this, Eve?' He'd take whatever advice was on offer.

'Babies don't come with an operations manual—you have to deal with everything as it comes. You'll be fine.' Eve shot him a smile and turned away.

He retreated to his office, making a mental list of all the things he needed to do now that he was back at work. Then his phone vibrated. Callie had sent a video of Riley. Ben stared at the notification, his finger hovering over the play icon. Then he threw his phone down onto the desk, hearing the bell ring as he did so.

The crew had been summoned to a small fire on one of the few pieces of waste ground left in the densely populated city. It was a simple enough job to extinguish the flames but it seemed somehow surreal.

'Steady on, boss...' Ben almost tripped over a coiled length of hose and he turned just in time to see Jamie flash a knowing smile towards Eve. Yeah, okay. He still had his baby head on.

And Callie hadn't exactly helped. He'd managed to get

his head around not seeing her and Riley for five days, but now all he could think about was that video.

'Sorry...' Ben decided that if he couldn't watch where he was putting his feet the best place for him was out of the way, standing next to the tender. He was used to the fact that Blue Watch could operate perfectly well without him, he'd encouraged that during their training exercises. Being a liability was new, though.

This couldn't go on. Compartmentalisation was the way forward. When he was on duty he had to be a leader. Off duty was the time to be a father. Ben decided not to look at his phone again until the shift was finished.

That evening, when he retrieved his phone from his locker, there was another text from Callie. Before he had a chance to look at it, the phone buzzed again.

How was your day?

Callie was probably feeling the same as him, that all this was unbearably strange. They both had to find their feet, but it was just as well to start as they meant to go on.

Good. Can't text while working.

He sent the text before he had time to think that it sounded a little curt. His phone buzzed again, almost immediately.

Sorry.

Ben cursed under his breath. He'd upset her now.

It's okay. Busy day.

It hadn't been a particularly busy day. If he was starting as he meant to go on, a little honesty would be better than excuses. But the text had been sent now. He typed another.

Thanks for the video. Looking forward to seeing you on Wednesday. Eve sent a present. I'll bring it with me.

His phone buzzed again. It would actually be easier to call Callie but something stopped him.

That's so kind. What is it?

So Callie didn't know that they were supposed to open it together either. Ben smiled. They were both on a learning curve.

I don't know. She says you have to open it. Wait until Wednesday.

He added a smiley face and put his phone in his pocket, slamming his locker door shut. Wednesday seemed a long time away, and he'd just ruled out any possibility of more texts in the meantime. That was how it should be, though. They were both adults, and surviving for a few days on their own shouldn't be that hard.

CHAPTER SIXTEEN

IT HAD BEEN five days since she'd seen Ben, and Callie had spent much of that time thinking about him. Perhaps it was her hormones.

The texts had been a mistake. Ben had made it very clear that he didn't want to indulge in the to and fro of sending videos and *How are you?* messages on the days he was working. And Callie had decided that she needed to clear the air, leave nothing unspoken, because it was the things that were left unsaid that generally did the most damage to a relationship.

He was on her doorstep at exactly two o'clock on Wednesday afternoon. Ben was nothing if not prompt.

'How are you?' That was always his first question, and always accompanied by a tight smile.

'Fine, thanks.' Callie stood back from the door to allow him in. As he passed her in the hallway she caught a delicious curl of his scent. She needed to ignore that. He was Riley's father, and that was bound to flip a switch somewhere.

'Where's Kate?' He walked into the sitting room, looking around.

'She's popped out for some shopping. Riley's sleeping.' Maybe he wouldn't notice that this opportunity to talk had been carefully contrived.

If he did, he gave no hint of it. Ben's smile was inscrutable, calculated not to give anything away. Inscrutable was probably a lot easier for him than it was for her at the moment as he didn't have raging hormones to contend with.

'I wanted to say…' Callie lowered herself carefully onto the sofa. 'I'm sorry about the texts.'

He shook his head. 'It doesn't matter. That was a great video of Riley.'

It *had* mattered. Callie had known it almost as soon as she'd sent it, and when he hadn't replied straight away it had confirmed her fears.

'Ben, I wish that…'

'What?' He gave her an innocent look.

'I wish that we could have an adult conversation. There are things that we need to work out and… Can't you just tell me how you feel about this?'

'I don't matter. You and Riley are the ones who matter.'

'Stop it. You *do* matter.' Callie could feel tears in her eyes and she blinked them away impatiently. 'Look, there's no walking-away option here. Not for me anyway. Riley will always be my daughter and you'll always be her father.'

He looked at her thoughtfully. 'I don't have a walking-away option either.'

'Right, then. In that case we both need to say how we feel. Because that's the only way forward.'

'You're right.'

Callie puffed out an exasperated breath. Ben had been letting her off the hook about things, telling her that everything was okay for the last three weeks. He couldn't keep this up and at some point he was going to explode.

If he couldn't do it now, maybe he'd think about it and do it later. Callie wondered whether she should get up and make a cup of tea, and decided that the effort of standing could wait a little longer.

'I'm angry.' His quiet words didn't sound all that angry but at least he'd said them. It was a start.

'About?' Callie felt herself starting to tremble.

Ben sucked in a deep breath. 'Were you really so afraid of me that it took eight months to work up the courage to tell me you were pregnant?'

'I'm not afraid of you. After what you went through with Isabel, I decided to wait until…you could be sure.'

'I imagine it had been obvious for a while.' He shook his head, clearly trying to understand but unable to. 'Isn't it just that you wanted to be the one to provide for Riley? You didn't want me to have any part in her life?'

The quiet vehemence in his tone shocked Callie. But this was what she'd wanted, to clear the air between them and for Ben to tell her how he felt.

'Yes, I want to be able to provide for Riley on my own. There's nothing wrong with that, is there? But you had a right to know, and you have a right to be able to see her as well. You're her father.' The sudden thought that Ben might have been questioning that struck Callie. 'You can take a test if you're in any doubt…'

His face softened suddenly. 'I'm in no doubt. I trust you, Callie, but I just wish you'd trusted *me* a bit more.'

'I tried. I sent you a text but you didn't reply.' Now she thought about it, not replying to uncomfortable texts was Ben's modus operandi. She should have taken that into consideration.

'It was one text.' He spread his hands in disbelief. 'You said you wanted to meet for lunch, not that you were pregnant.'

'Because it would have been such a good idea to tell you that I was pregnant by text, is that what you're saying?'

They fell silent, staring at each other. Callie was the first to give in. 'Look I know I did this badly but I did the best I could at the time. I'd hoped that we'd have a bit more time to get used to this but... I failed there as well, I couldn't even make the full term of my pregnancy...'

The nurses had told her that it was common for women who'd undergone emergency deliveries to feel a sense of failure. She'd said the very same thing to women herself when she'd attended emergency calls. Callie hadn't realised just how all-consuming and corrosive the feeling was until now.

Ben shook his head, running his hand through his hair in a gesture of frustration. 'That's not a failure, Callie. But not telling me...it made *me* fail. I wasn't there for you during your pregnancy and now...it's a lot to get my head around in such a short time. I'm struggling and I need some...distance.'

Callie's mouth felt suddenly dry. Failure. Distance. It hadn't taken Ben long to change his mind and now he was backing away.

'What kind of distance?'

'I just need to compartmentalise a little. When I'm at work I need to concentrate on that. When I'm here I can concentrate on you and Riley.'

That didn't sound so bad. One box for Ben's job and another for her and Riley. Callie could live inside that box for Riley's sake. She'd even decorate.

'That's okay. I can live with that.'

'Really?' He looked almost surprised.

'Yes. I need some time to myself too and...that sounds like a good arrangement.'

Her head approved of it at least. Her heart and her hormones wanted to know where he was at any given point in the day and wanted Ben here when he wasn't at work. But her head was her best and strongest ally.

The sound of a key in the front door made them both

ump. Ben smiled a hello as Callie's mother walked past, towards the kitchen, and then he got to his feet. 'I should go...'

'No, Ben. You're not going anywhere.'

'Your mum's here and I don't want to argue.' His face was impassive again. Closed off.

'Fair enough. But you're here to see Riley and I don't want her to be one of those kids who gets caught up in her parents' problems. Whatever happens between the two of us shouldn't ever affect your time with her.'

He nodded. 'You're a great mother, Callie.'

The compliment made her want to burst into tears. Not now. Not when they seemed to be making progress.

'Then be a good father and go and fetch her. I dare say that Mum's making a cup of tea.'

Ben had smiled a lot since Riley had been born, but none of his smiles had had the carefree warmth about them that Callie had seen in his face last Christmas. But this one... He was getting there. A weight had obviously been lifted from his shoulders.

They were making progress. Maybe not quite in the direction that Callie had imagined, but that was what compromise was all about.

CHAPTER SEVENTEEN

AGAINST ALL ODDS, they were making it work. Ben wondered if that would be the one thing that he looked back on as the crowning achievement of his life.

They were doing it for Riley. She meant more than his anger and Callie's independent streak. More than their confusion and the feeling that neither of them were a match for the situation. And he told himself that Riley meant more than the tenderness that he saw in Callie's eyes from time to time, and which echoed in his own empty heart.

As late summer gave way to autumn and then winter, they were turning their uneasy truce into a way of life. Callie started to organise afternoon photography shoots, starting with portraits and visits to the hospital to talk about the possibility of using her portraiture as therapy. She always worked on Ben's days off, and after some weeks of having Kate there to help him look after Riley while Callie was gone, he took the plunge and cared for his baby daughter alone.

The times that Ben had come to treasure were when Callie wasn't working. When all three of them could spend time together. The everyday things that had meant so little to him took on a touch of magic. Going shopping for food or for a walk in the park. Watching as Riley began

o notice that there was a world around her, and seeing
her discover it.

'I have to pop in to the hospital before we drop Riley
off with my mum. There are some notes I need to pick up
from Dr Lawrence in preparation for this evening.'

'You're sure your mum's happy to look after Riley this
evening?' Callie was working, taking photographs with a
man who was recovering from severe burns.

'She's always happy to look after Riley. I don't know
what time I'll finish, and you're working tomorrow.'

'You're going to be great.' He could see that Callie was
nervous. He'd felt much the same when he'd gone back to
work after Riley was born, and he'd had far less reason.
This new project, in partnership with the burns unit at the
hospital, had taken a lot of work and planning.

'Thanks. I just hope… I just want to do this right.'

Callie gave him an apprehensive smile. This was one of
the times when he wanted to fold her in his arms and tell
her that he believed in her. But Ben couldn't, because hugs
were for Riley. If he and Callie happened to touch during
that process, it was an electric pleasure that he never allowed himself to think about.

'Trust me. You'll do it better than right.' Ben shook off
the temptation that was pounding in his veins and lifted
Riley out of her baby bouncer.

Watching him trying to bundle Riley into her snowsuit seemed to take Callie's mind off her own self-doubt
for a moment. Ben heard a stifled giggle behind him as
the little girl managed to pull her left arm back out of the
sleeve for the third time.

'I think she must get this from you,' Ben joked, finally
managing to get both Riley's arms into the snowsuit at the
same time and pulling the zipper up.

'And I thought that she'd inherited her uncooperative

streak from her father.' Callie laughed and Riley started to wave her arms, joining in. That was one thing that the little girl definitely got from her mother. Her smile, and the way that it made Ben's heart turn to mush.

Ben concentrated on his daughter, leaving his feelings for Callie out of the equation. 'Do you want to walk to the hospital or take the car?'

'Shall we walk?'

'Yes. I could do with stretching my legs.' His arms and legs still ached a little from his efforts at a factory fire two days ago. But that wasn't for Callie to know.

As they drew near the hospital gates she seemed more buoyant, talking about her work and the new opportunities and challenges it would bring. That was Callie all over— the closer at hand the challenge, the better she rose to it. It was good to hear her so excited now. Maybe in time he'd share some of the challenges that his work brought...

No. Keeping that separate worked for both of them. Ben didn't function well at work when he was thinking about Callie. They'd been through that already.

In front of them a car wove across the road. Ben instinctively put his arm out, pushing Callie and the pram behind him, although the car wasn't going at any great speed. It drifted to a halt halfway across the pavement, pointing towards the entrance to the hospital.

He felt Callie start forward and he pulled her back, gripping her arm tightly. 'Stay here with Riley. I'll go and see...'

She looked as if she was about to protest and then she nodded. Ben ran towards the car, seeing a man slumped across the steering wheel as he neared it.

He tried the door and it was locked. But the front window was slightly open, as if the car's occupant had been in need of some air. He forced it down, reaching in to switch off the engine and open the driver's door.

'He hasn't crashed, the airbag hasn't even been activated,' Ben called back to Callie, knowing somehow that she'd wouldn't have stayed right where he'd left her. She couldn't help coming a little closer.

'Maybe taken ill at the wheel.' Callie's voice was even closer than he'd expected and when he looked around she was craning to look inside the car, one hand on the pram.

'Callie, will you—?'

'Stay back? No.'

Ben gave in to the inevitable. Callie was better qualified to do this anyway. He took hold of the pram while she knelt down beside the car, examining the man quickly.

'Looks as if he's had a heart attack. Maybe he felt unwell and tried to drive himself to the hospital.' She looked up at Ben. 'Get my phone, will you? It's tucked in the side of the pram.'

Ben felt for the phone and found it. Callie grabbed it from him and made a call, speaking quickly. Then she put the phone back into her pocket.

'They're sending someone down straight away.' She unzipped the man's jacket, pressing her head to his chest, her fingers searching for a pulse. 'We can't wait. He's in cardiac arrest.'

'We need to get him out of the car?' If they were going to attempt resuscitation, they couldn't do it while the man was still in the driver's seat.

'Yes.' Callie pre-empted Ben's next thought and stood back. 'You can lift him better than I can.'

Ben knew that the scar from the Caesarean still pulled a little sometimes, and reaching into the car meant she'd have to lift and pull at the same time. He let her take charge of the pram, thankful that she hadn't ignored her better judgement. Carefully he manoeuvred the man out of the car, laying him down on the pavement, and Callie slipped a baby blanket under his head.

'Should I start resuscitation?' He wasn't going to allow Callie to do that either. Ben had enough training to do the job.

'Yes. You want me to count?'

'Yep.' Ben felt her eyes on him as he positioned his hands on the man's chest in the way he'd been taught. Callie started to count and he followed the rhythm that she set for him.

'Keep going, you're doing great. They're coming...' He heard Callie give an impatient huff. 'Stay back, will you? There's nothing to see here. Let the paramedics through.'

Ben smiled grimly, briefly aware that the small crowd that had formed behind them on the pavement had suddenly begun to disperse. There was the sound of voices and then a man knelt down beside him.

'Swap on three.' Callie counted the beats and Ben sat back on his heels, letting the paramedic take over. An ambulance was approaching the gates and its crew were unloading a trolley, ready to take the man into the hospital.

He stood up, retreating to where Callie stood with the pram. She smiled up at him and Ben felt her hand slip into his.

'Good job, Ben.'

'Great counting.' He smiled down at her. 'I'm impressed by the standing back, too.'

'Don't push it.' He felt her elbow in his ribs and a sudden tingle ran down his spine.

Riley's first medical emergency. She'd come through it with flying colours, dozing in her pram the whole time. He and Callie had come through it too, relying on each other and working as a team. It had stirred an ache in Ben's chest. Memories of when they'd been more to each other than just Riley's mum and Riley's dad.

Callie reappeared from her meeting with Dr Lawrence, a manila envelope in her hand. It was only a short walk to Kate's house, and once they'd handed Riley over to her grandmother there was no reason for him to stay. He'd pick up his car keys from Callie's and go home.

As they walked up her front path, Callie's phone rang. She answered it, cradling the phone between her ear and her shoulder as she opened the front door and motioned him inside, listening intently to someone at the other end of the line.

'No… No, Eric, that's absolutely fine. We'll do this when you're ready, not before… It's no inconvenience. It's really important that you take whatever time you need.' She was smiling into the phone. 'Give me a call tomorrow when you're feeling better. If you want to talk about things a bit more, I can always drop in and see you…'

A few more reassurances and then Callie finished the call. As she met Ben's enquiring gaze, the smile faded from her face.

'What's up?'

'The guy I was going to take photographs with this evening just cancelled. He's had a bad day and doing things when he isn't ready is just going to be counterproductive.' Callie shrugged. 'That's okay. He still wants to do it, just not this evening.'

She was clearly disappointed. Callie had prepared for this so carefully and now that it wasn't going to happen she seemed at a loss as to what to do next. Ben made for the kitchen. 'I'll make you a cup of tea before I go.'

There was no excuse to keep Ben there now but Callie suddenly didn't want him to go. That was a sure sign that she should send him on his way as soon as politely possible.

'It's good that he felt able to phone and cancel.' She sat

on the sofa, her coat and gloves next to her on the cushions. 'I suppose I'd better go and get Riley.'

Ben put two mugs of tea down on the coffee table. 'Drink your tea first. There's no rush. Kate's got a full programme of baby activities planned, and she won't much like it if you turn up on the doorstep before she's had a chance to try Riley out with the baby learning centre.'

Callie chuckled. 'True. Mum's determined that she's going to be a genius.'

'I'll settle for her being able to do whatever she wants.'

'Yes, me too.' That was one thing that she and Ben could agree on without any danger of their shared ambitions starting to look like a relationship.

'I know you've done a lot of preparation for this evening. You must be disappointed.' He leaned back on the sofa cushions, sipping his tea.

This crossed the boundaries that she and Ben had set for themselves. But maybe she needed him to put a toe across those lines at the moment.

'I just feel…' She shook her head, trying to work out exactly how she did feel. 'I'm rather hoping I haven't lost my edge. That man this afternoon…'

'Lost your edge? Seriously? From where I was standing, it looked as if you were in charge the whole time.'

It was nice of him to say so. She'd stood by, counting helplessly, clinging to the pram, while he'd done all the real work. 'I'd have had him out of the car and started resuscitation without even thinking about it once upon a time.'

'And you'll do it again, but not before you're fully fit.' He held up his hand as she protested. 'I know you feel as if you are, but these things always take a bit longer than you think. You were exactly where you needed to be, and where Riley needed you to be.'

What would she have done if Ben hadn't been there,

though? Callie dismissed the thought. He wasn't the only person who could have helped, even if, at the time, it had felt that he was the only person she needed in the world.

'Do you want to stay and watch a film with me?' She could allow herself that at least. 'Then I'll go and pick Riley up.'

It was a departure from their usual way of doing things, and he took a moment to think about it. Then he nodded. 'I'd like that. Why don't you choose something and I'll go and get us some snacks from the kitchen?'

CHAPTER EIGHTEEN

CALLIE'S IDEA OF snacks while watching a film usually extended to opening a packet of crisps. She flipped through the list of films, trying not to smile. It wasn't exactly unexpected that the man with the best-stocked fridge she'd ever seen had found the packet of popcorn at the back of the cupboard, and from the sound of it was putting it to use.

She still hadn't settled on a film when he appeared in the doorway of the sitting room, holding a bowl of popcorn in one hand and a large platter in the other.

'What's this?' She moved her coat so that he could sit down beside her.

'Just popcorn. And I raided your chocolate stash and found some bits and pieces in the fridge...'

To good effect. A thick, melted chocolate goo was in a small bowl in the centre of the platter, surrounded by an assortment of fruit, chopped and arranged carefully. Callie grinned at him.

'When it's time to teach Riley to cook, will you promise to do it?'

Ben chuckled. 'Taste it before you say that.'

He reached forward, taking half a strawberry from the pile and dipping it into the chocolate. When he held it to her lips the warm and cold sweetness, coupled with the scent of having him close, made her forget about everything else.

'Mmm… That's…very good.' Too good. Callie could feel heat rising to her cheeks, and she covered her confusion by reaching for the TV remote. They could draw back now and nothing would be lost. It would just be a moment that meant nothing.

'Have you chosen a film?' If Ben had felt anything then he too seemed unwilling to acknowledge it.

'How about this?' The first one on the list looked as good as any other, and when Ben nodded she pressed the start button. They'd watch the film and then she'd collect Riley and Ben would be on his way.

This was strong magic. The wish to take Callie's mind off her disappointment had turned into the sudden feeling that kissing her was the absolute next thing to do. If that was just an illusion, it was a hard spell to break.

He held out as long as he could. But Callie seemed about as interested in the vivid special effects on the TV screen as he was. All he could see was her.

'Carrots? Really?' They'd worked their way through the fruit on the platter now.

'I used whatever I could find…'

'So this is an experiment?' She dipped the baton into the chocolate and tried it. 'It's….different.'

Ben couldn't move. He didn't have the strength to resist when she dipped the rest of carrot into the fondue and held it to his lips. And by some sorcery he thought he tasted only Callie.

He should stop before he was completely beguiled. But the look in her eyes kept him motionless. And then the touch of her finger on the side of his mouth, wiping away a smear of chocolate, turned his blood to fire.

He could kiss her now, and then they could forget all about it and go back to what they'd been for the last three months. What had worked. *Yeah. Tell yourself that...* Ben ignored the voice of warning echoing softly in the back of his head.

She dipped one finger into the chocolate and put it into her mouth. And he was lost. When he reached for her, Callie was there, melting into his arms as if there had never been any other place she'd wanted to be.

Her body was different now, but it hadn't forgotten what it was like to feel Ben close. However had she thought it could?

She felt Ben's hands spreading across her back. Just the way they had before...

Not *just*. It was more. All they'd been through since last Christmas, all the hurdles they'd managed to over come lent a depth and an exquisite tenderness to his kiss. A slow burn, which couldn't be quenched.

He was holding her away from him a little, but seemed helpless to stop her when she moved closer, feeling his body hard and trembling against hers. Callie kissed him again or maybe Ben kissed her. They were so connected, so much at one with each other, that it was impossible to tell.

'I've missed you so much, Callie. But...'

Did there always have to be a *but*? Always some reason why they couldn't do what they both wanted to do? Callie couldn't bear to pull away from him. If he was going to reject her, he'd have to do it while she was still in his arms.

'But what?'

In the heat of his sudden smile nothing could hurt her. 'You couldn't be any more beautiful to me than you are now, Callie. But you've just had a baby and...to be honest I don't even know the right questions to ask.'

It was all right. Everything was all right again. Callie put her finger over his lips and shifted onto his lap. Face to face, staring into his eyes.

'You want to ask whether I'm ready. And how far we can go together.'

Ben chuckled softly. 'I knew I could count on you to come to my rescue. I don't suppose you have the answer, as well as the question?'

'My answer is that I feel ready, and I trust you to be with me and take each moment as it comes.' She kissed him, a new warmth flooding her body. She was safe with Ben, he'd never hurt her. And he'd never hurt Riley.

'I'm following your lead. One word from you and we stop. I'm trusting you to say that word.'

'Do I get to say "Come upstairs" as well? "Let me take your clothes off"?' she teased him.

'Yeah. You can say that as soon as you like.'

Their lovemaking hadn't been so physically active this time around. But Ben's tenderness had been deeper and wilder than before. He'd told her all the things she wanted to hear, that she was beautiful and that he desired her. And the connection was stronger than ever as he watched for her every reaction.

She wanted to stay curled up in his arms but the evening had slipped away in a slow burn of delight and it was getting late.

'I should go and fetch Riley.' She nudged at his shoulder.

'I can go if you want to stay here.' He opened his eyes sleepily.

'No, I'll do it. Mum's expecting me.'

Ben nodded. Maybe he too wanted to keep this between the two of them. Callie wasn't ready to make it a part of her everyday life, not just yet.

His gaze followed her as she got out of bed. Picking up her clothes from the floor, she instinctively held them across her stomach, hiding the scar and the stretch marks.

'Don't cover them up.' His murmured words made her stop. 'Or am I going to have to take a photograph to convince you?'

Callie dropped her clothes back onto the floor.

He grinned, blinking his eyes as he imitated the sound of a camera shutter. 'That's the picture I want...'

Ben refused to think about the complications. This felt right. Getting out of bed, he threw his clothes on and went downstairs. The sitting-room light was still on and he cleared away the scattered remains of the popcorn and fondue. Still wrapped in the satiated warmth of their lovemaking, he sat down on the sofa and began to doze.

He didn't hear Callie coming back. When he felt tiny fingers on his face, his eyes snapped open in alarm and he heard Callie's laughing admonition.

'Don't punch Daddy in the face, sweetie.'

Two different pieces of his life crashed together head-long. He rubbed his eyes, trying to make sense of the gorgeous chaos.

'Sorry.' Callie was sitting on the edge of the sofa, one hand on Riley's back to steady her. 'Did we startle you?'

'I must have dozed off.'

And woken to find that the simple, comforting rules that he'd built his life around didn't hold true. He could follow the pattern he'd used to keep his work and his private life separate, and put his relationship with Callie and his relationship with his daughter into two separate boxes all he liked. Keeping them there was an entirely different prospect.

But somehow it didn't matter. He reached for Riley,

picking her up for a hug. It seemed suddenly possible to hold everything that he most loved in the world in his arms. When Callie moved closer, nestling against him, that possibility became a reality that took his breath away.

'This…is nice.' Callie looked up at him as he put his arm around her shoulders. 'Different…'

He kissed Callie's cheek and then bent to kiss the top of Riley's head. 'You want to take a moment to get familiar with it? I'd like to.'

She laughed suddenly, and Riley imitated the sound in her own sing-song way. 'Yes. I could definitely get used to this.'

Riley was crying. And then the bed heaved as Ben got out of it and she heard the sound of him pulling on his jeans.

'I'll go…'

Callie muttered an acknowledgement. This moment ranked with all the others that she wanted to keep. She could hear Ben singing quietly, and when she opened her eyes she saw his silhouette, rocking their baby in his arms.

'I'll take her downstairs. You get some sleep.'

She heard Ben chuckle. 'You'll do no such thing.'

The bed moved again as he sat down on it, and Callie wriggled over towards him, still wrapped in the duvet. All the love in the world seemed to reside within the circle of his arms.

Love? Was this what this was? Or was it just two people thrown together who wanted to make a family from the materials to hand? At the moment the future seemed like a distant ogre that could be fought later.

'I'll have to go soon.' Ben's voice rang with regret and Callie glanced at the clock beside the bed. It was an hour's drive home and then he had to get to the fire station to start his shift.

'How long?'

'Not yet. Half an hour.'

He seemed to want that half-hour to last as much as she did. Riley quietened suddenly in his arms, as if she too knew that this was something special.

'When will I see you again?' The question she'd been determined not to ask came naturally suddenly.

'Maybe we can…spend the day together when I'm next off shift?'

Five days. Probably six, to give him the chance to sleep after his night's work. It seemed like an age but Ben was probably right. This was too fragile a thing, too precious, and they should go slowly.

'Yes, I'd like that. Give me a call then?'

She felt him move and his lips brushed her forehead. 'Yeah. I'll give you a call.'

CHAPTER NINETEEN

No thought went into it. Ben's training kicked in as soon as he realised he was falling, and he bent his knees, landing on his feet and then rolling.

The pain came soon enough. He couldn't stand so he crawled, dragging his useless leg behind him. There was only one aim in his head. Get out. If he wanted to hold Callie and Riley in his arms again, he had to get out...

Blind, dogged effort gave way to relief when he felt himself being lifted and carried the final few yards out of the building. Eve's voice penetrated the haze of pain. 'Stand down, boss. We've got you.'

He realised that he'd been fighting, still trying to get to his feet even though he was well clear of the building now and he could see the sky. Hands found the place where his ribs hurt most and he groaned...

Sirens. The ambulance was running on a siren and it was making his head hurt. Why couldn't they just turn it off? He managed to pull the oxygen mask from his face, getting out just one word before the ambulance paramedic gently put it back in place.

'Callie...'

Callie ran from the hospital car park, making straight for the ambulance crews' entrance into A and E. She hadn't heard from Ben since he'd left her early yesterday morning, and she hadn't expected to. When Eve had called, it had felt like a physical blow.

As luck would have it, her mother had been there, and she'd been able to leave Riley with her. The roads had been clear and she'd made the drive to the hospital in just over half an hour.

An ambulance had drawn up and the crew was wheeling a gurney through the automatic doors into A and E. She recognised Ben's shock of dark hair and put on a final sprint for the doors before they swished closed again, feeling the scar across the base of her stomach pull a little as she ran.

'Callie Walsh. I'm a paramedic...' She fumbled in her bag, showing her ID to the ambulance driver, who was standing next to the gurney. 'I'm...with him.'

Luckily *with him* was a good enough explanation. Callie wasn't sure how else to describe herself.

'Okay. We're finding a doctor now....' The driver nodded towards his partner, who was navigating through the melee of people, all of whom seemed to have something to do.

'How is he?' Callie could see dressings on Ben's arm and an immobiliser on one of his legs. An oxygen mask obscured his face and his eyes were closed.

'He's breathing on his own, no critical injuries that we can see. His arm's burned and his leg's broken.' The man allowed himself a tight smile. 'I'm glad you're here.'

Before Callie could ask why, Ben stirred. He seemed to be trying to reach for something, and she caught his flailing hand, telling him to stay still. At the sound of her voice he opened his eyes suddenly.

'Callie...?'

'Everything's all right, Ben. You're at the hospital and you're safe.'

He seemed to only half comprehend what she was saying but half was enough. Ben's fingers tightened around hers and the urgency of his movements subsided.

'What happened?' Callie murmured the question to the ambulance driver.

'A floor gave way and he fell from the first to the ground floor. He crawled a fair way before the crew could get to him and bring him out.'

And Ben was still on autopilot. That steely determination of his hadn't quite worked out that he was safe yet.

'He's been like this all the way here?'

'Yeah, he's been drifting in and out. When he was awake he was thrashing around, calling for you. And Riley...?'

'That's our daughter.'

'Right.' The ambulance driver looked round, seeing his partner approach with a young doctor. 'Here we go...'

Callie followed as the doctor shepherded them into a cubicle with the gurney. She could hardly breathe. Ben hadn't called out for his work family, the team he'd come to rely on. He'd wanted her and Riley.

It was nothing, an automatic reaction. She'd heard patients call out for all kinds of people. The doctor introduced himself as Michael, and Callie flashed her paramedic's ID again, when it looked as if the next thing he would do was to tell her to stand back.

The doctor thought for a moment. 'We're very busy and it's not as if I couldn't do with your help.'

Could she keep her tears under control and think like a medic? Right now she'd do whatever it took. 'I won't get emotional.'

Michael nodded. 'Okay. I want you to step back if that

changes, Callie. We all have our limits, and I can deal with whatever needs to be done.'

Barely. It would be quicker and better with two. But Callie nodded her head. 'I understand.'

'In that case, I want you to try and keep him conscious and focussed.'

Michael was giving her a task that involved as little medical intervention as possible. That didn't matter, as long as she could be close to Ben. And it would be a lot easier for the doctors and nurses if he could react to their questions, rather than alternating between a semi-conscious state and trying to fight them.

As Michael turned his attention to the nurse who had just arrived with a burns trolley, Callie surreptitiously reached for the penlight on the counter. Keeping him conscious wasn't so very different from checking for a concussion.

She tapped his cheek with her finger. 'Ben... I've got you now, and you're safe. Look at me...'

He opened his eyes. Clear blue, in stark contrast with the grime streaking his face. They held all the need that she'd seen when he'd cried out for her in the night, but this time he needed her in a different way, one that was a lot harder to respond to. He was hurt, and it was up to Callie to pull him back from a precipice that she hadn't dared think about.

Callie swallowed hard. She knew her job, even if she knew nothing else at the moment. She just had to do her job.

'Do you know where you are, Ben?'

His lips formed one word. 'Hospital...'

'Great. That's right.' Callie caught his free hand in hers. 'I want you to squeeze my hand if you feel any sudden pain.'

He nodded, his gaze fixed on hers. When she shone the

penlight, his pupils reacted correctly to the light and Ben appeared to know what was going on around him. More than that. His gaze seemed to know everything, the way it always had…

Tears threatened, and Callie made an effort to stop thinking that way. If she showed any signs of distress, Michael would have to make her stand back.

'What's the date today?' She covered her confusion with a question, moving the face mask a little and leaning in to hear the answer.

'First of December. The monarch is Queen Elizabeth. My name's Benjamin David Matthews and my daughter's name is Riley.' Ben caught his breath in pain. 'She has the cutest smile.'

Okay. She got it. Ben had been through this procedure before and he knew all the answers to the questions.

'Your middle name's David, is it?' She forced a smile. In all the hundreds of little details about their lives that they'd exchanged, middle names had never come up.

'Yes.'

'Just stay still for a moment…' Callie let his hand drop and felt him clutch at her blouse. Fair enough. How many other patients had reached for her, holding on as if that was all that was keeping them safe. She carefully examined him for any cuts or bumps on his head, finding nothing.

'Your leg and your arm hurt…' She could see from his eyes that they did. 'Anything else?'

She was caught again in his gaze. 'Nothing…hurts.'

Nothing had been able to hurt her either when she'd been in his arms. 'Ben, cut the macho act. What else?'

His eyelids fluttered down in a sign of acquiescence. 'My side…'

Callie turned, and saw that Michael had uncovered a large, rapidly forming bruise on his ribs. It could be a sign of a cracked rib or even internal bleeding. He was probing it with his fingers and Ben groaned, his hand clutching tighter onto her shirt.

'I want you to breathe in…' Michael caught his attention and Ben's gaze turned to him. But however hard she tried, Callie couldn't get him to loosen his grip on her.

As Callie had anticipated, the break was a bad one, and his leg was going to need surgery. The doctor thought that they could get Ben down to the operating theatre straight away, and left Callie with him to wait for news.

He was slowly coming around. Warm, and about as comfortable as pain killing drugs and pillows could make him, Ben began to loosen his grip on her shirt. Then he let go.

'It won't be long now.' Callie had gone to speak to one of the nurses to find out what was happening.

'I'm sorry, Callie.'

'Be quiet. You have nothing to apologise for.' Callie heard a tense edge to her voice. Ben must know as well as she did that her greatest fear was that the father of her child wouldn't come back one day, and that it was agony to see how close he'd been to that possibility today.

'You should go… Riley…'

'Riley's fine, she's with Mum. You're the one I'm worried about.' She bit her lip as tears sprang to her eyes. Callie had resolved not to mention the word 'worry'.

He reached for her hand, squeezing it tightly. 'I'll be okay…'

She wanted to raise his fingers to her lips, but she couldn't. Instead, she laid her hand lightly on his forehead. It was a gesture of comfort that didn't seem too dangerous at the moment.

'I'll be here when you come out of surgery. I called

Eve to let her know how you were doing and she said that some of the crew would be coming down here later as well.

'No fuss, Callie...'

'You're not the boss here, Ben. You'll do as you're told and we'll make as much fuss as we want to. You're in no position to stop us.'

He frowned, clearly searching for an argument. Then Ben's lips quirked into a smile. 'Yes, ma'am.'

'That's better.'

When she was alone she could cry. She could think about the ramifications of seeing the father of her child injured in the line of duty. How it felt more awful than she could ever have thought it would. But for now she had to be strong.

Yesterday afternoon and evening was a blur. The only thing that had been in really sharp focus was Callie. Ben had woken up in his hospital bed this morning, and as Eve had promised him before she left last night, he was hurting in places he hadn't even known he had.

Ben submitted to all the doctors' and nurses' requests of him, but his mind was elsewhere. His injuries had changed everything between him and Callie. She'd done everything to reassure him, but he had seen through the façade. He'd made a reality out of her worst fears.

When visiting time came, he couldn't help but watch for her, almost hoping that she'd decided not to come. But she did, and when she walked through the doors of the ward, carrying Riley in a sling, his heart took over from his head and beat wildly.

He couldn't take his eyes off her. As she sat down next to his bed, she smiled at him. 'How are you today?'

'Much better, thanks. What about you?' Callie looked tired. As if she hadn't had a wink of sleep last night.

'I'm fine.' The hint of protest in her voice told Ben that she very definitely wasn't fine. He reached for her hand, feeling it cold in his.

'No, you're not.' He flashed her a *Don't argue* look, and she quirked the corners of her mouth down. 'I know that this isn't where you ever wanted to be.'

He'd put her here, though. He'd made love to her, and now she was sitting by his hospital bed. The different strands of his life had become tangled and knotted and it was time to unravel them.

'I don't know what you mean.' She bent down, reaching into the bag she'd brought with her, but she couldn't disguise the flush in her cheeks.

The worries that had been swirling in his head consolidated into certainty. Callie would make an effort to ignore her fears, but she couldn't overcome them. She might stay with him because of love, or from a misplaced sense that it would be better for Riley. She might stay to nurse him back to fitness. Whatever the reason, she'd get to the point where concerns over his safety made her feel threatened and unsafe, the way she had when she'd been a child, and that would break them apart. There could only be one thing worse than never having the family he wanted, and that was having them and then losing them.

'We have to talk about this, Callie.'

She puffed out a breath, one hand moving protectively to the back of Riley's head. The little girl was curled against her chest, fast asleep.

'Okay. It's difficult, Ben, is that what you want to hear? I'm dealing with it.'

No. She wasn't. The only way forward was to rely on what he knew worked. Compartmentalisation.

'Callie, neither of us can deal with this, we both need

to back away. What happened between us the other night can't happen again. We can't take that risk.'

She caught her breath. He could see the question in her eyes. *Don't you care?* If she didn't know that he cared for her, she didn't know anything about him, but Ben couldn't say it. Callie could ask him anything, but that was the one question he wouldn't answer.

'We can't take the risk with Riley, you mean?' Eventually she settled on an easier question.

'No, we can't. We promised that our relationship wouldn't ever hurt her, and a week ago that promise was easy to keep. I think we should make sure it stays that way.'

'But…we already…' She looked around at the other beds, as if to check that no one was taking an interest in their conversation. 'We've already spent the night together and things were fine… They weren't just fine, they were great.'

'And now they're not. After one night we can go back and pick up our lives. After six months or a year… I couldn't make it back from that.'

'But what if we *can* make it work?' She was frowning, her face haggard with lack of sleep. Callie was so intent on just getting through this, but he could see in her eyes that she was fighting a losing battle with herself.

'Can you honestly tell me that this is what you want for Riley? Having her mother worry like this every single day? Because it's not what I want for her and it isn't what I want for you and me either.'

'I…' Callie's protest died on her lips. 'No. It's not what I want.'

'So let's make things easy, shall we? Go home. I'll give you a call in a couple of days when I'm out of here. We'll work from there.'

Her back stiffened suddenly. 'I can't do that. You need someone to look after you, Ben.'

That was the least of his worries right now. He reached for his phone, switching it on and showing her the texts. 'What I *need* is an appointments system.'

She flipped through the texts, a tear rolling suddenly down her cheek. 'I guess the fire service looks after its own.'

'Yes, we do.' Ben had always thought of his crew as family. Now they seemed a shadowy second-best to the one he was sending away. The one that couldn't ever be.

'Okay.' She began to unclip Riley's sling, running her finger across the little girl's cheek to wake her. Then she held her closer to the bed so that Ben could reach her. 'I want you to kiss your daughter, Ben. Tell her you'll see her very soon.'

'So how's Ben?'

It was a natural enough question. When Callie had accepted an invitation to lunch at Eve's, she'd expected she would ask and had her answer ready.

'I haven't seen him for two weeks. My mum and her partner have been taking Riley over to see him. We decided that it's best for all of us if we just stick to our access arrangements.'

'That's what he said when I saw him last. I just wondered what your side of the story was.' Eve flashed Callie an apologetic smile.

Even in the quiet agony of their parting it seemed that she and Ben were maintaining a united front. Callie hugged Riley tight. She was the one thing that made any sense in any of this.

'It is what it is. He's a great father to Riley, and that's what matters.'

'Yep. I can't imagine Ben would be anything else.' The oven timer sounded from the kitchen and Eve got to her feet. 'That's our lunch…'

Thankfully, there were no more questions about Ben. But Callie was learning that not talking about him didn't stop her from thinking about him. All roads seemed to lead back to him at the moment.

'Doesn't your husband worry? About your job?' Eve had been talking about how they managed Isaac's care when she was on shift, and Callie couldn't help asking the question that was pounding in her head.

'Yes, he worries. I worry about him as well.' Eve grinned in response to Callie's questioning look. 'He's a civil servant. Desk jobs can be tough, too.'

'Not as tough as your job surely?'

'I don't know about that. He's not as fit as I am, and he doesn't get to work off the stress. I'm a bit concerned about his cholesterol.'

'What level is he?' Callie asked automatically, and then thought better of it. 'Sorry. Professional interest.'

'That's okay. He's at five point five.'

'That's not so bad. It could be lower, particularly at his age, but a bit less saturated fat in his diet and some exercise should bring it down.'

'I'm sending him to the gym.' Eve grinned. 'I reckon that I might as well get the benefit of this health kick of his, and I'm looking forward to a little finely toned musculature.'

Callie almost choked on her food. Ben did finely toned musculature well. Very well. Thinking about it wasn't going to help.

'So it's not really an issue for you, then?'

'Yes, of course it's an issue. But I was a firefighter when I met Danny, and we both knew what we were signing up for when we got married.' Eve shot Callie a knowing glance. 'And I'm not Ben.'

'Is there a difference?'

'Ben's a leader. He's responsible for everyone, and he's the one who makes the hard decisions. Do you know why it was him who fell through that floor the other day and not his partner?'

'No. Why?' Callie almost didn't *want* to know.

'Because Ben goes first. He always does. He never asks any of us to do anything that he won't do, and he never gives up. That's not an easy thing to live with.'

Callie could feel the flush spreading across her cheeks. Ben was a true hero. That *was* hard to live with, but she couldn't be more proud of him.

'If you see him…'

'I'm dropping in tomorrow. The guys are great at going round there and ordering in a pizza, but Ben's probably worked his way through most of the fresh food I left him last time. You want a status report?'

'Yes… Yes, please. But please don't tell him.' The least that Callie could do was to watch over Ben from afar. It couldn't hurt if he never knew about it.

'I won't. I'll call you tomorrow evening.'

CHAPTER TWENTY

Christmas Eve

BEN WAS SPRAWLED on the sofa, looking miserably at the Christmas tree. It was still bare, looking like something that had wandered in and settled itself by the hearth but had no real place there.

He'd had such hopes for this Christmas. This year, Blue Watch had Christmas Eve off, and he'd been planning to see both Callie and Riley. The day would be full of sparkle, all the pretty things that Riley loved. After their night together, he'd briefly hoped that he and Callie would be able to share some magic of their own, too. It would be the best day of the year.

Instead, it was shaping up to be the worst. Ben shifted uncomfortably on the sofa, the cast on his leg cumbersome. His leg throbbed and the burns on his arm were still painful.

The buzzer sounded and Ben laboriously made his way over to the intercom. That was one of the disadvantages of a large, open-plan living area. Everything was so far away.

Whoever it was didn't buzz again. They must know that he was slow at the moment. Perhaps it was one of his crew, coming to try and cheer him up. He'd done his best when

Eve had popped round the other day with her little boy but when she'd left he'd felt even more upset and alone.

'Ben. Are you there?' Despite the crackle of the intercom, he recognised Callie's voice.

'I'm here.' His hand hovered over the door release and then dropped to his side. He'd made his decision about seeing Callie, and he wasn't going to change it just because he was at a low ebb.

'Are you going to let me in?'

'No. Go home, Callie.'

'I've just come from home. It's taken me an hour to get through the traffic…' Her voice rang with dismay. 'I have Riley with me, and she's freezing cold. And she's crying.'

Ben couldn't hear any crying. But Callie obviously wasn't going away and he couldn't leave her on the door step. Despite himself, Ben felt a little thrill of excitement as he pressed the button to release the main door.

'Thank you!' He heard Callie's final words before the intercom cut out. They were laced with frustration and he could just imagine her rolling her eyes.

It would be a few minutes before she got herself and Riley into the lift and back out again. Ben used the time to stack that morning's breakfast things into the sink and dump the newspapers that littered the sofa onto the coffee table in something that resembled a tidy pile. It was the best he could do to make it look as if he was managing for himself.

He'd barely got settled, back onto the sofa, when the door drifted open and Callie appeared. She was carrying Riley in a body sling over her red coat, a richly patterned skirt grazing the tops of her fleece-lined boots and a large bag over her shoulder. Riley was dressed in green, with a little elf hat on her head. When Callie pointed toward Ben, Riley stretched one arm out and began to chuckle.

Ben hardly dared move. He watched as Callie kicked the door closed behind her and walked towards him. A short struggle with the body sling and then she put Riley down on the sofa next to him. 'Look, Riley, there's Daddy.'

Riley reached for him, and Ben lifted her onto his lap. He hugged his little girl tight, kissing her.

'She doesn't look as if she's been crying.' He decided to call Callie's bluff.

'She cheered up when she saw you.'

From the little jut of her chin it seemed that Callie found Riley's sudden change in mood just as unlikely as he did. She shrugged, looking around the apartment.

'Nice tree. You've decided to go for the minimalist look this year?'

'The guys brought it round but they had to get to work and I haven't got around to decorating it yet. Sorry about the mess, I wasn't expecting company.'

'That's all right. I can tidy up a bit...' Callie seemed intent on finding something to do.

Enough. He couldn't bear this. 'Callie, why are you here?'

'I knew you'd be disappointed about not seeing Riley, and Mum's busy. I brought some shopping as well. Eve said you were running out of a few things...'

'*Eve* said?'

'You know I speak to Eve.' She flushed, putting her bag onto the kitchen counter and starting to empty it.

He knew it. Callie and Eve had struck up a friendship, and had seen each other regularly since Riley had been born. It had been hard, in the last three weeks, not to ask Eve how Callie was and clearly Callie had been similarly tempted.

'Callie, you didn't need to come all this way to restock

my cupboards. And it's great to see Riley, but that coul
have waited until Kate was free to bring her.'

She froze, staring down at the groceries that she'd take
out of her bag. 'Yes. You're right.'

'So what *are* you doing here?'

Callie felt her cheeks burn. This was the biggest risk she'
ever taken in a life dedicated to avoiding risk.

She swallowed hard. If he was going to send her away
she might as well say what she'd come to say first.

'I've made a decision, Ben. I couldn't do anything abou
it when I lost my father or my home, but I can do somethin
about losing you. You said to me once that there are som
things that are important enough to take risks to achieve
and without that a life can become meaningless…'

Callie stopped for breath. Ben was staring at her, an
Riley was suddenly still in his lap. The little girl was look
ing intently at her too, knowing maybe that this was a mo
ment that could change their lives.

'Go on, Callie.' At least he was going to hear her ou
That was something.

'Eve told me that you were injured because you alway
go in first. You never ask anyone to do anything you won
do.'

Annoyance flashed across his face. 'That's not quit
how it is.'

'Don't try to protect me, Ben, that's exactly how it i
And you're exactly the kind of man that I want in Riley
life. Someone who isn't afraid to lead and who'll be ther
for her whatever happens.'

He nodded. 'I *will* be there for her.'

Callie took a deep breath. Now or never… 'You're ex
actly the kind of man I want in *my* life, too.'

'Callie, we've been through this already—'

'Yes, we have. But I was wrong to let you go. All I could think about was that I might lose you, but... I never thought that the only person who could make me happy enough to deal with my fears was you.'

He shook his head. She'd messed up all over again. Callie began to panic, as the consequences of the risk she'd taken began to swell in her heart.

'Say something, Ben. If you want me to go...'

Suddenly he smiled. 'Stay here, Callie. With me.'

She could feel heat spreading from her cheeks to her ears and then around the back of her neck. She'd taken the first step, and Ben had responded with another one. She wanted to fling herself into his arms, but it was all too soon for that. If he just let her stay for a little while, she could show him that she wasn't going to pressure him any more.

'Right, then. So you'll tell me where the decorations are?'

Ben nodded towards the door that led to the other side of the apartment. 'There's a big cupboard. Through there...'

She hadn't been through there since last Christmas. Then it had seemed a concrete reminder for Ben of all the things he hadn't believed in any more. Now maybe it was a reason for hope.

'I'll...go and get them, shall I?' She was still standing yards away from him, in the kitchen area, but Callie couldn't shake the feeling that they were closer now than they'd ever been.

'That sounds great. We can decorate the tree together.'

That sounded wonderful. Callie almost ran towards the door, twisting the key feverishly in the lock, before Ben changed his mind.

seemed that Callie couldn't sit still. Ben knew exactly how she felt, but it was a little more difficult for him to give in to the temptation to quiet the pounding of his heart with physical activity.

Callie had changed everything. The tearful grin she'd given him had made him realise why his life had been so dark recently. Without her, Christmas was just another drab winter day. But she'd turned it into a time of hope.

In a whirl of energy she fetched the decorations and examined the contents of his fridge, while the coffee machine dribbled the last of his fresh coffee into two cups. Then she declared the food situation to be worse than she'd imagined and decided they should go out, because he couldn't possibly go without turkey sandwiches at Christmas time.

'It's too late. We'll never get a turkey on Christmas Eve.'

'It's early still and when I drove down the High Street the shops were heaving. Look at Ebenezer Scrooge—he managed to find a turkey on Christmas morning.'

Ben chuckled. 'As I remember, he sent a boy to find the turkey. And that was a long time ago. Things have probably changed.'

'Yes, they've changed. We have supermarkets now. Do you have a sock that I can put over your cast to keep your foot warm?'

Ben gave up. It was hard enough to resist Callie when she wasn't around, and now it was downright impossible.

'Upstairs. I'm afraid it's a bit of a mess...'

Callie chuckled. 'I'll survive. Running up and down the stairs to tidy up isn't exactly a priority when you're on crutches.'

'I'll have you know that my physiotherapist was very impressed with my grasp of stair climbing techniques. She may even have mentioned the word *perfect*...' He called after her.

Ben could hear the sounds of pillows being plumped

and the duvet being rearranged. 'Don't bother with that. Socks are in the top drawer of the dresser.'

'Okay...' It sounded as if Callie was ignoring him because she was still walking around, probably picking up the clothes he'd left on the floor. 'We'll go shopping and then we'll decorate the tree.'

Callie knew that she was pushing things further than she'd meant to go. But Ben was smiling, that luminous blue-eyed smile that she remembered from last Christmas. The moment he stopped, she'd take a step back, but she couldn't while it was still on his face.

Ben's car was bigger than hers and he could get into the passenger seat more easily. Callie manoeuvred the SUV into a parking space as close to the supermarket entrance as she could. It went without saying that leaving him in the car with Riley while she got the shopping was too much time apart. And even if everything did take a little longer, Ben made good use of the opportunity, dropping things they didn't need into the trolley and making faces at Riley.

'I can hear carol singers.' He was looking around as Callie loaded the boot of the car, trying to work out from which direction the voices were coming.

'Perhaps we can drive past...'

'Can't we take a walk over?' They must be at the Market Square on the High Street.

'How far is it? Can you make it?'

He nodded. 'This is Riley's first Christmas. I'll make it.'

Riley had seen carol singers already, but Callie decided not to take away the magic. This was the first time she'd see them with her father. She flipped the remote to lock the car doors and put Riley into the body sling, feeling her daughter's hands to make sure that she wasn't too cold.

The little girl was as warm as toast and as cute as a button in her green elf hat.

The carol singers were obviously an established choir and they had a band with them. The music swelled as they got closer, and the crowd around them let Ben through when they saw his crutches. Callie stood close. Even if he couldn't hold Riley, he could at least touch her.

She began to hum along with the carols, and Riley followed her example, tuneless and wavering, not pausing when the singers finished and the band turned the pages of their music sheets. Ben's smile made Callie's heart quiver.

Maybe it was just Riley who made him smile. But Ben slipped the crutch out from under his left arm, putting it with the other one under his right. Callie felt his arm curl lightly around her waist, a little tighter when she nestled against him. She'd missed this so much, his scent and the taut strength of his body. It had seemed like an impossible dream that he would hold her again, and that Riley should be with them in a circle of warmth between her mother and father.

But they couldn't stay long. Ben began to shiver, from the cold and the effort of standing like this, and when Callie led him away, he didn't protest. It had been a few precious minutes, but whatever the future held for them, that could never be taken away.

CHAPTER TWENTY-ONE

ɪᴛ ᴡᴀꜱ ᴀʟʟ his Christmases rolled into one. Callie had decorated the Christmas tree, and Ben had helped as best e could. Riley had wanted to touch all the decorations, nd he'd carefully held them in front of her, allowing her ᴏ play with the felt ones he'd bought for her.

'*Ew...* This one's all slimy.' Riley had handed Callie a abric star, pointing at the tree. She was getting the hang f this quickly. 'She's been sucking it, hasn't she?'

'Yes, I think she's hungry.'

'I'll make up a bottle.' Callie grinned at him and headed ᴏr the kitchen.

'Don't bother with that, I'll make myself scarce. She's lready had one bottle today.' However much he wanted ᴏ recreate the feeling he'd had watching Callie feed Riley ᴛ the hospital, he shouldn't rush things. If Callie wanted ᴀis space, he had to respect it.

'Don't you want to feed her?'

'Yes, but...' He realised suddenly that it wasn't space ᴀat Callie wanted. She'd suggested a bottle so that he ᴏuld feed Riley. Warmth rushed through his veins and ᴇ nodded.

'Well, then.'

Callie prepared a bottle and put Riley into his arms. ᴀhe little girl tugged at his shirt, pressing herself against

him. This was the best time in the week. Along with a
the other best times that he had with Riley.

He glanced up at Callie, and suddenly the world tippe
and he slid helplessly into her smile. *She* was watching *him*

Riley had fallen asleep, and Callie reckoned she'd hav
at least an hour before she woke up again. She knew tha
Ben wouldn't do this in front of his daughter.

'Let me see your arm.'

'No need. It's okay.' Apparently he wasn't intending t
do it in front of Callie either. But if Riley clearly had he
father wrapped around her little finger, Callie had a fe
more weapons in her arsenal. Being able to form word
was a start.

'When did you last have it dressed?'

'A few days ago. It'll be all right until after Christmas

'I'm sure it will be, but *I* want to take a look. The healt
visitor left some sterile dressings?'

Ben grinned. 'In the cupboard, over there. You treat a
your patients like this?'

'Not all of them. The firefighters are generally th
worst, they're a pretty stroppy crowd. I keep my specia
tactics for them.'

'Special tactics?' He chuckled, and Callie fought to kee
a straight face.

'You don't want special tactics. You're not up to it
the moment.'

'No, I don't think I am.' He undid the zip of the warr
sweater he was wearing and slipped it from his shoulde
rolling up his sleeve.

Callie carefully peeled off the tape that secured th
dressing pad, making sure that nothing was stuck to th
wound. The burn looked better than she remembered
but it was still red and painful.

'And the health visitor's happy with your progress?'

'I don't much care what the health visitor thinks. Since you've decided to take a look, I'd like to know what *you* think.'

Callie stared at his arm. She wasn't accustomed to being fazed by any degree of injury, a paramedic who was wouldn't be of much use. But this healing burn had turned her stomach to jelly.

'I think…you're doing well. If it keeps healing like this there won't be any scar. How's your leg feeling?'

'It feels…like a broken leg. It'll heal.'

'And I don't need to make a fuss?' She grinned up at him, and saw laughter reflected in his eyes.

'Consider it your sole prerogative to make as much fuss as you like.'

Callie re-dressed the burn as gently as possible. Ben didn't make a sound, although she knew it must still hurt.

'How does that feel? Not too tight?'

'No, it feels fine.'

She pulled his sleeve back down again carefully. As she reached to help him back into his sweater, she felt his fingers on the side of her face, tipping it up to meet his gaze. All the tenderness that she'd missed so much.

'Thank you, Callie.'

She felt her fingers turn clumsy. Liquid fire was running through her veins, not burning but warming her after that seemed like a very long winter.

'How's your side? Since it's my prerogative to make fuss.'

'Still a bit painful. They said that this kind of bruising would take a little while to heal.'

Callie nodded. 'It is healing, though?'

He nodded, pulling the side of his shirt up a little, and Callie carefully pulled it a little farther. The bruise that had covered most of his left side was blotchy and beginning to disperse. Callie felt a tear run down her cheek and turned her face downwards so he wouldn't see it.

'Hey. What's this?' His fingers brushed her face again and this time they were trembling. 'Please, Callie. Don't cry, I'm not going anywhere. Riley's going to have to put up with me for a good while longer. So are you, for that matter.'

'Of course we are.' Callie wiped her face with her sleeve. 'I think I just needed to look and... I needed to face what happened to you. I never really did, not at the hospital, I was too afraid of breaking down.'

'And now you have faced it?' Ben's voice was tender.

'I can leave it behind.' She sat down next to him on the sofa, feeling his arm curl around her shoulders. She already had more than she could have hoped for, but she was greedy. Callie wanted one more thing.

'I was going to take Riley over to Mum's tomorrow morning for lunch with her and Paul. She asked me if you'd like to come.'

'She...did?' He raised his eyebrows in disbelief.

'Well... Actually, she said it was a shame that you were alone this Christmas, and she wished you could be with us. If she knew I was here, she would have told me to ask you to come.'

'You're sure about that?'

'Yes, positive. You'll be more than welcome, Ben. And it's Riley's first Christmas. If you'd like to come, I can pick you up in the morning.'

He was silent for a moment. Callie felt her heart thump in her chest.

'I'd love to come. But you can't make a two-hour round trip on Christmas morning.'

'It's okay. The roads will be clear.' Perhaps she shouldn't push it.

'You could, but if you'd like to stay here tonight, you and Riley can take the spare room.'

'I suppose…that might be more convenient.' The pounding of her heart seemed to be blocking her throat.

'Let's do that, then. Thank you.'

Ben's head felt as if it was about to explode. Was it really possible that so much could change in the course of just a few hours?

When she'd looked at his injuries, she'd cried. She'd let herself feel something, and that had helped her to move on. If Callie could be that brave, he could too. Whatever difficulties stood ahead of them, they could be no match for love. He could face the risk of losing her if it meant he had a chance of keeping her.

Suddenly, from being sure about nothing, Ben was very sure about everything. Last Christmas had seemed like a bubble and the New Year a return to reality. But it was the other way around, and Christmas was the reality.

'I need you to do something…' He wondered if she'd guess what it was.

She moved in his arms, looking up at him. 'What's that? You'd like something to drink?'

'No.'

'Switch the gas fire on? It's getting a little chilly in here…' Callie grinned suddenly. She knew now, and she was just teasing him. Making the delicious anticipation last.

'No.' Ben tightened his arm around her shoulders in case she took it into her head to move anyway.

'This?'

She moved closer, pausing before their lips finally met.

The thought that this was so much more than he could ever deserve flitted briefly through his mind. And then there was no thought, just the feel of her arms around his neck and her body pressed close to his.

The kiss lasted until they were both breathless. And when she drew back, the look in Callie's eyes was almost as intoxicating.

'You're going to do that again?' Ben needed to be reminded that this wasn't all a dream.

'How soon?'

'Now…'

There was no doubt any more. When Callie kissed him again, he knew that this was a promise that wouldn't be broken.

'Please don't ever doubt me, Callie. I love you, and that's never going to change.'

'I love you too, Ben. That's never going to change either.'

Ben wound his arms around her. The here and now had just turned into for ever.

Ben's kiss was all she needed. Callie almost danced through the evening, cooking for them while he played with Riley, and Christmas carols echoed softly from the sound system. She'd taken the wreaths from the boxes of decorations and wound them around the balustrades at the edge of the mezzanine floor, the way they'd been last year.

He helped her bathe Riley and put her down to sleep, and then the evening was their own. Callie returned to the sofa, and Ben's arms, and he kissed her.

'There's something missing.'

'What's that? I'll fetch it immediately.'

He laughed. 'You'll need superpowers, if you're going to make it snow.'

Tonight it felt as if Callie really could conjure up snow. She could do anything she wanted to.

'I'll attend to the snow a bit later. I have something a little more pressing on my schedule.'

'Yeah? What's that?'

As if he didn't know. Callie kissed him, and Ben trailed kisses across her jaw. She felt his mouth on her neck and she shuddered with pleasure.

'You remember last year, lying in bed, with just the Christmas lights from the balcony…?'

She remembered. He'd traced the patterns that they made across her skin with his finger. And she'd watched the smooth ripple of light and shadow that had accompanied every move he'd made.

'Why do you suppose I put them up there?'

He chuckled. 'I'm not sure I can manage what came next…'

Callie put her finger over his lips. 'I doubt you can, but this'll be better. I'll arrange a few pillows to make you comfortable… You don't have to worry about anything, you'll be in the hands of a trained paramedic.'

He gave her a questioning look. 'That…could work.'

'Then…' she leaned in, whispering in his ear '… I'll rip your clothes off, and have my way with you. You might hurt a bit in the morning…'

He pulled her against his chest, holding her tight in his arms. 'That's very definitely going to work. Tomorrow can take care of itself.'

Just the two of them. Together. Callie had a feeling that everything was going to be just fine.

EPILOGUE

Two years later. Christmas Eve

THE PARTY FOR Ben and Callie's first wedding anniversary had wound down. Plates and glasses were stacked in the dishwasher, and after Riley had fallen asleep in her father's arms, Ben had put her to bed. He walked up to the mezzanine and found Callie, wearing a bright red cosy dressing gown and sitting cross-legged on the bed, stuffing Riley's Christmas stocking.

'That's very cute.' The dark blue felt stocking had an appliquéd Santa and his sleigh on it, along with sparkly snowflakes and shining golden stars.

'Isn't it just? Mum made a great job of it. Are you going to put it in her bedroom now?'

'I thought I'd give it an hour. Just to make sure she's fast asleep.'

Callie nodded, putting the stocking to one side. 'One year, Ben.'

'It couldn't have been a better one.' He took the small package out of his pocket, sitting down on the bed next to her. 'Happy anniversary, darling.'

She turned his gift in her hands, shaking it to see if it rattled. Her shining excitement made Ben smile. Then she undid the wrappings and opened the box, her hand flying to her mouth when she saw what it was.

'Ben! This isn't paper!'

'I couldn't wait another fifty-nine years to give you diamonds. I reckoned it would be good enough if I just wrapped them in paper.'

'They're beautiful, thank you.' She wrapped her arms around his neck, kissing him. 'So do you want me to try the earrings on or the paper?'

'Earrings first. If you don't like them we always have the wrapping paper to fall back on.' Ben watched as Callie took off her stud earrings and replaced them with his present. 'You look gorgeous.'

'Thank you. I love them. Would you like to come and see yours?'

'I have to come and see it?' Ben wondered what on earth Callie could have given him that he had to go to it, rather than it coming to him.

She took his hand and led him downstairs, tiptoeing past the open door of Riley's room and unlocking the door to the other side of the apartment. She'd been overseeing the last of the building works here while Ben had been busy with work. Every time he'd thought of coming in here to see the progress that was being made, Callie had headed him off, telling him she wanted him to wait until it was finished.

The faintest smell of new paint still hung in the air, and Callie led him past the new bedrooms and the playroom to the door that led to the new master bedroom. She made him close his eyes and then guided him into the room.

'You can look now.'

Ben opened his eyes and his breath caught suddenly. 'A wall? You've given me a wall! It looks fabulous...' The simplicity of the cream colour scheme set off the far wall perfectly. It had been sandblasted and sealed, something that Ben and Callie had talked about doing but had decided that they didn't have the funds.

'It's not just the wall.' She almost danced over to the far end of the room to a line of four photographs hung in plain, dark frames. The first was the one that Callie had taken of Ben that first Christmas at the fire station. Then Riley's first Christmas, followed by a photograph of Ben and Callie's wedding day. The fourth was one that Callie had taken of Ben and Riley together just a few days ago.

'We'll add to it. One photograph every year.' She was hugging herself, grinning broadly at Ben's delight.

'There's plenty of space…'

'Then we'll have to make a lot of memories to fill it, won't we?'

A whole wall of Christmas memories. This was their future together, the one that they'd both taken a leap of faith to make possible.

'I love you, Callie.' However often he said it, those four words still seemed to take on a deeper, richer meaning every time. And Ben never tired of her reply.

'And I love you.'

He took her in his arms, holding her tight. 'It's been the best year, Callie. Your book deal, and the recognition of your work with burns patients.'

'And your new job. I hope you'll have a bit more time to spend at home now that the initiative's off the ground.'

'I will. Depend on it.' Ben had accepted a new job, heading up a task force to promote fire safety for the elderly. Callie been concerned that he might be taking it for her sake, and had insisted that he follow his own heart. But this was what he'd wanted to do, and the position had turned out to be even more challenging, and rewarding than he'd hoped.

'I'll be wanting you here.' She stretched up, kissing his cheek. 'We've just built three new bedrooms, and I can't fill them all on my own…'

A little brother or sister for Riley. If Ben could have predicted the one night of the year when that shared dream would come true, it would be this one. He smiled, gazing into her eyes.

'Are you ready for it, darling? Our future?'

She smiled up at him, and his heart almost burst with happiness. 'I can't wait…'

* * * * *

COMING SOON!

We really hope you enjoyed reading this book. If you're looking for more romance, be sure to head to the shops when new books are available on

Thursday 29th November

To see which titles are coming soon, please visit
millsandboon.co.uk

MILLS & BOON

Coming next month

THE BILLIONAIRE'S CHRISTMAS WISH
Tina Beckett

'Theo?'

'Actually, I'm struggling with something.' Maybe it was the revelations about her mom that cast Madison in a different light—the reasons for the slight standoffishness he'd noticed from time to time suddenly making sense. Or maybe it was the stress of dealing with Ivy's illness that had his senses out of whack. But he found himself wanting to do something crazy and impulsive, something he hadn't analyzed from every angle before acting on it.

'With what?'

'The way your thoughts dart from one thing to the other so fast that I can barely keep up.'

'I—I'm sorry.'

'Don't be. I like it. But it also drives me…insane. In ways I should be able to control.' Letting go of her hand, he curled his fingers around the nape of her neck, his thumb sliding just beneath her jaw to where he knew her pulse beat. He let his fingers trail down the side of her throat, along skin that was incredibly soft. 'But right now I don't want to control it. And that's the struggle. So…I need you to tell me to back off.'

She moistened her lips and started to say something, then stopped. Her eyes met his. 'I don't think I can.'

Something inside him leaped to attention and he lowered his voice, aware that they were still completely alone. 'You can't tell me to back off, or you don't want to?' He leaned forward, employing light pressure to bring her nearer until their lips were a mere centimeter away.

'I don't want to tell you...want you to...' Her hand went to his shoulder, fingers pressing through the thin fabric of his button-down shirt. Warmth bloomed and traveled. And then, with a feeling of déjà vu, her mouth touched his.

Senses that had been dormant for years erupted in a huge array of lights that rendered him blind for several seconds.

When he could see again, he was kissing her back and Theo knew at that moment he was in big trouble. He should stop this before it went any further, but his limbs wouldn't co-operate. Neither would his mouth.

So there was nothing else to do but sit back and enjoy the ride. Because any time now Madison was sure to realize what a mistake this was and call a screeching halt to it.

All of it.

And when that happened, Theo had no idea what he was going to do.

Continue reading
THE BILLIONAIRE'S CHRISTMAS WISH
Tina Beckett

Available next month
www.millsandboon.co.uk

LET'S TALK

Romance

For exclusive extracts, competitions
and special offers, find us online:

Get in touch on 01413 063232

For all the latest titles coming soon, visit
millsandboon.co.uk/nextmonth